Beyond the Western Sea: Lord
Kirkle's Money
Avi,
AR B.L.: 6.1
Points: 18.0

Lexile

690

Lexile
940

BEYOND THE WESTERN SEA
◄► Book II ◄►

Lord Kirkle's Money

AN AVON CAMELOT BOOK

AVON BOOKS, INC.
1350 Avenue of the Americas
New York, New York 10019

Copyright © 1996 by Avi
Published by arrangement with Orchard Books, New York
Library of Congress Catalog Card Number: 95-36058
ISBN: 0-380-72876-1
www.avonbooks.com

First Avon Camelot Printing: April 1998

CAMELOT TRADEMARK REG. U.S. PAT. OFF. AND IN OTHER COUNTRIES, MARCA REGISTRADA, HECHO EN U.S.A.

Printed in the U.S.A.

CONTENTS

Friday, January 24, 1851

Saturday, January 25, 1851

Monday, January 27, 1851

Wednesday, January 29, 1851

Thursday, January 30, 1851

Saturday, February 1, 1851

Thursday, February 6, 1851

Monday, February 10, 1851

Monday, February 17, 1851

Thursday, February 20, 1851

Saturday, February 22, 1851

Sunday, February 23, 1851

Monday, February 24, 1851

Tuesday, February 25, 1851

Wednesday, February 26, 1851

Thursday, February 27, 1851

Friday, February 28, 1851

Saturday, March 1, 1851

Saturday, March 8, 1851

BEYOND THE WESTERN SEA

—•❖ *Book II* ❖•—

Lord Kirkle's Money

Chapter 75
Farewell, England!

A brisk, chill wind and a strong tide bore the *Robert Peel* down the Mersey River, away from the city of Liverpool and out upon the rolling Irish Sea.

On the main deck stood three hundred and fifty emigrants, most of them Irish. They were of all ages, from children in mothers' arms to the old and hobbled. Virtually everyone was dressed shabbily, though here and there—like plump plums in an otherwise poor pudding—could be seen those of a richer sort. Well-off or poor, most were cold, many weak and ill. All were pondering what would happen to them next. But now that England had been left behind—and the ship's gray sails bulked large even as her high, stout prow plowed the waves—there was little the passengers could do but wait anxiously for some word from the ship's captain.

Maura O'Connell, her brother, Patrick, and their friend, Mr. Horatio Drabble, pressed side by side against the ship's bulwark, each lost in thought.

Mr. Drabble, long, lanky, expanded his thin chest and breathed deeply of the rich sea air, hardly believing his good fortune. Just a few days ago he had been trapped in the insufferable misery of Mrs. Sonderbye's Liverpool basement. Now he was sailing to America, the fulfillment of a dream long held. Watching England's coast fade in the distance, he felt the weight of past disappointments drop away. As far as he was concerned, he had already become a new man. His smile was as wide as his face.

Maura O'Connell—brown hair blowing, red shawl aflutter—thought of her mother back in Ireland. While Maura could envision the woman wrapped in black, saying her beads, the girl could not imagine where in the ruins of Kilonny Village she might have found shelter. The thought brought tears to her eyes.

And was not her brother, Patrick, too young, too headstrong? And did she not bear full responsibility for him?

Then there was the actor, Horatio Drabble. Though he had been truly kind and helpful to them in Liverpool, Maura was not certain she knew him. There were times he seemed to be from quite another world, not because he was English, but because he, like Patrick, struck her as more boy than man.

Then Maura thought, with some self-chiding, that soon they would be in America with their father, and she could turn over all her responsibilities to him. How well he'd care for them! Maura wanted little but some peace, some quiet, and some work to call her own. How fine that her father, rich man that he was, would provide it. The idea prompted one of Maura's rare smiles.

Patrick O'Connell had no interest in observing either the passing scenery or the other passengers. Nor was he pondering the future. He could think of nothing but Laurence hidden belowdecks. So it was that he stared fixedly at Captain Rickles—splendid in gray uniform and red mustache—who was standing before the main mast, calling commands to the sailors in the high rigging. As Patrick watched, the first mate approached the captain, who introduced him to Mr. Drabble's friend, Mr. Grout, and his stout companion whose name Patrick did not know.

So great was Patrick's worry about Laurence that he simply assumed the subject of their discussion was stowaways. The notion filled him with dread. He must free Laurence.

Satisfied that Maura was intent upon her own thoughts, Patrick murmured, "I'm going to watch from over there."

"Don't go far," Mr. Drabble cautioned. "They'll be letting us below soon."

Small and wiry, Patrick had little trouble slipping through the crowd to the opposite side of the ship. Once there, he climbed the ratlines a ways and held on, toes curling over the ropes. From this roost he studied the main deck in search of some entry into the bottom hold. Only now did he admit to himself that he had no clear idea where or what the bottom hold was. In all his twelve years he had never been on such a boat. The words had made sense in Liverpool, when Fred told him where he'd hidden Laurence. They didn't make sense now.

Looking about, Patrick noticed a sailor emerge from a closet-like structure almost directly below the main mast. Would that be a way? he asked himself.

As soon as the sailor moved on, Patrick climbed down from the lines and stole a look inside the small structure. A narrow stairway led down. After checking to see if anyone was watching him, Patrick stepped into the alcove, made the sign of the cross, grasped the guide rope, and started to descend.

The first level he reached was dim. Long rows of what appeared to be wide shelves stretched forward and aft into darkness. As for cargo, he saw none. The steps continued down. He went on.

At the next level Patrick discovered a few candles set in wall-mounted glass bulbs. Their small yellow flames illuminated neat rows of boxes and crates. Here, surely, was the bottom hold.

Taking up one of the candles, Patrick made his way toward the bow of the ship only to come to a sudden, heart-pounding stop. Before him gaped an open hatchway. One more step and he would have plummeted down.

From the open square of the hatch a ladder dropped into darkness as black as his hair. Was there yet another, third hold below? Fred's words echoed in his mind: *the bottom hold*. Patrick stepped onto the ladder and began to climb slowly down.

Candlelight revealed a dark cavelike expanse embraced by enormous arching timbers. Countless casks, barrels, and chests, piled one atop the other, were deployed in rows that seemed to vanish, fore and aft, into murky blackness. The air was humid, clotted with the stench of rot and filth. Sounds of sloshing bilgewater, the creaks and groans of the plunging ship, filled his ears. This, Patrick told himself with dread, *must* be the bottom hold.

Leaving the ladder, Patrick moved warily in the direction he thought was forward, for Fred had also said *the bow*.

As Patrick crept along—the rough planking pricking his bare feet—he tried to examine each and every crate in fear of missing the one that bore the telltale X in a circle.

Upon reaching the bow, Patrick held the candle up. A few feet from where he stood he saw a coffinlike box wedged between two great beams as far forward as possible. On the side facing him, Patrick could just make out Fred's mark.

Patrick ran to the box and tapped on it. "Laurence!" he called. "Are you there, Laurence?" When no answer came, he began to claw away at the boards.

Chapter 76
In Search of Stowaways

O n the quarterdeck Mr. Murdock, the first mate, assembled his stowaway search party: two sailors, Mr. Grout, and Mr. Clemspool. One sailor carried a long sharp stick, the other a heavy hammer. Mr. Murdock held a lantern.

"All right, gents," the first mate began, "yer welcome to come along to search for stowaways if it's Captain Rickles's pleasure. I'm just warning yer to keep behind me and the lads. If we find someone, they're liable to be desperate. Yer'll want us to deal with 'em, not yerselves."

"No need to worry about me, sir," Mr. Clemspool replied heartily. The further the ship drew away from England, and Mr. Pickler, the more the man's cherublike face resumed its cheerful demeanor. "My friend, however, who cannot claim more than twenty years of life, is quite another matter."

Indeed, Mr. Grout was finding the ship's motion most upsetting. His stomach was queasy, and his face had turned a pasty white. As the *Robert Peel* pitched and rolled, he was continually reaching out for support. "Will this 'ere search take long?" he fretted.

"I wouldn't think so, sir," Mr. Murdock told him, taking pleasure in the landlubber's uneasiness. "But yer welcome to step out at any time and go to yer stateroom. Just take yerselves a pull of fresh air before we go, 'cause we start in the bottom hold. And it's not particular pleasant there."

5

Chapter 77
Laurence Found

F rom inside the crate a weak and dazed Laurence blinked at the candle flame. His muscles were cramped. His stomach ached from hunger. His throat was parched. "Is that you, Patrick?" he beseeched hoarsely.

"Aye, it's me," Patrick replied, much relieved to have found his friend. "And you, Laurence, are you all right?"

"I thought you'd never come," the English boy managed to say.

"Didn't I tell you I would?" Patrick returned with pride, though as he spoke he looked nervously back over his shoulder.

Carefully, he helped Laurence from the crate. But the boy sank to the floor, too weak to stand.

"I'll be needing to put the boards back on," Patrick cautioned. "Else for sure they'll know you've been in the box." He set his candle aside and worked to shove the crate boards back into place.

"Now, Laurence," he said, kneeling before his friend, "you must listen to me, because I can't be staying long. I don't know where we're to be yet so I can't take you with me. And faith, I'm thinking it wouldn't be safe for you there. Maybe you'd best bide some time here."

"Where?" Laurence asked, too numb, too confused to think for himself.

"I'm not sure exactly," Patrick admitted. "You could try among the barrels over there. Only you'd best hurry, Laurence. They'll be searching for you."

"For me?" whimpered Laurence.

"For any stowaways."

The miserable boy stared into the murky darkness.

"Laurence, you must look at me and listen! I'm going now or my sister will be wondering where I am. You can hide yourself, can't you?"

"Patrick! Will you come back soon?"

"Don't you be worrying about that," Patrick assured him as he retrieved the candle and backed away a few steps. "You can be sure I'll come as often as I can."

"But—"

"Just hide yourself, Laurence!" Patrick whispered with urgency as he moved further into the dark. "Do you hear me? Hide yourself!"

Laurence struggled to his feet. "Patrick!" he called. But the Irish boy had disappeared, though where Laurence was not sure.

Enveloped by inky blackness, Laurence stood where he was, sensing little more than the ceaseless pitching and yawing of the ship. The motion made him disoriented. It was hard to grasp what was happening. "I'm going to America," he said out loud. "To America," he repeated as though trying to convince himself. Then he added, "I have no family. I've no money. My name is Laurence, and I—"

Suddenly he heard voices coming from above. Terrified of being caught, Laurence looked up and saw a beam of light cut down a ladder like a golden spike. Then he saw boots descending. Close to panic, he scrambled along the aisle in search of a hiding place.

Chapter 78
Mr. Murdock on the Prowl

I magine people hiding in such a pestilential hole!" Mr. Clemspool exclaimed.

"But they do," Mr. Murdock said as he swung his lantern beam about to illuminate the cargo.

The smell in the hold was so nauseating that Mr. Grout pinched his nose. " 'Ow can yer find anyone 'ere?" he wondered as he gawked about. "More a place for ghosts than livin' people." Nervously, he reached out and rapped his knuckles upon wood, then grasped the same timber to keep himself steady.

"Aye, ships do have ghosts," Mr. Murdock solemnly assured him.

"They do?"

"It's a sailor's belief, sir, that ships are haunted by the souls of those who died trying to get on board. Not to mention those who drown during a voyage."

"Lord 'elp us!" Mr. Grout cried. "Are yer speakin' the truth?"

The first mate tipped a wink to Mr. Clemspool, who in turn encouraged the teasing with a grin.

" 'Course it's true!" Mr. Murdock insisted. "And yer had best be on the lookout for them, sir."

In dread, Mr. Grout shut his one good eye.

"Now, gentlemen," Mr. Murdock said, "to business. Stowaways always think themselves clever by trying some-

8

thing different. Except it's just those differences that help us find 'em. See these barrels here, gentlemen, stacked one atop the other? All neat and regular. Little likelihood of anyone being in 'em. Consider yerself." He measured the large Mr. Grout with gleeful eyes. "Yer could hardly get in one of 'em barrels, now could yer, sir? And if yer did," he added ominously, "we'd never pry yer out alive. Regular bit of salt cod, yer'd be."

Mr. Grout shuddered.

"No, sir," the first mate continued, "what we do is look for what's irregular. Stowaways tuck themselves into corners, thinking they won't be noticed. We usually find 'em up forward or aft by the bread and spirit larders, where there's some open space. Yer'll see."

Holding his lantern before him, Mr. Murdock led the way down the central aisle between the rows of cargo. Now and again he nodded to one of his crew and pointed to a box or bale. The sailor either banged the box or poked a staff deep into it. But though they tried many times, no one was found.

When they went as far forward as they could, the first mate suddenly gave a snort and pointed to an upright crate standing quite isolated in the bow. Its position had the look of irregularity even to Mr. Clemspool's and Mr. Grout's unpracticed eyes.

Grinning broadly, Mr. Murdock beckoned to the sailors. They hastened forward and crouched at either side of the crate.

The first mate gave a curt nod, reached out, took hold of one of the crate's slats, and yanked. The board clattered to the floor. All five men leaned forward to see what was inside.

It was empty.

"By God," Mr. Murdock swore with rage. "*Someone* was here. And whoever he is, he's on board somewhere. Don't yer fear, gents. I'll get him. And when I do, I'll make him jig to a lively tune."

Laurence, crouched deep among rows of barrels amidships, heard every word. To keep himself from sobbing, he bit hard into his lower lip.

Chapter 79
A Proposal Is Made

Mr. Drabble could not help himself. While Maura was caught up in her thoughts and worries, he had gazed at her intently, smiling broadly from time to time. Miss Maura O'Connell was the angel who had dropped through the miasma of Mrs. Sonderbye's basement and led him out of loathsome Liverpool toward the promised land. Without her, the actor was convinced, he would have perished. Indeed, it was far more than gratitude that he felt toward her: In a matter of days he had fallen in love with her.

The idea of loving Maura thrilled him. Was not he a gifted actor? Was not she a heroine? Was not her rescue of him the stuff of great drama? So he believed.

Here they were embarking on an epic voyage—the play. Here they were on a ship—a stage. There were the passengers—the audience. Here was his leading lady—Maura. Was not he—Horatio Drabble—destined to play the role of devoted lover? Was not loving this young woman the part he'd prepared himself for all his life? To each of these questions Mr. Drabble answered a resounding "Yes!"

Now, as the ship sailed toward the Western Sea—the second act of the play—he felt compelled to speak the lines fate had written for him.

10

"Miss O'Connell," he called gently.

Maura, hearing her name, turned.

Even as she did, Mr. Drabble gathered up one of her hands in both of his and embraced it with his long fingers. Solemnly, he pressed the hand to his lips, kissed it—then allowed himself a prodigious sigh.

Maura was shocked.

"My dear Miss O'Connell," Mr. Drabble began again, his face suffused with a pink glow that heightened the intensity of his brown eyes, "though we've known each other but a short time, it has been long enough for me to discover your great virtues. The bard expressed it far, far better than I ever shall when he said, 'Love goes toward love.' May I, even as we set upon this voyage together, beg your permission to extend it through the rest of our lives?"

Maura looked at him incredulously.

Oblivious, Mr. Drabble smiled sweetly and went on. "What I am suggesting, my dear Miss O'Connell, in humbler words, is this: Will you bestow upon me the honor of your hand in marriage?"

Maura's reaction shifted from shock to offense. How could this man—all but a stranger—speak to her, a girl alone, in such a way? But a stab of guilt quickly followed her sense of affront. What had she done to encourage this man? The answer was immediate and clear. She had allowed herself to become too familiar.

In fright, she snatched her hand away and pressed it against her throat as if to feel her words as she spoke them. "Mr. D-D-Drabble," she stammered, "you must not say such things. You mustn't! If we're to be friends at all—and you've been a generous one—you cannot address me so. I'm but fifteen years of age. I'll not hear it!"

Mr. Drabble sank to his knees. "Shakespeare's Juliet," he reminded her, "was a mere fourteen."

"By the Holy Mother, Mr. Drabble, I'm afraid I don't know this Juliet you're speaking of, and besides—"

Maura's words were interrupted by a voice that rang out across the deck.

"Attention! Attention!" As one, the crowd of emigrants turned to see Captain Rickles addressing them through his speaking trumpet.

"My first mate," the captain announced, "has informed me that there's a stowaway upon this ship. I warn you: Do not aid this person! If you do, it will go as hard on you as on him when he's found, as he surely will be.

"But we are well off, and there will be no more green seaweed till we reach America! For now, all is in readiness for you to go below. Once there, you will be permitted to claim your berths. We expect orderly behavior. There's room for all."

The captain's words galvanized the crowd. The emigrants snatched up their belongings and began to surge toward the steps that would take them below.

Maura turned back to Mr. Drabble. The actor, still upon his knees, was gazing up at her as if he had not heard anything she or the captain had said.

"Please, Mr. Drabble, *please* . . . ," Maura begged in an agonized whisper, "you must get up! I'll not think of it again, nor, I beg, will you. Please!"

Maura felt a pull on her arm. It was Patrick.

"And where have you been?" she demanded, the harshness of her voice masking the great relief she felt that her brother was by her side again.

Breathless from rushing up from below, Patrick could not speak. He could only shake his head.

"Are you ill?" Maura asked, instantly alarmed.

"It's the rolling of the ship," he gasped.

A trembling Mr. Drabble pulled himself to his feet. "Miss O'Connell," he managed to say in a voice barely above a whisper, "we had best go below ourselves."

Patrick looked from his sister to the actor. Though he had come too late to hear their exchange, he had seen the man on his knees and observed his sister's great agitation. Neither one would look at the other.

He's asked her to marry him, Patrick thought with dismay, and she's accepted. Even if he had had the courage to inquire about it—which he did not—there was no time to do so. They gathered up their bundles and joined the crowd surging toward the entryway, the same that Patrick had used before. Slow as their descent was, the trio at last stepped upon the steerage deck, where they were to live during the long weeks of the voyage. What they beheld made them gasp in astonishment.

Chapter 80
The Steerage Deck

The few oil lanterns dangling from the low ceiling cast a dull, smoky light, making it impossible to see for any great distance. What was visible were two long rows of platforms—forty-five to a side—set up like bunk beds, upper and lower. On the foot of each platform section a number was chalked.

These platform berths were built of soft and splintery wood and measured six feet by six, boxed in by wood strips so as to keep occupants and their possessions from tumbling out. Wooden braces—none too strong—ran from floor to ceiling to hold the platforms up. As for the space between bottom and top—where one might hope to sit up—it was hardly more than a few feet.

Patrick thought there must be two hundred passengers

already jammed into the narrow area between the facing rows of berths. Goods were being passed about, sorted, tearfully lost, searched for, loudly found, then lost again. Unwieldy mattresses were being unrolled. Trunks were opened and rummaged through, their contents spewing forth as from horns of shabby plenty and further scattered by the constant rolling and pitching of the ship.

And the noise! Babies were crying, children squabbling, adults shouting to make themselves heard above the din. The air was close, stinking with the crush of too many people in a space too small with too little ventilation. Mr. Drabble could barely breathe.

"Keep going along! Keep going!" a sailor at the foot of the steps repeatedly cried. "Take yer berths. Four persons to each! Keep moving! Keep moving! Four persons to a berth."

The newcomers struggled forward, loudly proclaiming this or that platform as the one assigned them and crawling in, whether others were there or not.

"Where are we to go?" Maura demanded of the sailor.

"What's yer number?" he cried.

"Seventy-four!"

"To the forward, lass!" he shouted. "And yer'd better be quick. Nothing lasts long here."

Mr. Drabble exclaimed, "Do you mean to say, sir, that these open platforms are our berths, where we are expected to live?"

"Yer can live or die on 'em, for all I care, mate," the sailor retorted. "It's yer place so yer can do wot yer likes. Now move yerselves or yer'll be trampled! There's a hundred or more behind yer."

Propelled forward, Maura, Patrick, and Mr. Drabble struggled through the crush of people. Each berth they passed was packed with occupants, pushing and jostling to establish themselves in some degree of comfort.

"Here's our number," Mr. Drabble announced finally. "Do you wish the top or lower berth?"

"Together?" asked a horrified Maura. Only minutes ago this man had shocked her nearly to death with his proposal.

Mr. Drabble glanced back. More passengers were pressing forward. "It's either me or someone else, Miss O'Connell," he said.

Maura, furious at him, at herself, at everything, blushed to the roots of her hair. "Mr. Drabble, it's not decent!" she cried.

Then, embarrassed by her outburst, she turned away and stared back into the area toward the steps. Never in her wildest thoughts could she have imagined anything like this. She had considered Mrs. Sonderbye's house ghastly. The steerage deck was ten times worse.

Chapter 81
Berth Mates

S omething crawled over Patrick's bare feet. Startled, he looked down just in time to see a brown rat scurry across the wooden floor and disappear beneath one of the lower platforms.

"Miss O'Connell," Mr. Drabble urged with a nervous glance at the flow of newcomers. "If we don't choose quickly, we'll be pushed aside."

Maura gave way. "The top," she whispered.

"Up you go," Mr. Drabble told Patrick. More than glad to leave the floor, the boy hauled himself to the higher berth. Once there, he looked down along the teeming deck only to see Mr. Murdock working his way through the crowd in their direction. Certain he was coming for him, Patrick, heart hammering, crammed himself into a far corner. As it was,

15

the first mate pushed past, but Patrick was sure he looked right at him as if to say, "I know what you know." It frightened him terribly.

"Patrick!" Maura cried. "Pay some mind!" She was handing up their few belongings. Then Mr. Drabble worked his way into the berth. He twisted about but did not try to sit. There was no headroom.

"Can I help you up, Miss O'Connell?" he said to Maura, his voice stiff with formality.

"No," she replied, full of mortification. As she stood there, another Irish family arrived, a man, his wife, and two young children.

"Would you be holding this spot?" the man asked Maura, indicating the lower berth.

Maura shook her head.

"In you go then," the man instructed his family. All four hastily squeezed in, leaving their two trunks and three sacks to block the aisle.

Another family appeared. It consisted of two boys, a girl, a large fleshy-faced man with a mop of curly hair, and a woman who seemed to be in charge. The woman's long, tangled gray hair and ragged dress hid nothing of her squalidness. Though her appearance was one of frailty, her fixed and sullen eyes revealed a ferocity that promised argument.

"How many would ye be having up there?" she demanded of Maura.

"The three of us," Maura felt obliged to reply.

"And wouldn't you know that each berth is meant for four?" the woman cried shrilly as she pushed the small dirty girl forward. The girl, no more than eight, Maura thought, bore such a marked resemblance to the woman, it was clear she was her daughter. But it was fright not fierceness that Maura saw in her eyes.

"This will be yours then, Bridy Faherty," the woman informed her bewildered child, indicating the top berth where

Patrick and Mr. Drabble already were. "Get yourself in before someone steals that from us too."

"But, madam," Mr. Drabble tried to object, "we're already three." To Maura's further embarrassment, he added, "And we are a family."

"Begorra, you could be the queen's horse guards for all I care," Mrs. Faherty snapped, her face flushed with anger. "There's to be four in each berth, and since we'll be berthing down a ways, the girl will be stopping here, thank you." Without further ado she picked Bridy up and thrust her onto the platform.

The girl crawled into a corner opposite Patrick and shrank down.

Maura, seeing how frightened the child was, reached up and touched her hand.

"It's all right," she said softly. "It's the same for us all. But you need not fear. We'll soon be getting to America, where all will be fine."

Chapter 82

Laurence in the Hold

*T*hough Laurence was pretty sure that the stowaway search party had gone above decks, he was afraid to stand up and stretch himself. Suppose the searchers came back? As it was, he remained crouched down between two barrels, listening intently, all the while aware of the taste of blood from his bitten lip.

After ten more minutes he cautiously raised his head and looked about. By the light of the open hatchway above, he gazed at the cargo. It seemed endless, row upon row of

17

crates, boxes, barrels. There was also a considerable amount of litter, sticks, staves, and blocks of wood. Moreover, the entire hold was so terribly foul, with such a ghastly stench, the rasping and grating of wood timbers so irritatingly incessant, that Laurence hardly knew what to cover first, his eyes, his ears, or his mouth.

Growing bolder, he began to roam. At the stern of the boat he found a room with a door partially ajar. Curious, he pulled the door open. Though he could see nothing, he smelled the distinct sweet smell of bread. It was strong enough to make his stomach growl.

Feeling his way, Laurence entered the room and banged into something hard. Groping blindly, he felt what seemed to be stacks of small, light, and very hard squares of wood. Was it what he'd seen before? Wood blocks? He couldn't tell. He picked one up and sniffed it. It was something breadlike. Once again his stomach growled. Laurence put the square to his mouth and tried to bite into it. It was as hard as a rock.

Convinced that no matter how hard it was, he'd nonetheless found bread, Laurence took a few of the squares and continued wandering through the dark, eating—or trying to—as he went. Bit by bit, the bread softened, until at last he was able to break off a piece. He felt something wiggle. It was a worm. Hastily he plucked it out. Though it made him queasy to eat, he was so hungry, he did anyway. The bread had a sour taste and gritty texture. He continued to eat, finding and throwing away two more worms before he gradually consumed an entire square. Having eased his hunger a trifle, he began to work on a second.

The more he ate, the thirstier he became. Harking to the continual sound of water sloshing below his feet, he lay down and pushed his fingers between the planking. When his fingertips touched wetness, he pulled back his hand, eager to suck at the moisture. The smell proved so offensive he could not.

His thirst now raged. Feeling desperate, he began to search for another source of water. Midships he came upon two great metal tanks very much taller than he was, as well as wider. He had no idea what they were. As he groped his way by, his hand drew across the surface of one. It was cool and wet. When he sniffed his fingers and sensed nothing bad, he licked the moisture off. The taste of water! Excited, he pressed both hands flat against one of the tanks, then hastened to lick more from them. He tried again along another part of the tank and licked the water off. He smiled, recalling his sister's cat washing herself. Twenty minutes later his thirst was slaked.

Continuing to explore, Laurence came upon a narrow ladder leading up into darkness near the stern of the ship. He wondered what would happen if he climbed it. But he thought of the searchers and refrained.

As he stood there, he heard a high-pitched squeaking noise. It was different from the sound the ship timbers made. And it came from first one place, then another.

Something ran over his foot.

Involuntarily, Laurence screamed. The squeaking stopped abruptly. He knew then what the sound was. Rats.

He decided he must find a permanent place to hide, somewhere he might sleep safe from men, and rats. First he made his way to the bow and located the crate in which Fred had stowed him aboard. For a brief moment he thought of climbing back in. But the notion was repugnant. He wanted nothing more to do with that box, ever.

He wandered back among the barrels. Though many of them were taller than he, Laurence tried now and again to lift a lid. Not one of them budged. He tried some crates too but with no better results.

Returning to the barrels, he set about checking each one,

row by row, avoiding those along the aisles. After a full hour he found one whose lid was open a crack—hardly wide enough for his fingers. He pulled, but it would not give.

Counting barrels by rows until he reached the aisle, Laurence searched out a stick to pry the lid open. Again by counting he found his way back to the barrel, eased the stick into the crack, and pulled down. With a sudden pop, the lid flew off.

Excited by his success, Laurence hauled himself up the barrel side and fished inside with his hands. What he touched was straw. It smelled sweet and clean. Plunging his hand down into the straw, he felt some crockery, grasped it, and pulled out a teacup.

One by one he removed the cups and saucers—he took out a hundred all together—and stashed them individually and in groups about the hold, behind timbers, into nooks and crannies, anyplace he thought would be out of sight. By the time he was done, he was able to crawl into the barrel itself, press the straw down, and sink upon a scratchy but pleasant-smelling soft cushion. He found it quite roomy, big enough to allow him to sit comfortably if he drew up his legs.

Pleased with what he'd achieved, Laurence stood up and drew the barrel lid partway over the opening. It was easy then to maneuver the lid atop the barrel and, even as he squatted down, to pull it back as it had been. He could only hope it was not noticeably open.

Sitting in total darkness, Laurence took from his pocket the last of his bread squares and began to suck on it—on the alert for worms. As he ate, his thoughts drifted, and he tried to remember—for it seemed so long ago—when it was that he had left his home. To his astonishment it was but three days past! Impossible. He counted the days again, and again. Three days. . . . Amazed, he shook his head.

He thought then of his London house, where the rooms

were so many. This is my room now, he said to himself, touching the side of the barrel. He made up his mind that each day the ship sailed, he would pretend the barrel was a different London room. He would start with his own room, recalling each and every object just as it had been . . . three days ago.

He began by thinking about his bed in London. It was high. It was plump. It had lacy pillows. . . . By the time Laurence thought of the pillows, he was fast asleep.

Chapter 83
An Identity Revealed

The two staterooms on the *Robert Peel* could be found beneath the quarterdeck, near the stern of the ship. The rooms had no windows, though in each a large overhead oil lamp provided sufficient light. The woodwork—of well-finished mahogany, satinwood, and maple—was replete with carved scrolls and capitals, some even edged in gold. A washstand with saltwater pump, a chest of drawers, a writing desk supplied with paper and ink, a sofa, and two beds, one on either side of the room, made up the furniture. Everything, including a rug, was bolted down.

"I rather like it," Mr. Clemspool announced as he sat on one of the beds and kneaded the soft mattress with his fleshy fingers. "But then I deeply believe that if he pays a fair price, a gentleman should expect something decent. Don't you think?"

Mr. Grout lay stretched out upon his bunk, feeling miserable. His stomach was still queasy. His head was dizzy. "It's bloody small and crowded if yer asks me," the young man said between clenched teeth. "I could 'ave done much better in London at 'alf the price. And I wouldn't be pitchin' and rollin' neither."

"Ah, but, Mr. Grout, consider: Here you are, free from the restraints of your past. Far better than sitting in jail," Mr. Clemspool suggested.

"Beggin' yer pardon," Mr. Grout said peevishly. "I wasn't goin' to no jail."

"Now, sir, let us not forget that *money*." He looked slyly at his friend. "Where would you be, sir, without it?" The portly man smiled sweetly and looked about with a deadpan air. "I must confess," he said, hastening to change the subject, "I do wish I'd had the time to gather my personal belongings."

"No one said yer 'ad to come," Mr. Grout replied, still smarting from his companion's remark about jail. "Yer might 'ave gone back to London and done wot yer do. It would 'ave saved me a pretty penny."

"Me? Go back? Not I," Mr. Clemspool returned. "That investigator—Mr. Pickler—made it perfectly clear that he was going to bring an action against me."

"Fearful, are yer?"

"To be frank," Mr. Clemspool admitted, "it was not *him* I feared. It was Mr. Pickler's employer."

"Which is why yer 'eadin' for America."

Mr. Clemspool pondered the remark. Then, as much to himself as to Mr. Grout, he said, "But, to make my point precisely, perhaps I *can* strike back."

Mr. Grout raised himself on an elbow. "Wot's that supposed to mean?"

"Is it not worth considering," Mr. Clemspool asked, examining the idea even as he proposed it, "how Mr. Pickler's venerated employer would react to the knowledge that his rude cur of an elder son endeavored to send his second son out of England . . . *permanently?*"

Mr. Grout shook his head. "Wot was the boy's name?"

Mr. Clemspool considered. Then he said, "No harm in your knowing now. It was Sir Laurence Kirkle."

Mr. Grout sat bolt upright. "Kirkle!" he cried. "Of the government?"

"The same," returned Mr. Clemspool smugly.

"Yer mad to touch that kind!"

Mr. Clemspool plucked the air as if it contained an invisible harp. "He may rot at the bottom of a ditch for all I care."

" 'Ere! Do yer think 'e's dead?"

"I sincerely hope so," Mr. Clemspool said.

"The dead can come back at yer," Mr. Grout warned.

"Nonsense. Anyway, I am engaged upon a greater purpose. My new life. I suppose I could inform the boy's father or—" He stopped short, his mouth open, his fingers extended.

"Or wot?" Mr. Grout asked. The talk of death and ghosts had unnerved him.

Mr. Clemspool snatched at the air as if it held the very answer he was looking for. "Yes! Perhaps it would be better if I communicated with the older brother, Sir Albert Kirkle."

" 'E the one who 'ired yer?"

"He was, indeed. Yes, I shall write Sir Albert and say I have his brother with me."

"But yer don't!"

"Of course not, you fool! He's in Liverpool, somewhere, thank goodness. But I will tell Sir Albert that I shall inform his father about his scheme—engaging me to dispose of Sir Laurence—unless he sends me a sum of money sufficiently large to cover my losses."

"Blackmail," said Mr. Grout with a nod of his head.

"Sir!" Mr. Clemspool returned with a withering glance. "I do not engage in illegalities like some I might mention.

No, I am merely desirous of finding some means of defraying losses that have been brought down about my innocent head. It will be no more than what he owes me."

"One lump of money or a regular allowance like?"

The question prompted a wide smile. "Mr. Grout, I do sometimes believe you can actually think! Indeed, it is always better to have a steady income. Such befits a gentleman."

"Gentleman! Who yer talkin' about now?"

"Me."

Mr. Grout pushed himself up from his bed and snatched up his hat. "I needs to look about," he announced, and, somewhat unsteady, went out of the room.

Mr. Clemspool was quick to follow.

Chapter 84

Mr. Clemspool about His Business

M r. Grout groped his way up to the quarterdeck, to a room maintained for first-class gentlemen passengers. A small space, it contained little more than a U-shaped sofa—built into the walls—where passengers could smoke the cigars set out for them in a canister.

Mr. Grout arrived with Mr. Clemspool at his heels. "Now see 'ere, Clemspool," Mr. Grout said, his back braced against the wall and his one good eye fixed upon his companion, "yer do wot yer want in yer business. But I want nothin' to do with it anymore. Messin' 'round with swells like the Kirkles ain't smart. They've got ways to punch back that's 'ot and 'eavy."

"Ah, Mr. Grout," said Mr. Clemspool, sitting and selecting a cigar, "you are a callow youth. Much too timid!"

"Me? Timid? Not by yer life. It's just that I knows about live folks as well as dead ones and pays heed to both kinds."

Mr. Clemspool waved his unlit cigar grandly. "You need not worry, sir. I have no intention of being dependent on you."

"Don't yer?"

"You, sir, are—to make my point precisely—beneath me."

Flushing with anger, Mr. Grout pushed himself away from the wall. "Just don't forget—"

At that instant the door was flung open, and another man entered. His top hat, greatcoat, and silk muffler proclaimed him a gentleman. Moreover, though he was not tall, his considerable bulk and a mane of flowing graying hair helped give him a look of authority. His face was square with a firm chin and smooth, waxen cheeks, rather like the sculptured head of an ancient Roman. Of smile there was none. As for his eyes, they were small, gray, and set together closely, giving him a hard, disdainful expression.

The newcomer nodded briskly to Mr. Clemspool and Mr. Grout as he rubbed his hands vigorously to create some warmth. "I fear I shall be chilled until home comes into view," he announced in an American accent. "The sea air cuts to my bones."

"I am sorry to hear it, sir," Mr. Clemspool allowed.

"I hate these voyages," the man informed his listeners, as if they needed to know his mind, "as you must. But when you have as many responsibilities as I do, you are in demand. A man's business is his own. I trust my mother, sir, but no one else's. No doubt you've come to the same conclusion."

"I certainly have," Mr. Clemspool hastened to say as he rose and offered his hand to the stranger. "Mr. Matthew Clemspool of London. A pleasure to make your acquaintance, sir."

"Ambrose Shagwell," the man announced as he shook the proffered hand so hard it was all Mr. Clemspool could do to keep from crying out. "You must be the other first-class passengers. My home is in Lowell, fairest city in the great Commonwealth of Massachusetts, the United States of America. Engaged in the manufacture of cotton textiles. And you, sir?"

"Not in any particular business, sir," replied Mr. Clemspool, waving his hand airily. "I am sailing to America to see what might engage me. That's to say, I have large funds at my disposal."

Mr. Grout snorted at the man's boldness.

The American, however, cast a newly appreciative eye upon Mr. Clemspool. "You are an investor then."

"I am, sir," returned Mr. Clemspool with a nod that seemed to imply much.

"With large funds, you say?"

Mr. Clemspool plucked at the air. "Do you consider fifty thousand a lot?"

Not only did Mr. Shagwell extend his hand to Mr. Clemspool a second time, his grip was quite tender.

"You are more than welcome to America, sir," he said. "We have room for men of enterprise. Just understand that our ways and means are advanced and distinct from yours. Seek to impose Old World ways upon us, and we shall have trouble. America first and always!" Mr. Shagwell concluded, pointing to one of his eyes, then his nose, and with the same hand shaping his thumb and first finger into a circle. Finally, he nodded portentously, as if these signs held some significant meaning.

Mr. Clemspool, though puzzled, chose to ignore them. "I'm not here to dispute you, sir," he returned with an engaging smile.

"Well then," Mr. Shagwell enthused, "our friendship shall

flourish. But you, young man," he said to Mr. Grout, "I don't have the pleasure of *your* acquaintance."

"Toby Grout," a baleful Mr. Grout replied.

"Also in business?"

"Nothin' in particular."

"I hope, Mr. Grout, that you're not one of these lazy, ill-educated fellows who come to my country merely to gawk. We do not appreciate laziness there. Hard, *honest* work has made us great. Hard, honest work will make us greater."

"Excellent philosophy," Mr. Clemspool applauded. "Mr. Grout will be indebted to you for your advice."

"Happy to be helpful," Mr. Shagwell said. "But I was taking my walk about the deck. I intend to do so three times a day regardless of the weather. Gentlemen, since we three constitute the first-class passengers, I trust I shall see you at the captain's table. Good day." So saying, he left the room.

The moment the door shut Mr. Clemspool laughed.

"I don't see wot's funny," Mr. Grout complained. "Sayin' yer 'ave fifty thousand! Yer 'ave nothin'!"

"Give me a man who has nothing but answers," Mr. Clemspool observed, "and I shall show you a man who has no questions. I enjoy doing business with a man like that. Where are you going?"

"I'm going to find that Mr. Drabble and fix up them readin' lessons as 'e promised."

"Do so, Mr. Grout. You heard what that Shagwell fellow said. In America, laziness is not appreciated."

For his part, Ambrose Shagwell, striding about the quarter-deck, speculated if this man Clemspool were not the answer to his great problem, his pressing need for money. He rather thought he was.

Chapter 85

Mr. Drabble at the Bowsprit

*A*t the bowsprit of the *Robert Peel*, a thin spray of sea blew upon Mr. Drabble's forehead like a cooling hand. This was a considerable blessing, since the actor's whole mind still burned with Maura O'Connell's rejection of his proposal. To add insult to his sense of injury, she was now bestowing much attention upon Bridy—the girl who had been foisted on them. The actor, feeling jealous, had left the steerage to go up on deck.

The despondent man entertained the idea of throwing himself into the waves and thus ending his misery. Though the gesture suited his mood, he was not so wretched as to believe that such an act would inspire love in Maura. Even if it did, how could he rejoice in it at the bottom of the sea?

Instead, Mr. Drabble thought about his life. He was willing to acknowledge that he had been a failure in England. In fact, the more he thought about it, the more certain he was that Maura had refused him for exactly that reason. Or was it because that runner, Toggs, had knocked him down so easily at Mrs. Sonderbye's? Oh, why hadn't he put up more of a fight? Because, he told himself, he was a coward.

Perhaps, the actor mused, he should have remained in Liverpool. There, at least, he'd earned a few pennies. It was a kind of living. What could he possibly do in America?

A line from *Hamlet* crept into his head: "When sorrows come, they come not single spies, but in battalions." The words soothed him. Emboldened, he recited other lines from

28

Shakespeare. The more he spoke, the better he felt. Soon he was emoting in his most flamboyant manner, extending his hands and arms, presenting his profile to the wind until, when he was finished, he felt obliged to take a deep bow. To his surprise he heard applause. He turned. There was Mr. Grout.

"Bravo!" the man cried. "Yer in as fine a voice as ever."

"I am happy to see you, sir," Mr. Drabble returned, though he was, in fact, not overjoyed to have company. There was something comforting in reciting tragic lines to an uncaring wind.

"Practicin' for yer American performin'?" Mr. Grout asked.

The actor smiled grimly but was unable to resist someone's interest in him. "Mr. Grout, sir, I confess I don't know exactly what I shall do in America."

"Can't say I know wot I'll do meself," agreed Mr. Grout. "Right now I'm feelin' sick with the way the ship heaves. It's all I can think of."

"Surely your friend can provide some relief."

Mr. Grout snorted. "My friend—if yer want to call 'im that—ain't concerned with much but 'imself. Wot I need is to strike out on me own."

"Going alone," Mr. Drabble agreed, "is the fate of mankind."

"I still want yer to be teachin' me some readin'. It might 'elp."

"Mr. Grout," Mr. Drabble exclaimed with weariness, "you must not place me too high in your esteem. I am nothing—no more than the lowest of low." He bowed to demonstrate the fact.

"To tell the truth," Mr. Grout said, "I'm glad to 'ear it."

"Why is that?" asked Mr. Drabble, who, though eager for sympathy, was grieved to be taken as deserving of his own doleful estimation.

" 'Tween yer and me, Mr. Drabble, I'm not so 'igh as yer

might think. Someday I might tell yer all I've got to answer for. Avoid the dead and take wot yer can of the livin'. That's me way. So if yer thinks yerself low, why, I'm low too, which is reason enough we could be comrades."

Mr. Drabble extended his hand warmly. "Nothing would give me more pleasure, sir."

"Just don't forget I still wants those readin' lessons. I can pay for 'em too. And I'd rather give the money to yer than some other people I know."

Chapter 86
Mr. Clemspool Writes a Letter

*M*atthew Clemspool stood before his stateroom desk and removed a sheet of paper from the pile in the drawer. How much, he asked himself, should he reveal to Sir Albert about what had happened to his brother? After some deliberation, he decided indeed to claim that he had Sir Laurence with him. So what if it were a lie? Sir Albert expected the boy to be on his way to America. That had been the assignment from the start, after all.

After dipping his pen in the blue ink and trying to accommodate his hand to the rolling of the ship, Mr. Clemspool wrote:

My dear Sir Albert,

I send you greetings from the sea.

I wish to inform you that I have the property about which you were concerned safely with me. Indeed, I decided I could best serve your interests if I myself carried it to America and disposed of it there, as you so much desired.

Now, sir, since I am going to such considerable lengths to do your bidding, I must ask you for some payment as soon as possible. I require a fee of one thousand pounds. Then, in addition, I ask you to pay me the sum of one hundred pounds monthly until such time as I alter the arrangement.

I entreat you to do this quickly, for the post across the Atlantic is slow and I have incurred considerable expense on your behalf. In return, you have my word as a gentleman that no information regarding your desires shall ever reach the esteemed ears of your lord father.

But of course, sir, if you do not see fit to pay your bills promptly, I will be forced to inform your father directly about what you paid me to do. *I'm sure you can appreciate the complications that might result.*

Mr. Clemspool read and reread what he had written, making only a few minor adjustments. After due consideration he added:

As to my address in America, I have yet to determine upon a permanent abode or even whether I will remain in the country. But you should write to me in the care of Mr. Ambrose Shagwell, in the city of Lowell, Massachusetts, USA. I am sure word will reach me. Mr. Shagwell is a highly esteemed gentleman and a good friend, a man I trust and, sir, a confidant in all *my affairs.*

Trusting you are, sir, continuing in good health, I remain,

Faithfully yours,
Matthew Clemspool, Esq.

The letter written, Mr. Clemspool stepped out of the stateroom into a long galley way. On the other side of the galley way was the dining room where the three first-class passengers would eat their meals with the captain, first mate, and ship's doctor.

At the forward end of the galley was a large door providing access to the main deck. At the stern end was the captain's quarters. The galley itself was windowless, lit only by a single oil lamp, far forward.

Mr. Clemspool turned toward the captain's cabin. When he heard voices from the inside, he knocked.

"Enter!" a voice commanded.

Mr. Clemspool opened the door. Captain Rickles and his first mate, Mr. Murdock, were conferring.

"Yes, Mr. Clemspool," the captain said, looking up. "What can I do for you?"

"I don't wish to trouble you, sir, but I understand that from time to time as we sail, we meet with other ships."

"We do, sir," the captain replied. "And when we meet them, we heave to and share information."

"Do they ever carry letters?"

"Always and happily."

"Then," Mr. Clemspool said, holding up his letter to Sir Albert, "might I request that this be sent to England when the first opportunity presents itself. It concerns important financial matters."

The captain took the letter and looked at the name and address. Mr. Clemspool noted that he was impressed. "I can assure you, sir, you may count upon me. The shipping lanes are full this time of year. We shall certainly bespeak someone. Your letter will be passed on."

"I am much obliged," Mr. Clemspool said, and bowed his way out, shutting the door behind him. Once beyond the door, however, he lingered and listened.

"As I was saying, Captain"—it was the first mate speaking—"that stowaway is about somewhere. And I'll ferret him out even if it's in Boston Bay."

Mr. Clemspool, having not the slightest interest in the topic of stowaways, turned back to his own stateroom, confident of his future.

Chapter 87
7:35 P.M., Lowell, Massachusetts

C rowds of workers, women mostly but men and children too, poured out through the gates of the Shagwell Cotton Mill Company, the night air frosting their breaths. With their way lit by glowing curbside gas lamps and handheld flares, they headed for boardinghouses, rooms, or shanties, whatever it was they called their homes in the gloomy town of Lowell, Massachusetts.

Amid the throng walked two men. The older was Gregory O'Connell, father to Maura and Patrick, whom they called Da.

Though barely fifty years of age, Mr. O'Connell had the sad and grizzled look of a tired, broken man. A small slip of a fellow, he had stooped shoulders and a round creased face with dark hollows beneath his eyes. His boots and jacket were old and patched. The muffler about his neck was torn. His companion, Nathaniel Brewster, had never seen him laugh.

A tall, gangly, broad-shouldered seventeen-year-old, Nathaniel had an awkward, often clumsy walk, unruly brown hair, lively hazel eyes, and a quick smile.

Born and raised on a farm in Maine, he was the youngest

son of a large family. Having no expectations of an inheritance and wanting neither a sailor's life nor a fisherman's, he decided he'd go to the new state of California in search of gold. With little more than his poor parents' blessing, he had set off by way of Boston, in hopes of getting a ship.

On the docks, however, he discovered that he would have to raise a fair amount of money before he could sail, for the voyage around Cape Horn was costly and of several months' duration. Nathaniel promptly sought employment. It was in Boston, in cheap lodgings, that he met Gregory O'Connell.

Mr. O'Connell, being much bewildered and lonely in the New World, welcomed the bold but caring kindness of one who knew American custom. As for Nathaniel, he felt better in the company of a dour elder. So it was that the two men had begun their winter-spring friendship nine months before. Together they struggled to establish themselves by sharing bed and board. For the past few months they'd worked steadily in the mills of Lowell, thirty miles to the northwest of Boston.

That evening, as the two men negotiated the pits and holes in icy Adams Street, neither spoke. Toiling from five-thirty in the morning till seven-thirty at night had quite exhausted them.

Suddenly—though still some distance from their rented room—Mr. O'Connell stopped. "No," he announced as if he had come to a decision after much debate, "I'll never get used to it."

"What's that?" Nathaniel asked. Though his thoughts were on dinner, he paused in deference to the elder man.

"It's the dreadful noise and cotton dust in the mill," Mr. O'Connell said. "A man can hardly breathe or think. Or," he added ruefully, "even live."

"Mr. O'Connell," Nathaniel said with his good-natured

laugh, "seems to me you're forgetting we're being paid for our work."

"In faith," Mr. O'Connell replied, "I was raised on the land. Worked my bit, may the Holy Mother bless it. An old-fashioned life, you're forever saying, Mr. Brewster. But here, it's eight hundred machines banging and crashing fourteen hours a day. Doesn't the floor itself tremble?" He lifted a hand, only to drop it when unable to find words to express himself.

"You've said it all before, Mr. O'Connell," Nathaniel reminded him, eager to move on.

The Irishman held his ground and shook his head. "By the blessed saints, Nathaniel, I don't suspect you'll be hearing me say it for very much longer."

"You've said that too, so often," Nathaniel replied. "I reckon you'll be saying it fifty years from now."

"You don't understand," Mr. O'Connell insisted. "I'm a doomed man."

This woeful prediction brought another laugh from Nathaniel. "Mr. O'Connell," he said, "keep in mind that things are different here in America."

"They are."

"And the biggest difference," the young man reminded his elder, "is that you're employed."

"I'll not deny it."

"For hard cash."

"Four dollars a week."

"And you eat."

"I do."

"While in that Ireland of yours—so you've told me—there was no work, cash, *or* food."

"There are those, Mr. Brewster, who have no love of the Irish."

"Now, Mr. O'Connell, you have many a friend at the mill."

Mr. O'Connell looked up at Nathaniel. "Faith, lad, don't you miss your family?"

"Of course I do," the young man returned. "But before I left, my father took me aside. 'Nathaniel,' says he, 'don't waste your time missing us. We'll be here forever, alive or dead.' "

"A kind man you have for a father," Mr. O'Connell said.

"He is," Nathaniel agreed with a touch of impatience. "But we should get on, Mr. O'Connell. I can smell snow in the wind, and I'm roaring hungry."

Mr. O'Connell, however, would not move. "By the living Jesus," he cried, "I wish I had never left home!"

"Mr. O'Connell," Nathaniel said, "how many times have we agreed, we did the right thing by leaving our homes. Besides, your wife and children will be with you soon."

"God willing."

"Look how quick you raised the cash for their passage!"

"But hundreds die on those coffin ships," the Irishman said.

"Mr. O'Connell, you're living proof that not everyone dies. You'll be reunited soon."

"No more faithful wife than Annie O'Connell," Mr. O'Connell was quick to acknowledge. The thought was sufficiently soothing that he began to walk again.

"And there's your lovely daughter, Maura," Nathaniel added with care, "tall and strong, with thick brown hair and blue eyes. There, you see! You've told me so much about her, I sometimes think I'm already in love with the girl."

Mr. O'Connell stopped abruptly.

Nathaniel, alarmed, asked, "Did I speak too free?"

"Lad," Mr. O'Connell said with considerable difficulty, "the truth is, I never felt so ill as I do now. Weren't there moments today when I was certain the machines were about to snap me soul from me heart? I could hardly keep up, I was that dizzy with confusion. Terrible pains too," he added,

touching his heart. "Aye, I'm a beaten man," he concluded sadly.

"Mr. O'Connell," Nathaniel said lightly, "you've been
dying since I met you." He moved on.

Mr. O'Connell did not. His heart seemed to contract in
pain. His breathing grew difficult. "Mr. Brewster!" he cried
out in alarm. The young man stopped and looked back. "If
something happens to me . . . ," he managed to say, "happens before my family comes, it's your vow that you'll always
be their friend. . . . It's that I'm waiting to hear."

Nathaniel ambled back. "Of course I'll be their friend,"
he replied. "And if a decent Catholic is willing to shake the
hand of an equally decent Protestant, you can have my hand
on it!"

A trembling Mr. O'Connell held out his hand. Nathaniel
grasped it gladly. Then, having recovered his breath, and
the pain subsiding, Mr. O'Connell went on with his friend.

But as whirlpools of old snow spun like tops all about
them, Gregory O'Connell prayed under his breath. "Holy
Mother," he whispered, "just let me live till my family
comes."

Chapter 88
A Meeting in Lowell

That evening the snow Nathaniel had predicted for Lowell
arrived. It was borne on the edge of a sharp sleet-edged
wind that sliced through the wide expanse of Merrimack
Street, the city's principal thoroughfare. Windows rattled,
doors banged, store signs whipped like the wings of fright-

ened birds. The few people and horses out and about were forced to bow their heads in submission as they struggled to find warmer, kindlier refuges.

Though it was an evening designed to keep citizens at home, a meeting was being held in the back room of the Spindle City Hotel and Oyster Bar on the main street. It was a hotel that catered to the itinerant salesman, the mechanic, the traveling businessman. Public gatherings were often held there.

This meeting, however, was not a public one. Indeed, a ragged boy had been posted next to the entryway with clear instructions to give an alarm if anyone else tried to enter. By the boy's side was a box upon which was written SHINE, 2C.

There were four people gathered. Of the three men and one woman seated at the square table in one corner of the room, three wore hats and coats. Whether they did so because the room was cold or because they wanted to be ready to flee at a moment's notice was not clear. But now and again, as the wind blew by with its low, dirgelike sound, they lifted their heads, listened intently, and were inwardly pleased: The storm would be the most effective guardian of their meeting. Who, upon such a night, when hearths at home were heated, would desire to engage in a discussion about the menace of immigrants?

The four shared one small lighted candle. It stood on the table close enough to illuminate the one bareheaded person in the room. His name was Jeremiah Jenkins.

The shaggy white hair and full fringe of white whiskers about Mr. Jenkins's face suggested he had reached advanced years. Not so. His skin was smooth, and his eyes, beneath bushy dark eyebrows, were as bright as candle flames. He appeared to have a fire within, the strength of which helped him command the rapt attention of his small audience.

"And what I'm telling you, friends," Jeremiah Jenkins was saying in a voice that oozed confidentiality, "is however refined it is to *talk* about these problems, what truly counts in this world is the *action* you take.

"Friends," he ventured, looking into each of his listeners' faces, "may I suggest the time for action is at hand!"

"Hear, hear," came a murmured reply from one of the men, a stooped, shrunken fellow who had something of a rat's appearance.

"Do I have to remind you people," Mr. Jenkins continued, "of the decrease in wages now offered working men and women, the increase in crime, filth, and illness in this once-great city of Lowell?"

"Not me, you don't," responded another of the men warmly—a beefy round man, middle-aged, who wore his hat perched high on his head.

"I'm pleased you agree," said Mr. Jenkins, reaching across the table to shake the man's hand with something that suggested gratitude. He then swiveled about in his chair. "You there," he called across the room to the boy sitting by the door.

The boy, who had been daydreaming, started up. "Yes, mister."

"Do you have a name?" Mr. Jenkins gave a wink to his tablemates.

"Jeb Grafton." The boy had a raw red face that seemed to have been recently peeled to expose a perpetual pout. His trousers were ragged, his thin jacket frayed and split at the elbows. The cloth cap he wore was pulled so low that he seemed to look upon the world as if from under a ledge.

"Come over here, boy," Mr. Jenkins said kindly.

The boy shuffled over and stood sheepishly by the man.

"Do you go to school, Jeb Grafton?"

Jeb gave a contemptuous grunt. "I suppose I did—for a while. I'm thirteen now."

"And how many in your school were foreigners?"

Jeb screwed up his face. "Pretty much half."

"Is that why you left?"

The boy shrugged. "They were too stupid for me."

"There, you see," Mr. Jenkins said with a slap of his hand on the table so loud and sudden it made his listeners jump. "*That's* what it's come to! The foreigners have even taken over the schools from *our* children. Now, friends," he continued in a somewhat modulated voice, "you know very well who the worst of these foreigners are: the Irish." The word *Irish* was spoken slowly, in two equally stressed syllables, the second slipping out with a hiss.

"Even as I speak, they are crowding onto our shores. By the thousands. By the tens of thousands! Starving beggars, each and every one of them. All expecting to live on handouts from the government, *your* government.

"Are they grateful? Not a bit. To whom do these Irish give *their* allegiance? To the Roman Church, that's who. To priests, nuns, bishops, and popes. Friends, I'm here tonight to warn you that the republic is under attack by these people. I say we must fight back."

"And what are we supposed to do about it?" The woman who asked the question was named Betsy Howard. She was young, with a broad open face and dark hair. "They take low wages, and they don't mind how fast the machines go," she added.

"Where do you work?" Mr. Jenkins asked.

"Shagwell Cotton Mill."

The smile on Mr. Jenkins's face withered. He leaned forward. "Are they taking on Irish there too?" he asked.

"Quite a few."

Mr. Jenkins sat back in his chair, visibly shaken. For a moment he seemed lost in thought. His eyes flashed. His fingers fidgeted. Then, as quickly as the emotion had come, it subsided. He smiled wryly.

"What are we to do?" he said. "I'll tell you what *I* do. There's an inn in Boston, the Liberty Tree Inn. Right on the docks. The immigrants often head there directly from the ships. I wait for them there, and when I see them— you can always recognize them—I tell them to get out." He chuckled silently.

"But there's something we can *all* do. It's a new movement, friends, a new spirit aborning of which I have the pleasure to be a part. For the time the movement is secret, as this meeting is secret. Understand, we only want pure Americans, which is why I selected *you* to be here." He looked at each of his listeners in turn and smiled. Each was pleased to be so included.

"Friends," Mr. Jenkins continued softly but with determination, "people like us are coming to power in this land. Join us, and as we grow strong, you'll grow strong. When we grow strong enough, we'll drive these Irish from America and restore the nation to all its ancient republican virtues."

The ratlike man shifted uncomfortably. "What's the name of this organization?" he asked.

"A reasonable question. It's the Order of the Star-spangled Banner. But if anyone asks about it, all you need to do is this." Mr. Jenkins pointed to his right eye, then to his nose, and then made, with his thumb and forefinger, the shape of a circle.

"What's that supposed to mean?" the woman asked.

Mr. Jenkins smiled slyly. Once again he pointed to his eye. "I," he said. He pointed to his nose. "Knows," he said. Finally, he made the circle with his fingers. "Nothing," he said.

"Which means?" came the question.

"I know nothing," Mr. Jenkins exclaimed with triumph. "But the good joke is, my friends, we know a great deal. It's merely that we're *saying* nothing."

"And what do we know?" asked Betsy Howard.

Mr. Jenkins allowed himself his broadest smile. "We know that in Lowell—and *soon*—we shall drive the Irish out. Not by words, but action!" Mr. Jenkins sat back and nodded to affirm the prediction.

Chapter 89
Mr. Jenkins and Jeb

*T*he meeting was over. Those who had sat around the table, listening to Mr. Jenkins, were gone, though the gentleman himself remained slumped in his seat. The room was perfectly quiet, save for the mournful rise and fall of the winter wind and the pinging sound of icy snow upon the windows. Now and again the candle hissed and sparked as it burned through a bit of corrupted tallow.

Jeb Grafton waited nervously for the payment he had been offered for his guard duties. He was only hoping that the gentleman who'd done all the talking had not forgotten him.

In his mind Mr. Jenkins was brooding over whether he had achieved anything with his small audience. There was so much to be done for his cause. At times he felt he was the only man dedicated to the momentous task. The news about Irish being taken on at the Shagwell Cotton Mill had caught him by surprise. No doubt it was only happening because Mr. Ambrose Shagwell had gone abroad. As soon he returned, he needed to be informed of the treachery.

Mr. Jenkins stared at the candle flame. The thought came to him of how fine a thing fire was, that it was a great purifier and thus a great power. How often fire was the weapon of the ancient gods. It all depended—Mr. Jenkins told himself—on how one used it.

Jeb, wanting only to get home, stepped forward. "Mister?" he said.

Mr. Jenkins turned in the boy's direction. Seeing him, his dark thoughts lifted.

"Please, mister, you said you'd pay me something for my guarding the door."

A smile came to Mr. Jenkins's lips. "How much did we bargain for?"

"You didn't say."

Mr. Jenkins reached into the pocket of his vest. He selected one coin and held it out. "Here's a half dime." Jeb put the money into a pocket and headed for the door.

"Boy!"

Jeb stopped and looked back.

"I'll buy you some bread. Fetch up your box."

Mr. Jenkins squeezed the burning candlewick with his bare fingers. There was a momentary hiss, and the light was snuffed.

Man and boy went into the oyster bar, a large room with a long bar counter and many tables. Paintings of horses, hunters, fish, and soldiers covered the walls. Because of the weather, only a few people were there.

For a penny Mr. Jenkins purchased two pieces of stale bread from the barman. He flipped them to Jeb, who ate both hungrily.

"Where do you live?" Mr. Jenkins asked the boy.

"Howard Street."

"I'll walk a ways with you. Get your coat."

"Don't have one."

"Don't you?"

"It ain't bad," Jeb insisted, pulling his cap lower over his eyes.

Mr. Jenkins contemplated the boy for a moment, then turned back to the barman. "Got any left coats?"

"Always," the man said.

"A dollar if you give the boy one."

The barman measured Jeb with his eyes, then knelt behind his counter before coming up with a drab green coat with a torn collar and one seriously frayed cuff. He offered it to Mr. Jenkins, who in turn handed it to Jeb.

The boy held back. "What do I have to do for it?" he demanded.

Mr. Jenkins grunted. "I want to show you a house."

"What kind of house?"

"An Irishman's house," he said, his voice suddenly thick with anger.

Taken aback, Jeb stared at the man, but then shrugged, took the coat, and put it on. It was much too large for him, reaching far below his knees. He had to roll back the cuffs, and even so his fingertips barely peeked out. Nonetheless, he'd never had a coat of his own before.

"Come on," Mr. Jenkins said, pushing open the door.

The moment they left, a man who had been sitting at a table nearby got up and quickly donned his own coat and hat. He hurried out, muttering a thanks to the barman.

The barman shook his head.

It was hard to see outside. The velvet darkness swirled with snow. Street lamps were shrouded. Slick swatches of ice lay concealed underfoot. The wind blew down at a hard angle, insinuating snow into collars and shoe tops. As he and Mr. Jenkins walked, Jeb had to bow his head. Neither knew they were being followed.

Cold as it was, Jeb was deeply engrossed in the pleasures of wearing the coat. Once, twice, he shifted his shoe-shine box, stole a grateful look at Mr. Jenkins, and decided he liked him.

They trudged in silence. Now and again the man growled,

44

"This way," or, "Next turn." Finally he said, "There," and pointed across the street.

Jeb wiped his eyes free of snow, which was fast changing to sleet. He saw a large house, its whiteness ghostlike in the night, windows glowing with the warmth of candlelight. As far as Jeb could make out, there was nothing new or fancy about the place—the kind dwelled in by better-off working people in Lowell. Jeb could only wish he lived there.

"What about it?" he demanded, pulling his cap lower over his eyes.

"That house," Mr. Jenkins said, "belongs to an Irishman. I was born here, and I don't have one. Do you live in a house like that?"

Jeb shook his head.

"Do you see that front room, the one on the left, the one with the fire?"

Jeb looked at the room, then up at Mr. Jenkins. What he saw startled him. Despite the cold, the man's deep-set eyes seemed to be smoldering with their own fire.

"The man who owns that house," Mr. Jenkins said, "that's his room. His name is James Hamlyn, and he's an Irishman. Jeb, how do you think an Irishman came to a house like that?"

"I don't know."

"He took my job, that's how. I used to work in the mills. Then there was an accident." For a moment Mr. Jenkins could not speak. Then, with a trembling voice, he said, "That man in there was the cause. The accident was his fault. I couldn't work anymore. But he got rich.

"Do you know what he does with that house? He takes in boarders, *Irish* boarders. People who work in the mills. Do you have a father?" Mr. Jenkins suddenly asked the boy.

"I guess I do."

"Where was he born?"

"Up by Concord."

45

"Does he work?"

"Not much."

"Because an Irishman or Irishwoman took his job. You can be sure of that. Jeb Grafton, you know my name. Jeremiah Jenkins. I can use a boy from time to time. Where can I find you?"

"I'm on the street where you found me before. In front of the hotel. With my box. Prime spot."

"Don't you worry. I'll find you," said Mr. Jenkins, and without another word he walked off, his broad back unyielding to the elements.

Jeb watched him go until the man became lost in the whirling sleet. Then he turned and looked again at the house. He was quite sure he hated Mr. James Hamlyn too.

Chapter 90
Mr. Tolliver Calls

James Hamlyn lay upon his bed, back propped up against two pillows. He was a small man with a small head and but a few strands of white hair dangling down the back of a scrawny neck. A white stubble frosted his chin and a certain sleepiness dimmed his gray eyes. Now and again he blew his nose—which had become quite red from a cold—and reached out to drink from a cup of honey-sweetened hot cider that had been set out for him on a side table. He hated having colds, and he was always getting them.

On his bald head he wore a nightcap, its strings tied beneath his chin. An old muffler was wrapped around his neck, and though he was in bed with quilted blankets pulled high, he wore a jacket as well. On his lap lay a small book, which he glanced at from time to time, alternating the reading of pages with the reading of the flames that danced in the fireplace. By force of habit he occasionally looked toward his feet. He had but one now, and even the one he had was useless.

A quiet knock came at the door.

"Come in."

A gray-haired woman, rather delicate in appearance, looked in upon him.

"Yes, my dear?" Mr. Hamlyn asked his wife.

"It's your friend, the police captain, Mr. Tolliver. He's come to call."

Mr. Hamlyn reacted with surprise. "Mr. Tolliver?"

"He says it's rather urgent."

"What hour is it?"

"Past nine. And snowing."

Mr. Hamlyn sipped some of his hot cider, made a face, and said, "Best stir up the fire then, Mrs. Hamlyn." His wife obligingly poked at the grate with an iron rod, then withdrew.

Moments later there was another knock. Instead of waiting for a reply, Mrs. Hamlyn reopened the door and ushered in the man known as Mr. Tolliver. He was a big burly man with broad shoulders and a large expanse of chest and waist. The look on his face was carefully guarded, and his generous mustache—which curled down along his fleshy cheeks until it curled up again to merge with thick sideburns—served him as a mask. He wore a jacket that was somewhat too small for him and a vest likewise, from the pocket of which dangled a chain with a number of seals. The man's hands were plunged deep in his pockets, and as he stood considering Mr. Hamlyn with shrewd eyes, he rocked slightly back on his heels.

"You're looking well, Mr. Hamlyn," the police captain said in a robust voice.

"Then you're either blind or a liar," Mr. Hamlyn replied

gruffly with something of a smile about his thin lips. "Is the weather out there bad?"

"Not very pleasant, sir. An icy snow, maybe two or three inches."

"Then there's some comfort in being forced to lie abed," Mr. Hamlyn said. "A man without legs hasn't much fun on ice, Mr. Tolliver. But the storm keeps the thieves in too, I suppose."

"That's a fact, sir. Your thief is like your ordinary person. Prefers to go about his work in good weather."

"But I'll warrant you didn't come to talk about the weather, Mr. Tolliver. Pull up a chair by the fire and unburden your mind."

Mr. Tolliver set the chair near the fire but close to the foot of the bed. Instead of speaking, however, he tilted the chair back and thrust both hands again into his pockets as if he might find his thoughts there.

Finally he said, "Sir, does the name Jeremiah Jenkins mean anything to you?"

Mr. Hamlyn's eyes widened. He cocked his head to one side. "Mr. Tolliver," the man in bed began, "I need to know whom I'm talking to. Is it Mr. Tolliver of the Lowell police? Or is it Mr. Tolliver, Jim Hamlyn's old friend?"

"Can't it be both?" the man replied.

"I suppose it can. Why don't you lay the case out before me. Then I'll tell you what I know."

"Very well," agreed Mr. Tolliver, and he sprang from the chair and paced about, hands in pockets.

"Mr. Hamlyn, sir, it's a delicate situation. Mr. Jenkins is a troublemaker. But the fact of the matter is, to the best of my knowledge, he has not committed any crime."

"To the best of your knowledge."

"But"—Mr. Tolliver paused in his pacing to rock back on his heels—"I do know he's stirring up something, some secret society."

48

"The country is full of them," Mr. Hamlyn replied.

"True, true. It's our way here in America. But this one, sir, is aimed full out at the Irish, and aims at nothing less than shipping them all back home."

"All?" Mr. Hamlyn said with a snort.

"All."

"And how does he intend to do that?"

"I have no idea."

Mr. Hamlyn stared into the fire. "Jeremiah Jenkins is a deeply unhappy man," he said. "Worse, he's ready to blame anything and anybody for his own failings. Would you like to know what happened?"

"I would, sir."

"At the mill where he and I worked, he appeared one day with his son. A child. A sweet-looking lad. It's not generally permitted. But exceptions are made. . . . That day I allowed the exception."

Mr. Hamlyn closed his eyes at the painful memory. "Anyway, along about midday an overhead pulley belt slipped. Though rare, it does happen. A serious accident resulted. The boy, who had been playing about the machines, was killed. Jenkins became half-mad with the loss. It turned his hair white. What's more—since I was the overlooker and allowed the boy to be there—he blamed me for being the cause."

"Were you?"

"No. And when I tried to extricate the boy, I lost the use of my legs."

For a moment Mr. Tolliver said nothing. Then he said, "He's a good friend of Ambrose Shagwell's."

"Is he?"

"Mr. Shagwell gives Jenkins money."

"Why?"

"Mr. Shagwell likes to keep his operatives nervous. Agitated. I believe that's Mr. Jenkins's job."

"When I had problems with him," Mr. Hamlyn continued, "he tried to raise up the other operatives—this was at the Boott Mill—and I had to turn him out. Do you know what he began to accuse me of?"

"No."

"Of being Irish."

"Are you?"

"I was born in Ireland. Came here when I was two."

"Mr. Hamlyn," the police captain said, "if all the man is up to is talk—no matter how foul—it's no concern of mine. But if there is anything else . . ."

"You'd like to know."

"I would, sir."

"And how might I, from where I now lie, be of use to you?" Mr. Hamlyn asked.

"The man's in Lowell—tonight. He was holding a meeting at the Spindle City Hotel. A secret meeting."

"Hardly a secret if you know of it, Mr. Tolliver." Mr. Hamlyn laughed.

"I'm a collector of secrets," replied his friend with the utmost seriousness.

"What do you think might happen?"

Mr. Tolliver considered. "Violence, sir. Violence."

"In any particular direction?"

Mr. Tolliver paced again, hands in pockets. Suddenly he stopped. "Well, sir—you might wonder why I should be visiting you at such a time. The truth is, I followed Mr. Jenkins from the hotel. A boy was with him. Mr. Jenkins made his way through the snow, sir, to this house."

Mr. Hamlyn sat up. "This house!"

"Across the street anyway. And, sir, I believe he pointed to this very room."

"But why?"

"That's an answer I have yet to learn, Mr. Hamlyn. But I am determined to find out."

Chapter 91
Jeb Grafton

J eb Grafton hurried up the shadowy narrow steps to the second floor of a tenement building on Howard Street. The stairwell walls were dirty, and the plaster so full of holes that in many places the cold night air whistled through. Though it was dark on the steps, the boy hardly looked where he was going. Excited, he paid scant attention to the babble that rang out from many directions in the building. Instead, he all but ran down the hallway and pushed against the door that let him into the place he called his home.

It was a two-room apartment, one none-too-clean room behind the other. There was an old Franklin stove, but it was small and gave but a meager measure of warmth. Not far from the stove a boy, a year old, sat on a thin blanket. He wore a tattered man's shirt—much too big for him—but nothing else, and the chill that set upon him could be seen in his raw red hands and blue lips.

There was a table and chair by the room's only window, which was boarded up. Such light as there was came from a candle set in a cracked dish.

Seated in the chair before the table was Jeb's father, Henry Grafton. Thin, scantly bearded, he wore an old army coat over his shoulders, a battered derby on his head, and a tattered muffler around his neck.

Mr. Grafton was reading a Lowell newspaper, *The People's Voice*, by the light of the candle. Now and then he glanced toward the back room, from which an occasional cough could be heard. When it came, he listened intently. When it subsided, he turned back to his reading.

He was still reading when Jeb burst in.

"Look!" Jeb cried. He had a great grin on his face as he showed off his coat.

"Where'd you get that?" his father asked.

"New friend."

"Get it honest?"

The boy's face flushed. "What do you think?" he replied. "The fellah who gave it to me is so rich he just gives money away."

"Who is he?"

"Mr. Jenkins. Jeremiah Jenkins."

"Never heard of him."

"Paid me money—good money—just to sit by a door and make sure no one barged into a meeting."

"How much?"

"A whole half dime. And he says he'll hire me again."

"To do what?"

"I don't know. But I bet he does."

"What about the rest of today?" Jeb's father asked.

"Fair."

Mr. Grafton held out his hand.

Ignoring it, Jeb came farther into the room and set his shoe-shine box down in a corner. "How is she?" he asked, nodding toward the back room, from which coughing had erupted again.

"Got through the day."

"They speed the machines up again at the mill?"

"She didn't say."

"I hate them mills," Jeb said.

"Some are worse than others."

"Then I hate the Shagwell Cotton Mill," Jeb said decidedly. He crossed the room and sat on the floor next to the child. The youngster chortled and crawled onto his brother's lap. In response, Jeb opened his coat and drew the infant close, then wrapped him in his arms as well as the coat. "You read all day?" he asked his father.

"It fills the mind," the man replied dryly.

"You could work."

"That so?" Mr. Grafton asked. "Where?"

"I heard they were taking on at the Appleton Mill."

The man shook his head. "Only Irish."

"Mr. Jenkins wants to get rid of the Paddies."

"Does he now? Well, they're hungry too, I suppose."

"Not as hungry as us," Jeb declared.

"I don't know," Mr. Grafton said with an indifferent shrug. "I ain't never seen into a man's belly, but I expect they're all the same." He tapped the newspaper. "Got a good yarn here, this week," he said. "It's about a ship at sea in a storm."

"Mr. Jenkins is a powerful man."

" 'Cause he gave you a half dime? Pshaw!" Mr. Grafton read a bit more to himself before folding up the newspaper. "Look here, Jeb, let's see your money."

Jeb smoothed down the child's curly hair, then gently put him aside, took off his coat, and wrapped it around him. From his pocket he drew out his earnings, went to his father, and dumped the money onto the table.

Mr. Grafton counted the coins carefully. "Twenty-five cents," he said approvingly. "You did fine."

"You could go to California," the boy blurted out. "Find some gold for us. Not right that just me and her"—he nodded toward the inner room—"do all the work."

"It costs money to go to California."

"You could walk. Lots are."

"Walk? Three thousand miles? Pshaw!"

Frustrated, Jeb grabbed the candle in its cracked saucer and, with his cap pulled low, crept to the doorway of the back room and looked in at his mother. Sarah Grafton sat on the bed, her back propped against the wall. A blanket was drawn around her. Her long black hair lay in disorder and contrasted sharply with her pale thin face. About her mouth Jeb saw specks of blood. Now and again she coughed, deep racking coughs, but she made no movement to suppress them.

Her son went to her side and sat on the bed. Mrs. Grafton looked at him with dark enormous eyes. "Jeb, darling, you mustn't go at him so," she whispered. "It ain't his fault."

"I know," Jeb returned.

"Is it a nice coat you got?"

"Best in the world."

She smiled. "I'll look at it later. I was just waiting up for you. But I'm tired. Go on now," she said. "I'll be fine." She closed her eyes.

Jeb watched her face—which was full of pain—for a while. Then he went back into the front room. "Do you think a doctor would come?"

Mr. Grafton shrugged. "To cure the cotton cough? Don't you think I've asked? The doctor, with his medicine, costs ten dollars. Have any notion where to get that?"

"I could ask Mr. Jenkins."

"Maybe you should," his father said. "Truth is, Jeb, they say the only cure is to get away from the mill."

Jeb said nothing.

"Look here, son, I was turned off at the mill for objecting to the speedup. They've got my name down. Blacklisted. That's why I can't find work. Anywhere. If she got turned off too, where would we be?" He scooped up the pennies and stood. "I'll fetch some bread and tea. Maybe some milk. You stay home now, do you hear?"

A series of coughs came from the inner room. Father and son exchanged looks but no words. Mr. Grafton went out the door.

For a while Jeb remained motionless. Then he turned to

his brother and gathered him up on his lap once more. The baby laughed and waved his hands in glee.

"I hate them Irish," Jeb whispered into his brother's small ear. "I hate them. But that Mr. Jenkins said he'd do something. And I'm going to help him. Won't that be grand?"

Chapter 92
Whispered Words

*I*n one corner of his small room, Mr. Jenkins knelt before a shrinelike assemblage upon a low table, a cluster of multicolored ribbons, silk flowers, and seashells. In its very corner was a Daguerreotype of a dead boy's face: Mr. Jenkins's son.

As he stared at the image, the man clasped his hands together, not in prayer, but in a tight fist. "Revenge . . . ," he whispered over and over again. "Revenge. . . ."

Chapter 93
Meetings

A ll during his first night on the *Robert Peel* an uproar of
singing and coughing, groaning and weeping and praying had interrupted Patrick O'Connell's sleep. On one side
of him, Bridy Faherty tossed restlessly. On the other side
stretched Mr. Drabble, one arm dangling down from the
platform, long legs twisted awkwardly. His breathing was
loud.

The family below them never seemed to quiet. Even the
sound of people scratching—lice, no doubt—had irritated the
boy. Everything on the platforms—people and possessions—
shifted and stirred continually.

Patrick dozed. When he awoke again, both Maura and Mr.
Drabble were gone. With a spurt of resentment, he recalled
the scene he had witnessed earlier, the actor on his knees
before his sister. Sure, but she'll be having less time for me,
he thought.

Then he considered Bridy. She was at the opposite end
of the berth now, hunched against a post, staring at him.
"Bridy Faherty," he asked, "how old would you be?"

"Eight," she whispered, so low he almost could not hear
her.

"You need not be fearful of me," he said. "I'll not do you
any harm."

The girl said nothing.

"Well then, did you see where my sister or that Mr. Drabble went?" he asked.

Bridy shook her head.

"Wouldn't it be fine if they were getting some food," he said.

When the girl gave no further response, Patrick thought of Laurence. His friend must be famished!

Lowering himself to the floor, Patrick made his way to the central stairway, then down to the first cargo hold. Just as he started toward the open hatchway, Mr. Murdock loomed before him.

The boy jumped back in fright.

"Where do you think yer going?" the first mate demanded.

"Just looking about, Your Honor," Patrick stammered, afraid to raise his eyes.

"Look at me when yer speak," Mr. Murdock snapped, jerking up Patrick's chin. "Yer allowed on the steerage deck, the main deck, and the forecastle deck. Nowhere else. Go poke where yer allowed," the officer growled. "If I catch yer out of place again, I'll break yer neck. Get on now!"

Patrick turned, ran to the steps, and hurried back to their berth. But seeing that neither his sister nor Mr. Drabble had returned, he again left the steerage deck.

The main deck was crowded. People were milling about or silently watching the sea. Some were in line for the two privies available to the steerage passengers. Set on the forecastle deck and enclosed on but three sides, they afforded little privacy.

Yet another line led to the fireplace, the only cooking space made available to the emigrants. It consisted of a metal grill surrounded by bricks stacked loosely on three sides of a brick-and-mortar floor. Ashes and smoke spewed onto anyone near it. Regardless, the line of passengers waiting to cook on the fireplace lasted all day and into the night. Now and again people did try to slip into the line or bully their way forward. Then harsh words and fists erupted.

When Patrick saw neither his sister nor Mr. Drabble on either of the lines, he took himself up to the forecastle deck. Near the billethead he spied the actor deeply engaged with his gentleman student, Mr. Grout.

Patrick watched them from a distance, glad that the actor was not with his sister. But he did wish he knew where she was.

From the height of the forecastle deck Patrick was able to look across to the quarterdeck at the aft section of the ship. It was there he saw his sister. She was not alone. A gray-haired gentleman was talking to her. Two sailors stood near as though on guard. Immediately, Patrick recalled what the first mate had just told him, that steerage people were not allowed there.

Worried, he watched. From the way Maura's head was bowed, her hands tight together, he sensed she was in trouble.

He hurried down from the forecastle deck, ran across the main deck, then dashed up the steps toward his sister.

"Here now," a sailor barked, trying to keep him from coming closer. "Get off with you!"

Deftly, Patrick darted around him and reached his sister's side. She gave him a quick glance, lifting a hand in warning.

"And who is this?" the man who had been talking to her demanded. It was Ambrose Shagwell.

"He's my brother, if it please Your Honor," Maura said.

The man grunted. "Another one going where he's not wanted. Well, you can repeat what I've been telling you, that you Irish are making a mistake coming to America."

Maura looked up. "It was our father who sent for us, Your Honor."

"Your father!" the American scoffed. "He shouldn't be there either. Take my advice, girl, and board the first boat back home. You'll be better off—and good riddance." Mr. Shagwell turned on his heels and walked away.

"All right now," one of the sailors said harshly, "get along. The two of you. And don't come back."

Maura turned stiffly and led Patrick down the steps. Neither spoke a word. Only when they reached the main deck did her brother say, "And what was that all about?"

Maura said nothing at first. Instead, she leaned over the bulwark and stared out at the waves.

"Maura . . . ," Patrick pressed.

"I was just wandering," she said at last. "Faith, no one told me we weren't allowed up there. Then that wretched man stopped me, and didn't he make me listen to his ugly sermon."

"Did he do you any harm?" Patrick asked, studying his sister's face.

Maura jerked her head to toss her hair out of her eyes. "Not a bit," she said. "Sure, but he's just a stupid man with no courtesy about him. I don't intend to pay it any mind. And neither should you. It'll take more than that to stop us."

Chapter 94

In London, Mr. Pickler Makes
His Report

*M*r. Phineas Pickler, new bowler hat in one hand, a paper-wrapped package in the other, stood before Lord Kirkle in his lordship's study. Upon the desk between them lay a few pinned sheets of paper—Mr. Pickler's report regarding the running away of Sir Laurence Kirkle.

Having just read the report, Lord Kirkle sat with his hands clasped before him. Pain filled his red watery eyes. As Mr. Pickler waited—and he had been standing quietly for several minutes—his lordship, in an agitated state, kept lifting up and putting down the papers.

Restless, Mr. Pickler glanced about the room. He contemplated the cost of the heavy furniture. He wondered if anyone actually read the many leather-bound books that filled the shelves. He ventured to ask himself if the green velvet curtains covering the front windows were ever pulled back so as to let sunlight in, thereby making unnecessary the fireplace, with its hot, glowing coals. Finally—and not for the first time, for he had read it on his earlier visit to this Belgrave mansion—Mr. Pickler pondered the family motto, chiseled below the gleaming marble mantel.

FOR COUNTRY, GLORY—FOR FAMILY, HONOR

What price honor? Mr. Pickler asked himself silently, and thought of his own home, of his wife and two children.

Lord Kirkle stood up. The light cast by the fireplace flames caused his black silken waistcoat to gleam and the gold watch and chain that stretched over his stomach to glow. Slowly, he asked again in anguish, "And you are quite sure, Mr. Pickler, that my son has left England?"

"I do not have absolute proof of it, my lord," the investigator replied. "But all indications lead me to that conclusion."

"And where has he gone, do you think?"

"I believe he boarded the packet ship *Robert Peel*, which is bound for the American city of Boston."

"*Boston* . . . ," his lordship murmured. "As a stowaway."

"I fear so."

Lord Kirkle shuddered visibly. "And that one thousand pounds he . . . borrowed?"

"As my report indicates, it was apparently stolen from him. By whom, I cannot say."

"How . . . how could he do this to me?" Lord Kirkle sighed.

"My lord, he had help."

Lord Kirkle looked up sharply. "From whom? And why doesn't your report say that?"

Mr. Pickler stared into his new bowler. Recollecting that Lord Kirkle had not told him the truth about the circumstances of Sir Laurence's leaving, he felt constrained to be wary. "In the last instance," he said, "he received help from a street urchin by the name of Fred."

"*A street urchin?*" Lord Kirkle asked incredulously. "A boy by the name of Fred?"

"That seems to have been his only name."

"And who is *he*, sir?"

"My lord, I believe Sir Laurence became a pawn in a struggle within a local organization in Liverpool called the

Lime Street Runners Association. This . . . Fred was a member, if you will."

Lord Kirkle took up and dropped Mr. Pickler's report as if it were a leaden weight. "All this is beyond my understanding," he admitted. "What I need to know is *why* my boy left. You don't say that in your report either, do you?" He looked right at Mr. Pickler. The investigator slowly lifted his eyes. The two men stared at each other.

It was Lord Kirkle who turned away.

"No, it is not written there," Mr. Pickler allowed.

Lord Kirkle moved from behind the barrier of his desk and approached the fire. He held his hands out and washed them in the warmth, his breathing labored. "I appreciate your tact," Lord Kirkle said at last. "All the same, sir, I desire you to say what needs to be said."

Mouth dry, heart beating rapidly, Mr. Pickler squeezed the rim of his bowler. "My lord," he began, "just before your son left this house he was—I believe—beaten." Though Lord Kirkle's body stiffened, he said nothing.

Emboldened by the silence, Mr. Pickler continued. "His clothing was cut in many places, my lord." Putting aside his bowler, the investigator unwrapped his package and drew forth Laurence's filthy torn jacket. He laid it upon the desk.

Lord Kirkle held up the jacket. Light showed through the rents. The man groaned.

"Moreover, my lord," Mr. Pickler went on nervously, "the boy bore a disfiguring welt upon his face. Presumably . . . it came from that beating."

In the stillness of the room, the clock's ticking sounded like a heartbeat. "My lord," Mr. Pickler ventured after a moment, "if what I said is untrue and I have brought an unjust accusation, I will withdraw from your house immediately."

Lord Kirkle stroked the torn jacket, even looped his fat

fingers through the rips. In a choked voice he said, "It is true, sir."

The investigator allowed himself a deep breath. "It is my judgment," he continued in a stronger voice, "that the beating as well as the wound on his face not only propelled Sir Laurence from this house, but made it easier for another to prey upon him."

Lord Kirkle looked up sharply. "Another, sir?"

"I have come to the conclusion, my lord, that while in the first instance Sir Laurence desired to leave London, he was aided by someone."

"Who?" Lord Kirkle demanded.

"My lord, does the name Matthew Clemspool mean anything to you?"

"Never heard of him."

"My inquiries have informed me that he has a business called Brother's Keeper. On Bow Lane. In the City. Its principal purpose is to exploit the conflicts between younger and older brothers in families of wealth."

"I don't grasp your meaning, sir."

"If," Mr. Pickler explained, "a younger brother wishes to trouble or push aside an older brother, he engages Mr. Clemspool. By the same token, if an older brother wishes to trouble or push aside a younger one, he also engages Mr. Clemspool."

From his pocket Mr. Pickler drew out the tincture of rhubarb. He held the bottle up. "This, sir, was procured for your son by this Mr. Clemspool. A chemist has advised me it contains something beyond the tincture. He suspects a sleeping potion."

"Despicable! I will have this Clemspool fellow arrested!"

"He seems to have vanished."

"I'll track him down!"

"He is not to be traced."

"Are you implying, Mr. Pickler, that this scoundrel *abducted* Laurence?"

Mr. Pickler bobbed his head and swallowed hard. "No, sir, I am not saying that."

"Then, good heavens, man," Lord Kirkle thundered, "what *are* you saying?"

"My lord, you have another son."

"What about him?"

"Perhaps, my lord," the investigator offered, "it would be wise to ask—" He hesitated. Then, speaking more softly, he added, "Ask Sir Albert if *he* has had any dealings with this Matthew Clemspool."

It took a moment for Lord Kirkle to absorb the thought. When he had, his face turned fiery. "Mr. Pickler," he cried, "are you fully aware of what you are saying?"

"My lord, this Mr. Clemspool informed me himself that he helped Sir Laurence leave London and reach Liverpool. He was employed to do so, I believe, by . . . your elder son. Once in Liverpool I am quite sure Sir Laurence got on a ship that sailed for America—as a stowaway."

The blood drained from Lord Kirkle's face. His body sagged. He would have fallen if he had not grasped the edge of the desk. Only with great effort did he pull himself up to his full height.

"Mr. Pickler," he whispered in a breaking voice, "do you think my boy is . . . alive?"

"To the best of my knowledge, my lord. But they do not treat stowaways kindly. And . . . many die on these emigrant boats." Mr. Pickler looked into his bowler, which, for security, he had retrieved from the desk. "Even if your son survived the voyage and reached America, I don't know how we could find him." The investigator looked up. "America is a measureless place. We have only the *Robert Peel*'s destination to go on."

For several minutes Lord Kirkle said nothing. Then,

speaking very slowly, he said, "Mr. Pickler, I thank you for your efforts. Your services are no longer required. Consider yourself dismissed."

Mr. Pickler was so astonished by Lord Kirkle's words that he had no breath to respond.

"Leave my home *immediately*, sir," Lord Kirkle croaked hoarsely. "At once! You are not to share your speculations with anyone—*anyone*. If you do, it shall be worth your life."

"My lord," Mr. Pickler gasped, "I only beg to say—"

"Go!" Lord Kirkle shouted. "Leave me!"

Though it took every ounce of his willpower to keep from bursting into tears, there was nothing else for Mr. Pickler to do but turn toward the door. When he reached it, he paused and attempted to speak. Lord Kirkle prevented him.

"You will be well paid for your trouble, Mr. Pickler. Double your fee. I will give you a good character if asked. Now remove yourself from my house. And do not return. *Ever*."

Mr. Pickler murmured a final, "My lord," bobbed his head, and crept from the room.

Lord Kirkle remained leaning on the mantel for a long while. Utterly wretched, he crossed to the corner of the room and pulled upon a braided rope. A servant entered.

"Richards," Lord Kirkle managed to say. "Is Sir Albert at home?"

"I believe he is, my lord."

"I wish him here. At once."

Chapter 95
Enter Sir Albert

A weary Lord Kirkle sank upon his chair, drew Laurence's tattered jacket toward him, and buried his face in it.

The door to the study soon opened. Sir Albert clumped in, a complacent smile upon his face.

"My—," he began to say, but stopped short when he saw his father's anguished look. And the familiar jacket. Albert's first thought was that Laurence had been found. Perhaps dead. It took all his strength to keep from smiling. "My lord . . . ," he tried again.

Lord Kirkle stared at his elder son with bloodshot eyes. "Sir," he said, his voice trembling, "I intend to ask you some questions. You had best answer me truthfully."

"Of . . . course, my lord," Albert stammered.

"Albert, does the name Matthew Clemspool mean anything to you?"

Taken by surprise, Albert swallowed hard and squeezed his hands until his knuckles cracked. "I . . . I . . . am not sure."

"What does that 'not sure' mean, sir?" Lord Kirkle demanded. "Do you or do you not know him?"

"Well, perhaps I have heard the name, but—"

Lord Kirkle sprang from his chair so suddenly that Albert jumped back. "Have you had *any* dealings with this scoundrel?" his father demanded.

"I don't know that—"

"I have been informed that this Matthew Clemspool

helped your brother leave London and reach Liverpool, from which point the boy went to America as a stowaway."

Sir Albert gasped. "But, sir . . . what has that to do with me?" His knuckles cracked again.

Lord Kirkle continued. "I have been further informed that Mr. Clemspool's business is to involve himself in older-younger brother tensions on behalf of one or the other. It has been suggested, sir, that you and Mr. Clemspool have had business dealings."

"He's a liar and swindler," replied Sir Albert. "If you knew him as I do—"

"Then you *have* dealt with him!" Lord Kirkle roared.

"Well, yes, I suppose, in some—"

"Do you admit, sir, that you conspired to have Laurence spirited away from London, that he might go off to America?"

Albert gulped for air. "No, sir . . . not at all," he stammered. "It wasn't that. It was only to teach the nuisance his proper place. I had no intention of—"

"Do you know what you have done?" Lord Kirkle shouted. "Do you?"

"I didn't do anything, my lord," Albert whined. "Nothing. I swear I didn't. I—"

"Because of you, your brother is a beggarly stowaway on a ship for Boston. Alone! At the mercy of any and all! Quite possibly dead! And even if by some happy chance he does reach America alive, he will be lost to us—forever."

"I'll . . . I'll go find him," Albert cried. "I will. I'll leave right away."

"By God, sir!" Lord Kirkle shouted, his face contorted with rage. "You had best do exactly that! Consider yourself cut off from every penny you think is yours save what you need to bring your brother back. Do you understand me, sir? Find your brother! Now remove yourself from my sight!"

"Yes, sir."

"Go!"

Sir Albert hurried from the room—and met his mother in the hallway. The small woman was looking alarmed. "What is it?" she asked. "The servants are saying something has happened."

"It's Laurence."

"Has he been found?"

"The fool has actually gone to America."

"America!"

"And would you believe, Mama, the governor has asked me to fetch him back."

"You? But how can he expect that you . . . ?"

"Never mind. He's asked, and of course I'll go. Now excuse me. Duty calls," he said sarcastically, "and I must prepare myself."

As Albert hurried on, all he could think was that he must do something and do it quickly. He knew well that his father preferred Laurence to him, knew that his father's will gave his brother too much and him too little. Yes, he would go to America. He would find Laurence. But once he found him—if he found him—he would make sure his dear brother *never* came home.

Chapter 96

Mr. Shagwell Asks a Question

D inner in the *Robert Peel*'s first-class dining room was done. The food had been more than ample: soup, fish, meat, potatoes, followed by a sweet. Of the regular diners, Mr. Clemspool, Mr. Grout, and Mr. Murdock were gone. Three remained, Mr. Shagwell, Captain Rickles, and the ship's doctor, Mr. Woodham.

The doctor was a young man, fresh from his licensing exam, on his way to America to make his fortune. Long curls fell about his ears and neck. Dressed meticulously in black waistcoat and ruffled cravat, he had discovered as part of his studies that a haughty demeanor was as important a part of his professional attire as anything else.

Just as the captain was rising, Mr. Shagwell said, "A word with you, sir. Just a moment."

"By your leave," the captain said, and sat.

The doctor moved to go.

"Do stay, sir," Mr. Shagwell said. "I should value your thoughts too."

The doctor brushed away crumbs that had fallen on his waistcoat and resumed his seat.

"Gentlemen," Mr. Shagwell began, "this is a matter of some delicacy." He settled his bulk more comfortably in his chair. "I need only tell you the subject's money for you to understand."

The captain laughed good-naturedly. "Money is always delicate, sir."

"I'm glad you agree." Mr. Shagwell picked up a fork, poked it gently against his fingers, laid it down, and said, "It concerns one of our fellow passengers."

The captain pulled at his red mustache but said nothing.

Mr. Shagwell went on. "I am, sirs," he said, touching his hand to his chest and dipping his head, "engaged in the manufacturing of cotton textiles. Mine is a most important mill."

"In what city, sir?" inquired the doctor.

"Lowell, Massachusetts."

The doctor nodded as if he knew the place exactly.

"You see, sirs, Mr. Clemspool has intimated to me that he is seriously considering investing funds—his funds—in my company. Naturally, I am interested. What, gentlemen, do you know of this Englishman?"

The doctor leaned back in his chair and brushed a crumb from his sleeve. "English—as you've said. Very friendly fellow. Always asking questions. Somewhat prying. Seems to make his home in London with a business office in the City."

"Ah, the City . . ."

"He did tell me he was going to America on matters of high finance."

"Do you know what exactly is his business?"

"Seems to deal with the wealthy," the doctor said. "Family matters and the like."

Mr. Shagwell placed his hands upon the table. "Did he say that?"

"That's what he told me too," said the captain. "You will recall that two days ago we bespoke a ship. . . ."

"Going to England."

"Mr. Clemspool specifically requested we do so. He had a letter he wished sent to London. Said it concerned very important financial matters."

"Did he?"

"His very words."

"And, sir, did he say what the matters were?" asked Mr. Shagwell.

"No, sir. But he impressed me with a sense of its urgency. And, sir"—the captain offered up a shrewd, knowing look—"the letter was addressed to Sir Albert Kirkle."

The doctor looked around. "Did you say *Kirkle*, sir?"

"I did."

"Do you know the name?" the doctor asked Mr. Shagwell. The American shook his head.

"One of the most important names in Her Majesty's government."

Mr. Shagwell could not help but smile. "What you have said pleases me, Doctor," he allowed. "It confirms my understanding of the man. Very much so. Gentlemen, I will make the best use of this information. I thank you."

Chapter 97
Maura's Morning

*H*aving slept fully clothed, Maura groped in the darkness for her shawl only to discover that Bridy had managed to wrap it around herself. She gave a brief tug, then decided to leave it with the child.

Maura tried to see through the cold, dank gloom of the steerage deck. Her feelings of claustrophobia had grown greater. Everyone reeked with the sour stench of sweat, filth, and tobacco. Maura sighed. Hadn't someone said there were at least thirty more days to sail?

As quietly as possible, she lowered herself to the floor. The wood planking chilled her bare feet. When she stepped into the central aisle—clotted with people's possessions—she sensed other people stirring. Sure enough, women and girls were making their way to the steps that would take them to the main deck and then the forecastle deck above it. Since the privies afforded so little privacy, the women preferred to use them at night or just before dawn. They lined up silently, avoiding one another's eyes.

On deck, the ship's bell rang twice, sounding hollow and bleak. Lanterns, one on the forecastle deck, another at the stern by the wheelhouse, provided the only dull light. The two small safety lamps on the ratlines on either side of the ship were useless. Here and there icicles hung from the lines. The only hint of the day to come was a thin yellow streak of sky in the east.

Maura looked across the dark ceaseless waves. Though they had already met one ship—and, apparently, even exchanged letters—the empty vastness of the sea frightened her. She often worried if they would truly get to land again.

Aloft, she saw the shadowy forms of sailors going about their work amid spars and sails, chipping away ice. They seemed to Maura like ghosts among the clouds. Others were stoking up the steerage fireplace on the forecastle.

Maura craned her neck to see if the privy line was moving, only then realizing that the woman just before her was Bridy's mother. Not since she had placed her daughter on their platform had the two spoken.

Feeling the need to talk, Maura reached out and touched the woman's shoulder. "Morning to you, mother," she whispered.

The woman made a half turn, saw who it was, and nodded. "And to you," she said curtly.

Refusing to be put off, Maura said, "I need to be saying your daughter's no trouble at all. She's as sweet a soul as ever was."

"You're kind to say so," the woman replied, softening. "And hasn't she been telling me you share provisions with her. May the blessing of the Holy Spirit be upon your kindness." The woman crossed herself.

"Kindness is never extra," Maura replied.

"It's the saintly way," the woman agreed. Then, after a moment, she said, "Perhaps, mistress, it's an apology I should be making to you. I'd no intention of being harsh when we first set her in your berth. Begorra, it was all I could do to keep my wits. It's not just the girl, but her brothers too. And my husband, poor soul, is ailing."

"I'm sorry to hear it," Maura said.

"Our name is Faherty, you know," the woman said. "From Blarney, not all that far from Cork."

"My name is Maura O'Connell. We're from county Cork too. Kilonny, which was tumbled."

"God give you comfort, Maura O'Connell," said Mrs. Faherty.

For a while neither woman spoke. Finally Mrs. Faherty turned to Maura. "If I'd known how hard this voyage would be, I'm not so sure I'd have come."

"In truth," Maura said, "my mother chose not to."

"Then is it just your husband you're traveling with?"

Maura blushed. "He's not my husband," she said.

"Ah," Mrs. Faherty said, speaking kindly and without any hint of censure, "but it's hardly fit for unwed girls to be traveling this way. Where is your father then?"

"In America," Maura explained. "He sent us the money to come. From Lowell, Massachusetts."

"May heaven speed all," Mrs. Faherty whispered, crossing herself.

As they waited for the privies, Maura explained how she came to be traveling with Mr. Drabble. For her part, Mrs. Faherty related how she and her family came to emigrate. "It was the landlord who paid for our going. By the Holy Faith, it was either that or perish."

"And what made you choose to go to Boston?" Maura asked.

The woman smiled grimly. "Wasn't it more the case of the ship choosing us. Sure, the first one we had tickets for never sailed. The second neither. We took the one we could. In the name of Jesus, I don't suppose it matters as long as it's to America. Aren't they saying it's the land of promise. Food so plentiful no one starves. Full of decent employment and wages as well as honest places to live for the asking. Surely a paradise on earth."

"And have you no family there at all?" Maura asked.

"In faith, we're all we are."

Silently, Maura thanked God that her father was waiting.

Chapter 98
Mr. Gregory O'Connell

I n that section of Lowell, Massachusetts, known as the Acre stood many a three- and four-decker wooden building. These leaned one against the other like sleepy folk who know that if one falls all will fall. At the curb, dirty snow lay in piles.

After their day's work, Gregory O'Connell and Nathaniel Brewster moved slowly toward one such structure. The younger man all but guided the older around a street lamp, whose blue flame hissed feebly against the gloom.

Suddenly, Nathaniel said, "Hold it."

Mr. O'Connell stopped and looked up. Ten yards before them, they saw three boys. They were standing side by side, effectively blocking the way, their shoe-shine boxes at their feet.

Mr. O'Connell peered at them through the darkness. "And what may they be wanting?" he asked Nathaniel.

"I'm not sure," Nathaniel replied. "They don't have a pleasant look, though."

"If you're Irish," one of the boys called out, "you might as well learn that no Paddy can pass this way."

"Hooligans," Nathaniel said under his breath.

"But . . . what do they mean to do?" Mr. O'Connell whispered.

Before Nathaniel could answer, a snowball splattered on the ground not far from them. The first was quickly followed by another, then another. One struck Nathaniel on the chest. It felt like a rock.

"Out of America!" one of the boys called.

Mindful of Mr. O'Connell, Nathaniel grabbed his companion's sleeve. "We'd best go this way," he urged, and all but dragged the man down an alleyway.

More snowballs followed at a faster rate.

As they hurried along, Nathaniel turned to see the boys coming after them. "Run!" he cried to Mr. O'Connell.

The two men scrambled down the alley. Mr. O'Connell lost his muffler. "Over here!" Nathaniel panted, ducking into a recessed and shadowy doorway. Struggling for breath, Mr. O'Connell followed. "Jesus, Mary, and Joseph," he gasped, "I—"

"Shhh!" Nathaniel warned. The boys' footsteps grew louder. The two pressed their backs against the wall. The boys raced past them.

When the sound of their footfalls grew dim, Nathaniel poked his head out. The way was clear. "Come on now," he said to Mr. O'Connell in a low voice. "We better move before they return."

The man remained where he was. "You'll need to . . . to be . . . needing to give me . . . another moment," he breathed. "My heart's aflutter."

Anxiously, Nathaniel waited, all the while checking up and down the alley to make sure the boys had not returned.

"Now why . . . should they be doing that?" the older man asked, his pulse still racing.

"They're nobodies," Nathaniel replied. "You don't need to pay them any mind. Can you walk now?"

"Faith, I think so."

"Let's get you home."

Upon reaching Adams Street, Nathaniel checked again for followers. Satisfied none were there, the two entered the back door and began to climb the poorly lit stairs. Every few steps, Mr. O'Connell paused to catch his breath.

"Go on," he urged his companion. "You needn't be waiting for me."

"I'm in no rush," Nathaniel insisted. He was watching his friend's face with increasing concern.

At the third floor Mr. O'Connell halted yet again. Despite the cold he was sweating. Gently, Nathaniel took his arm. The older man made no resistance. Together, they shuffled through the dark hallway until they reached their room. Once inside, Nathaniel lit the single oil lamp.

It was a small cold room without windows. The walls were covered with peeling paper of some muddy color. The only decoration was a faded hand-colored religious print Mr. O'Connell had nailed up over his bed.

Other than the beds there was no furniture. A wooden box under Nathaniel's bed held the men's few possessions. Against the rear wall stood a small iron stove, a tumbled supply of sticks, and a few lumps of soft coal.

Exhausted, Mr. O'Connell subsided onto his bed. Perspiration stood on his brow. After remaining motionless for a long while, he struggled to remove his boots. Not having the strength to do it, he uttered a deep sigh and lay back.

Nathaniel, glancing quickly at his friend, strove to build a fire so as to bring some warmth into the room and make their dinner.

"Faith," Mr. O'Connell murmured, "I'm thinking there are more people in this whole house than in all of Kilonny."

"Your old home."

"I hardly know them here."

"They're right neighborly folks, Mr. O'Connell."

"By the Holy Mother, haven't I just been learning it."

"Just boys," Nathaniel insisted. "We're a friendly folk."

"Aye, but who will sit by me side in death?"

Nathaniel shook his head. "Mr. O'Connell, you're only suffering from what's called homesickness."

"Me lad, you're a braver man than I."

"Not so."

"Younger for sure. It's one and the same."

The fire was lit now. The room began to grow warmer. From under his bed Nathaniel drew out a paper bundle and unwrapped half a loaf of bread and a sausage. After sniffing the sausage to make sure it had not gone bad, he took a thin sharp poker from his box of possessions. Skewering the meat, he laid it atop the stove. Soon it was sizzling and popping, filling the room with its pungent smell.

"Jesus, Mary, and Joseph," Mr. O'Connell groaned. "I wish I were home!"

The depth of Mr. O'Connell's cry stirred Nathaniel. "And what would you be doing if you were?" he asked over his shoulder.

"I'd have me family around. . . ."

"How many times do I have to remind you, Mr. O'Connell, they'll be coming to Boston on the packet *Robert Peel*, out of Liverpool! The twenty-sixth of February. Just as your priest wrote. It's not so long now."

"I'd have me family around," repeated Mr. O'Connell, "and then . . . I'd die in peace."

The deep sadness in the man's voice caused Nathaniel to pick up the lamp and go to his friend's side. Mr. O'Connell's eyes were shut. His face was pinched, almost mustard yellow in color.

"Mr. O'Connell?" Nathaniel asked, kneeling beside him. "Is this worse than before?"

"Aye . . . I felt terrible weakness the whole day. Pains here. A numbness there." He did not open his eyes.

"It will pass," Nathaniel assured him, though he was beginning to doubt his conviction.

"Nathaniel," Mr. O'Connell called softly, beckoning the young man to draw closer, "you'll not forget—God willing— that promise you made to look after me family when they come. And you'll give them the money I have."

"Of course I won't forget. Mr. O'Connell, should I go fetch a doctor?"

"It's a priest I'll be wanting now."

"Why? What do you mean?"

"Ah, Nathaniel, me lad, I've never felt so ill in all me life."

Nathaniel Brewster stared at his friend until, with a shudder of fear, he tore from the room in search of help.

Chapter 99
Jeb and His Gang

Wonder where them two Paddies got away to," Nick Boswell said as he and his two companions—Jeb Grafton and Tom Pelkerton—pushed their way into the ramshackle shanty that was, for them, a kind of haven.

The three had built it from discarded bits of wood in the corner of a yard not far from Adams Street. There was barely enough room for them all. Aside from a bottle with a candle stuck in its neck, there was little more than rubbish about: a rope, candle ends, two other bottles, and, when the boys were there, their shoe-shine boxes.

"We'll get them another time," Tom said. He was a thickset thirteen-year-old boy with a face almost babyish in its roundness and soft features. Having picked up Mr. O'Connell's tattered muffler from the alleyway, he now flung it into a corner.

"Think they *were* Paddies?" asked Jeb.

"Had to be," Nick assured them as he lit the candle in the bottle, "or they wouldn't have run." Though Nick was

shorter than Jeb, he was the toughest, ready to take on anyone. But then all he did was done with certainty, his speech,
his way of walking, his willingness to use his strength to get
what he wanted.

"I wish we had got 'em," Tom said, pulling his box close
to the candle and sitting on the top of it.

"What would we have done with them?" Jeb asked.

"I'll tell you," said Nick. "Remember that one we got
last week?"

The other boys grinned.

"I suppose he was sorry he tried to slip by us," Nick went
on. "Bet you most anything he's still soaked and shivering."
He laughed.

At the memory, Jeb trembled, drew his coat up to his
neck, and stared into the flame.

"Make anything today?" he asked Nick.

"Hard when it snows," Nick replied. "Just fourteen
cents."

"I got ten," Tom said.

Jeb looked up. "I did better than that," he bragged. "Got
me twenty-four cents."

The boys grew thoughtful. "How's your ma?" Tom
asked Jeb.

Jeb stared hard at his friend—as if to make sure how the
question was meant, kindly or nosily. Then he shrugged.

"They say it's worst in winter," Tom offered with
sympathy.

"Suppose. . . ."

The reminder of illness silenced them. It was Jeb who
said, "I saw Mr. Jenkins again."

"The one who gave you that coat?"

Jeb nodded. "I did up his boots. He gave me a dime."

"He's something," Nick said with ill-disguised envy.

"What'd he say this time?" Tom asked.

Jeb stayed quiet for a while, enjoying the attention of the others. "He's waiting for someone to come back."

"Who?" Nick demanded.

Jeb stared into the candle flame, biding his time.

"Come on, tell us!" Tom cried, cuffing Jeb's shoulder.

"Ambrose Shagwell, that's who," Jeb said.

It took a moment for the name to sink in. "The man who owns the Shagwell Cotton Mill?" Nick asked.

Jeb grinned.

Tom whistled. "They friends?"

"Close as anything," Jeb said.

Tom leaned in toward the candle. "Hey, Jeb, do you think he could get us regular jobs?"

"I suppose he could . . . if I asked," Jeb bragged.

"Well then, why don't you ask?" Nick demanded.

" 'Cause I'll do it when I'm good and ready," Jeb replied. "Well, maybe he could get your father a job," Tom said after a moment. "Or mine."

"He could. Sure thing," Jeb assured him.

Nick's eyes narrowed. "They got Irish working there at Shagwell's."

"So what?" Jeb said. "They're everywhere."

"I'm just saying—"

"Mr. Jenkins is planning on something, something big."

Tom's eyes grew wide. "What kind of big?"

Though Jeb did not know, he smiled knowingly all the same. "I'll tell you when I want to, that's what. And the thing is, I'm going to help him. And when I do, that's when I'll ask about getting jobs. Get my mother some medicine. Get my father money to go to California—"

"California!" Nick cried.

"Sure, to lay his hands on some of that gold. It's there, isn't it? And all you have to do is get there and put it in your pocket. And people say it's a lot warmer than this place is."

Nick let forth a low whistle. "You'll be doing fine then, won't you?"

Jeb grinned and nodded.

Tom said, "If you want me to help Mr. Jenkins, just say the word. I'll be there."

"Me too," said Nick. "Sure thing."

Jeb smiled. "I'll talk to him. He's my friend." And he drew his coat about himself a little tighter.

Chapter 100
Patrick Goes to the Bottom Hold

*L*aurence? Laurence! Are you there? It's me, Patrick."
His voice echoed through the darkness, becoming lost in the creaks and groans of the continually shifting ship.

Hearing no answer, Patrick moved lower, trying to see through the shadowy light dispelled by the single candle he carried. Six days had passed since he had last visited Laurence. Each time he'd started to come, he'd seen Mr. Murdock lurking about and had to retreat. This time he was sure no one was watching.

When he reached the floor, he called again.

"Over here," came a soft answer.

Candle before him, Patrick made his way along the central aisle toward the sound of the voice. Suddenly, a hand gripped his ankle. Patrick dropped the candle. The flame, hitting bilgewater, went out with a hiss. What remained was a smell of smoke and wax. The only illumination came from the hatch high above.

Heart pounding, Patrick looked down. A ghostlike Laurence was lying on the floor between two barrels. He was grinning.

"Faith, you scared me," Patrick said.

"I had to be sure it was you," Laurence replied as he pulled himself up. Patrick could see that his hair was a tangle, his cheeks pale. The clothing that the minister had given him in Liverpool was filthy and torn.

"Men come down here every day," Laurence said. "They take up bread or spirits or other things. And I've seen the first mate twice. From the way he prowls about, I'm pretty sure he's looking for me."

"Where do you hide?" Patrick asked.

"I've fitted up a barrel. It's perfectly dry. I'll show it to you if you'd like. It's over here."

They cut around three rows of barrels. "Here it is," Laurence said.

Patrick looked about. "Where?"

Laurence giggled. "You can't tell, can you?" He lifted the lid of his barrel. Patrick saw that it was empty save for some straw.

"That's my home," Laurence said with pride.

Patrick said, "What do you do all day?"

Laurence shrugged. "I've counted the barrels lots of times. Sometimes I sing songs or try to recall things I've read. Or I try and think of all that's happened. Other times I just sit and remember my family."

"Laurence," Patrick said, "you never did tell me of them. Or why you had to run away. Faith, was it something to do with the mark on your face?"

Laurence touched his cheek. "I have to forget all that," he said softly.

"Oh." Patrick emptied his pockets. "I brought you some food," he said. "Bread and cooked rice."

As Laurence reached for the food, he asked, "How many days have we been traveling?"

"This is the seventh day."

"It feels like a month," Laurence said. "Where do you stay?"

"Ah, Laurence, you never saw such a place for noise. Sure, it's crowded beyond belief and terrible dirty."

"Is it warm?"

"Cold. And rats, Laurence. I've seen a lot of them."

"They're down here too. Once I read in a book about sailors taming them."

"Faith, I wouldn't."

"I should like to try. It would mean company. I've been leaving some food near where I think one comes. I call him Nappy, for Napoleon. . . . Patrick," Laurence said, abruptly changing the subject, "could I come visit you?"

"Wouldn't risk it," Patrick warned. "You said yourself they were looking for you."

Laurence sighed.

After a moment he asked, "What place are we going to?"

"Boston."

"Is that a country?"

"A city, I think. My father will meet us there."

"What's he like?"

"Faith, not a big man. Nor one for smiling or singing songs. Nor can he read, not like Maura or me. For all of that he's a God-fearing, kindly soul."

"Patrick?"

"What?"

"When we get to America, can I go with you?"

For a moment Patrick was silent. Then he said, "The thing is, Laurence, I'm sure my sister is to marry that Mr. Drabble. I'm not so fond of the man," Patrick confessed. "And I don't know what all of that will bring."

"Patrick . . . ?"

"What's that now?"

"Why did you leave Ireland?"

"Sure, you know of the terrible times there."

Laurence shook his head.

"Jesus, Mary, and Joseph! I would have thought everyone knew. It's something truly bad. When we had all but nothing, Da left for America to find work. And then didn't he do fine enough to send for us? Ah, Laurence, it must be a grand country. The promised land they call it."

Laurence wondered what Patrick would say if he knew his father owned land in Ireland. Then he reminded himself he had nothing to do anymore with any of that.

"Laurence," Patrick said after a while. "I had better go."

"Will you come back tomorrow?"

"You know I'll try. But I can't always."

Laurence said, "I didn't mean to frighten you."

"I wasn't frightened. Not really."

"It was just something to do."

"I'm sure. Look for me then."

"I will."

Patrick made his way back down the center aisle of the hold, found the ladder, and began to climb up. "Bye!" he called.

"Bye," Laurence echoed. For a moment, he just stood in the dark. "I am like poor Robinson Crusoe," he said, remembering his favorite book at home. "Just the same."

Chapter 101
Sir Albert Kirkle in the City of Liverpool

In Liverpool, England, Sir Albert Kirkle, tall hat in hand, leaned over the quarterdeck railing of the packet ship *Yorkshire* and watched Irish emigrants board below him.

He was angry at his father and at Laurence. Why couldn't his brother simply have accepted the fact that he *was* a younger brother? Why should he be forced to go find him and deal with him in America? As was his habit, Albert squeezed his knuckles so hard they cracked. Let them all go hang!

For a while he studied the people filing on board. It made him think of a parade of beggars. That he should even be close to such people disgusted him.

As Albert looked on, he observed a hansom carriage race up to the quay. The carriage bore the royal insignia, an indication that its mission was government business. A man in livery leaped out, holding a portfolio. He scanned the *Yorkshire*, then began to push his way through the crowd, which gave way before him. When he reached the gangway, he conferred with the sailors on guard, showing them the portfolio. He was allowed to pass through immediately. Albert presumed he was watching the delivery of a government document, some matter of diplomacy, no doubt. It made sense: The *Yorkshire*, Captain Bailey commanding, had a reputation for being the fastest ship in the North Atlantic trade.

He turned away and allowed his thoughts to drift elsewhere but soon felt a tap on his shoulder. It was the man with the portfolio.

"Sir Albert?" The man saluted him.

"Yes."

The man bowed and held out the portfolio, which bore the stamp of the government. "A message from Lord Kirkle."

Albert started. He held out his hand. Perhaps Laurence had returned on his own. Upset by the possibility, Albert opened the portfolio. Inside were two letters. The first was from his father:

Sir,

I send you news. The enclosed letter—which I intercepted—establishes your guilt in this affair beyond question. But it also provides some information that I presume will be of use to you. Remember, I do not expect to see you again unless you bring back your brother.

Lord Kirkle

Albert hastily looked at the second letter. It was the one Mr. Clemspool had written to him. Not only did it make him blush, it was a disappointment to learn that his brother was alive. Nonetheless, he paid particular attention to the last part of the note.

As to my address in America, I have yet to determine upon a permanent abode or even whether I will remain in the country. But you should write to me in the care of Mr. Ambrose Shagwell, in the city of Lowell, Massachusetts, USA. I am sure word will reach me. Mr. Shagwell is a highly esteemed gentleman and a good friend, a man I trust and, sir, a confidant in all my affairs.

Trusting you are, sir, continuing in good health, I remain,

Faithfully yours,
Matthew Clemspool, Esq.

"Will there be any reply?" the messenger inquired of Albert.

"You may tell his lordship that I'm much obliged to him."

As the messenger went off, Albert wondered where Lowell, Massachusetts, was. It did not matter; he would go there. He would find Laurence and make sure the boy did not come back. As he mused, he suddenly had a thought: What, he wondered, had happened to all the money that had been taken?

Chapter 102
Bridy Listens

*I*n the afternoon, Maura and Patrick left the steerage deck to go after daily provisions. Mr. Drabble was gone again, murmuring something to Bridy about giving a lesson. She was not sure what he meant but was content to be alone in the berth, full of idle thoughts.

She thought about Maura O'Connell, so strong and beautiful, so sure of herself. Bridy thought that if she ever grew up, she would like to be like Maura.

She gazed at the ceiling, the dark crisscrossing wooden beams. She felt the swaying of the boat, and while she knew they were going to America, she had no idea what America was, only that her mother said they would be happy there. Bridy was not sure she knew what being happy meant. Taking a deep breath, she wondered if she would ever know anything. So much seemed uncertain.

Deciding to ask her mother about America, Bridy made her way to her family's berth. Her father and two brothers lay asleep. Her mother was not there.

In the dull light, she studied her father's face. It was a face she loved: the heavy-lidded eyes, the soft cheeks, the curve of his lips. Though Bridy often sensed his disappointment—and knew how tired he most always was—she never knew his anger. Now, as she looked at him, she saw that his sleep was restless and that there was sweat on his brow.

Her brothers—fourteen-year-old Brian and fifteen-year-old John—were thinner, taller than their father. They were the best of friends, always together, whispering off in corners, full of private jokes. She loved them too.

Bridy reached over to stroke her father's brow. It was hot. At her touch, he opened his eyes, saw her, made a small grimace—Bridy was sure it was a smile—then dropped back into fitful sleep. Bridy let him be.

Half an hour later her mother returned. She stood at the foot of the bed and stared fixedly at her husband, unaware of Bridy sitting in the shadows. After a few moments she crossed herself. From the way her mouth was working, Bridy knew she was saying prayers. "Mother . . . ," Bridy spoke softly.

Mrs. Faherty looked about.

"I'm here," Bridy said.

Mrs. Faherty beckoned the girl to her side. Then she sighed. "Come now, Bridy," she said, touching her daughter on the shoulder, "we'll take a bit of a walk."

They went along the central aisle, then up the steps to the crowded main deck. There were the inevitable long lines for food, for the fireplace, for the privies. Ignoring them, Mrs. Faherty led the child into a corner, from which the quarterdeck rose. It was a gray, cloudy day, and seas were low. Now and again the sails above fluttered languidly.

Bridy, knowing her mother had something to say to her but would speak only when she was ready, waited patiently, staring out at the waves.

"Bridy, love," her mother said at last.

The girl looked around.

"Faith now, are you still faring well with that Maura O'Connell?"

Bridy nodded.

"And is she kind to you?"

"She's very kind," Bridy said. "And, Mother, they do share their food with me."

"And her brother?"

"He's fine too."

"What about the other one, the Englishman?"

Bridy considered a moment. "I don't always understand the way he talks."

For a while Mrs. Faherty said nothing. Then she said, "Bridy, you need to know. Your father is doing poorly."

Bridy stared up at her mother.

"Ailing. Not well at all," her mother said. "But you mustn't tell a soul. Begorra, I wanted you to know, but I'm also wanting it to be a secret. Can you keep it?"

Bridy nodded.

"Didn't I hear a priest say once, 'When an angel speaks, it's silence you hear, 'cause it speaks to your heart and not to your ear.' It was a fine thing to say." Mrs. Faherty sighed, then went on. " 'Cause most of what people like us hear is silence. Sure, isn't it a great comfort to know it's God who's speaking so much to us."

Bridy pressed her face against her mother's belly. "You'll do fine, Bridy Faherty," her mother said, squeezing her close. "Just fine." Then she pushed the girl away. "Look at me, love."

The girl looked up.

"You must keep away from us. Even from me who loves you so. You must. If it's a sickness we're having, you need to keep yourself clear of it. Stay with them, do you understand? You'll be safer."

Bridy heard the words, but even as she gazed at her mother, she listened intently to the silence that followed. What she sensed was dread.

Chapter 103
A Warning

This morning in the privy line Mrs. Faherty kept looking past Maura, fastening on the distant red dawn. "When a sky's as wounded as that one," she said mournfully, "there's sure to be a storm sowing and sorrow reaping. Here's a prayer that it comes after they give us our oatmeal portion." She crossed herself.

Before returning to the steerage deck, Maura looked out at the weather. The sky was indeed gray, ominous. The sea was up, and the waves high now, flicking foam. Wind whistled through the lines, and the ship plunged like a galloping horse.

More and more steerage passengers were anxiously crowding the deck to wait for their rations of water and oatmeal. They carried a variety of pots, pans, and earthen jars.

Worried that, if she and Mr. Drabble did not hurry, they would not get their portions, nor get to cook if a storm came, Maura hurried down to the steerage deck.

Patrick and Mr. Drabble were awake, though still on the platform. Bridy was asleep.

"Are they handing out water yet?" the actor asked Maura.

"People are gathering now," she informed him. "I was speaking to Mrs. Faherty. She thought today was the day for oatmeal." Then she added, "They're speaking of a storm."

"I had better get our provisions," the actor said immediately. He found one of their sacks and emptied it of their belongings.

"Go with him," Maura told her brother. "You'll be saving some time. I'll join you soon."

The two went off, Patrick taking their can for water.

Maura yawned. The thought of an almost empty platform proved irresistible. She climbed into the berth. For a while she was content to listen to the surging winds and the sounds of the ship responding with groans and creaks. Remembering the storm when they had crossed from Cork to Liverpool, she was grateful that this time they would be belowdecks. Maura whispered a prayer, made the sign of the cross, closed her eyes, and soon fell asleep.

On the main deck Mr. Drabble and Patrick found apprehensive passengers pointing off to the east, watching the swelling waves rise and fall with ever-increasing force. As soon as the water, food, and fireplace were made available, lines formed. They could see that people were nervous. Mr. Drabble sought Patrick's hand, but the boy pulled away, turning to where water was being distributed below the main mast. There, two sailors stood next to a barrel they had hauled up from the hold. They were using a bucket to dole out meager portions.

At the other side of the deck, another sailor was scooping out measured rations of oatmeal from a huge sack.

"Make sure you get your full share," Mr. Drabble called after Patrick. "If that storm comes, who can tell when we'll get our due again."

Patrick joined the water line. There was the inevitable jostling and pushing. Every time the ship lurched, someone lost his footing and often his place.

Slowly, Patrick moved forward in the line. He could smell the water now, laced as it was with vinegar to keep it drinkable. Patrick hated the taste.

The wait seemed endless. The sailors were taking delight

in teasing passengers by doling out the water even more slowly than was their custom. Patrick, trying to be patient, passed the time by listening to those about him.

"And didn't one of the crew tell me it was a big storm brewing," he heard a man say.

"How big?"

"That he wouldn't foretell. Nothing to worry about, says he. Said we'd be perfectly safe in steerage, and to thank our particular saints we weren't down in the bottom hold."

"Small mercies," said the other man, casting a wary look at the scudding clouds.

Patrick thought at once of Laurence. If the hold was an unsafe place to be in a storm, shouldn't he warn his friend? He looked up. Sailors—more than usual, he thought—were climbing the lines and beginning to reef in sails. Captain Rickles was barking orders over an increasingly loud wind.

"Come on, Paddy boy," a voice suddenly growled into his ear. "Move yerself!"

Patrick, who had not been paying attention, realized he was at the head of the line. He stepped forward, holding his can before him.

The sailor, a grizzled old man with few teeth, dunked his wooden bucket into the water barrel, then drew it up.

"Hold your can out farther, won't you!" he shouted.

Patrick stretched forward.

Unexpectedly, the sailor flipped his bucket over. The water gushed out so quickly, the force of it knocked Patrick's can to the deck. His water portion flowed away. Enjoying his joke, the sailor laughed loudly, as did his companion. Patrick, hands and wrists soaked, stood helplessly.

"Away with you, Paddy boy," the sailor cried. "Yer had yer portion. There's a line behind you."

"But, Your Honor, I . . . ," Patrick tried to protest. Before he could say more, one of the sailors kicked him aside.

Angry, Patrick retrieved his can and scuttled across the deck to find Mr. Drabble.

The actor was incensed to hear the boy's story. "You're going to have to handle things better, Mr. Patrick," he scolded. "Your sister and I can't always be looking after you."

Handing over the oatmeal he'd received, he took the water can from Patrick. "Take the meal down," he instructed. "Once there, you can rid it of worms. I'll fetch the water."

Patrick, already upset by the sailor's treatment, resented Mr. Drabble's words. Who was he to be scolding and ordering him about? Even if he was to become Maura's husband, the man had no right to be lording it over him. Patrick decided to complain to his sister.

When he reached their platform, however, Maura was asleep. Bridy was awake, but he had no wish to talk to her. For a time Patrick remained by his sister's side, hoping she would get up, rehearsing what he would say. But Maura slept on, and the tossing of the ship grew more turbulent.

Feeling he must warn Laurence about the storm, Patrick set off for the bottom hold. He stopped, took a fistful of oatmeal, and thrust it in his pocket.

Certain he hadn't been observed, Patrick started down the steps. Suddenly, the ship shuddered. It was as if a great hand had grasped the vessel and shaken it. Patrick almost lost his footing, but he reached the level below. As usual, he took up one of the wall candles and brought it to the head of the ladder.

The ship heeled once, twice. Patrick held tight, his heart thumping. After a moment he peered down the ladder again into nothingness. It made him want to turn back.

But, reminding himself that he must warn Laurence— then retreat—Patrick gathered himself and began to descend. He hated the ladder.

The deeper he went, the louder grew the grinding and groaning of the ship. Halfway down he held out the candle in hopes of seeing his friend. He saw nothing but the confusion of cargo.

"Laurence!" he called. The name echoed up and down the hold. "Laurence!" he cried again, louder. Was Laurence playing his hiding game? Not now, Patrick prayed.

He descended a few more rungs. Unexpectedly, the ship gave a violent heave. Patrick was swung wildly about. Without thinking, he grabbed for the ladder with the hand that held the candle. The flame guttered out.

Before he could catch his breath, the ship pitched in yet another direction. This time the hatchway door above—with a reverberating bang that sounded like a pistol shot—slammed shut. Alarmed, Patrick scrambled up the ladder and pushed against the hatchway. It would not budge.

Chapter 104

The Storm

*B*ursts of lightning shattered the sky. High winds sliced through the lines, making them hum. Thunder came next, pummeling the ears.

The sailors reacted speedily by whisking away water casks and the oatmeal sack. In a matter of moments the fireplace fire was doused with buckets of seawater.

"All passengers below!" bellowed Captain Rickles from his place before the mizzenmast. "All passengers below!"

Like a stiff broom, an icy rain swept the decks of the ship, all but pushing the emigrants down the stairway to the steerage deck.

"Shorten sail!" the captain cried through his speaking tube as he tried to make himself heard above the howling wind and thudding waves. "Stand by to take in royals and flying jib! Take in mainsail and spanker!"

The sailors wrestled with the heavy rain-soaked sails, struggling to reef them in before the wind gusted again. Enormous waves began to smash broadside against the *Robert Peel*. With each blow the ship shuddered, pitching and yawing wildly.

As the last frantic passenger tumbled down the steps into steerage, sailors leaped to the doors and hatches, slammed them shut, then secured them tightly with ropes so as to keep the interior decks from flooding. Anything on the main deck not tied down would be quickly washed away.

On the steerage level, the rain beat a tattoo against the ceiling. The hanging lamps gyrated, some so wildly that they guttered out. The shifting and tilting of the ship set trunks, pots, food, water to flying.

The emigrants crouched down upon their platforms and the floor planking, clinging to their possessions. Some became sick. Many began to cry, to pray. If they kept their eyes open, they saw, even through the gloom, the increasing havoc and destruction all about them. If they closed their eyes, they heard sudden shrieks and moans and could only imagine the worst: that they were about to sink.

A drenched Mr. Drabble was one of the last to get down the steps. When he reached the platform, he found Maura alone with Bridy. The girl was clinging to a platform post with two hands, crying for her mother, who, tending to the rest of her family down the way, could not come. Maura struggled to keep the child calm.

As soon as she saw Mr. Drabble, Maura called, "And where is Patrick?"

"I thought he was with you."

"Jesus, Mary, and Joseph!" Maura moaned. "I never saw him. Do you think he could still be up on deck?"

Mr. Drabble shook his head. "They sent everyone below."

Ignoring Bridy's whimpers, Maura scurried off the platform. "I'll be worrying till I find him," she declared.

But by the time Maura reached the central stairway, she had seen no sign of her brother. Feeling compelled to search further, she pushed her way back into the aft section of the deck.

Again she told herself that she need not worry, that Patrick would turn up safe and sound as he always had. But in spite of her own assurances, she kept thinking the worst, that he was on the deck.

She struggled back to the central steps. Upon reaching the top, she pushed against the door, but it remained shut. First she knocked on it, then she pounded. No one came. In desperation she threw herself against the door. It still would not give. The realization dawned on her that they had been locked in. Had the crew abandoned them? It could not be, she told herself. It could not. She slumped on the top step, buried her face in her hands, and began to pray.

When a sudden plunge of the ship knocked her off the step, she knew she must return to their berth. Should she inform the others below that the door was locked? If she did, she was certain to cause a panic. She decided to say nothing.

The stench of people's sickness was overpowering. With almost no light she had to grope her way back to the platform.

"Did you find him?" Mr. Drabble called.

Maura shook her head. Then, once again, she began to pray.

Chapter 105
In the Bottom Hold

*F*aintly, as though from a great distance, Patrick heard the cries from steerage as the *Robert Peel*'s timbers moaned and groaned in twisted agony. So severe was the ship's movement that a barrel broke free, careened wildly across the central aisle, struck a post, and shattered, spewing its contents in all directions.

Patrick, barely able to stand, fell to his knees. "Laurence!" he shouted over the tumult. There was no answer. "Laurence!" he fairly screamed. "It's me, Patrick."

"I'm here," came a faint reply.

"I'm by the ladder," Patrick called. "I can't see."

"Stay where you are," Laurence replied. "I'll come to you."

Staring hopelessly into the absolute darkness, Patrick propped himself against the ladder and waited, breathing hard. When he least expected it, he felt the touch of a hand. He jumped. "Laurence?"

"What is it?" Laurence asked. "I keep hearing shouts from above. Why is the ship moving so wildly?"

"It's a storm," Patrick explained.

But Laurence only said, "Did you bring me anything to eat?"

Patrick reached into his pocket and pulled out as much oatmeal as he could. "Here," he said.

Laurence found Patrick's hand, cupped it in his, and gathered up the food. Dry and uncooked as it was, he pushed the oatmeal into his mouth.

The ship lurched heavily. From a distance panicky cries rose and fell. Then something else closer at hand broke loose and smashed. Patrick jumped, recollecting suddenly the sharp crackling sounds of Mr. Morgan's soldiers shooting at him back in Kilonny the day they left.

"Laurence," he gasped, "we need to be getting ourselves away from here."

"Why?"

"Didn't I hear a man say that during the storm it would be worst down here. It's why I came to warn you. By the blessed Saint Martin, it's come on fast."

"Lots of things have been breaking loose," Laurence said. "Barrels keep smashing."

To Patrick, Laurence's voice seemed unnaturally calm. It was almost as if he didn't care.

"Back there," Laurence went on, "a whole chest of dishes broke to bits. It did sound awful."

"That's what I'm telling you, Laurence, you have to find a safer place."

"But won't they discover me?"

"Sure but there must be somewhere to hide you that won't be as bad as down here," Patrick said.

"Where?" Laurence asked eagerly.

"I'm not sure," Patrick admitted. "That hatch above is shut and jammed. Maybe someone closed it. I couldn't lift it at all."

"There is another ladder," Laurence said. "To the rear."

"Where does it go?"

"I don't know. But do you think it's safe?"

"Laurence, it can't be worse than this. Do you think you can find that ladder now?"

"I think so."

"Go on then," Patrick said. "Better give me your hand. I can't see a thing." Groping for Laurence, he found his friend's arm.

Laurence led the way down the littered aisle. Twice, Patrick stumbled.

When they were halfway along, the ship gave a tremendous shudder, and Patrick lost his grip. Behind them, a barrel broke free, rumbled down the aisle, and struck Patrick from behind. With a scream he fell.

"Patrick!" Laurence cried.

"I'm . . . here," Patrick breathed. "I can't move." The barrel had come to rest atop his foot, pinning him down. "Get it off!" Patrick pleaded against the searing pain. "Get it off!"

Laurence fumbled through the dark. Once he found Patrick, he threw all his weight against the barrel. He could not move it.

"Please!" Patrick implored.

Laurence tried again. As he did, the ship heaved. The combined movement was enough to shift the barrel, causing it to rumble on down the aisle.

"Jesus, Mary, and Joseph, the leg hurts bad," Patrick whimpered.

"Can you move at all?" Laurence asked.

Patrick dragged himself forward. "I need your hand."

Clinging to Laurence, Patrick managed to pull himself up. But when he put weight on his right leg, a bolt of excruciating pain shot through him. "Holy Mother," he managed to say. "It's something truly bad. Where's the other ladder?"

"This way."

They inched along. Every time Patrick put his foot down, the pain seemed to explode.

"Here it is," Laurence finally announced.

Patrick reached out and touched a ladder. It was considerably smaller than the central one.

"Where do you think it goes?" Patrick asked.

"I don't know. Will you be able to climb?" Laurence asked.

"Faith, I'd better. I'm not staying here," Patrick replied. He was breathing hard, trying to keep from crying.

Laurence said, "Let me go first."

"You?"

"I think I'd better." Without waiting for a response, Laurence reached up and began to climb. Patrick, following, put his good foot on the bottom rung and hauled himself up. Then he tried the hurt foot. The pain had not eased. "Don't go too fast," he called.

Gradually, the two boys worked their way up, now and again pausing for the ship to desist in its wild tossing.

Laurence knew he'd reached the ceiling only when he banged his head against it. "I'm at the top," he yelled down.

"Faith now, see if you can find a hatchway," Patrick told him.

Laurence stretched up and felt about until his fingers touched what he thought was a trapdoor. "I found it!" He gave it a shove. Though very heavy, the trap rose slightly. "It moves!" he cried.

"Get it open!"

Moving higher on the ladder, Laurence bent his head forward so that his back came up against the hatchway. Then he pressed down on both legs even as he pushed his back up. The hatchway lifted. Twisting awkwardly, almost falling, he shoved the door with all his strength.

"I've got it upright," he hollered to Patrick. "I'm going to see where it leads."

Chapter 106
Seasick and Smiling

*T*oby Grout lay stretched upon his stateroom bed in awful misery. One large hand gripped the bed frame; the other covered his good eye. Now and again he groaned.

In contrast, Mr. Clemspool sat on his bed, his round, rosy face completely relaxed as he observed his roommate with detached amusement. "I trust you've heard what Mr. Murdock said?" he asked.

"I couldn't eat," Mr. Grout returned. As far as he was concerned, the only valid question to be asked was, Would death come by the sinking of the ship, or by the sinking of his stomach?

Mr. Clemspool went on. "He insisted this was just an ordinary storm, that it will last a few days, but it will make the voyage go faster. May I therefore suggest, sir, that you pull yourself together."

"Yer do wants to plague me, don't yet?" Mr. Grout groaned.

His companion laughed.

"Ain't no shame in sayin' I'm sick!" Mr. Grout cried. "I'm frightened too," he added as the ship heaved in such a particularly wrenching way that the ceiling lamp swung over his head like a decapitating ax. "I don't like it. Yer don't 'ave to keep tryin' to make me worse."

"Mr. Grout, you should save your fears for something worthy, like the ghost of a sailor rising from the sea. Mr. Murdock informed me it happens during storms."

Mr. Grout pushed himself up on an elbow. "Did 'e?"

"To make my point precisely, sir—you are an ignorant man. I should think you are rich enough to get that tutor of yours to teach you some proper religion."

"I just knows wot to be fearful of!"

"You could be worse off," Mr. Clemspool taunted. "You could be with all those ignorant Irish down below. You'd be at home with them."

Mr. Grout, feeling yet another wave of nausea rise within him, fell back on his bed.

"*My* only complaint about this storm," Mr. Clemspool went on, "is that it keeps me cooped up with you."

The ship took a sudden drop, as if into a crevasse. Mr. Grout leaped up in terror.

"You need to be as calm as I am, sir," Mr. Clemspool suggested scornfully. "Like a gentleman."

"I needs to get away from yer, that's wot I need," Mr. Grout declared. "I'm goin' into the galley. Anywhere would be better than 'ere." When Mr. Clemspool only laughed again, Mr. Grout, feeling both wretchedly sick to his stomach and furious, hurried out of the stateroom, slamming the door behind him.

The galley way was deserted. Overhead, on the quarterdeck, beat the unceasing rain. From below, as though from a great distance, rose the frightened cries from steerage.

The gloominess of the galley, the distant shouts, the tumultuous, incessant rocking of the ship, all convinced Toby Grout that his death from drowning was foredoomed.

Desperate for peace of mind, the one-eyed man staggered along on wobbly legs, bracing himself against the walls each time the ship heaved abruptly. The more he thought of the fact that he was caught in a raging storm in the middle of the Atlantic Ocean, the greater became his dread.

Why am I 'ere? he kept asking himself. Then the frightening thought occurred to him that perhaps the storm was aimed at *him!* Was not that how God dealt with Jonah when the man had sinned?

Just to contemplate his criminal past made Mr. Grout quake. Images of his criminal life on London streets careened through his mind. A fit of remorse gripped him, shook him. In particular, he fastened on the way he had come by the money in his cabin now, the money that had brought him to this point of suffering. That thought in turn reminded Mr. Grout of the London boy he had robbed in the street. He began to wonder—with a deepening sense of guilt—what had happened to him. Perhaps he was dead. The idea of it made Mr. Grout tremble.

Chapter 107

Out of the Bottom Hold

*L*aurence poked his head up through the hatchway opening. A small oval window on the far wall shed a feeble light into a small room. Some two dozen seamen's chests as well as traveling trunks shifted about on the floor as the ship rolled. One large chest had already tipped and broken and now lay open. Its contents, gentlemen's fine shirts, lay strewn about in disorder.

Seeing in a glance that no one was there, Laurence scrambled into the room. "It's all right!" he called back down the opening.

Slowly, painfully, Patrick dragged himself up. As he did, his left foot caught on the hatch door. It banged shut with a thump that made the boys flinch.

"We'd best keep it open," Patrick advised. "There's no telling when we might have to get back down fast."

Laurence dug his fingers around the hatch. "It's stuck," he said, then sat back against one of the trunks. "Where are we?" he asked after a moment.

"I'm thinking it's a storage place for rich people's things." Patrick examined his foot. When he moved it, the pain was severe.

"Does it hurt a lot?" Laurence asked, holding off a trunk that had slid up against him.

With a shake of his head, Patrick ignored the question. Instead, he listened to the sounds of the raging storm. "Jesus, Mary, and Joseph!" he whispered as he crossed himself. "Isn't that wind something fierce?"

In a far corner he spied yet another ladder leading up. There was also a door in the forward wall. "Do you think that door opens?" he asked.

Laurence tried. It would not give.

Patrick said, "I suppose you'd best try the ladder."

Laurence stood at the foot of it and gazed up. "There's a door in the ceiling. I'll go up."

"Be wary," Patrick warned.

Laurence climbed. At the top of the ladder he pressed his hand against a small square in the ceiling. It was a door indeed, and it lifted. Moving higher, he stuck his head up and looked down a long dim hallway.

Chapter 108

Mr. Grout in the Galley

U pon reaching the forward end of the galley, Mr. Grout pushed against the door, opening it some two inches. Small as the gap was, a blast of wet wind momentarily blinded him, though not before he glimpsed a deck awash with wild water. In haste, he pulled the door back shut.

Attempting to wipe his face dry, Mr. Grout turned and stumbled back toward his stateroom. All he wanted to do was to curl up on his bed and hide from everything—his past included.

As he tottered toward the stern of the ship, Mr. Grout stopped short. At the far end of the shadowy galley way something was moving. Low and indistinct, it was difficult to make out exactly, except that the thing seemed to be rising out of the floor.

Hardly believing what he was seeing, Mr. Grout, heart pounding, took a few hesitant steps forward, straining to see more clearly through the dim light.

What he observed was a rising head, shoulders, then hands. Here were his most fearful superstitions coming true! *Here was a ghost.* Mr. Grout could barely breathe. His heart nearly burst from hammering. Oh! Here was the boy from London—the same dirty face, the same look of fear, the same severely marked right cheek—the boy from whom he had stolen the money!

Staggered by the force of the vision, Mr. Grout stumbled in the direction of the ghost only to see it vanish through the floor. At that moment, the ship lurched. His legs weak and shaky, Mr. Grout slipped, saving himself from a fall by clawing at the wall. Feeling as though he were suffocating, he tried to cry for help, but his throat was too constricted.

Shaken to his soul, Mr. Grout propped himself against the wall and stared at the place where he had seen the ghost— as he believed it to be. Then the boy *was* dead! Such a visitation could mean only one thing. He—Toby Grout— bore the appalling responsibility.

Whatever was left of the one-eyed man's courage evaporated. He floundered back to his cabin, snatched the door open, stepped inside, slammed it, and leaned his full weight upon it so nothing could follow.

Chapter 109

Patrick and Laurence Search for Safety

What's the matter?" Patrick asked when Laurence dropped down to the floor of the luggage room.

For one brief, terrible second Laurence was certain he'd seen the man with the eye patch, the man who'd robbed him in London. "Patrick," he bleated hoarsely, "there's someone in the hallway."

"Who?"

"A . . . a man," Laurence stammered, hardly knowing how to explain. He wasn't sure he wanted to.

"Did he see you?"

"I don't know. He ran away."

"Where?"

Laurence shook his head.

Patrick pulled himself up. His foot throbbed. "We have to find a way out of here," he said. He pointed to the forward wall. "Try that door again." When Laurence, lost in thought, simply stood there, Patrick repeated, "What's the matter with you?"

"It's nothing," Laurence said, trying to shake off his fright. He pulled at the door again. It still would not move. He looked around at Patrick for advice.

"Faith then," said Patrick, "the only way to get out is up the ladder. Go on. Best check to see if there's anyone there now."

Instead, Laurence closed his eyes, intent upon the man he had seen in the galley. Surely he was the one-eyed man who took his money. Hadn't he seen the thief's face—albeit falsely bearded—that night in London? Hadn't he seen it again at the Liverpool railroad station and still again through the keyhole when Mr. Clemspool had locked him in the hotel room? He couldn't confuse that face with any other. It had to be the same person! But how could that be?

Recollecting closely was a skill that Laurence had practiced and developed to pass away long, lonely hours in the dark hold. So it was that when he cast his mind back to the hotel room in which Mr. Clemspool had kept him prisoner, trying to recall what he had seen and heard, he was able to envision much: the hotel room's size, the color of its walls, the soft luxury of the bed, the room's two windows, the curtain he'd used for his escape. He saw the room's door and the keyhole through which he had seen the thief and heard his voice.

Slowly but surely the scene unfolded in his memory: The thief was speaking to Mr. Clemspool, telling the villain that he was going to America. Would Mr. Clemspool come with him? No, Mr. Clemspool refused. Laurence was not sure what the one-eyed man's name was, Gout or Grout or Clout.

But he said he would go to America anyway and would, moreover, "deal" with Laurence there.

That was why the thief was on the ship.

Then a new thought tumbled upon him: Did the man know Laurence was on board? Only Fred, Patrick and Maura, and that Mr. Drabble knew he'd stowed away, and he didn't think any of them would have told the one-eyed man. No, unless the man had just recognized him during their brief meeting in the galley, he could have no idea that Laurence was on the ship too.

Then another notion came, one so extraordinary, it took the boy's breath away. Could the thief still have the money he'd stolen? To think that the money he'd taken from his father might not be far from him at this moment! Oh, if he could only get it back!

He understood now that he'd taken a great sum, enough to live on for a long time. It could buy his passage home to England, and still he might be able to return most of it to his father.

Or should he stay in America once he got there and do— what? Laurence pushed aside all such speculations. Instead, he concentrated on how he would get the money back.

His thoughts were interrupted by a poke from Patrick. "Laurence," the Irish boy warned, "stop your dallying and get on with it. There's no choice. If we stay here, we'll be found, certain. The more so if that man you saw reports us. Go on now."

Chapter 110
Mr. Grout Learns Something

As Mr. Grout retreated into the stateroom, Mr. Clemspool glanced up and laughed. "I've never seen anyone look so sick in all my life," he said.

"I'm not ill," Mr. Grout barely managed to whisper.

"I assure you, sir, you look like death itself."

"It's possible. I did see death."

"Did you now?" Mr. Clemspool mocked.

"A ghost," Mr. Grout said.

"A ghost!" Mr. Clemspool hooted. "Was it the ghost of a fish?"

"I seen the ghost of the person I took the money from."

"What money?"

"The fortune as I got in London."

"I never asked you where you got your money, Mr. Grout." Mr. Clemspool sneered. "I don't want to hear about it now."

"But I seen 'im. Right out there. I could describe 'is every particular."

"Spare me your remorse, sir."

"It was a warnin'," Mr. Grout cried with anguish. "A warnin' to change me ways from the sinner I am."

Mr. Clemspool waved his hands about in annoyance. "You are absurd!"

"And I will change!" Mr. Grout shouted. "For one thing, I'll 'ave nothing more of yer schemin', connivin', and swindlin'!"

111

"All this for a mere ghost," Mr. Clemspool returned with contempt.

"That ghost was a boy no bigger than I once was. A scrawny pale-faced tyke. Filthy like 'e just came out a London sewer. With a long welt right 'ere." Mr. Grout pointed to his right cheek.

Mr. Clemspool sat bolt upright. "*A welt!*" he cried. "Did you say *welt?* On the right side of the face?"

"I seen it."

"What kind of clothing was he wearing?"

"Then? When I cleaned him out in London? All fine, like 'e was going to some swell's bash. But all the same muddy, like 'e'd slept in a ditch."

"Not then, you fool! Now! When you just saw him."

"I didn't see *'im*," Mr. Grout replied. "I saw 'is ghost. In tattered rags."

"Good God!" Mr. Clemspool fairly screamed. "Show me where he is!"

Mr. Grout blocked the door. "Don't go messin' with me ghost, Clemspool. Leave it alone."

Too excited to take heed, Mr. Clemspool shoved Mr. Grout aside and yanked the door open. Once in the dim galley he looked up and down. It was deserted. Annoyed, he returned to the room. "Nothing," he announced.

"Because it was meant for me one good eye and no one else's!" Mr. Grout shouted.

"It was your imagination, sir," Mr. Clemspool said with a derision that disguised his relief. "Your *guilty* imagination."

"*I am guilty!*" Mr. Grout cried.

"But that face you described," Mr. Clemspool said evenly, "is the face of the boy I had with me in Liverpool, Sir Laurence Kirkle."

"Not true!" cried the one-eyed man with terror.

"If your description is accurate, it's so."

"Then 'e's dead," Mr. Grout said with quaking remorse. "And 'e's come to 'aunt me. To get back 'is money."

Mr. Clemspool lowered himself onto his bed. "And I say if the lad is dead, so much the better. But frankly, sir, I am pleased to discover you have as much to do with this business as do I." He shook a plump finger at Mr. Grout. "To make my point precisely, sir, if you ever try to pretend you do not, it shall be my pleasure to tell the world *where* you got your money."

"I don't deny it," Mr. Grout returned bitterly. "I repent it!"

"How much did you take?"

"A thousand pounds!"

"One thousand!" cried Mr. Clemspool.

"If I could give it back to 'im, I would."

"See here, Mr. Grout," the man said with exasperation, "if you feel so bad about it, give me the money!"

"Not a chance," Mr. Grout said. "I knows wot I'm going to do with it."

"What?"

"As soon as we gets to America, I intends to send it back."

Incredulous, Mr. Clemspool shook his head. As for Mr. Grout's intentions, they were one thing. His own—for the money and for himself—were quite another.

113

Chapter 111

Into the Storm

O nce again Laurence lifted the hatchway just enough to peek out. Half of him wanted to see the one-eyed man. The other half shrank from the idea. But the galley was empty. "No one's there now," he called down to Patrick, not sure how he felt.

"Then we'll go that way," Patrick said. "You crawl out first."

Laurence shoved the hatch door completely open, then pulled himself onto the galley floor.

"Give a hand here, will you?" Patrick whispered.

With Laurence's help, Patrick struggled out of the luggage room. Once on the galley floor, he studied the area. There were seven doors. It was difficult to know which way to go.

"Where did you see this man?" Patrick asked, keeping his voice low. There was muffled shouting from behind one of the doors.

"At the far end," Laurence answered.

"Do you think he came from the outside?"

"I don't know." Laurence looked at the stateroom doors, wondering if the man he'd seen was behind one of them.

"We might as well try that way," Patrick said, pointing at the forward door. He crawled to the far end of the galley. Laurence struggled to calm himself. Over and over again he kept seeing the one-eyed man.

Patrick noted the water at the threshold of the forward door. "I think this one goes out," he whispered. "Your man must have been coming in. Help me open it."

114

The boys pushed hard. Wind and rain burst upon them. Laurence tried to duck back, but Patrick, just behind him, shoved him forward. "Go on," he urged. "It's the only way."

Leaving the protection of the galley, the boys discovered a murky gray world flooded with water. From above poured the rain, raw and cold. Foaming waves crashed over the bulwarks and washed across the deck.

Instantly drenched, pawing at their eyes in order to see, the boys struggled to stay together.

"Which way?" Laurence shouted into Patrick's ear.

Patrick tried to determine where they were—not far from the steps that led down to the steerage deck.

"We need to get to the other side!" he shouted, pointing.

Laurence nodded to show he understood.

"Stay close to me!" Patrick cried. Struggling, he edged away from the doorway. His bare feet made the going slippery. Laurence followed just as a massive wave struck the side of the ship, a mountain of foaming white water that rose up, then crashed down upon the deck. Patrick, who was not putting his full weight on his hurt leg, stumbled. The deck water lifted him bodily and, as the vessel pitched to one side, swept the helpless boy along as it began to sluice overboard.

Laurence sprang forward and threw himself on Patrick, trying to hold him back. Thoroughly entangled, the two went tumbling, only halting when they crashed into the bulwarks.

Groggy, spitting water, Laurence staggered to his feet. Wiping his face clear, he held Patrick, who sought to stand.

"Jesus, Mary, and Joseph, you saved me," Patrick sputtered.

"Can you move toward the door again?" Laurence asked.

"I'll try."

Bent almost double against the wind, the boys inched back toward the steerage door. This time they had much more distance to cover. And when they finally reached the door, they discovered it had been lashed shut with a great knotted rope.

As Patrick—his teeth chattering, his foot throbbing—clung to the wall, Laurence began to pick frantically at the knot. Again and again he had to wipe water from his eyes just to see his own fingers.

Strand by strand the knot began to give. When at last he pulled it apart, the door flew open. Caught by the wind, it swung wildly against a wall and began to bang like a drum.

Patrick dived forward, all but falling into the stairwell. Holding tightly to the guide rope to keep his balance, Laurence came right behind.

The steerage deck was dark, the foul air thick as molasses. Groans, whimpers, and murmured prayers rose from everywhere. It was impossible to move without stepping on someone.

"How many people are here?" Laurence asked in astonishment.

"Too many," Patrick answered between gritted teeth.

Patrick found their berth. "Maura," he called.

Maura—who had been dozing fitfully—sat up immediately and looked down on her brother. She hardly knew what she felt, anger or relief. "And where have you been?" she demanded.

A sleepy Mr. Drabble peered down at the boys too.

"I got caught out on the deck," Patrick said. "And almost washed away. Laurence saved my life."

"*Laurence?*" Maura repeated. She stared at the English boy.

Trembling with the wet and cold, Laurence lifted his face and grinned sheepishly.

Though Maura felt the urge to tell him to go away, to leave her brother alone, she restrained herself. "Sure, it was a kindness you've done," she said instead. "May you be blessed for it."

Only then did Patrick confess, "I've hurt my foot."

"And how did you do that?" Maura asked, the anger finally breaking through.

"Something struck it," Patrick answered evasively.

"How bad do you think it is?"

"I don't know."

"Patrick O'Connell, you'll be the death of me!" Maura cried with exasperation.

Mr. Drabble climbed down and, with help from Laurence, got the dripping, shivering Patrick onto the platform. Once there, the actor examined his foot. Maura hovered close.

"He had best stay where he is and not move," Mr. Drabble urged Maura.

She crawled to the foot of the platform to relay the news to Laurence. "And have you been hiding?" she whispered.

"Yes," he replied.

"Are you alone?"

Laurence nodded.

"You need to know," she said, "that the sailors and that first mate, Mr. Murdock, come through from time to time. Is it you they are looking for?"

"I think so," Laurence said. "Can I say a word to Patrick?"

"If you'll be quick about it."

Laurence climbed up at the end of the platform. Patrick was lying on his back, eyes closed. Sitting next to him was Bridy. She stared wide-eyed at Laurence.

"You can see how crowded we are," Maura said.

"Who's she?" Laurence asked, pointing to the child.

"A friend," Maura replied, reaching out to touch Bridy's hand.

Briefly, Laurence and Bridy exchanged looks.

"Patrick," Laurence called. Patrick opened his eyes and

117

looked around. "I'm going back below," Laurence said. "I have to. There's no choice."

"Do you know your way then?"

"No."

"You'll need to use the steps in the middle of the ship. Then there's the ladder. Only you'll have to open the hatch."

"I'll do it," Laurence said. He slid down to the floor. After a final look at the O'Connells' berth, he began to make his way back along the steerage deck.

"Why did you send him away?" Mr. Drabble asked Maura.

"Sure, Mr. Drabble, you know yourself there's no room for him here," she replied.

"But didn't he just save your Patrick? Ah, Miss O'Connell, you can be hard." The actor sighed.

Stung, Maura turned to look after Laurence, but he was already lost in the darkness.

Chapter 112
The Sickness

The storm on the Atlantic continued unabated. Hatchways and doors remained sealed to prevent the flooding of the lower decks. With no one permitted out, the steerage deck grew more and more polluted. No food or water was distributed. Steerage passengers had little choice but to go thirsty and hungry. The ones who did have extra provisions, such as the O'Connells and Mr. Drabble, fared better. But when other passengers saw that some of their company had food, they begged and pleaded for a portion—anything. Maura shared as much as she dared but made sure she kept enough for their own needs and Bridy's too now.

After four days the winds slackened, the seas flattened, the rain gentled, and the air grew mild. The crew threw open all hatches and doors and ordered the passengers—first class as well as steerage—out on deck. Extra water and food, they announced, would be available. There was a rush to get to fresh air.

"You better go first," Patrick told his sister. "With my foot, I'll need time." He'd hardly stood on it for four days.

"All right then," Maura agreed.

As she climbed down from their berth, she felt a pull on her skirt. It was Mrs. Faherty.

"Miss O'Connell," the woman urged in a low frightened voice, "it would be a kindness if you'd step down the way. It's me husband. He's faring poorly."

With a nod, and wrapping her shawl tightly around herself, Maura followed.

She remembered a big full-faced man with thick curly hair. It was a shock to see Mr. Faherty now. Lying full-length upon the bare platform, he clutched his gaunt shivering body as though trying to keep warm. Now and again his hands moved listlessly to scratch himself. What she could see of his body was covered with sores. By his side, the two Faherty boys huddled. While they did not look as ill as their father, their expressions too were strangely vacant.

Unsettled, Maura was afraid to draw too close. "How long has your husband been this way?" she asked in a hushed voice.

"The man was none too well when we came aboard," the woman confessed. "Sure now, with so little food, he gave what he had to the children. Then with the storm, and no food or water at all, he hardly ate a thing. Hasn't it made him worse then."

"I heard someone say a doctor was on board," Maura told her. "You'd best be speaking to him."

"And do you think, miss," Mrs. Faherty asked bitterly, "any doctor would be coming to help the likes of us, who haven't the least penny for his fee?"

Maura hardly knew what to reply.

"Maura O'Connell," the woman went on, her voice breaking under the strain of her misery, "for Jesus' sake, would you have the kindness to go to this doctor for him? I'd only get me anger up. It'd do no good at all."

"I can try," Maura agreed, glad to be able to do something.

After standing in line to get up the steps, Maura was astonished to see that the sky was a clear, brilliant blue. The seas were easy and seemed to sparkle. The *Robert Peel,* under full sail, drove through them with a steady rollicking rhythm.

On the quarterdeck Mr. Clemspool was walking arm in

arm with Mr. Shagwell, listening, always listening. On the main deck, where most of the emigrants were, long lines had formed. The longest were for the privies. But the lines for water, for the bread ration, and for the use of the fireplace were almost equal in length.

Ropes had been strung about and passengers encouraged to bring out clothing and bedding to air. The ship looked like a rag shop.

As Maura gazed about, she noticed Mr. Murdock standing at the foot of the steps to the quarterdeck. Despite his scowl, she went up to him.

"Please, sir," she said, "there's a sick man below in great want of a doctor. His wife asked that I fetch him."

The first mate looked at Maura carefully. "What kind of sick?" he demanded.

"Sure, he's just lying there, all cold and shivery, with the look of the lost upon his face."

"Shivering, did yer say?"

"So it seems to me, sir. In berth eighty-two. On the bottom."

Mr. Murdock swore an ugly oath. "Ship fever," he said with loathing. "It comes from the way yer Irish keep yer-selves. All that filth and squalor." He spit on the deck to show his contempt.

Maura wanted to object but held back. Getting the doctor to come was more important. "I wouldn't know, Your Honor."

"Well, I know," the officer said. "But having the fever won't be all bad, Miss Paddy. Yer'll get some good out of it."

"Faith then, and what might that be?" Maura asked.

"If some of yer died, yer'd have more room."

Chapter 113
A Death

When Dr. Woodham went down to the steerage level, not only was he frowning, he had placed a perfumed handkerchief to his nose. Mr. Murdock, lantern in hand, was by his side.

"Pestilential place," the doctor declared as he peered through gloom made thick with tobacco and tea leaf smoke. "Can't there be any better ventilation?"

"Take my word for it, sir," Mr. Murdock replied, "yer could put these people in the queen's palace, and it would be a pigsty by the end of a week. I've seen it again and again. They don't know better."

"If there is real illness here," Dr. Woodham observed, "it will spread rapidly."

"Don't I know it, sir. That's why yer never see the captain here. Now, sir, if yer'll just come this way, I'll show yer the berth that's got the reported contagion. Here now, make way for the doctor. Make way!"

Passengers hastily stepped aside. Maura followed in the doctor's wake.

"All right, mistress," Mr. Murdock called to Mrs. Faherty when they had reached her berth, "we've had a report of sickness here."

From her place near her husband's head, Mrs. Faherty shooed her two boys away, then attempted a clumsy curtsy. "If it please Your Honor, it's me husband."

"Put the light on him," Dr. Woodham ordered.

Mr. Murdock aimed his bull's-eye lantern on Mr. Faherty's face, then his body. The face was swollen, as were his fingers and joints. A distinct, disagreeable odor—beyond the stench of the steerage—was discernible.

"How long has he been this way?" the doctor demanded with revulsion, his handkerchief still held to his nose.

"Please, Your Honor," Mrs. Faherty replied, "from the second day of the storm."

"You should have reported it earlier," Dr. Woodham said. "Has he had water? Food?"

"Your Honor, there was none to be had. . . ."

Dr. Woodham frowned, lowered his handkerchief, and looked to Mr. Murdock for corroboration.

"Not safe for them on the deck in a storm, yer know," the first mate explained. "Liable to be washed away. Captain can't allow it. As it was, someone managed to open the door to the main deck during the storm. We had to lash it down double."

Dr. Woodham nodded with understanding.

"Please, Your Honor," Mrs. Faherty asked in a low fearful voice, "is it what they call the ship fever?"

"I suspect so, yes."

"Jesus have mercy," the woman breathed, and reached out to touch her husband's hand. Even as she began to weep, she looked up at the doctor. "Is there anything to be done, Your Honor?"

The doctor stared again at the man's flushed face. "It's too late," he answered brusquely.

The woman groaned. "Is there nothing to make him easy?"

With a curt shake of his head, Dr. Woodham turned and marched down the aisle, the handkerchief again pressed to his face.

Mr. Murdock lingered by the platform. "Yer'll want to

123

keep me informed of any change," he told Mrs. Faherty. Then he too left in haste.

Even before the doctor had reached the steps, the words *ship fever* passed quickly among the passengers. At first there was a hush, then sounds of praying and moaning.

Maura approached Mrs. Faherty timidly. "Is there anything I can do?" she whispered.

"Would you be knowing if there's a priest on the ship?"

"Faith, I've not seen one."

"It's terrible cruel," the woman said with bitterness, as much to herself as to Maura. "He keeps asking for water. Other than a priest, it's all he's wanting."

"I'll try to get some," Maura said.

Before she reached the water barrel on the main deck, the supply gave out. A second barrel had to be hoisted up. By the time she returned to the steerage deck with her can, a full hour had passed.

As Maura approached the Fahertys' berth, she saw that a crowd had gathered. Only when she'd worked her way through it did she discover that Mr. Faherty had died.

His widow sat by his body. She seemed to be in shock, not crying, but staring bleakly before her. Her three weeping children were pressing close.

A deeply distressed Maura came forward and held out the can of water. "I could get it no faster," she murmured apologetically.

Mrs. Faherty made a small nod. "Give it to the children," she said. "They've been terrible thirsty too."

Maura looked at them. Bridy alone appeared relatively healthy.

Maura offered the can to them. One by one they drank. Mrs. Faherty merely shook her head in mournful resignation.

Maura, not wishing to intrude, began to leave.

"Maura O'Connell," the woman called softly.

Maura turned.

"Sure, but it will be the same for me in quick time. Will you, for Jesus' sake, be willing to take Bridy under your care? You know she don't say much. And she promises to mind you."

Maura stared at Mrs. Faherty. The look in the woman's eyes was exactly like that in her mother's on the night Timothy, her brother, had died, the same as when her mother fled the Cork dock.

"She's only a child and will be needing someone."

"I'll look after her," Maura whispered.

"A blessing on you," Mrs. Faherty said, crossing herself.

Two sailors appeared at the edge of the crowd. One carried a folded piece of sailcloth. The other bore a heavy sack over his shoulder. "Where's the body?" one of them called. The crowd parted to allow the two men to step to the platform.

"Forgive us, mistress," one of them said with rough kindness. "Captain's orders. The remains must be got rid of. He don't want the disease spreading."

Mrs. Faherty remained unmoving.

"Did you hear me, mistress?" the sailor asked quietly.

This time she returned a tiny nod.

The man beckoned to his companion, who quickly unfolded the sailcloth and stretched it full-length alongside Mr. Faherty. The other sailor, with a quick push, rolled the body onto it. Then he took from his pocket a leather case of sail needles and thread. Working together, the men folded the cloth over the body, then began to sew the edges of the cloth together with crude but effective stitches. Before closing it up, one of the sailors opened the sack he'd brought. From this he pulled some stones, which he stuffed by the dead man's feet.

"What's that for?" asked one of the onlookers.

"You don't want him bobbing about for the sharks, now

do you?" the sailor replied. "The weight will get him down quick and keep him there till Judgment Day."

Throughout this procedure Mrs. Faherty continued to stare vacantly before her. It was the sniffling children who watched the sailors intently, their eyes wide with fear.

Once the body had been sewn into the cloth, one sailor asked, "Will you be coming, mistress?"

"Faith, I've not the strength."

"What about the children?" she was asked.

"They should go," she murmured.

From the crowd of onlookers four men stepped forward and hoisted the awkward body bag to their shoulders. A way was cleared. Behind came the sailors and the three Faherty children. Others followed to make a motley funeral procession. Among them were Maura and Mr. Drabble.

Mr. Faherty's body was carried to the main deck. Near the bulwark a board had been laid out. Under the sailors' direction, the body was placed upon the board.

Mr. Murdock now appeared. "Is there anyone wanting to say a few words?" he asked. No one spoke.

"All right then," he said, "do yer duty." The sailors came forward, picked up the board with its load, and brought it to the top rail, feet forward. With a grunt and a sudden lift, they tilted the board up. The body slid off and plummeted over the side. There was a rush to see it descend, but too late. Mr. Faherty's mortal remains had been swallowed by the sea.

Chapter 114
Mr. Murdock
Makes a Discovery

E ager to get away from the deck and the greatly agitated steerage passengers, Mr. Murdock prowled about the cargo hold. Lantern in hand, he took note of the storm-wrought damage. Chests and barrels were strewn about, like so many ninepins struck by a bowling ball. While most were intact, there were a fair number destroyed. Their contents— from dishes to hats to toys—had been scattered about and broken or were now filthy from bilgewater. Indeed, the amount of wreckage was so great, Mr. Murdock realized it would not be possible to clean it up until they reached Boston.

As the first mate picked his way along the starboard aisle, he noticed four teacups and four saucers tucked tightly between two arching beams. For a long time he just stared at them. Something was wrong. The symmetry of the numbers alone—four and four—suggested they were not tossed there by the random pitching of the ship in the storm. Then too, not only were these dishes *not* broken, they appeared to have been carefully wedged one atop the other by someone. How else could they be there and in such good condition? The more Mr. Murdock considered, the more convinced he was that he knew who that someone was. . . . *The stowaway.*

Turning, the first mate plied his beam about the hold. He would search again.

Chapter 115
Laurence Goes Looking

*L*ater—as soon as Mr. Murdock was gone—Laurence climbed up the luggage-room ladder and lifted the trapdoor just enough to see if the galley way in the first-class passenger compartment was empty.

When he saw that it was, he lifted the trap higher. A small light was burning. It was enough for Laurence—who in any case had grown very accustomed to the dark—to see the seven doors that lined the way. Behind one of them, he hoped, was the one-eyed man, and with him Lord Kirkle's money.

Wanting to catch his breath and calm himself for the task ahead, Laurence rested on the edge of the trapdoor. He wished he was not alone. He had considered taking Patrick into his confidence. But that would have meant explaining everything to his friend. He had resisted that, fearful that if Patrick learned who and what he was, he might turn against him. For Laurence just the thought of that was unbearable.

For the moment, however, the only question was which door he would try first. One by one he considered them, but they told him nothing. He would simply have to take a chance.

Leaving the trap open—for a fast escape if necessary—Laurence crawled onto the galley floor. When he approached the nearest door, he grasped its latch and drew himself up.

Softly, he twisted the latch, but his heart was pounding so frantically, he had to pull back in order to regain self-control. Finally, he pressed his shoulder to the door and pushed. It opened.

The ship bell struck seven times, causing a tremor of nervousness to course through his body. When he was calm again, he edged the door open farther, leaning forward to try and catch some sound from within.

What he heard was regular rhythmic breathing intermixed with the ever-present shifting and creaking of the ship. The breathing continued evenly, and at last Laurence swung the door wider and stuck his head directly into the room.

The only light seeped in from the galley way itself. Laurence could make little sense of the room. It was smaller than he had expected. A lamp—not lit—hung from the ceiling and swung gently back and forth. He saw, obscurely, a washstand, a sofa, and a chest of drawers as well as what might be a writing desk.

To either side of the room were beds. Only one was occupied. Under a heap of blankets, the sleeper stirred. Laurence froze, then pressed a hand to his heart to keep it from beating so loudly.

After a few moments, he crept farther into the room, moving silently toward the occupied bed. He stared intently at the passenger, trying to determine if it was his thief or not.

Though the sleeper shifted, the face remained hidden. Laurence stood motionless, waiting. Nothing! Carefully he reached forward—his hand shaking—and attempted to flick the blankets away. Though he managed to do so, he also brushed a cheek.

The sleeper sat up abruptly. He was a heavyset man with a mane of flowing gray hair. His face was somewhat square with eyes—only barely open—set together closely.

In haste, Laurence took a side step out of the man's line of vision. The man remained sitting for a moment before dropping back upon his pillow.

Breathless, Laurence waited for the sounds of regular

sleep to resume. When they did, he inched his way toward the galley way and made his way out.

Deciding he had done enough for one night, he scurried back to the hold. When he reached his barrel, he removed the lid and climbed in. But instead of squatting down, he remained standing. With tongue and teeth he made a clicking sound.

In moments there was an answering squeak. Laurence called again. It brought the sound of scampering. The next moment a large brown rat was sitting on the barrel lid next to him.

"Good for you, Nappy," Laurence whispered. He reached down and retrieved a bit of hard bread. "Here's your dinner." He held the bread bit out to the rat, who sat up on his hind legs to take it. "Let me tell you what I did," Laurence whispered.

Chapter 116

Sarah Grafton

In the Shagwell Cotton Mill of Lowell, Massachusetts, Sarah Grafton—along with other women operatives—was almost two hours into her day at the drawing machines. Her long black hair, parted in the middle, was pulled behind her neck in a bun. She had tied an apron over her skirt.

The room in which she worked was vast. Just below the high ceiling, leather belts flapped, looking for all the world like gigantic looped brown noodles. The power to move them came from canal water turning a huge wheel at the basement level. The belts rolled and twisted through pulleys and gears that in turn drove the smaller belts that dropped down to run the machines.

These machines—second carders, drawers, and double-speeders—twisted and pulled raw cotton into thick thread, rocking and shaking upon their metal and wooden legs with such violence and loud crashing that the entire wooden floor vibrated. Clouds of cotton specks floated in the air, making it hard for the operatives to draw a clear breath.

The room, moreover, had its windows nailed shut to keep the humidity high. This made the cotton pliable and helped prevent the fragile fibers from breaking.

Sarah Grafton's job was to take up four or five of the cotton strands from the carding machines—slivers they were called, each one thicker than her arm—and feed them into the drawing frames. These not only stretched the cotton slivers by means of a series of rollers, but gradually combined them into one finger-width cord, which was wound then onto large bobbins. Once full, the bobbins were taken to the double-speeding machines to make a finer thread for the looms on another floor. Each day Sarah Grafton was required to produce at least two hundred bobbins.

She worked standing, pacing up and down before the machines she was responsible for. Because the slivers kept breaking, she was continually obliged to stop the machine by pushing a heavy lever, then quickly twisting the broken ends of the sliver together. Then she started the machine again.

She also had to be sure the rollers worked at even speeds. To look away could mean disaster. The slivers would tangle or break or, worst of all, become lumpy. What was wanted was a single uniform cord spooled neatly on the bobbin.

For the most part, Sarah ignored her cough, though during the last five months it had deepened. But rarely did it keep her from coming to work in the predawn darkness. She could not afford to give in to it.

Behind her, striding up and down along the rows of drawing machines and their operatives, was Mr. Osmundson, the floor overlooker. He was making sure that the pace of the work was steady. A fat jolly fellow with a derby perched on the back of his head, he liked his operatives—girls he called them—and bestowed many a smile and word of encouragement upon them. If any of the machinery broke, he hurried to fix it. If he could not fix it, he called for help. And, if any of the women lagged at their work, he was there to remind them of their duty, calling out a rebuke as he saw fit.

"Sarah, my girl," he shouted as he came down the line, "how are you today?"

"Fair enough," she returned without looking around at him.

"And the baby?"

"He's got a new tooth."

"I remember how that can keep you awake. Watch your third roller, darling. It's balking!"

Sarah leaped forward to make the adjustment.

"And your husband, has he found work?"

"He's all but given up."

Mr. Osmundson shook his head in sympathy. "Once they've turned you off and marked you down, it's awful hard on a man. Look there! You've got a thick spot on sliver number two!"

Sarah, coughing, reached out and pulled at the sliver, her thin fingers deftly teasing the lump until it melted away.

"Your cough is no better, darling," Mr. Osmundson called to her. "You need to take good care!" With that, he moved along to the next machine and chatted with Betsy Howard, the operative stationed there.

At seven-thirty the breakfast bell rang. As soon as it did, Mr. Osmundson threw the floor's main lever. Though the power belts still whirled above, all the machines slowed to

132

a halt. On the instant, most of the operatives hurried toward the doors. They had no more than thirty-five minutes to eat.

Sarah did not leave with them. To save strength, she sat down on the floor, back propped against one of her machines. From the base of it, she took up a handkerchief, in which Jeb had wrapped her breakfast. The meal consisted of a piece of bread and a cold sausage. She ate slowly.

Betsy Howard came to sit next to her with her own small meal.

"How are you doing today, my dear?" she asked Sarah as she bit into her piece of meat pie and simultaneously began to brush the white cotton lint from her blouse.

"Good enough," Sarah answered without looking around. No sooner did she speak than she coughed, then patted her mouth with her handkerchief. She inspected it.

"Blood?" Betsy asked softly.

Sarah shook her head. "Not yet," she whispered.

"Cotton cough. What you need is some fresh air. That's the only thing to make you better. Get out of the city somewhere, Sarah. Or go for that walk along the river. It's good air there."

"Perhaps," Sarah said. "On Sunday."

"You can take your baby."

For a while, the two women ate without speaking.

"I think there's been a speedup again," Betsy said, keeping her voice low.

Sarah looked around. "I thought it was just me getting dull," she said.

"It isn't you. Considering, I don't know how you can keep up."

"Did you ask Mr. Osmundson?"

Betsy shook her head. "I've tried. He gave me a warning."

"What kind?"

"Too much complaining will get me turned off. He was kind about it, but he meant it."

133

"They wouldn't do that to you," Sarah said. "You've been here five years. More than most. And you're too good."

Betsy laughed grimly. "He said there's plenty an Irish girl to take my place."

"That there is," Sarah said. Finishing her meal, she tilted her head back and closed her eyes. "My boy Jeb hates the Irish. Goes on about them all the time."

"I don't like them either." Then Betsy Howard said, "Get some rest now," and patted her friend on the arm. "Only five more hours till lunch bell."

Chapter 117

Mr. Jenkins Makes a Visit

It was early evening. Partially hidden by the darkness, Jeremiah Jenkins stood across the street from James Hamlyn's house, staring at it as if his eyes alone could blast the structure to bits. But since his look could not accomplish the task, he brooded the more on his anger and his cause.

As the wind scattered the gray snow at his feet, he watched the mill girls and women passing by, returning from work.

With a grunt of frustration, Mr. Jenkins spit and trudged off to another, more affluent section of town, coming to a stop at a large stone structure of three stories with a steeply pitched roof. A grand columned door stood close to the ice-rutted street so that one could step directly from a carriage onto the stone front steps.

Mr. Jenkins climbed the steps and knocked sharply upon the door. It was opened by a serving girl in a simple brown dress, mobcap, and apron.

"Has Mr. Shagwell returned from England?" he inquired.

"If it please you, sir, he's not," answered the young woman.

"Are you Irish?"

The woman smiled. "Only recently come over, sir."

"Bloody hypocrite," Mr. Jenkins mumbled.

"Would you be wanting the mistress?" the young woman asked.

Mr. Jenkins shook his head.

"I can only tell you the master is expected soon."

"How soon?"

"It's not for me to be saying for certain, sir. Might you like to leave your card?"

"I don't have a card," Mr. Jenkins said.

"You could be leaving your name, sir."

"Just tell him Jeremiah Jenkins called. On urgent business."

"I'll do so, sir. Mr. Jenkins."

Angry, the man set off again, entirely unaware that Mr. Tolliver—as had become his habit—was following him.

Chapter 118
Night at Sea

Midnight. The *Robert Peel*'s sails fluttered and whipped in the wind. A salt spray—soft and cool like an angel's wings—floated across the deserted deck. High in the southwestern sky, the moon cast a golden road of light across the rolling waters, a road that ran directly from the ship to the edge of the sea and beyond. It seemed to be the road the *Robert Peel* was following.

The helmsman, his two large red-raw hands grasping the spokes of the great steering wheel, stared straight ahead along the moonlit way. The second mate rang the ship's bell eight times. Now and again he examined the compass with a lamp, gazed up at the sails and stars but found nothing to say to the helmsman.

The door from the steerage deck opened. A sailor emerged, looked about to make sure no one was watching, then beckoned to someone. Quickly he was followed on deck by four men carrying a long closed sack. They bore this to the bulwarks, where, in hasty unison, they hurled it into the sea.

Their task done, the sailors rubbed and blew on their hands for warmth, then hurried off to their forecastle bunks.

The helmsman, who had heard the splash, asked the second mate, "How many is that?"

The other man shrugged. "Thirty-two, I should think."

The helmsman spit over his shoulder.

"I heard say a whole family went. First the father. His wife and two sons too. Just a young girl left."

The helmsman shook his head and gripped the wheel spokes a little tighter. Save for the sound of the ship sliding through the sea with a consistent hiss, all was quiet again.

Chapter 119

Mr. Grout Has a Lesson

'*O*w am I doin'?" Mr. Grout asked Mr. Drabble across the table. The two men were in the first-class dining room. After the lunch had been served, Mr. Drabble had been called there from steerage to give the young man another reading lesson. On the table were the cluttered remains of Mr. Grout's lunch: plates of meats, pickles, boiled eggs and assorted meat pies, bread, and drink.

"You are a good student, Mr. Grout," a hungry Mr. Drabble replied. Feeling as though he'd not eaten for weeks, he was distracted by the food. "And though you have a considerable way to go, you progress rapidly."

"I'm wantin' to progress," Mr. Grout said with solemnity. "I'm needin' to progress. I've been told to progress."

"Have you now," the actor said casually. "By whom?"

Mr. Grout looked about furtively. "Can yer keep a secret?" he asked.

"As well as any man," Mr. Drabble returned.

Mr. Grout leaned across the table and fixed his one good eye on his teacher. "I've 'ad a vision," he revealed in a hushed voice. "From the other side."

Mr. Drabble drew back. "Why . . . what do you mean by that?"

"Right 'ere. On this ship. A spirit came to warn me of me sinful ways."

Mr. Drabble, suddenly uncomfortable, pushed the hair out of his eyes. "It's nothing I should make sport of, Mr. Grout," he cautioned.

The one-eyed man put a hand to his heart. "Mr. Drabble, accordin' to me lights, yer gets these warnings but once. If yer don't 'eed 'em, yer doomed."

"Then you had best heed it," Mr. Drabble replied, having no desire to contradict his benefactor.

"I intend to," Mr. Grout said loudly, as if he wanted the spirit itself to hear. "And yer a part of my 'eedin'. I've never 'ad much in the way of schoolin', not so much as yer little finger's worth, do yer know. But now . . . I can read some. Ship," he proclaimed. Then haltingly but proudly he said the letters. "S-H-I-P. Is that right?"

"It is."

"Yer've helped me, Mr. Drabble, and I'm thankin' yer. Sometimes I think I might set up as an innkeeper. I'd get to 'elp people that way. I can see meself lookin' rather decent dolin' out the victuals."

Mr. Drabble looked up. "Why then, sir, I suggest we practice a little of that right now."

" 'Ow do yer mean?"

"Why not stand up where you are, behind the table, while I act—you do recall that I am an actor?—while I act a guest, famished, of course, and you can serve me."

Mr. Grout nodded. "I can see that," he said with some gravity. Standing, he removed his jacket.

"Good!" said Mr. Drabble, standing himself and crossing the room. "I'll act a man who has just come in from a storm. I'm wet, ragged, and hungry, eager for my 'cakes and ale,' as the bard put it. You'll want to arrange the food a bit."

Mr. Grout gathered the plates of food before him. "All right now. 'Ere we go."

Mr. Drabble approached the table and bowed. "A very good evening to you, sir. Terrible weather we're having."

"It surely is," Mr. Grout replied uncertainly. "An' wot can I do for yer, sir?"

"I am very hungry, sir."

"Wot do I say then?" Mr. Grout asked as an aside.

"Something along the order of, 'Make yourself at home, sir. Eat whatever you desire.' Then you offer all those plates to me."

"I've got it!" Mr. Grout said, and did as his friend suggested. In turn, Mr. Drabble resumed his seat, drew the food plates toward him, and began to eat ravenously.

For a while there was no more talk. At last Mr. Grout asked, "Is there anything else I should be sayin'?"

"You might inquire if I was enjoying myself, or if I'd had enough. Something of the sort. And . . . and if you were really generous, you might even suggest I take some away with me."

Eager to oblige, Mr. Grout followed his tutor's directions. Accordingly, the actor stuffed his pockets with whatever food he could manage to hold.

"You've done very well," he enthused, pushing himself from the table, his stomach and pockets equally full. "You will make an excellent innkeeper."

"It's 'ard to wait. The captain told us 'e's 'opin' to see land in a few days."

"Did he?"

"Maybe sooner. I 'ope so, 'cause I'm wantin' to start me new life, Mr. Drabble. Wantin' it bad!"

Hands over his bulging pockets, Mr. Drabble hurried back down to the steerage section. Both Maura and Patrick were on the platform and Bridy too, off in her corner.

Mr. Drabble hauled himself halfway up the berth. "I bring good news, Miss O'Connell," he said, keeping his excited voice low. "There are but a few days more of this voyage. Better yet, my pockets are full of decent food."

"Sure, that news is grand, Mr. Drabble. But where would you be getting food from?" Maura asked.

"From my student, Mr. Grout."

"I can't say I care for the man, Mr. Drabble, but I'm not too proud to take his food," she said.

"Can I have some for Laurence?" Patrick asked.

"Ah, yes, the stowaway. For our sakes, I do hope he is not caught."

"Sure, but he hasn't been caught yet," Patrick replied with annoyance. "And you just said it's only a few more days."

"Mr. Patrick," the actor allowed with a quick glance at Maura, "I admire your loyalty."

"Well, I for one don't think we should be talking about him," Maura warned.

Feeling rebuked, Mr. Drabble silently laid out the food he had brought. It consisted of bread, slices of meat, and a hard-boiled egg.

Patrick's eyes grew large. "By the Holy Mother, it's a feast," he exclaimed.

Mr. Drabble put a finger to his lips. "If you don't keep your tongue tight, Mr. Patrick, you'll be sharing it with the entire deck."

Maura took up the egg and beckoned to Bridy. "Come on then, Bridy. Here's decent food."

The girl shook her head. Since her family had perished, she rarely ventured far from her corner. She neither cried nor spoke, even when addressed. She ate little. Her eyes were forever staring into a distant place as though she were engaged in private prayers. By her side she kept a small pile she'd saved of her family's clothing. This she had folded neatly and often used as a pillow.

"Faith, the poor girl hardly wants to live," Maura confided to Mr. Drabble.

"She should be made to eat," he said sternly, "or she'll suffer the same fate as the rest of her family."

"You need to be kind to her, Mr. Drabble," Maura urged. "But won't you be eating any yourself?"

"None for me, Miss O'Connell," he said grandly, "I've already eaten enough. It's all for you and yours."

"Truly, Mr. Drabble, you've been the saving of us again and again. You'll be blessed in the hereafter, I'm sure."

"I'd rather be blessed now, Miss O'Connell," he returned. Blushing at his own boldness, he hurried away.

"What did he mean by that?" Patrick asked, looking after the departing actor.

"I'm sure I don't know," Maura answered evasively. "Now here's your food. Eat it and then get on with you. It's the girl I need to be tending."

Patrick divided his food in half, ate one part, then carried away the rest, intent upon finding Laurence.

Maura, alone on the platform with Bridy, considered the child. Her uncombed hair hung about her wan face like a ragged shroud. Her eyes were half-closed, her mouth turned down. Now and again she rubbed her nose but made almost no other motions.

"Bridy," Maura coaxed softly, "the ones who eat resist the fever best, they say."

The girl stared at her with empty eyes.

Maura gently touched her small fingers. They were rough and cold. "The Lord knows it's been a terrible thing," she said. "Surely, He'll help you. But there's no harm in taking comfort from me too. And sure, you have to eat." Maura held up the egg.

"But . . . ," the girl whispered, only to falter.

Maura leaned closer. "But what?"

"I don't want to be living."

"Now, Bridy," Maura said softly, "it's a sin to say so. You know it sure as I. And didn't I promise your poor mother I'd be a comfort to you and keep you well?"

The girl only wiped her nose.

"It's not just an egg I'm offering."

142

Bridy looked at her. "What then?" she asked.

"We'll not cast you off, Bridy. You can be with us. Never a word need come from your lips, not unless you're wanting to speak. But think of it, you can grow into something fine, an honor to them that brought you into God's world."

Bridy made no reply.

"And to tell you the truth, Bridy Faherty," Maura continued, "it's a friend of my own that I'm needing. Don't you know but I'm scared to my soul about where we're going as much as you. There's many a tear that I've shed when none are looking."

The words made Bridy stare at Maura for a long while.

"It's the earth that needs to know you, Bridy," Maura coaxed. "Not the sea."

A tear trickled down Bridy's cheek. When Maura stroked it gently away, the girl trembled. Then she reached out and took the egg. It lay moonlike and smooth in the palm of her hand. "I never ate an egg," she confessed.

Maura reached over and cracked the shell, then peeled the egg. Crumb by crumb she fed it to the girl.

Chapter 120
An Unexpected Meeting

Before getting onto the ladder that led to the cargo hold, Patrick wiggled his foot. Though it was still somewhat sore, and caused him to limp, it was not nearly as bad as it had been.

He looked about to make sure he was not being observed. Satisfied he was not, he started down, this time not taking a candle.

The stench was worse than ever. He wondered how Laurence managed to bear it, then he thought of the news: only a few days to go. That would surely cheer him.

Upon reaching the foot of the ladder, Patrick waited and listened. The only light available came from the open hatchway above. When he neither heard nor saw anything suspicious, he called, "Laurence!"

There was no answer—but nothing unusual in that. Patrick knew that Laurence would appear from the direction he chose and at any moment he wanted. It was a game the English boy had not tired of playing. As far as Patrick could tell, it was one of the few pleasures Laurence had.

Growing impatient, Patrick called again, and added, "I'm by the ladder!"

A hand reached out and touched his shoulder. Patrick turned. "Lau—," he started to say, only to realize it was not Laurence at all but a sailor. The man, grinning broadly, said, "Thought no one ever noticed, did you, laddie?"

Speechless with shock, Patrick tried to break away. "Not yet," a second sailor said. "Someone wants to talk to you. 'Ello!" he called. "We got 'im! 'E's over 'ere."

Mr. Murdock stepped out of the dark. He flashed his bull's-eye lantern into Patrick's face, blinding him.

"What's yer name?" he demanded.

Heart hammering, Patrick stammered, "P-P-Patrick O'Connell, Your Honor."

"Who's this here Laurence yer've been calling to?"

"It's no one, Your Honor," Patrick replied, desperately trying to recover his composure and think what to do.

"Don't heave that to me, Paddy boy. Of course it's someone. Yer've been seen coming down here any number of times. Have yer been taking care of someone?"

Patrick shook his head.

Mr. Murdock gazed at the boy. "What's that yer have in yer pockets," he demanded.

Patrick said nothing.

The first mate called to one of the sailors, "Mr. Croft, empty them."

The sailor took out a thick piece of bread and two slices of meat.

Mr. Murdock frowned. "That's too good for steerage folks."

"Faith, Your Honor, it was someone who gave it to me."

"Stolen, yer mean."

"I didn't!" Patrick returned with indignation.

"That food was in the dining room," the first mate insisted. "Where did you get it?"

"It was Mr. Drabble, Your Honor. It's him that's berthed with us. And isn't he teaching that Mr. Grout, who's a first-class passenger. It was him that gave it to Mr. Drabble, and he gave it to us."

"Never mind that," said the first mate, stymied by the plausibility of the explanation. "I want to know who it's for."

"Myself, Your Honor. Sure, I was only being greedy and came to eat alone."

Mr. Murdock cuffed Patrick on the side of the head. The blow frightened the boy. The sailor behind him held him tight. "Yer telling nothing but lies, laddie," the first mate cried. "When we left Liverpool, I found an empty crate up forward. I'm willing to bet my last penny yer bringing food to someone. Where's the man?"

"There is no man," Patrick said stoutly.

"Answer quick, where's your father?"

"In Boston, Your Honor."

"Mother?"

"Back in Ireland. She wouldn't come."

"A brother?"

"Dead, sir."

The first mate's eyes narrowed. "Who yer traveling with then?"

"It's my sister, Your Honor. Maura O'Connell. She's in the steerage."

"Do you know, Paddy boy, what can happen to yer if I find that yer've been breaking the law?"

Patrick hung his head. "No, Your Honor."

"All I need do is inform the captain. He can have yer tossed overboard. Or maybe keelhaul yer. Do yer know what that is?"

"No, Your Honor."

"Dragged from one side of the boat to the other, underwater. Or he could put yer in irons, for that matter, and bring yer back to Liverpool. What do yer have to say to that?"

Patrick swallowed hard and stared at the floor.

"Anything at all to say?" the first mate prompted.

"Nothing, Your Honor," Patrick whispered.

Mr. Murdock looked about. "We're going to search every inch down here. If we find someone, I'll have yer tossed over if I have to do it myself. Yer understand?"

"Yes, Your Honor."

"Barkum," the first mate shouted to another sailor. "Bring him along but hold him fast. Croft, do you have yer pike?"

Mr. Croft held up a long pointed stick. "All right then," said the first mate. "Let's have ourselves a look." He aimed his lamp along the long jumbled rows of crates and barrels.

"Laurence!" Mr. Murdock called out, "or whatever yer name is. We know yer about. Just so yer understand, when we find yer—and we will—yer can join yer Paddy friend here when we toss him over."

He began to pick his way down the central aisle, pausing at almost every crate and chest. Patrick, his mouth so dry he could hardly swallow, was pushed along after him. Now and again Mr. Murdock stopped. "Try that one," he said to Mr. Croft. The sailor stepped over the crate and examined it closely to see if it had been tampered with. Finding nothing, they pressed on.

Slowly, the search party wound its way through the confusion of cargo toward the stern of the ship. More than once Mr. Murdock was certain he'd discovered the hiding place. Each time he was proved wrong.

"Look there!" he suddenly whispered, pointing to a barrel. "That lid's not fully closed." He beckoned Mr. Croft forward. The sailor moved cautiously.

Patrick, almost certain they had discovered Laurence's barrel, could barely restrain from shouting a warning.

But just as Mr. Croft drew close to the barrel, a large brown rat suddenly darted out of it.

"Rat!" shouted Mr. Murdock. "Get him!"

With a deft stroke Mr. Croft flung his stick and speared the rat, killing it instantly. Then he flipped the carcass into the bilgewater.

"That's one less stowaway," Mr. Murdock said with a laugh.

Back they went to the bow. Once they reached it, and still had found no sign of Laurence, the first mate cursed profusely. "Let the Paddy go for now," he said, and spit. "This place will be the death of us."

Patrick was shoved away into the dark, so hard he tripped and fell.

"If I catch yer down here again, Paddy boy, I'll bring yer to the captain. Do yer hear me? Yer'll get a lashing then."

Without waiting for an answer, Mr. Murdock turned about. With the two sailors he made his way to the central ladder and climbed out of the hold.

Patrick, on the decking, lay unmoving. Slowly his heartbeat returned to normal. Then he sat up. "Laurence . . . ," he called in a whisper. "Where are you?" There was no answer.

Chapter 121
From the Podium

.

*I*n Lowell, the main meeting room of Appleton Hall was full of people, mostly men but women too, including Betsy Howard. All were seated on long benches, eagerly awaiting the speaker. For the most part these were mill workers and shop owners. A few were dressed in their finest clothing, since the occasion was deemed a special one. Others in the audience, who had come directly from their work, were in rougher dress, spotted with bits and pieces of cotton and thread as if they had just come in from a snow flurry. Men wore their hats. Women still had their work aprons on.

At the back of the room stood Jeb and his two friends, Tom and Nick.

Gaslights were blazing, illuminating the picture of George Washington placed upon the speaker's podium. Red, white, and blue bunting ran from the stage to pillars on either side of the hall.

The hum and buzz of the crowd was stilled when a man in a dark frock coat and top hat walked to the podium, leaned over it, and announced, "Ladies and gentlemen, it is my pleasure to introduce you to that great American, Mr. Jeremiah Jenkins."

There was a round of applause as Mr. Jenkins strode forward. He placed his right hand upon the podium and, with his left, touched his heart and bowed slightly, just enough to show he appreciated his reception, but not so much as to suggest he was in awe of it. Then he squared his shoulders, grasped one lapel of his jacket, looked upon the audience with a long penetrating gaze that seemed to bore into every person's eyes at once, and began to speak.

"My fellow Americans. We meet today in the birthplace of the American Revolution, Massachusetts. It is here that we struck a blow for liberty. It is therefore our special duty not just to defend that liberty, but to make sure that our children and their children enjoy it too.

"Here, in this great state, we still have some semblance of peace and plenty. It is ours to share. We must protect the rights of all but give privilege to none. This touches upon an issue that goes beyond the political parties. The issue, my fellow Americans, is immigration.

"Are you aware that most of the beggars in this state today are . . . immigrants? That most of the crimes are committed by immigrants? That the very health of our cities is endangered by immigrants? True, all true.

"And we are tired of hearing languages other than English upon our streets. Moreover, these foreigners lower the tone of American feeling. Their willingness to take low pay lowers the pay for true Americans.

"Here in Massachusetts, here in Lowell, we are particularly threatened by the Irish paupers being brought here by the boatload by our old enemy, England. Half the students in Boston schools are foreigners. I say, we do not want these immigrants!

"Yes, my friends, America must stand together against this tide of inferiors. Those of us in the majority—true Americans—should resist minority demands.

"We must exclude these foreigners from the electoral process. We must restrict citizenship, particularly for those whose allegiance to the Roman Church destroys the very foundation of our republican ways! It would be far better to send them back where they came from. Let England take them back. The lords of England should not be allowed to ship off these ignorant, filthy people to our golden shores!

"We are Americans. Not Europeans!

"And I say, if the government in Washington or in Boston cannot deal with this problem, the people of Lowell themselves should see to it and get rid of all immigrants!"

At this the audience rose up and applauded wildly.

The speaker, smiling grimly, went on.

Chapter 122
Patrick Goes Searching

O n platform seventy-four in steerage Patrick lay wide awake. Most deck lamps had long ceased to burn. The area was shrouded in gloom. The creaks and groans of ship timbers mingled with the sighs and murmurs of restless sleepers.

Two days had passed since he had looked for Laurence and not found him. His clash with Mr. Murdock had made him afraid to go below again. All the same, he kept thinking about his friend, wondering where he had been that time, wondering what he could be doing.

Patrick had another worry. The evening before, another passenger had died of ship fever, bringing the total number of deaths to forty-four. The thought of Laurence being alone and sick deeply upset Patrick. What if Laurence had died? It would be on his head. Once that idea lodged in him, Patrick was resolved to seek out his friend.

At the sound of the fourth bell, Patrick sat up slowly, taking extra pains not to disturb Bridy, who was sleeping restlessly on one side of him, or Mr. Drabble, on the other. Once up, Patrick reached over by Maura's head and fumbled among the provision bags. When he found a moldy piece of bread, he drew it out and stuffed it in his shirt. Then he wormed his way down to the foot of the platform, swung over the rail, and slipped to the deck.

Moving so as not to step on those who slept there, Patrick crept to the central stairwell. Quickly now, he went down the steps to the first cargo deck. There he found himself a candle. Though he neither saw nor heard anyone, he kept thinking that he hadn't seen anyone the last time, and Mr. Murdock *had* been there in the dark.

When he reached the ladder to the bottom hold, he halted to look and listen. Absolutely convinced it was safe to proceed, lighted candle in hand, he started down. Among the shadows of the confused mass of barrels and crates, he could see no sign of Laurence.

Once on the cargo floor, Patrick leaned against the ladder to rest his aching foot. "Laurence," he called in a whisper. He saw nothing, nor heard anything but familiar ship sounds.

"Laurence!" he called again, louder. That time he heard a faint echo of his own voice—but no more.

Crawling over and around the chaos of cargo, he inched his way to Laurence's barrel. It was empty. Had Mr. Murdock found him? Had he thrown Laurence overboard as he'd vowed to do? Was Laurence lying sick somewhere?

"Laurence!" Patrick called again, louder still. No answer came.

The candle was burning low.

Near the stern he came upon the ladder to the luggage room. He looked up and was just able to make out the hatchway.

Patrick began to climb, then pushed against the door with his hand. It lifted. Moving higher, he eased the hatch completely open and stuck his head into the luggage room. Of Laurence he saw no sign. Still not satisfied, Patrick hauled himself up. The air in the room was musty. Trunks and cases lay strewn about.

Patrick crawled onto one of the trunks, held the stub of the candle up, then turned slowly to survey the room. This time he saw Laurence.

The boy was on his back, lying absolutely still upon a mound of clothing. His face was filthy, thin, his eyes closed. His hair had grown long and tangled. The canvas shirt and trousers Mr. Bartholomew had given him in Liverpool were in tatters.

The hairs on the back of Patrick's neck prickled. "Jesus, Mary, and Joseph," he murmured, crossing himself. "He's dead!"

Patrick's hand shook so the candle flame guttered out. For a while he did nothing, his heart was hammering so. But needing to know if Laurence was truly dead, he crept forward in the dark. When he thought he was close enough, he reached out. At his touch Laurence leaped up.

"Laurence!" Patrick cried. There was no answer other than quick, agitated breathing. "It's me, Patrick," he said hastily.

He heard a murmur. "You frightened me," Laurence said.

"Faith, I didn't know what had happened to you, Laurence," Patrick said, sighing. "I was afraid to come."

"Why?"

"Mr. Murdock caught me."

"Yes."

"Were you there all the time?" Patrick asked.

"I was waiting for you. But when I saw him coming, I had to hide in my barrel. I didn't know how to warn you without giving myself away. What did he say? I couldn't make anything out."

"Sure, they're still looking for you. Have they been back?" Patrick asked.

"I'm not sure. Most of the time I spend in this room. No one ever comes here. I only go down for water and some of that moldy bread."

"I thought you were dead," Patrick said.

Laurence sighed. "Sometimes I wish I were. That Mr. Murdock, he did kill my rat."

"A lot of people have died."

"How?"

"They call it ship fever."

"What's that?"

"It's a dreadful sickness. You turn to nothing at all and just lie there, weak and with filth oozing from everywhere on your body."

"How many have died?"

"They say forty-four," Patrick said. "Here," he added, remembering. "I brought some bread."

He felt the bread pulled from his hand, then heard sounds of Laurence eating rapidly.

"How long have we been sailing?" Laurence asked.

"I'm not sure. But people are saying it's only a short time before we see the land, and when we—"

"Patrick," Laurence interrupted, "when we reach Boston, I want to go with you."

"Laurence, I don't truly know if you can. I'll have to ask my da. But how will you get off the ship in any case?"

"I don't know."

"That Mr. Murdock will still be looking for you," Patrick cautioned.

Laurence closed his eyes and thought of the one-eyed man and his father's money. He wished now he had searched another time, or at least looked harder. Perhaps he should look once more. But what if the money wasn't there, or he just couldn't find it? And what if he were caught looking when they were so close to America?

"Patrick . . . ," Laurence said.

"What?"

"I'd rather die than hide anymore."

Chapter 123
The Thirty-first Day

D awn brought a cold, cloudless day. The *Robert Peel* was moving briskly forward. The air smelled sweeter than before. Though everyone could sense it, nobody could quite define what it was. "It's the smell of what's green and growing," someone insisted. Others claimed it was the shore itself. Regardless, the emigrants were sure America was near. There had been ship fever. Now there was a fever for land.

Though it was still early, some fifty steerage passengers had assembled on the forecastle deck. For the past few days, they had gathered each morning in hopes of being the first to sight America. Some leaned over the billethead. Another stood on the capstan. Others climbed the ratlines. All were searching.

Patrick had taken himself into the bow. As the ship dipped and bobbed, it churned up a heavy spray. Though he was getting a thorough cold soaking, he did not care. If being the farthest forward enabled him to spy land first, he was determined to do it.

Even as he watched, a wave rose. He felt a slap across his face. Reaching up, he pulled at a swatch of seaweed. He was about to toss it away when he realized it was green.

Wildly excited, he scrambled back from the bow and held aloft the green strand. "Seaweed!" he cried. "Green seaweed!"

Two hours later America, the promised land, was seen low on the horizon. Ten people claimed to be the first to see it.

Shortly thereafter, all steerage passengers were ordered to assemble on the main deck. Captain Rickles, resplendent in uniform and gloves, stood before the main mast and used his speaking tube to address them.

"We're fast approaching America!" he began. "When we reach Boston Bay, government health authorities will be inspecting the ship. If they learn we've had ship fever or that any passengers have died, they may not let you land. They could, indeed, send you back to England. If you are wise, you will say nothing if asked."

An unhappy murmur came from the crowd, but no one spoke up loudly.

"So mind yourselves! If you tell them about the ship fever, it will be you who suffer the consequence.

"These authorities will also be checking for cleanliness. Anything foul or dirty must be thrown overboard. Mattresses, clothing, food, whatever is soiled must go."

"But, Your Honor," a man cried out, "it's all we have."

"Nothing dirty will stay on my ship," the captain replied sternly.

"Sure then," came another plea, "and what happens if we don't throw the things out?"

The captain shrugged. "I told you, you'll be sent back to England."

To these words no one responded.

"Furthermore," he continued, "the steerage deck must be cleaned. This scouring will be done under the direction of Mr. Murdock and his crew. You are to follow his orders."

Mattresses were the first to go overboard. Then came ragged clothing, shoes, boots. It was Mr. Murdock, acting as judge, who settled disputes as to what had to go and what might stay. More often than not he insisted that the article in question be jettisoned.

"Faith, Mr. Drabble, there'll be some who'll have nothing left," Maura remarked after they had watched many passengers throw away most of their belongings. They themselves had just tossed the Fahertys' mattress into the sea. It broke apart instantly, its straw stuffing scattering on the water's surface like frightened minnows.

"Perhaps it's all for the best," the actor said as he heaved his tattered jacket into the water and watched it slowly sink. The sight mirrored his emotions, for he dreaded the impending disembarkation. "It's a brave new world, Miss O'Connell," he observed, placing hand on heart in his theatrical fashion. "Perhaps it's best not to carry old things and sentiments into it."

Maura kept her eyes on the coastline. "For a promised land," she said, "it doesn't have a look of beauty."

"It's early in the year," the actor reminded her, suppressing a sigh. "No doubt there are seasons here as at home. One must always think of spring, Miss O'Connell."

"To tell the truth, Mr. Drabble, it's me da I keep thinking about. I'm wondering if he'll look different or know us at all. It's more than a year now that he's gone."

"I assure you, Miss O'Connell," Mr. Drabble observed, "no one who has seen you can forget you."

When Maura made no response, he asked, "Do you know where your father has established your home?"

Maura wondered whether or not to answer the question. Then she said, "When he wrote to us in Ireland, bidding us come, he was living in a city called Lowell. That's where he found employment, though he did not say what he did."

"Well then," Mr. Drabble said, making an effort to sound casual, "perhaps I'll wend my way to this Lowell myself." He glanced at Maura. "Unless, Miss O'Connell, you have some objections."

"Mr. Drabble," she replied, "they say it's a big country. I've no doubt but you'll go wherever it suits you. Surely, it's not for the likes of me to be telling you either here or there." She turned and slowly walked away.

Mr. Drabble gazed after her longingly, afraid to ponder what he was sure would be a forlorn future.

Below them, on the steerage level, Patrick was on his hands and knees, using a large ballast stone to scour the floor with sand and seawater. The sanding brought up the natural whiteness of the wooden deck. For the first time in weeks, there was freshness in the air, a feeling of cleanliness. Everyone sensed it.

Tired from his heavy labor, Patrick sat up, rested his arms, and considered Bridy, who was working nearby. Not far from her side she'd set down the bundle of her family's clothing. She carried it everywhere.

"You can allow yourself some rest, Bridy," Patrick suggested. The girl, without looking at or speaking to him, paused in her work.

"Faith," Patrick said, "but it is all looking better, don't you think?"

Bridy made no comment. Instead, after a brief rest, she resumed work as doggedly as before.

Not to be outdone, Patrick bent over his stone and continued his scouring too. As he labored, he thought about the problem uppermost in his thoughts: how to get Laurence off the boat. With another glance at Bridy, an idea struck him.

Chapter 124
Mr. Grout and the Money

*M*r. Grout sat on his stateroom bed, arms folded over his chest. He had already packed his carpetbag in eager preparation for his arrival in Boston. Mr. Clemspool stood before the small washstand mirror, shaving with a straight-edge razor.

"Yer 'ave any notion as to where yer'll go when we get to land?" Mr. Grout asked.

"I'm not exactly sure, Mr. Grout," Mr. Clemspool replied with a flourish of his razor. "I need to see which way my prospects lie."

"Just so yer knows that once we're in Boston, yer on yer own."

With one finger, Mr. Clemspool pushed the tip of his nose up, the better to shave over his lip. "Casting me off, are you?"

"Clemspool, yer one of them dogs that always lands on yer feet."

"I could not agree more, Mr. Grout. Besides, our partnership has not flourished recently. Granted, you have been kind to me—"

"Glad yer know so."

"Kind to me," Mr. Clemspool continued, "with other people's money."

"Yer do go on about that, don't yer?" Mr. Grout said sullenly.

Mr. Clemspool sneered. "It was you who had a ghostly visitation, not I."

"It was a warnin'," Mr. Grout insisted hotly, "that I intend to 'eed. I'll just keep a bit of that money to get me started. The rest goes back to that dead boy's family."

"You do know, don't you, that Lord Kirkle has no need of it?" Mr. Clemspool said with annoyance.

"All I know is that I took it from 'is boy and that there boy is dead."

"You don't know that for certain."

"I saw 'is ghost!"

Mr. Clemspool laughed. "Mr. Grout, to make my point precisely, you are a fool."

Mr. Grout fixed the man with his glittering eye. "Clemspool, I don't want to 'ave anything to do with yer in America."

"Nor I you," Mr. Clemspool said brightly. "Save for one thing."

"Wot's that?"

"Never forget I know where you got your money."

A furious Mr. Grout leaped up.

"Touch me," Mr. Clemspool warned while coolly holding the razor before him, "and you will find yourself in great difficulty."

"If I was me old self, I'd be thrashing' yer easy," cried Mr. Grout. "But yer'll get off 'cause I'm tryin' to progress." So saying, he left the stateroom, banging the door behind him.

Mr. Clemspool gave a grunt of satisfaction, then quickly put aside his razor, locked the door, and immediately began to search among Mr. Grout's possessions. It was in the carpetbag that he found a small package wrapped up in a sheet of London newspaper. Smiling broadly, Mr. Clemspool unfolded the wrapping, saw that inside was indeed Lord Kirkle's money, and hastily put the package in his own pocket.

Chapter 125
Mr. Grout and Mr. Drabble
Make Plans

Mr. Grout, seething, leaned upon the quarterdeck rail and stared glumly at the New England coastline. To be called a fool! Someday he should like to show Clemspool who was the fool. As he calmed down, however, he had to acknowledge that it was time to think out some plan of action for himself.

The first thing he decided he'd do upon landing was sell his fine London clothing and dress himself as the person he really was. Then he would search for honest work. Once established, he would send as much of the stolen money back to Lord Kirkle as he could afford and work hard to pay off the rest. To begin he needed to find a lodging.

"Yer there, laddie," he called to a passing sailor, "wot's a place to stop in Boston?"

The sailor touched his hat in deference. "The Liberty Tree is good enough for the likes of me, sir. She's a cozy inn, snug off the Long Wharf on Commerce Street, not far from the customhouse. Only it might not do for you, sir."

"It'll be fine for me," Mr. Grout assured him, and he began to pace the quarterdeck, the better to focus on his future.

While doing so, he noticed Mr. Drabble leaning over the bulwark on the main deck below. The actor's expression was desolate. Feeling sympathy, Mr. Grout went down to him.

"There yer be," he cried as he clapped a hand on Mr.

Drabble's shoulder. "Yer seem to be a terrible moody piece."

Mr. Drabble shrugged. "I must confess, sir, I was speculating about what will happen to me when I reach land."

"Were yer?" Mr. Grout said. "I was worryin' the same meself. We're as like as two brothers."

"You are more kind than I deserve," Mr. Drabble said in his best melancholy tones.

"Yer and yer gal have no place in mind then?" Mr. Grout inquired.

Mr. Drabble blushed red and swallowed hard. "I—I—I am afraid, sir," he stammered, "she is not, as you would have it, my gal."

"Ain't she?" said Mr. Grout, surprised. "I was thinkin' she was."

"Though it was she who provided my passage, our being together has been no more"—the actor's voice faltered—"no more than a bit of sunshine in an otherwise cloudy life. Or, as the bard put it, 'the short and the long of it' is . . . she has . . . rejected me as a husband."

"Then she don't know 'er right mind," Mr. Grout assured his friend. " 'Ow could she think of refusin' a fine-speakin' man like yer?"

"It's not for me to say, sir," Mr. Drabble replied sadly.

" 'Ow many times 'ave yer asked for 'er 'and?"

"It was but once. Yet, I can assure you, Mr. Grout, that once was sufficient to decide my fate. She was most emphatic."

"Look 'ere, Drabble," Mr. Grout exclaimed, "yer 'ave to go at it again."

"Why?"

"Askin' once don't do. These gals need to be convinced yer in earnest."

"But, Mr. Grout," Mr. Drabble cried in despair, "she's to be met by her father. Then off they go into the wilds of

162

someplace called Lowell. I shall never see her lovely face again!" Tears filled his eyes.

"My friend, yer should follow 'er there and keep courtin' 'er," Mr. Grout advised. "She'll 'ave to come 'round when she sees 'ow well you do."

A ray of hope touched Mr. Drabble's heart. "Do you really think so, Mr. Grout?"

"I know so."

The actor considered. Mr. Grout's idea was attractive to him. Besides, Maura had not expressly forbidden him to go to Lowell. If he were there, he might try to win her anew. "Very well then, Mr. Grout, I'll take your advice and go to this Lowell, wherever it is."

"Yer do so," Mr. Grout agreed. "And if we're to be chums, I'll go along. I intend to see yer through with it all."

"You are more than kind, sir."

"Now see 'ere, Drabble, when I gets off this ship, I'm 'eading for a place they call the Liberty Tree. It's supposed to be decent. I'll wait for yer there."

"Mr. Grout, sir," exclaimed Mr. Drabble with true enthusiasm, "never have I had a better friend!"

Much pleased by the remark, Mr. Grout removed his hat and set it on the actor's head. "There yer are, Mr. Drabble. A token of me friendship. It looks better on yer than it does on me any day of the week."

Chapter 126
Business Plans

M r. Clemspool—Lord Kirkle's money deep in his pocket—hastened to the smoking room. Once there, he helped himself to a cigar, lit it, extended his legs, and waited. He was considering giving the money to Mr. Shagwell for safekeeping. It might be wise.

He did not have to wait long. Ambrose Shagwell appeared just as he had done every morning, eager as always to regale Mr. Clemspool with tales of his prosperous Shagwell Cotton Mill Company.

"The captain has informed me we should be in Boston by tomorrow," the American announced when he came in.

Mr. Clemspool waved away the smoke from his cigar. "I'm looking forward to it."

For a moment the two men sat in silence. Then Mr. Shagwell said, "Mr. Clemspool, do you expect to be visiting Lowell in the near future?"

"I have no particular objections," returned Mr. Clemspool casually, "saving that some important Boston bankers are hoping to meet with me and—"

"Never mind Boston bankers," Mr. Shagwell interrupted. "You should visit Lowell first. It offers the best hospitality. Indeed, sir, if you would be willing to be a guest in my house, I'm sure we could make you very comfortable. You could consider it your home. I'll show you about our mill, and you may see for yourself what a thriving enterprise looks like."

164

Mr. Clemspool took pains to suppress a smile. "Well now," he allowed, "you take me completely by surprise. Are you sure . . . ?"

"I'll not hear it otherwise. Come," Mr. Shagwell pressed, "say that you will."

"I should certainly like to," Mr. Clemspool said in his most nonchalant fashion. "You've made it sound most attractive, both as a place to visit and"—he stroked his invisible harp with plump fingers—"as an investment."

"I'll admit," Mr. Shagwell said, "that we've had our troubles with too many Irish of late. Increase in crime, disease, filth . . . not to mention their deplorable religion. A sad business, sir. Not like the American worker. But they present one advantage. They take less in wages. It keeps the others in line. But, of course . . ." Here Mr. Shagwell pointed to his eye and his nose and made the figure of a zero with his thumb and first finger.

"No doubt . . . ," Mr. Clemspool agreed, still wondering, but not asking, what the gestures meant.

"Very well then, Mr. Clemspool, when we reach America," Mr. Shagwell said, "it will be my great privilege to escort you to Lowell."

Mr. Clemspool offered up his best smile. "To make my point precisely, it shall be *my* very great pleasure."

"And if what you see makes you desire to risk—"

"I will take it," Mr. Clemspool said emphatically. "You may have little doubt about *that*."

Mr. Shagwell frowned. "I do have one small question."

"Please, sir."

Mr. Shagwell arched his eyebrows so high, they almost turned into question marks. "Your young traveling companion . . . Mr. Grout . . ."

Mr. Clemspool laughed lightly. "Pay not the slightest attention to him, sir. I took him along as a means of—what shall I say . . . education. The cousin of a distant relation.

165

But I hasten to assure you, sir, once we reach Boston, Mr. Grout and I go our separate ways. No, sir, I would not for a moment think of allowing him access to your home."

Mr. Shagwell bowed slightly. "I admire your judgment, Mr. Clemspool. I do."

"And I, sir," Mr. Clemspool said, "admire yours. Indeed, I look forward to a profitable partnership."

"In Lowell," Mr. Shagwell added.

"In Lowell," Mr. Clemspool agreed.

As Mr. Clemspool extended one hand to Mr. Shagwell, his other hand clutched Lord Kirkle's money. It was perfectly clear to him that the American coveted the cash. Good! thought Mr. Clemspool. The more Mr. Shagwell sought it, the easier it would be for him to swindle money from the American.

Chapter 127

Mr. Clemspool Sees Something

Mr. Clemspool—in his nightshirt—lay rigid upon his stateroom bed beneath his blankets. Though it was nearly midnight, he was too anxious to sleep. He had stashed Lord Kirkle's money under his pillow. Every few minutes he gave the packet a squeeze to make sure it was still there. Even so, there were moments he wished he'd put the money in a better hiding place.

Mr. Clemspool took consolation by telling himself that a loss of sleep was but a small price to pay. Once he got away with the money, he would be a rich man. And when Sir Albert Kirkle began to make payments, he'd be richer yet.

That thought set him to musing about how Sir Albert had received his letter. With a sigh, Mr. Clemspool acknowledged that, after all, Sir Albert was yet another unpleasant young person, not to be fully counted upon. Indeed, there were times Mr. Clemspool felt that the young people of the world were causing all his problems. He recalled the boys of the Lime Street Runners Association in Liverpool. He had paid good money for their assistance to find Laurence. What did he get? Nothing!

"Am I my brother's keeper?" he murmured. "No, absolutely not."

The ceiling lamp had been turned low, not off. Mr. Clemspool preferred it that way. It enabled him to make sure Mr. Grout remained asleep. For though the one-eyed man looked asleep, Mr. Clemspool could not be sure. Mr. Grout could be cunning.

Mr. Clemspool propped himself up on an elbow, the better to contemplate the man. Deciding to check, he swung his legs out from under the blankets.

No sooner did he do so than he heard a noise, a click. He listened intently. Again! It was the door. He waited. Sure enough, the door edged open.

Mr. Clemspool's first instinct was to cry out an alarm. But his curiosity made him hold back. Noiselessly, he swung his legs back upon the bed and pulled the blankets over his head but arranged them so he could peek out.

The door opened wider. Certain that someone was about to enter, Mr. Clemspool held his breath. Sure enough, a head appeared around the door and looked inside. All Mr. Clemspool could see was that the person was quite small. Immediately he decided it was one of those beggarly Irish children he'd noticed among the steerage passengers. The thieves! he thought contemptuously.

Constraining his anger, Mr. Clemspool watched and waited. The young person stepped fully into the room. He looked in Mr. Clemspool's direction, thereby illuminating his face. What Mr. Clemspool saw caused his heart to all but explode: The intruder was none other than Sir Laurence Kirkle!

At first the man thought he was dreaming. He pinched one hand to make sure he was not. As it was, he needed every bit of his willpower not to move.

Laurence, having looked in Mr. Clemspool's direction, now turned to Mr. Grout. When he saw the face, he stood absolutely still, staring.

Mr. Clemspool's mind raced, trying to comprehend how Sir Laurence could be in his stateroom. Dimly, he recollected that in Liverpool Sergeant Rumpkin spoke of the possibility of Laurence's seeking to stow away. And had not the *Robert Peel*'s first mate—Mr. Murdock—insisted from the first day of the voyage that there was a stowaway on board? Though Mr. Grout had believed the boy he had seen during the storm was a ghost, it must have been Laurence—alive! So here he was—Sir Laurence Kirkle himself!

Nearly in a panic, Mr. Clemspool wondered, Should I seize the boy? Ignore him? Cry an alarm? All these thoughts thundered through his brain while Laurence continued to gaze at Mr. Grout's face. But before Mr. Clemspool could make up his mind, Laurence began to search under Mr. Grout's bed, in his boots, and finally in his traveling bag. To Mr. Clemspool's astonishment, he saw the boy open the bag, put his hand inside, and rummage through it. The effrontery! He's looking for the money, Mr. Clemspool thought, and reached gingerly under his pillow to reassure himself that it was still there.

Tiptoeing to the desk, Laurence opened its drawers. Then he turned again toward Mr. Clemspool's bed. Under the covers, the man held his breath. His limbs trembled from tension.

Laurence moved to the door only to pause, look about,

and—to Mr. Clemspool's intense irritation—return to make a second foray into Mr. Grout's traveling bag.

At last, and with a sigh, the boy stepped out of the room and closed the door behind him silently.

Only when he heard a click did Mr. Clemspool dare to move. He threw back the covers and sat up. His mind was a whirl. What should he do? One fact stood out clearly: In a matter of hours he would be disembarking in Boston. What was to be gained by taking hold of the boy now? Nothing. He was sure Laurence did not know he was on the ship. Good. Let the boy focus all his attention on Grout. As for himself, Mr. Clemspool decided that *his* energy must be directed toward keeping out of Laurence's sight.

But there was one other thing Mr. Clemspool realized he must do. Removing the packet from under his pillow, he carefully unwrapped it. After placing the money back under his pillow, he looked about for a substitute, at last recalling the notepaper in the desk drawer. He wrapped a stack of this in the same London newspaper Mr. Grout had used for the real money. When he was done, Mr. Clemspool was quite sure it looked like the original. This new packet he placed in Mr. Grout's traveling bag.

At the sound of eight bells, and resolved upon his next steps, Mr. Clemspool sought and found some sleep—his hand still clutching the money.

Chapter 128
Patrick's Idea

*I*t was close to ten in the morning when the *Robert Peel*'s anchor splashed down off Governor's Island in Boston Bay. Within the hour, a revenue cutter with a spanking blue hull and new white sails brought word that government medical authorities would make an inspection of both ship and passengers the following morning. If all went well, first-class passengers would be allowed to leave immediately, taken off by a coastal lighter. Steerage passengers would wait to disembark at the Long Wharf in Boston.

By early evening the cleaning of the vessel was complete according to Mr. Murdock's stipulations. The *Robert Peel* seemed a new ship, clean and bright. To celebrate, Captain Rickles ordered extra helpings of bread and rice and as much vinegar water as remained. Even the sailors took on a more kindly manner, chatting amiably with passengers they had so recently mocked and abused.

That night the air was cold, but full of the sweet scent of earth. The moon, at three-quarters, brought sparkle to the water, while across the bay the city seemed alive with light.

Though the hour grew late, the deck remained crowded as the immigrants feasted their eyes on their future.

"Doesn't Boston look to be a fine place," Patrick said to Maura as the two gazed at the city from behind the bulwark. "I heard some folk saying it would be hard choosing from

170

all the work they'd be offered, when the food is there for the bending down and picking up. But tomorrow we'll be there ourselves."

"We will," Maura agreed.

"Do you think Da is there now?" Patrick asked.

"Faith then, if he's not, he's fast approaching," his sister assured him.

"Would he be walking there from that Lowell, the way we did to Cork, do you think?"

Maura smiled. "If he's rich enough," she suggested, "he might have a horse and cart."

Patrick laughed at the pleasure of it. Then he said, "Maura, I was wondering if we'll need to tell him about Mother right off."

Her smile faded. "I think so," she said sadly.

Patrick looked at his sister. "Maura," he asked, "will you tell him you're going to marry Mr. Drabble?"

Maura, blushing, tossed the thick brown hair away from her eyes. "And why," she demanded fiercely, "should I be saying that?"

"Faith then, isn't it so?"

"Patrick O'Connell, if you're going to call yourself my brother, I'll thank you to know there's not a bit of truth to that!"

"Isn't there?"

"And if that's what you've been believing the whole voyage, you've altogether lost your senses. Marry Mr. Drabble! Saints look down! Not at all!"

A pleased Patrick turned his eyes on Boston again. When he sensed his sister was calm, he said, "Maura, there is something else I've been worrying about. It's the boy. Laurence. We need to help him get off the ship."

Maura sighed. "Patrick O'Connell, you're a plague of questions and thoughts this night, aren't you?"

"You can't imagine the terrible time he's had," Patrick

pressed, "being in all that dark and filth for so long. We can't leave him, can we, Maura, with him coming so far?"

"Faith, didn't the boy choose to come himself?"

"But wasn't I the one who offered him Mother's ticket?"

Maura sighed. "It's many a time I wish you hadn't."

"Maura," said Patrick, "I did think of a way to help him off."

"Did you?"

"Bridy is coming with us, isn't she?"

"That she is. To be sure, I made a vow to her poor mother that I'd take her on."

"I'm glad you did," Patrick said quickly. "But here's my notion. Let Laurence go off as one of her brothers."

"Jesus, Mary, and Joseph," Maura gasped. "Here's Bridy's grief so great she hardly says a word, but you're all for saying her brother's alive!"

"But don't you see?" Patrick persisted. "The captain said we weren't to say anyone died. Well then, there's Laurence to prove that a brother of Bridy's is alive indeed."

Though she tried to restrain herself, Maura smiled. "Patrick O'Connell, you could slip the heel off an English soldier's boot as he goes marching by."

Patrick grinned.

She studied her brother's face. "Why do you care so much for the boy?"

Patrick thought for a moment. "Maura, do you remember that statue of Saint George in Cork, the one slaying the dragon?"

"I do."

"It's as though this Laurence was being chased by a nest of dragons, and I'm the one to slay them. And surely," he added, "if I were so miserable and poor, you'd want someone to do the like for me, wouldn't you?"

Maura stared across the bay. "If I say yes and the boy comes off, will you be asking anything more?"

"No."

"And you'll promise not to go begging Da to have him come with us?"

"I did think of that," her brother admitted.

"By the holy saints! Isn't there the news of Mother? And we're bringing Bridy. How much can we be asking of himself?"

"But he's rich, Maura!"

"I'm only asking if it's fair, Patrick, and the boy being English at that."

"And I'm just wanting to get him off."

"Very well," Maura said after a while, "to that I can agree. But it's to Bridy Faherty you should be applying now."

When Patrick found her, Bridy was sitting alone on the platform berth. He hauled himself up. "Bridy . . . ," he began.

The girl, as mournful as ever, turned around to face him.

"I'm needing to ask you something," Patrick whispered. "You know we'll be in Boston tomorrow, don't you?"

Bridy's gaze was steady.

"Do you remember my friend Laurence?" Patrick asked. "That English boy? The one that kept me from being swept into the sea during the storm? Can you recall him at all?"

Bridy nodded.

"Then you know he's a poor, unfortunate creature, with nothing but rags on his back and all alone like you. So I was wondering, Bridy, if you'd be willing to let him pretend to be one of your brothers? That way, you see, he could get off the ship. But only if you don't object."

Bridy shut her eyes.

"Faith, Bridy," Patrick pleaded, "if he doesn't get off, he'll die. And sure, we've had enough of dying, now haven't we?"

Without a word the girl brought the pile of her family's

173

meager clothing forward. For a long time she gazed at it. Patrick waited patiently.

Bridy offered the clothing to him. "He can wear these," she said softly.

"For sure, Bridy Faherty, the gods will talk to you," said Patrick.

Chapter 129

A Change of Name

With the Faherty clothing in one hand, a lighted candle in the other, Patrick made his way down into the bottom hold, passed through the cargo, then climbed the ladder into the luggage room.

"Laurence!" he called as he popped up through the open hatchway. "It's me, Patrick."

"We're not moving," Laurence said right away. "What's happened?"

"Faith, it's Boston Bay we're sitting in now. America. And we'll be going ashore tomorrow."

To his own dismay, Laurence's first thought was that he would have only one more opportunity to search Mr. Grout's room for the money.

"Aren't you glad?" Patrick said when he saw the worried look upon his friend's face.

Torn between his twin desires, getting off the ship and the recovery of the money, Laurence hardly knew how to explain.

"But first," Patrick rushed on, "in the morning there's to be an inspection. Only after that can we leave the ship."

"If I have to," Laurence said grimly, "I'm going to jump off and swim."

Patrick laughed. "Look here," he said, holding up the clothing. "You can go off as one of Bridy's brothers."

"What do you mean?" Laurence asked.

"Sure now, you remember the girl who berths with us? The one who lost all her family to the fever?"

Laurence nodded.

"She's terrible sad and barely talks, her grief's so deep. All the same, she's willing to offer these to you. When you put them on, you can come up to steerage. That way, if anyone asks who you are, all you need say is you're her brother. The captain announced he wasn't going to admit anyone died coming over. Well then, he can't say you're not her brother without saying her brother's dead and gone, can he? Do you see that?"

Laurence laughed.

"I never saw you do that before!" Patrick cried with glee. "Go on now," he said. "Put them on."

Now excited, Laurence stripped himself of the clothing that Mr. Bartholomew had given him in Liverpool.

"There," Patrick insisted, when Laurence was newly dressed, "you're looking a whole different person."

"My shoes are tattered."

"Faith, keep what you have. I've none at all. Now what we need do is find a way to cut your hair and smudge your face to hide that scar. Once I tell you what you should be saying to my sister, we can go up."

"When?"

"Today. Soon."

Once again Laurence thought about the money. He frowned.

"Laurence, haven't you just been saying you wanted to get off?"

"I do want to," the boy said with a sigh of regret.

Two hours later Patrick led a nervous Laurence into the steerage area. Both Maura and Bridy were on the platform. Mr. Drabble too. Patrick hauled himself up. "Here's Laurence," he whispered.

Maura crawled to the edge of the platform and looked down. The Faherty clothing, shirt and trousers both, hung upon Laurence's body like an old sack. His smudged face and his hair, crudely hacked by a knife Patrick had borrowed, gave him the appearance of the most ragged street urchin.

"By the Holy Mother," Maura said to him, "from the looks of you, you've traveled a greater distance than over the Western Sea."

Mr. Drabble, by her side, agreed. "He certainly has changed much from Liverpool."

Patrick gave Laurence a poke, the signal for him to speak as instructed. "Please, miss," the English boy whispered haltingly to Maura, "for kindness' sake—may I stay with you?"

"As long as you understand, Laurence, that when you get off, you can come no farther. Our father will be there to fetch us, and we can't be asking him on your behalf."

Laurence nodded.

"Miss O'Connell," Mr. Drabble interjected with a surge of sympathy, "can you really abandon this boy on the dock?"

Maura's eyes flashed with anger. "Mr. Drabble, if you're so keen to feelings of kindness, why don't you take him with you when you go off?"

Accepting the challenge, the actor glared back. "That's exactly what I was going to propose," he said, though he had not thought of it before. "What do you say, boy? Don't you think it would be better for you to go with me than to be abandoned?"

Laurence, not fully grasping what was happening, looked

176

from Mr. Drabble to Maura, then back again to the actor. Finally, he glanced at Patrick.

Patrick nodded.

"Please, sir," Laurence said, "if you'll have me, I'll go with you."

"Of course I'll have you!" Mr. Drabble exclaimed, looking at Maura, not at the boy. "As the bard said, 'My friends were poor, but honest.' "

Maura, thoroughly irritated, said only, "But I'm thinking, Laurence, in case you're asked, that you'll have to take another name. Yours is hardly Irish. Have you thought of one?"

Laurence shook his head.

Maura felt a nudge. Bridy had come up by her side and had been staring at Laurence. "He could be John," the girl suddenly said. "John Faherty."

A surprised Maura looked at the girl. "Do you truly want the boy to take your brother's name, Bridy?" she asked.

Bridy nodded.

"Well then, Laurence, you're hereby christened John Faherty, and you can stay with us until we land."

Chapter 130
The *Robert Peel* Is Inspected

The sky was gray and the wind blustery when the medical inspectors—an older as well as a younger gentleman—arrived on board the *Robert Peel* in the early morning. Captain Rickles, Mr. Murdock, and Dr. Woodham were at the rail to greet them.

"Mr. Parker!" the captain cried hospitably to the older inspector. "Welcome aboard. A pleasure to see you again, sir."

"Mr. Rickles, sir," Mr. Parker returned as he shook the captain's hand, "a fair Boston morning to you. You've come in earlier than expected."

The captain laughed. "A storm at your back will take you home, sir."

"For those brave enough to ride them," Mr. Parker said. "My new colleague, Mr. Holmes," he added, introducing the younger man. Then, crisply, he asked, "Any sickness or deaths, sir?"

Captain Rickles turned to the doctor. "Dr. Woodham here has been our physician. He's the one to answer you."

"A short report if you please, sir," requested Mr. Parker.

Dr. Woodham smiled wanly. "The usual complaints," he said, gesturing indifferently to the crowd of immigrants behind him. "An ill-prepared people for sea travel, sir. But, be that as it may, I can assure you nothing untoward occurred."

178

"Delighted to hear it."

Mr. Parker shook hands with Mr. Murdock. "And you, sir. I trust you're well."

"Not complaining."

"Any stowaways?" Mr. Parker asked with a wink. He turned to his partner. "Mr. Murdock is famous for sleuthing out stowaways."

Mr. Murdock grinned. "Well yer might ask, sir. I thought I had one. But perhaps he jumped ship halfway over and fed the sharks. Otherwise yer can be sure I'll catch him when he tries to leave the ship. If so, I'll gain a cabin boy for the trip back to England."

The inspectors laughed.

"Gentlemen," Captain Rickles pressed, "would you care for some breakfast in my quarters before your inspection?"

"A pleasure, sir," Mr. Parker accepted promptly, and the five men set off.

The steerage passengers, nervous about what was happening, remained on the main deck, exchanging rumor and gossip. It was of no help to them that on the forecastle and quarterdeck, sailors kept watch like guards.

"Do you think those sailors are looking at us?" Patrick asked Maura.

"I shouldn't think so," Maura said, though she herself felt uneasy about Laurence's presence among them.

Once the captain's breakfast was enjoyed, the inspectors— accompanied by the doctor and first mate—made a quick check of the staterooms. Here, they were introduced to the first-class passengers, who thereafter were free to disembark. Their baggage would be sent on later.

To accommodate those departing, most of the immigrants were herded below. Laurence, hoping to catch a glimpse of Mr. Grout, tried to stay on deck.

"Laurence," Patrick whispered, "the less you're about, the

safer it will be." With reluctance, Laurence agreed, and he, Bridy, and Patrick went down to berth number seventy-four.

Up above, Mr. Shagwell led the departing passengers down the ship's ladder and into a steam lighter that had been signaled to come aside. Close behind came Mr. Clemspool, making considerable efforts to keep his face hidden. Then Mr. Grout stepped off. The captain saluted them all.

Observing the departure from the deck, Mr. Drabble waved his new hat after Mr. Grout.

"The Liberty Tree!" the actor called by way of reminder.

"I'll be there!" Mr. Grout assured him.

After the first-class passengers had disembarked, the medical inspectors, along with Mr. Murdock and Dr. Woodham, went to the steerage hold, where they found the air fresh, the deck scrubbed to whiteness. The few personal possessions remaining were clean and well ordered.

"My compliments to the captain, Mr. Murdock," Mr. Parker said. "The ship's a credit to him."

"I'll be pleased to tell him so, sir," returned Mr. Murdock, saluting crisply.

"You may weigh anchor and take her in," Mr. Holmes advised, "at your own pleasure and tide, sir. We'll be there to inspect the steerage passengers at dockside," he added. The two inspectors soon departed.

Once again the captain addressed the crowd on deck. "We've been cleared to land. Those still above must go to your places below so the decks will be free. Have patience. You are almost there."

The steam lighter spirited the first-class passengers swiftly to Boston's Long Wharf. As soon as they put feet on solid ground, Mr. Clemspool turned to Mr. Grout and held out his hand. "It's time for our farewells, sir," he said. "Do you know where you will be going?"

Mr. Grout—the ground beneath his feet still seeming to heave like the sea—fixed his former partner with an angry eye. "Clemspool, if yer'd be good enough to tell me where yer goin', yer can 'ave me promise it won't be anywhere close."

"Actually," returned Mr. Clemspool with care, "I haven't made up my mind. It's a big country, sir. There will be room—to make my point precisely—separate rooms for us both."

"There better be," growled Mr. Grout. And with a scornful refusal of Mr. Clemspool's hand, he marched away, a bit unsteady.

Mr. Clemspool, a smug smile upon his cherubic face, watched him go. As the one-eyed man disappeared from view, Mr. Clemspool put his hand into his coat pocket and touched Lord Kirkle's money. "Good-bye, Mr. Toby Grout," he murmured. "And good riddance. May I never see you again."

Chapter 131

Mr. Shagwell's Salvation

As soon as Mr. Shagwell made arrangements for his baggage to be sent on to his home in Lowell, he and Mr. Clemspool strode off, arm in arm. When they reached the end of the Long Wharf, Mr. Shagwell hailed a hansom carriage for the Barton Point Railroad Station, terminus for the Lowell & Boston Railway. The driver flicked his whip and off they went, the horse trotting briskly.

Hardly had they begun when Mr. Shagwell leaned out of the window and cried suddenly, "Stop!"

With a lurch the carriage halted.

"Just a moment, please," Mr. Shagwell called to the

driver. "Mr. Jenkins, sir!" he called out. To Mr. Clemspool he said, "An old acquaintance."

Mr. Clemspool glanced at the man approaching the cab, noting only that he had white hair and a fringe of white whiskers.

"Mr. Shagwell, sir," Mr. Jenkins exclaimed as he came up to the carriage. "I've been waiting for your return with some impatience."

"Only just landed, sir," Mr. Shagwell replied. "But I'm delighted to see you. Do you think you'll be in Lowell sometime in the near future?"

"It was my plan to be," Mr. Jenkins informed him. "Big doings brewing there. Big things." Then, with a glance past Mr. Shagwell's shoulder, where he dimly perceived Mr. Clemspool, he added, "There are problems—urgent problems—about which I must speak to you."

"All the more reason to visit me," Mr. Shagwell said with a forced smile. "At our office, sir."

Mr. Jenkins gave a knowing nod. "You can count on it," he said, and stepped away from the cab.

Mr. Shagwell called up to the driver to resume. Once again they clattered off. "An important person," Mr. Shagwell volunteered to Mr. Clemspool but gave no further information. The Englishman, though curious, made no inquiries of his own and dismissed the matter from his mind.

He contented himself by observing America through the carriage window. He was impressed by the quality of people's dress—varied and rich; the grand architecture—elegantly massive; the shops and stores everywhere. The city, moreover, was cleaner than London or Liverpool. To be sure, there was drabness to be seen, including a fair share of beggars—Irish perhaps. But by the time they reached the railroad station, Mr. Clemspool had little doubt that America was a place where a man with brains—such as himself—

would have ample opportunity to prosper. Having money in his pocket all but ensured it.

The Lowell & Boston Railway terminus, a long shedlike structure, was crowded with travelers. Green, red, and silver locomotives blew off white steam. Black smoke poured from enormous urn-shaped funnels. Bells rang loudly. Rail carriages banged together.

Mr. Shagwell insisted upon buying the tickets at a dollar apiece and assured his guest proudly that the ride would take no longer than one hour and five minutes.

Once they started, Mr. Shagwell informed his guest how much better American railways were than the British variety. For his part, Mr. Clemspool was impressed and reassured by the similarities. As on English trains, there was much swaying and rattling, considerable smoke, and flying sparks from the engine smokestack. The biggest difference, the Englishman noted, was that the seats ran from carriage side to carriage side, rather than end to end.

As they traveled, Mr. Shagwell provided Mr. Clemspool with an array of facts concerning Lowell. How the Merrimack River provided all the power for the many textile mills by means of an elaborate system of canals, and the resultant cleanliness of the city, which all could enjoy. How, at last count, Lowell had reached a population of thirty-two thousand people. How it was not just the first but the most important manufacturing center in Massachusetts. How the—as he called it—"Lowell system" of good relations between workers and factory owners was the envy of the manufactory world. How the textiles produced were the best in the universe.

All these facts and fifty more Mr. Shagwell poured into Mr. Clemspool's ear. The Englishman acknowledged all he heard with the briefest response and, in fact, paid very little attention. His mind was bent upon learning how he could best make use of his talkative host.

After considerable thought, Mr. Clemspool decided the best scheme would be to promise—not give—Shagwell his money. Any amount. But he would do so only when the mill owner gave him public backing for a business of his own. What the business was didn't matter. With public backing from such an important man, Mr. Clemspool had no doubt he could get others to invest. Once enough capital had been raised, he would take the money and go off. America was vast, and he would have his fortune.

In Lowell, there was little time to see more than a glimpse of the large redbrick mills before Mr. Shagwell secured yet another cab. The ride was brief, the American apologizing for the rush by explaining he'd been away from home for some months and was eager to return. "Home," he said, "after all, is home."

Mr. Clemspool was quick to agree with this sage sentiment.

His host chose to knock at his own grand front door. It was quickly opened by a serving girl. Mr. Shagwell introduced himself as the master of the house.

"Begging your pardon, sir," the flustered girl said with a blush, "I had no idea it was you, sir. Mistress employed me but recent. If you please, sir, I'll be getting her now." She fairly fled from the door.

Mr. Shagwell, muttering something uncomplimentary about Irish servants, urged Mr. Clemspool into the best parlor, a large perfectly square room with striped wallpaper and a rug of a vivid floral pattern. A rose-colored horsehair sofa, two chairs, and a tea table graced the room, as did some framed prints of birds upon the walls. Over the fireplace was hung a stern-faced portrait of a pale man dressed in a black suit.

Within moments of their arrival, Lavinia Shagwell hurried into the parlor and embraced her husband with cries of delight. She was a woman in her middle years, buxom, with rows of dark ringlets—like tassels—hanging to either side of a wedge-shaped face. Her long taffeta dress was black, set off with white lace at wrists and neck.

There were many exchanges such as: "My dear Mr. Shagwell—so soon—I hope you are well—and yourself, Mrs. Shagwell—all's well here—here is Mr. Clemspool—just from England—our guest—a pleasure, I'm sure—no, mine—to make my point precisely, I'm touched by your hospitality—be at home—your room—dinner at seven—I'm much obliged."

It was only later, when Mr. and Mrs. Shagwell were alone, that a more serious conversation took place.

"Well, Mr. Shagwell," his wife began, "I must know immediately, did things go well?"

"My dear," he returned bluntly, "my London ventures came to naught. The truth is, Mrs. Shagwell, unless I can raise forty thousand dollars quickly, all will be lost."

Mrs. Shagwell sank into the nearest chair as if she had been struck. "Mr. Shagwell," she gasped. "What are we to do?"

"Mr. Clemspool," was the answer.

"Who is he? And why did you bring him here at such a time?"

"*Because* of the time, Mrs. Shagwell. This Mr. Clemspool—I met him on the returning ship—is an investor. He represents the Kirkle family, a very important name in England. Mr. Clemspool is looking to invest Kirkle money here in America."

"Will he invest in you, Mr. Shagwell?"

The mill owner smiled with satisfaction. "I don't doubt it at all. And, once he has invested his money, I shall pump it into the ledgers, then sell the mill before the debts are paid. Let the buyer beware. We shall walk off with a handsome profit. Yes, Mrs. Shagwell, this man shall be our salvation. He admires me greatly. In short, we must do everything

185

in our power to lead him that way. He is not a very bright fellow. Quite easily led."

"And if that doesn't work?"

"I have more than one friend," Mr. Shagwell informed his wife. "Indeed, I spoke to Mr. Jenkins in Boston."

"Mr. Jenkins?" cried his wife. "Mr. Shagwell, the man is most unfortunate."

Her husband sniffed. "Perhaps. But he has his uses. In any case, I am hoping to see him soon. Just in case."

"Mr. Shagwell, you must be careful."

"I intend to do what needs to be done. But again, let me assure you, Mrs. Shagwell, the Englishman shall be our salvation!"

Chapter 132

Mr. Grout at the Liberty Tree Inn

M r. Grout, having made his harsh good-bye to Mr. Clemspool, walked off the Long Wharf content in the thought that he would never see his former partner again. Instead, he put his mind to learning how to walk on land again, and to finding the Liberty Tree Inn, the place recommended to him.

As promised, the inn was not far from the end of the wharf. An old building, it had a sagging roof and many windows, none of which looked square. A sign bearing both name and emblem hung over its door. Mr. Grout took it as a good omen that he could actually read the word *tree* for himself.

Upon entering, Mr. Grout found himself in a large tap-room. A low ceiling of blackened beams, a bright fire in a wide hearth, floors of polished oak planks all helped to present a picture of cheerful warmth. Being so close to the docks, the Liberty Tree was a favorite place for sailors, both those just coming off voyages as well as those about to embark. It was crowded twenty-four hours a day and was so when Mr. Grout arrived. Benches and chairs, scattered liberally about, were almost all occupied.

The first thing Mr. Grout did upon arriving was to take a room for himself and Mr. Drabble, making the arrangements with a rather unkempt, brusque fellow who stood behind the bar, dispensing food and drink.

After quickly inspecting his third-floor room and finding it acceptable, Mr. Grout left his belongings, locked the door, then returned to the taproom. There, he ordered as large a meal as the house could provide and requested a table at the side, the better to observe the crowd.

The meal, quickly served, began with stewed oysters, followed by a lavish plate of bacon, cod cakes, and beans and a loaf of bread, with a pitcher of ale to wash it all down.

Once feasted, Mr. Grout settled back to make his first real observation of Americans. Some differences were immediately obvious. He heard it in the way people spoke—louder, more bluntly, and with greater excitement than they did back home. Such was the rowdy, energetic clamor that at first he believed the whole room was engaged in a heated debate.

But the more Mr. Grout watched and listened, the more he realized he was witnessing the accepted way. Indeed, the men—and a few women—kept slapping one another on their backs, punching arms, even trading insults, though no one seemed to take offense. All was done in rough good humor. Mr. Grout was much amused.

Those who were eating and drinking did so quickly, as if

in a hurry to be off. Yet, when they had completed their meals, few moved to go but instead sat about and talked and argued as before, hawking and spitting into the brass spittoons scattered about the floor.

As for the clothing people wore, there were many tattered slouch and wide-brimmed hats and dented derbies—as if tattered were the current style. Most men wore square-tipped boots and baggy jackets and had tied different-colored strips of cloth around thin necks. Shirts of wool had buttons only halfway down the chest. More faces bristled with mustaches and beards than in London. And those not bearded were not well shaved.

Mr. Grout was quick to sense that he himself must appear quite different to the crowd. Though his boots were no longer shiny, his shoulder cape—with fur trimming on the collar—was hardly in keeping with his surroundings. Sure enough, there were those in the room who now and again cast a gaze upon him. It was no surprise then when at last a man did step forward and stood unabashedly before his table to scrutinize him. The man's fringe of whiskers made Mr. Grout think of a picture of the sun, though this fellow's flames were white, not fiery. Moreover, the man's dark eyes, set beneath bushy black brows, seemed to challenge him.

"Well, sir," the man began, "you seem to be a stranger."

"I suppose I am," the one-eyed man allowed, wondering at the aggressive air that emanated from the man.

"My name is Jeremiah Jenkins," the man announced. "What might be yours?"

"Toby Grout."

"And from what part of the world do you hail, Mr. Grout?"

"England."

"Our old enemy," Mr. Jenkins said with an easy smile. "Newly arrived?"

Other people in the room were now looking on and listening, but whether with amusement or hostility, Mr. Grout could not tell. "Just today," he answered.

"And ready to stay in America?"

"I 'ope to do so if yer 'ave no objections."

Mr. Jenkins's face darkened. He leaned forward. "Mr. Grout, sir," he said, "I should like to know if you have any particular church persuasion?"

Mr. Grout, who could not recall the last time he'd attended a church service, was taken aback. "Why, I suppose I was baptized Church o' England, not that I recalls it. Wot's yer concern?"

Mr. Jenkins, preferring to be the questioner, went on. "And did you come to America in hopes of getting employment?" he inquired.

"I can pay me own way, if that's wot yer askin'," replied a puzzled Mr. Grout.

Mr. Jenkins's stern features relaxed. He smiled. "Considering what you say then," he said, "you are welcome to the United States of America, Mr. Grout. I'm sure you'll find your way."

"Decent of yer to allow it."

"I hope you didn't mind my asking all those questions," he said casually, "but there's a reason for them."

"And wot might it be?" Mr. Grout asked.

Mr. Jenkins merely pointed to one of his eyes, touched his nose, and, with his thumb and first finger, made a circle. "Avoid the Irish," he warned with a knowing nod and grin. So saying, he backed away, turned, and disappeared into the crowd.

Mr. Grout stared after the man, trying to make some sense of what he had just heard and seen. Then he remembered: He had observed the exact same series of gestures from the hands of Ambrose Shagwell aboard the *Robert Peel*.

Chapter 133

Mr. Grout Makes a Discovery

U pon leaving word with the man at the bar that when his friend Mr. Drabble called he was to be directed to his room, Mr. Grout retired there himself.

The room was little more than a grubby box with a window that, if one wanted to rub away the dirt—and Mr. Grout did not—allowed the occupant to observe the congested street below. There was space, barely, for a pair of narrow hard beds set against opposing stained walls, a chair with unsteady legs, and, between the beds, a small pine table, its surface covered with initials, dates, and avowals of love. From an oil lamp a wisp of smoke fluttered like a nervous ghost. While the room had none of the luxury of the stateroom on the *Robert Peel*, it did have a floor that neither heaved nor tilted. Hardly a wonder then that Toby Grout felt a vast satisfaction to be in sole possession of such a solid piece of earth.

Full with his meal and at ease with himself, the one-eyed man removed his coat, flung it on the chair, and allowed himself the delight of stretching out upon one of the beds, hands beneath his head. Never before had he felt so free, so unburdened by his past. Quite quickly he gave himself over to daydreams and speculations as to what he might do with the rest of his life. Hadn't he begun training as an innkeeper with Mr. Drabble? Surely he had a better knack for it than the fellow downstairs here. But first, before any new life could begin, he must return the money he'd stolen from that dead boy, Sir Laurence Kirkle. The thought brought him to his feet, eager to empty his traveling bag of the sinful bills.

The packet, at the very bottom of his bag, was easy to find. Mr. Grout eyed it, hefted it, even sniffed it. Finally, and with great ceremony, he placed the packet at the table's center and began to unwrap it. Only when he had reached the very core of the package did he discover that the money, the nine hundred pounds he had not spent, was gone. In its place he found a useless wad of stationery.

Perfectly dumbfounded, Mr. Grout could at first only poke at it listlessly. Then, staggering, he collapsed on the edge of his bed. Mr. Clemspool, he was certain, had stolen the money.

The mere thought caused the desperate man to swallow great drafts of air, clutch his fists till his knuckles whitened, and grind his teeth before at last he bellowed, "Scoundrel! Villain!" to the walls of his room. If only he could get his hands on the man!

The next moment he rose up, tore down the steps and out onto the street, took one running step—and came to an abrupt, befuddled stop. He had no idea where to start a search in this vast country.

Seething with frustration, Mr. Grout slunk back to his room and fell upon his bed, his fingers clawing at the thin greasy pillow like the paws of a kneading cat. There he lay, muttering profane oaths, cursing Matthew Clemspool.

When his despair was at its deepest, he reached into his pocket and pulled out a few coins. They were all the money he had.

Chapter 134
Laurence and
Mr. Murdock

W hen the wind dropped to nothing and the tide shifted, the crew of the *Robert Peel* took to the longboats and hauled the ship in by oar power. At the wharf Captain Rickles shook hands with Mr. Murdock, the ship's bell rang, and the crew cheered. The voyage was over.

Soon after four o'clock Mr. Parker and Mr. Holmes reappeared on deck, even as the steerage passengers were ordered up from below. There, with a mix of eagerness and alarm, they gawked at the city of Boston. A multitude of houses packed close—and many a church spire breaking the monotony—it appeared to cluster around a hill upon whose summit stood a golden-domed structure.

Though none of the immigrants murmured a word, there was a general feeling of disappointment. Clearly, Boston was smaller than Liverpool and larger than Cork—but not all that different from either city. The golden dome excepted, it did not have the look of paradise.

The O'Connells, however, had little interest in the city, so intent were they on finding their father. Standing above the bowsprit, Patrick was sure he saw Gregory O'Connell twice. "Da!" he cried, and, "Da!" only to be disappointed each time.

"Passengers will assemble in orderly fashion by the steps," Captain Rickles announced. "Take all your possessions with you. Once you have disembarked, you will not be allowed back on board. Mr. Murdock will release you."

With much scurrying and confusion, a long line formed. Some pushed to the front. Some lingered. Regardless, they passed one by one onto the swaying steps that led them to the wharf. But before they reached it, all passed through a gauntlet composed of watchful sailors, Mr. Murdock, and finally the medical inspectors.

Maura organized their group. Mr. Drabble went first. Then came Bridy, Laurence, Patrick, and finally Maura herself. They wore what they owned. Mr. Drabble was the only one who carried something of value, his newly acquired hat and his tattered volume of Shakespeare, which he clung to as if it were a private anchor.

The line moved forward slowly. As it did, Maura watched Mr. Murdock study each and every face. She herself hardly knew where to look, at Laurence, who was right before her, or down on the dock, where she kept expecting her father to appear.

Mr. Drabble could think only of his imminent departure from Maura. Glum and quiet, the actor was passed through the inspection point with only a nod from the first mate.

Bridy came next. Mr. Murdock gazed at her with a show of kindness and even rested a hand upon her thin shoulder, then pushed her past the medical inspectors. The child twisted about to see that Maura was still coming.

Laurence, heart pounding, tried to keep his face averted. It was taking all his willpower not to clamber onto the bulwark and make a leap for freedom. Indeed, he had made up his mind that if the first mate attempted to hold him, he would make a run for it.

Mr. Murdock looked down at him. His brow furrowed; then he frowned. "Here now!" he barked. "Who's this scar-faced boy?" He stuck out one of his large hands to keep Laurence from moving forward.

As Mr. Parker and Mr. Holmes studied him, Laurence, despite his bold intentions, froze with fear.

Suddenly, Bridy turned and took hold of his sleeve. "It's me brother, John Faherty," she said, and yanked Laurence along after her.

Mr. Murdock opened his mouth to say something before catching Mr. Parker's inquiring eye. Turning red-faced, he merely watched as Laurence hurried down the steps with the girl. He was so flummoxed, he barely paid attention to a grinning Patrick and a much relieved Maura.

Chapter 135

On Land Again

The passengers—feeling stiff and awkward after so many days upon a continually pitching and yawing ship—found it difficult to adjust to the stationary wharf. Not that anyone was afforded the luxury of remaining still for long.

All seemed in chaos about them. Amid carts and wagons, mounds of boxes, crates, and barrels, some people embraced in grand reunions while others tried to assemble large families and what goods they still possessed. Runners—as in Liverpool—darted here and there, cajoling newcomers into lodgings. There were even baggage grabbers, thieves attempting to steal from the bewildered immigrants.

Mr. Drabble, attuned to his role as leader, shepherded the O'Connells to a relatively clear space. " 'Oh brave new world, that has such people in't!' " he quoted in a burst of enthusiasm. But while he meant to speak triumphantly, the phrase sounded hollow.

Laurence kept gaping about at everything, signs, people, buildings. But all he could think of was that he was at last free of the ship. "I am in America," he kept murmuring.

Bridy clung to Maura's shawl, but the older girl hardly noticed. She and Patrick were searching eagerly for some sign of their father.

Abruptly a young man appeared before them. "Can I help you find a lodging, folks?" he cried. "I know the best. The cheapest."

There was something about his brash and patently false cheerfulness that made the O'Connells as well as Mr. Drabble think instantly of Ralph Toggs.

"Be off with you!" the actor replied with furious indignation.

Startled by such vehemence, the young man shrugged and spit upon the ground. Muttering, "Filthy Paddies," he went off to corral another group of immigrants.

"Runners here too," Mr. Drabble said with disgust.

The day edged into dusk. The air grew chill, the wood of the wharf slick with mist. Dockside lamps were lit. Though the *Robert Peel* was still being unloaded of cargo, most of the immigrants had long dispersed. But Mr. O'Connell had yet to appear.

"Have you considered what might have happened to your father, Miss O'Connell?" Mr. Drabble asked.

Maura was so upset, she could only shake her head.

Patrick, wishing the actor would leave them, said, "He'll be here soon."

"I'm sure he will," Mr. Drabble replied, wanting with all his heart to be a comfort to Maura. The possibility that he might still be needed was impossible to resist. "You need not worry, my dear," he offered. "I'll not abandon you."

Maura bridled. "Mr. Drabble," she snapped, "now that we're here, there's no need for you and Laurence to be lingering on. I don't doubt but you want to go off for yourselves."

Turning pale, Mr. Drabble snatched off his hat and executed one of his deepest bows. "Miss O'Connell," he said in a trembling voice, "do you think I would leave you in such a parlous situation? How could I? Not after all we've gone through together."

The gallantry of the man only irritated Maura more. "In faith, Mr. Drabble," she cried, "you shouldn't concern yourself. My father will be here soon. Haven't I said there's no need of you!"

Mr. Drabble drew back. "Miss O'Connell," he managed to say, "I have no wish to offend you by my presence."

As tears flooded his eyes, he turned to Laurence. "Very well, my boy," he said in a breaking voice, "it's time for us to make our final farewells. 'Parting is such sweet . . . ,' " he began to recite, only to have his voice crumble with emotion. Incapable of further speech, and pressing his volume of Shakespeare to his heart, the actor turned about and attempted to walk away with as much composure as he could muster.

Laurence, suddenly confronted with this abrupt leave-taking, looked to Patrick with dismay. "G-G-Good-bye," he stammered.

"Laurence," Patrick replied, "you mustn't forget we'll be in Lowell."

Though Laurence was desperate to say something more, he found no words to speak. All he could do was turn and run after Mr. Drabble.

Maura, watching the two go off, felt her heart plummet. "Mr. Drabble!" she blurted out. "Sure, I didn't mean—" Remorseful, she ran a few steps after him. "I was not myself, Mr. Drabble. You must forgive me!"

The actor's pride had deafened him. Unswerving, he continued to march off the wharf.

Maura made her way quickly back to Patrick and Bridy. Fighting tears, she drew her shawl tightly about her. "We'll wait right here," she said, "where Da will find us."

Chapter 136
A Meeting at the Inn

L aurence hurried after Mr. Drabble. Once, twice, three times, the boy glanced back at Patrick, the only person in the world he considered his friend. He would have given anything to stay with him. But Laurence had nothing to give, and Mr. Drabble, propelled by his humiliation, was striding rapidly off.

For his part, the actor kept asking, How could Maura have been so cruel, so ungrateful? He hardly knew which he felt more, grief or fury. And now that he was in America, a terrible question beat against him: *What was he to do?* He had not the slightest idea.

Before them lay the crowded city of Boston. Both Mr. Drabble and Laurence stared at it. Gas street lamps were glowing. Candles and lanterns gleamed from countless windows.

"Where are we going?" Laurence asked.

Mr. Drabble looked down at him, trying to comprehend not just the question, but the person who had asked it. Why is this boy with me? Mr. Drabble fretted, deeply regretting that he'd brought him along.

"Do we have a place to go?" Laurence wondered aloud.

Mr. Drabble, to cover his confusion, mumbled, "A friend . . ." Turning, he gazed upon the great numbers of people rushing by, all of whom—in his eyes—seemed to know exactly where they were going. He was certain that he alone—in all the world—was lost.

He closed his eyes. "I am in America," he murmured to himself. "The promised land. Where everything is different." He repeated the phrases as though they were a prayer, letting the ideas stir him, fill him. Then he dredged up a line from his Shakespeare: " 'The miserable have no other medicine but only hope.' " The words comforted him, calmed him. Taking a deep breath, he vowed he would become a new man. And he would begin by putting Maura O'Connell out of his mind.

Mr. Drabble hailed the next person who passed. "Excuse me, sir, but I'm looking for The Liberty Tree Inn," he said. "Can you help me?"

"Just up there, half a block," the man replied, pointing the way.

The inn was easily reached. Mr. Drabble pushed through the double doors beneath the painted sign and stepped into the taproom. It was just as crowded and noisy as when Mr. Grout had arrived earlier in the day. The stench of liquor was thick, while clouds of tobacco smoke had reached thunderhead proportions.

For Laurence—who had spent so much time alone—the sight of so many people pressed into the confines of one room, talking and arguing all at once, was overwhelming. He had to stop at the threshold. Mr. Drabble said, "Wait here," made his way through to the bar, and addressed the man working there.

"Excuse me, my good man," he said. "A friend is lodging here. I'm supposed to join him. Would you be kind enough to tell me where I'll find him?"

"What's his name?" the man asked.

"Grout. Mr. Toby Grout."

"Englishman with an eye patch?"

Mr. Drabble nodded.

"Third floor, room sixteen. Take those stairs," he said,

indicating the steps at the far side of the room and providing Mr. Drabble with a lighted candle to help him find his way.

Collecting Laurence, Mr. Drabble began to climb, the candle's flickering light just enough to illuminate the narrow steps while creating grotesque shadows behind. At the third floor, the actor entered a gloomy hallway of many doors, upon each of which a number had been crudely painted.

"Here we are." As Mr. Drabble knocked, Laurence, feeling shy, stepped behind him.

From inside a voice called, "Who is it?"

"It's me, Horatio Drabble!"

The door was pulled open. "There you are," Mr. Grout cried. "I've been wonderin' wot 'appened to yer."

"The ship was late coming in," Mr. Drabble explained. "I've only just arrived."

"Don't yer worry none," Mr. Grout assured him. "I didn't give up on yer. Just step in so I can tell yer some amazin' news."

Mr. Drabble hesitated. "I need to tell you that I've brought someone."

Mr. Grout grinned. "Yer gal?" he asked.

The actor blushed. "N-N-Not at all," he stammered. "It's this boy." So saying, he stepped to one side and held up the candle. "His name is Laurence, and I should explain—"

Mr. Grout took one look and shrieked, *"It's him!"*

Chapter 137

The Rage of Laurence

There, to Laurence's utter astonishment, stood Mr. Toby Grout.

"Why—what's the matter?" asked the baffled actor, turning from Laurence's look of shock to Mr. Grout's look of terror.

"Take 'im away!" Mr. Grout wailed from the depths of his soul. "Take 'im away!"

"Take whom away?"

"The ghost!"

"My good man," Mr. Drabble sputtered in confusion, "what are you talking about? There is no ghost."

" 'E's standin' by yer side!"

When Laurence grasped the fact that it truly was Toby Grout before him, all the pent-up rage he felt against those who had tormented him—his brother, Albert; his father, Lord Kirkle; the London police; Mr. Clemspool; Ralph Toggs; Mr. Murdock—all that rage exploded.

"The money!" he shrieked. "Give me that money!"

Panicked, Mr. Grout began to retreat into his room only to have Mr. Drabble haul him back.

"Mr. Grout," the actor urged, "pray look and see for yourself. This is no ghost. Merely a wretched boy by the name of Laurence."

"I know 'is name!" Mr. Grout cried. "Get 'im away!"

"Thief!" Laurence screamed as he bore down upon Mr. Grout. "Thief!"

"Mr. Grout, I assure you," Mr. Drabble persisted as the one-eyed man struggled to get away, "this hapless boy is, like us, English and but newly arrived on the very same ship."

"I'm beggin' yer," Mr. Grout said, "take 'im away! I don't 'ave 'is money. It's gone!"

Laurence began to pummel Mr. Grout with his small fists. "The money!" he screamed. "Give me back the money!"

Hysterical, Mr. Grout waved his arms to protect himself from the rain of blows Laurence poured upon him. A lucky flail knocked the boy down. Sensing he was free, the one-eyed man fled from the room and sped along the hallway in search of escape but found only a dead end.

Laurence sprang up from the floor and attempted to pursue the man. Mr. Drabble blocked his way at the door.

"Mr. Grout, sir," the actor called down the hallway. "I beg you, explain!"

Cowering in the corner, Mr. Grout cried, "That money I 'ad—all me riches—I took it from 'im."

"From whom?"

"That there ghost!" Mr. Grout covered his face with his hands.

"Are you talking about this boy? But—I don't understand. Where? When?"

"In London."

"London?" Mr. Drabble looked at Laurence closely, but all he could see was the familiar beggar of a boy.

Breaking from his grasp, Laurence charged upon Mr. Grout yet again. The one-eyed man sank to his knees and extended his massive hands toward the boy in desperate appeal. "I've repented," he brayed. To prove it, he plunged a hand into a pocket, drew out his few remaining coins, and flung them to the floor.

"That's all I have," he cried. "Take it. Tell me wot else

to do, and I'll do it. Just don't 'aunt me anymore!" So saying he prostrated himself upon the floor in abject submission.

Standing over the groveling man, Laurence felt his fury melt. Abruptly, he turned and, wanting only to escape, ran back down the hall.

Mr. Drabble caught him. Though Laurence fought to free himself, imploring, begging, pleading, the actor held fast until, exhausted, the boy collapsed.

As if Laurence were a sack of potatoes, the actor hauled him into Mr. Grout's room. Once again Laurence rallied, but when he realized his way to the door was blocked, he spun about, flung himself on one of the beds, and gave way to deep racking sobs of despair.

Pale and quaking, Mr. Grout poked his head around the door and stared at the boy.

Mr. Drabble beckoned him in. "Shut the door," he whispered.

"Is it safe?"

"Of course it is!"

Mr. Grout crept forward.

"Lock the door."

A terribly nervous Mr. Grout complied.

"Now sit down," Mr. Drabble insisted, pointing to the empty bed. Mr. Grout did so, his gaze never leaving Laurence's shaking form.

Soon the sobs quieted, and the boy fell into a deep sleep, the only evidence of his misery being an occasional twitch.

Mr. Drabble sat upon the chair, but only after he had blown out the candle and trimmed the lamp low. Relit, it cast just enough illumination for the two men to see each other.

"Now, sir," the actor said softly, soothingly, "you must inform me about all this."

"Mr. Drabble," murmured Mr. Grout, keeping one wary eye upon Laurence, "yer don't know the truth of me life."

"Sir, I am prepared to listen."

"It ain't pretty."

"If you can speak it, sir, I am prepared to hear it. We are 'poor but honest.' "

" 'Onest, eh? 'Ear me tale, then yer can decide for yerself."

Chapter 138
Story of a Life

Y er see, sir," Mr. Grout began in a low, halting voice, "I was born maybe twenty years ago. In London, snug in the molderin' shadow of Newgate Prison.

"I 'ad lots of brothers and sisters, younger and older. None of us knew where the next feed might be comin' from. Yer see, me father and mother were both mud larks."

Mr. Drabble gave his friend a puzzled look.

"Mud larks goes into the Thames River, in London, yer know, winter and summer, gropin' and feelin' for things in the mudflats. Coal bits, old iron, rope, copper nails if yer lucky. Which they sells. It don't bring but farthings and ha'pennies, though once me father found a silver thimble. The best year, that were. But yer can believe we was always fightin' and scrapin' over wot we 'ad.

"Now," Mr. Grout continued, "when each of us tykes got to be nine years or such, me father 'eaves us out—boys and girls both—to live or die. 'Go muck fer yer own lives,' he says, givin' us 'is kiss an' 'is boot all in one blow. Me mother 'ad no say. She were a mute anyway.

"I did find me life, which was fightin' for prizes. Terrifyin'

203

Toby they calls me. I was that fierce. That's 'ow I lost me eye. I was maulin' Brawlin' Billy Bathwait when he slams me with a stake.

"Well, sir, yer can't fight much with one eye. And I couldn't find 'onest work for any price. Not wantin' the workhouse, I took to street thievin'. Me grift was an old man's disguise. After a while I meets up with this Clemspool."

"Your friend?"

"Clemspool ain't no friend of mine!" Mr. Grout cried so loudly that Mr. Drabble, with a glance at Laurence, had to remind him to keep his voice low.

"Clemspool runs a business for rich boys that don't like their own brothers. Brother's Keeper he calls it. For money—pots of it—'e'll nab yer brother, older or younger, 'e don't care. Maybe once a week 'e'd point them out to me on the street. I'd snatch 'em and bring 'em to 'im. Then 'e'd ship 'em out. To India. West Indies. Australia. America. Places yer can't get back from.

"One night, when I'm out on me own grift, I prigged a lot of money from that there boy." He pointed to Laurence.

"How much?"

Mr. Grout hesitated. "A thousand pounds," he whispered.

"A *thousand!*" Mr. Drabble cried in astonishment, and turned to look at Laurence again.

"Truth to tell, 'e's a young lord."

"A lord!"

"I thought me luck 'ad turned. But me luck had Clemspool bein' paid to send that very boy to America. Only the boy escaped, and somehow 'e got on board the same ship we did. Then I thought 'e'd gone dead, 'cause I was certain I saw 'is ghost rising up out of the floor on that ship."

"Mr. Grout, I assure you, if this is the boy you are speaking of, he's very much alive."

Mr. Grout shook his head. "I 'ardly know wot to believe.

204

I thought 'is ghost came to make me repent me ways, which I swore to do. Only now, if 'e ain't dead, I say, what's to be done?"

Mr. Drabble placed a comforting hand on his friend's shoulder. "Mr. Grout," he murmured, "as the poet said, 'Some rise by sin,' but I do believe repentance is the nobler path to redemption."

Mr. Grout looked earnestly at his friend. "And do yer think, Mr. Drabble, truly, I can be forgiven all the wickedness I've done?"

"The Bible teaches us so, sir. And does not the bard confirm this in the line 'When thou dost ask me blessing, I'll kneel down, and ask of thee forgiveness: so we'll live'?"

"I don't understand that, Mr. Drabble. To tell the truth, I never do when yer talks so. All the same, the sound of it soothes me wonderfully."

"Sir," Mr. Drabble asked gravely, "what happened to that money?"

"Some of it went into these very togs I'm wearin'. Other bits went to pay me way to America. And for Clemspool too. But just this afternoon, before you came, I discovered that same villain stole all nine hundred or so pounds remainin'!"

"Heavens above! Are you sure?"

"Somehow, Mr. Drabble, you believe in me goodness. Well, I believe in that man's wickedness."

"You say the boy comes from a noble family. What is his true name?"

Mr. Grout pondered the question for a time but finally shook his head. "Yer don't want to know. It'll only bring a fear on yer."

Mr. Drabble, so strangely fixed by the man's one bright eye, let the question drop by nodding his understanding that he was not to pursue the matter. "Mr. Grout," he said, "what do you intend to do now?"

"Thing is," Mr. Grout confessed, "I don't 'ave a penny. I'm shamed to ask, but do yer 'ave any of wot I paid yer?"

"I do," Mr. Drabble assured him. "And since you were kind to me, there's no reason not to be the same to you. The more so if you truly desire to change your ways."

"I do. Makin' just one exception."

"And what is that?"

"I'm goin' to find Clemspool."

"But how?"

"First I was in such a fit, I didn't know wot to do. Then I got to thinkin' 'ard. Clemspool made a friend on that boat. Name of Shagwell. An American. Said he came from a place called Lowell."

"Lowell!" Mr. Drabble caught his breath.

"It's slim pickin's, but I'm 'opin' that Shagwell fellow might know where Clemspool went."

"But, Mr. Grout," the actor said sternly, "I am bound to ask: Do you intend to do Mr. Clemspool some harm?"

Mr. Grout grimaced. "I'd like to. I would. Only as I swore a sacred vow to change me ways, I won't. But I do want that money so I can 'and it back to that there boy. As for Clemspool, I'm goin' to let the whole world know 'e's a scoundrel!"

"Well then, sir," Mr. Drabble said, "as we have become friends, we shall go together to this place called Lowell. The boy too."

Chapter 139

A Meeting on the Wharf

*F*or Maura, Patrick, and Bridy, it was a long night huddled together, attempting vainly to keep warm, on the Long Wharf. None slept well, Maura hardly at all. More than once she found herself wishing they were on the ship.

Suppose their father did not come. Maura had never considered such an appalling possibility before. How could she have? All they'd endured was for the sake of this reunion.

How long, Maura asked herself, should they wait on the wharf for him? One day? Two? What if he came on the third? What if he'd never received Father Mahoney's letter informing him of their sailing? Might it not be better then for them to go to Lowell, the place from which Da had written? But where was Lowell? How did one get there? Could one walk?

No, Maura told herself firmly, Da would come. To think otherwise was a sin. Yet as the hours passed, the impossible seemed more and more likely.

Maura wished she had not sent Mr. Drabble off the way she'd done. Had he not—for all his faults—helped them often? He'd deserved better.

Jesus, Mary, and Joseph, the girl prayed silently, help us in our hour of need.

Feeling pangs of hunger, she checked to see how much money she still had. What, she wondered, would a few English pennies buy in America? Very little, she supposed. "Oh, Da," she cried out softly, "where are you!"

From time to time she looked at Patrick and Bridy, both, for the moment, sleeping. She told herself that—no matter what—she would care for them. They were in America. There was no going back.

As the sky brightened to gray, Patrick stirred, opened his eyes, stretched, and looked about. They were the only ones on the wharf. "Has there been any sign of Da at all?"

"Not yet," his sister replied, struggling not to give voice to the panic she felt.

"Maura," Patrick asked in a low voice, as if there was danger in speaking too loudly, "what would you be thinking happened to him?"

Trying to sound hopeful, Maura dredged up a bit of a conversation she had overheard. "Sure, but someone on the ship was saying that storm blew us in sooner than expected. Maybe that's all it is. You mustn't be doubting, Patrick O'Connell, not for a moment. He'll be coming along today, tomorrow latest. There's naught to do but stay where we are. As for being hungry, sure, we've been that before."

"Is there nothing to eat then?" her brother asked.

"This is all we have," Maura said, holding out the English pennies in the palm of her hand. "I'm thinking we'd better see what the day brings before we use them. You might get some more sleep."

"I'm tired of sleeping," Patrick complained.

"Well then, you sit and watch. For my part, I could use some rest."

Though too tense to really sleep, Maura lay down and closed her eyes. Here was, in any case, a way to escape Patrick's painful questions.

The boy took measure of where they were. Nearby, floating quietly, lay the *Robert Peel*. The once bustling ship was

208

deserted. Puffed-up gulls strutted about as if claiming ownership.

Boston lay in shadow. Only the golden dome at the crest of Beacon Hill caught the early light, creating the illusion of fire. In the air there wafted a smell of bread baking. Patrick's stomach churned.

The sky brightened to blue. Patrick began to see a few people—they looked like dockworkers—straggle onto the wharf. One of them caught Patrick's attention. He was ambling along, hands deep in his pockets, as if he had all the time in the world. At first Patrick thought him old—he progressed so slowly—but as he drew nearer, Patrick realized he was a young man. Moreover, the way he was dressed— loose jacket, baggy trousers, blue cloth tied about his neck, cap perched on the back of his head—suggested nothing of either sea or docks.

The fellow seemed to be looking for something. When he reached the *Robert Peel*, he halted, yanked his hands out of his pockets, turned hastily, and began to survey the wharf.

Patrick realized that the young man was now staring right at them. He wished he'd turn elsewhere.

Instead, the young man drew nearer, inching toward them a few steps at a time, pausing, turning about only to come on again.

Patrick gave a poke to Maura. She sat up instantly.

"What is it?" she asked.

"There's a man staring at us," Patrick whispered.

Maura looked for herself. He had not been on the ship, of that she was sure. But then the young man gave a start of recognition, took a step back, whipped off his cap, and, with what appeared to be a great effort, moved closer. Not for an instant did he take his eyes from Maura.

"I . . . I beg your pardon." He spoke haltingly, crushing his cap in his hands and swallowing gulps of air. "Are you . . . are you . . . Miss Maura . . . O'Connell?"

"To be sure I am," she replied warily. "But . . . but . . . how did you know?"

"My name," the young man announced, "is Nathaniel Brewster. I'm . . . I'm bringing news of Gregory O'Connell."

Maura and Patrick leaped up. "That's Da!" Maura cried, her voice loud enough to wake Bridy. "And where is he?"

Nathaniel squeezed his hat nervously, looked at the O'Connells, looked away, looked again at Maura. "Miss O'Connell," he began again, only to falter. "I'm . . . afraid I have tell you that . . . some four weeks ago . . . your father . . . Mr. O'Connell . . . poor fellah . . . I fear he died."

Chapter 140
Unhappy Decisions

Nathaniel Brewster's words fell like a clap of thunder. "Died!" Patrick and Maura cried in unison. They stared at the young man in disbelief.

"I'm . . . terrible sorry," he stammered, "to be bringing such . . . awful news." He reduced his hat to a crumpled ball.

"But . . . how could that be?" Maura asked, unable— unwilling—to absorb the words.

"The doc said his heart failed him. To tell the truth, miss, long as I knew him he'd never been all that healthy. And homesick, well, something pitiful. And I guess too he was all worn out by the mill work. I reckon he'd want you to know that . . . he . . . died with a priest."

"Were you his particular friend?" Patrick managed to ask.

Nathaniel bobbed his head. "Guess I was. We worked and lodged together. A decent fellah, your father." He looked shyly at Maura. "Never stopped talking about you. . . . All of you. Why, when he first took on sick, he made me promise I'd come down to meet you. I took the day off. I guess your ship came in early, else, sure as shooting, I'd have been right here. I'm terrible sorry."

"Faith then, Mr. Brewster," Maura said, her voice quivering with emotion, "it's a kindness you came at all."

"But where—begging your pardon, miss—where's your mother?"

When Maura did not answer, Patrick whispered, "She . . . she did not come."

"And your brother . . . ?"

Patrick shook his head.

Feeling altogether helpless, Nathaniel said, "It's a powerful sad thing."

For a long moment no one spoke. Then the young man broke the silence. "Miss O'Connell," he said, "if you're wanting, I could take you to Lowell."

Maura, in tears, and unable to think of any other place, could only nod. As she did, she reached out and took Bridy's hand.

"I've money enough to go by railroad," the young man said.

"We've never been on one before," Patrick whispered.

"Where are your belongings?"

"We have none," Maura said. "Nothing at all."

"What about shoes?" he asked.

Maura shook her head.

Embarrassed, the young man stared off into the distance and rubbed the back of his neck. "Well," he said, feeling more and more tongue-tied, "if you follow, I can show you the way."

Maura did not move. "Mr. Brewster," she said, "you need to know we have no money."

"Don't worry about money, miss," Nathaniel replied.

"I've enough. And your father left some. It's up in Lowell. I guess I just thought you'd want to go there, else I would have brought it. Soon as I can, I'll get it for you."

The railway station was an hour's walk from the wharf. Maura barely saw the city or felt the cold. Bridy, clinging to her arm, and fearful about what might happen, had eyes only for her protector. Patrick stared mostly at the frigid ground.

At one point, Nathaniel turned to the boy. "Is it the cold that's making you limp?"

Patrick shook his head. "An accident on the ship."

Nathaniel said no more.

Once at the station, Nathaniel paid for the tickets, then guided his charges to the proper railway-carriage seats. It was much warmer there. The O'Connells and Bridy sat upon one bench. Nathaniel sat right behind. Though it was forty minutes before they began to move, no one said a word.

Nathaniel was having a difficult time. Ever since Mr. O'Connell had died, he'd dreaded the moment he would have to deliver the news to the family. Now that he had, he was convinced he'd done it wretchedly. Maura, he thought, must think him a clumsy oaf.

In fact, Maura was not thinking about Nathaniel at all. Her grief was too overwhelming. And she felt enraged. How could her father call them to an unknown world and not be there to guide them? What was she to *do?*

Despite his sorrow, Patrick was diverted by the train ride. The constant noise, the swaying of the carriage fascinated him. They were moving at an incredible speed, twenty-five miles an hour, or so Nathaniel had whispered into his ear. Not only did the thought make Patrick's heart race, he was dizzy with the sights that passed so quickly before his eyes. This was the America he had dreamed about, full of new and wonderful things.

Yet the stations they stopped at were hardly more than wooden platforms. The occasional house he saw was rather small and spare, not at all what he had expected. Fields were barren and appeared to be mostly mud. Patches of gray snow lay everywhere. There were few trees. Nothing was green. Nothing looked alive. Was this, he wondered, truly the promised land?

Chapter 141
What Laurence Does

*L*aurence lay still, listening. When he heard the sound of the others breathing, he shut his eyes and shifted about so as to face into the room but appear as though still asleep. Then he opened his eyes just enough to see.

Stretched out on the bed across from him was Mr. Drabble. His eyes were closed, his mouth agape.

Laurence peeked at the door. Sitting against it—blocking it—was the London thief, Mr. Grout. He too was asleep, his head thrown back, arms crossed over his chest, the patch slightly askew over his blind eye. Even in sleep he looked menacing.

All Laurence could think of was escaping. Then he realized *why* Mr. Grout was sleeping against the door: to make certain that he, Laurence, could not flee. With an angry twist he faced the wall again.

Mr. Drabble was the first of the men to awaken. He moved slowly, stiffly, stretching his arms, yawning many times. He swung his long thin legs carefully to the floor. Then he sat, motionless, bent forward, cupping his head in his hands, a glazed look in his eyes. Finally, he lifted his head and squinted across the room. Laurence was gazing right at him.

"Ah, yes . . . Laurence," the actor said in a whisper. "I trust you slept well."

Laurence offered no reply.

Mr. Drabble pushed his hair out of his face, yawned again, and extended his hands before him, wiggling his fingers to limber them. He glanced at the sleeping Mr. Grout.

"You need have no fear of him," the actor said. "He'll do you no harm. You know me for an honest man—he and I intend to care for you."

"I don't believe you," Laurence threw back.

With a pained look Mr. Drabble held up his hands in protest. "But I assure you, it's true."

"He stole from me."

Mr. Grout stirred. He rubbed his face, shook his head, adjusted his eye patch, then glanced over to find Laurence glowering at him.

" 'E's still 'ere," the one-eyed man exclaimed.

"Mr. Grout, sir," the actor said, "I believe this boy does not trust you."

The one-eyed man turned to Laurence. "Well," he said to Mr. Drabble, "that's all right, 'cause I'm fearful of 'im."

"Perhaps he has the greater reason."

Mr. Grout pondered this, then nodded. "I can see that. But 'e don't 'ave to. Not now. I wouldn't 'arm him. Not a 'air on 'is 'ead. I'll swear to that."

"There, you see," Mr. Drabble said to Laurence. "You have his word."

"He's a thief!" Laurence spit out, and indignantly turned his back on both men.

After a moment Mr. Drabble said, "Mr. Grout, sir, may I propose a plan?"

"It'd be a kindness if yer did, Mr. Drabble. I can 'ardly think to any measure."

The actor nodded. "Well, sir, you indicated that you desired to trade your clothing in for something better suited to your nature. May I suggest you do so now. It will bring us some money to pay our bill here. And some breakfast, if you please. Then I think we should hurry on to Lowell."

"And 'ow," Mr. Grout asked, "does the young gent—" He paused to correct himself. " 'Ow does the laddie feel about that?"

"You might ask him yourself, sir."

"I don't feel proper about that. It's going to take time for me to get used to 'im being wot 'e is, if yer get me meanin'." The one-eyed man rose to leave.

"Mr. Grout," Mr. Drabble called. "You must take the hat too."

"I gave it to yer."

"We need the money."

"Yer right there." Taking the hat and his traveling bag, Mr. Grout stepped into the hall, saying, "I'll be back as soon as I can."

Mr. Drabble sat back on the bed, hands clasped before him. He looked about vacantly, now and again glancing at Laurence.

Laurence rolled over, eyes open just enough to see that the door was no longer barred. He calculated how good his chances were for a successful dash to freedom.

But just as he was about to move, Mr. Drabble gave a grunt. "Mr. Laurence," he said, "I really don't think you should leave us. Besides, I need to ask you some questions. Perhaps, with Mr. Grout gone, it will be easier for you to answer."

Frustrated, Laurence rolled over again and closed his eyes.

"My friend Mr. Grout informed me that, in London, he took a great sum of money from you. Surely, Mr. Laurence, such a large sum—one thousand pounds—could not have been yours. Am I correct?"

Laurence's heart sank. Would he *never* be free of what he had done?

Mr. Drabble sighed. "You will recall that you and I met in Liverpool. You were being pursued by half the city because—I presume—you had committed some terrible crime. I understand now. The money."

Laurence still gave no reply.

"I wish to inform you—as Mr. Grout tried to last night—that he no longer has the money he took from you. It was stolen from him."

Laurence turned quickly and looked at the man.

"All three of us desire to go to Lowell. You to see your friend Patrick, I suspect. Mr. Grout has pressing business there—and I too—of a personal nature. If we go together, it would be best. On the other hand, if you were to take flight, where would you go? What would you do? May I humbly suggest you would be better off *with* us."

Laurence pondered Mr. Drabble's words. What troubled him most was the reminder that if he ran off, he would be alone. He'd had quite enough of that. And he did want to find Patrick. "I'll go with you," he said finally.

Chapter 142

Mr. Grout Buys Some Clothes

M r. Grout, traveling bag in hand, top hat upon his head, stepped from the Liberty Tree Inn onto the streets of Boston. Despite the early hour, stores were opening and streets were crowded, not just with those who, frowsy with recent sleep, were hurrying to work, but with shoppers too. Newsboys were hawking papers. Carts and wagons were on parade. How good it was, Mr. Grout told himself, to be on land! He even smiled at the policemen in blue frock coats, leather stars on their chests, sauntering by on patrol.

Mr. Grout paused frequently to note the signs everywhere—on placards, on windows, on walls—and found satisfaction in picking out letters and reading the words: *Flour. Fish Dealers. Fire Brick Clay.* In many shopwindows he read,

HELP WANTED
NO IRISH NEED APPLY!

" 'Ere there," he said, taking hold of a man who was passing by, "can yer tell me where I can trade in me clothing?"

"A rag shop?" the man said, annoyed by Mr. Grout's restraining hand.

"Yer might say."

"There's one around the corner."

Mr. Grout thanked the fellow and soon came upon a small wooden building. The shop bore a sign:

THINGS AND WORDS EXCHANGED

Wooden cowbells announced his entry with a noisy clatter. The interior was dim and chaotic with great mounds of clothing rising from the floor like ash heaps. From low rafters—so low that Mr. Grout had to remove his hat—hung a multitude of pots, pans, and kettles. Candlesticks, shovels, books, horse whips, and braces were piled about at random.

In the farthest recess of the room, appearing like a mole seeking fresh air amid the mounds, a woman, her long pointy-chinned face wreathed by a mass of gray hair, lifted her head. Tiny spectacles sat close to the tip of her nose, so that she seemed to be staring at the floor.

"And what can I do for you, sir?" the woman inquired.

"It's me clothes," Mr. Grout told her. "I got 'em in London. Only they're too good for the likes of me. Wot I'm needin' is something closer to me true person."

The woman tilted her head back so she could appraise his garments. "Ten dollars and twenty-five cents," she offered.

"Including what I've got in 'ere?" Mr. Grout asked, holding up his traveling bag.

"Depending on what you have," replied the woman, "I might go to twelve."

"I'll be wantin' stuff in exchange."

"Whatever you want, it's here. Even some glass eyes," she added with a blatant wink. "All you have to do is find them."

Grinning, Mr. Grout offered his traveling bag to the woman, who took it into exceedingly large hands. No sooner did she do so than she disappeared as though diving down a hole. The next moment she popped up again.

"Thirteen dollars even," she said. "And you can help yourself to a complete outfit."

Instead of immediately accepting, Mr. Grout asked, "Do you know 'ow far a city called Lowell is from this 'ere Boston?"

"Thirty, forty miles."

" 'Ow do yer get there?"

"A long day's walk or a short hour by railroad."

"Wot's it cost by railroad?"

"A dollar."

"Then I'll take yer offer," Mr. Grout said.

"Done is done," the woman said, and once again ducked out of sight.

Pawing among the piles, Mr. Grout readily found trousers, shirt, jacket, and hat. Newly clothed, he offered the woman his London attire. She took it all and in turn handed him the money promised. "You do look more yourself," she told him.

Pleased, Mr. Grout glanced at a cracked mirror on the wall

and agreed that now he did seem more like a man capable of bullying his way down any street.

"Wot about some boots for a boy?" he asked, recalling the tattered shape of Laurence's shoes and wanting to make some gesture of friendship.

"What size boy?" inquired the proprietor.

"About this 'igh." Mr. Grout held his hand as close to Laurence's height as he could recall.

"Piles of children's boots over there." The woman indicated them with a general flap of her large hand.

After finding a pair that he thought would do for Laurence, then negotiating a price and paying, Mr. Grout returned to the street.

Hardly had he stepped from the door when Jeremiah Jenkins accosted him.

"Well, sir," Mr. Jenkins called in friendly greeting, "you've cast off your foreign look."

Mr. Grout nodded. "More meself, yer mean."

A flash of suspicion crossed the older man's face. "Not looking for work now, are you?"

The Englishman shook his head. "I'm just 'eadin' for Lowell."

Mr. Jenkins's eyes lit up. "And why Lowell, sir, if I may ask?"

"I'm lookin' for a man there."

"To take his job?"

"Mr. Jenkins, yer do 'ave a nervous worry about jobs, don't yer?"

"Do you have children, sir?"

"Not one."

"If you were a native-born American, sir, and had lost your job to a foreigner, you'd worry about such things."

"It's not an American I'm lookin' for," Mr. Grout assured him. "And if I took anythin' from 'im, it'd only be the money 'e took from me."

219

"What's the man's name?"

"Clemspool, Matthew Clemspool, from England like meself and nothin' but a fraud and a cheat. The greatest scoundrel and swindler in the world."

"Clemspool, eh? I shall remember the name. And, indeed, I expect to be in Lowell myself this day," Mr. Jenkins allowed, "so I'll be on the lookout for him."

"Searchin' for work, Mr. Jenkins?" Mr. Grout asked lightly.

Mr. Jenkins smiled grimly. "I have my work."

"Which is wot?"

"There's to be big doings in Lowell, sir," said Mr. Jenkins with a mysterious nod. "Big doings." Once again he pointed to his eye and his large nose and finally made a circle with thumb and forefinger.

Mr. Grout shrugged, turned, and started off.

Mr. Jenkins watched him go. Suddenly a splendid idea struck him. It made him grin. "Mr. Grout!" he called.

Toby Grout stopped and looked back.

The American hurried up to him. "Mr. Grout, sir, in Lowell I shall be staying at the Spindle City Hotel and Oyster Bar. May I suggest you stop there. I think I could find a quick and easy job for you."

Mr. Grout beamed. " 'Ere now, Mr. Jenkins, are yer offerin' me money?"

"You don't appear to have much."

"Yer couldn't be more right. And are yer offerin' enough to live on?"

"For a short time."

"I'm not exactly yer native."

"You're not a papist, Mr. Grout, and you don't intend to take one of our jobs. That's to your account. As for me and my business in Lowell, I believe I can offer brief employment. Keep it in mind," Mr. Jenkins said, tapping Mr. Grout

220

forcibly on the chest. With that, he entered the old-clothes shop.

There now, Mr. Grout said to himself, there is luck and work to be found in America!

Chapter 143

Mr. Jenkins Buys Some Words

The moment Mr. Jenkins stepped into the clothing shop, the proprietor popped up again. Tilting her head back, she saw who it was and grinned.

"It's Mr. Jenkins," she cried, the tone of her voice containing just a hint of mockery. "Is the world still falling down?"

"Mrs. Brown," he returned as he gestured with his thumb toward the door behind his back. "You've had some early business."

"An Englishman with but one eye. I've got some glass ones, but he wasn't buying."

"I don't care about his eyes. What did he want here?"

"Mr. Jenkins, you're the nosiest man in the world. But I think this country still has its liberties."

"Some," Mr. Jenkins acknowledged.

"Then I'm not obligated to tell you what he came for."

"He was wearing new clothes when I first met him."

"When you buy your clothes at the tailor shop, Mr. Jenkins, they're new. When you walk out with them onto the street, they're old."

"I should just like to know one thing," the man pressed. "Was it you or Mr. Brown he had business with?"

"You are the most suspicious man, Mr. Jenkins!"

"There's much to be suspicious about," came the rejoinder.

"His business was with me," Mrs. Brown allowed.

"That's all I need to know. Is Mr. Brown in?"

"Oh, yes. In his regular fever, scribbling away day and night."

"I'd like to see him."

"You know how to find him, Mr. Jenkins. You've been often enough."

Mr. Jenkins proceeded though the stacks and piles of old goods as if he were working his way through a maze. When he reached the far end of a dingy corridor and came upon a small door, he paused and listened. What he heard was a continual scratching, as if a dog infested with fleas was trying to get rid of them. He knocked loudly.

"Come in!"

Mr. Jenkins entered a tiny room that consisted, in the main, of a large table. Upon it was a solitary spirit lamp and piles of handwritten pages. Behind the heaps sat a grizzled man not much bigger than Mrs. Brown. He had bleary eyes and a slit of a mouth. His tongue caused a bulge in his left cheek.

The man's right hand was dyed with blue ink up to the second knuckle of each finger so that the yellow of his flesh looked like a fingerless glove.

"Mr. Brown," said Mr. Jenkins, "good morning to you, sir."

"Is it morning?" returned Mr. Brown without looking up or ceasing to write for a second. "I've been working all night." Even as he dipped his pen into his inkwell, his tongue slid across his mouth—momentarily popping out like a snake's—and pushed into his other cheek.

"I assure you it's morning."

"You don't know what it is to live by deadlines, sir," Mr.

Brown said, putting aside one page, taking up a blank one, and continuing to write. "It's not for nothing they're called *dead*lines. When you reach the final line, sir, you are indeed dead. No wonder we're called ghostwriters."

"Mr. Brown," Mr. Jenkins said with impatience, "I need a speech written."

"How was the last one I wrote for you?"

"Excellent."

"I'm pleased to hear it." The writer dipped his pen and shifted his tongue.

"I need this new one quickly."

"Another deadline," said Mr. Brown, still scratching out the words. "What's the subject?"

"The Irish immigration. Crime. Illness. Poverty. The Papacy. The decay of the republic. The protection of our children. The need for radical reform."

"That's the one I wrote for you last time, Mr. Jenkins."

"This one needs a call to action."

"What kind of action?"

"Brimstone and fire. With a particular emphasis on fire."

For the first time since Mr. Jenkins entered the room, Mr. Brown ceased writing to look up. "*Fire?*"

"Fire," Mr. Jenkins repeated.

After dipping his pen, Mr. Brown returned to his writing. "I'm just composing another angry speech."

"What about?"

"Raising taxes on goods coming in. Or is it . . . lowering taxes on foreign goods? It hardly matters to me. Ah, it's an angry time, Mr. Jenkins, a time of blame. I have an antigold speech. To be followed by a progold speech. A speech in defense of slavery. A speech against. I tell you candidly, sir, the best way to write speeches is in pairs. Write one, then write the other—point by point—in opposition. Saves time. I'll do yours for the usual fee. When and where?"

"Within two days. Send it to me care of the Spindle City Hotel in Lowell."

"I'll have my usual advance, sir."

Mr. Jenkins produced two dollars, which he flung down before the speechwriter. "Done."

"Always a pleasure, Mr. Jenkins."

Mr. Jenkins turned to go, only to pause and look back. Mr. Brown was still bent over his manuscript, tongue in cheek again, writing. "A question, sir," Mr. Jenkins called.

Mr. Brown grunted.

"Sir, do you believe in anything?"

"I believe in words, Mr. Jenkins, and the power of words." For the second time Mr. Brown paused in his work and looked up. There was something about Mr. Jenkins's face—the fringe of white whiskers, the angry eyes—that caused the writer uneasiness. "And you, sir, is there anything *you* believe in?"

"Jeremiah Jenkins, that's who."

"Mr. Jenkins, sir, the pen *is* mightier than the sword."

"But fire," returned Mr. Jenkins, "is mightier still. It can consume all words."

Chapter 144

Laurence, Mr. Grout, and Mr. Drabble Go to Lowell

Mr. Drabble insisted that they travel on foot rather than by railroad.

"We don't have money to spare," he reminded Mr. Grout, "and one day more will make no difference in our quest."

"Wot's the laddie say?" Mr. Grout said, turning to Laurence.

"I'd like to walk," Laurence said. After the long confinement on the ship, the thought of being in the open air appealed to him. "I want to try out my boots."

"It's a done thing then," a grinning Mr. Grout announced.

By seeking directions from a variety of people, they made their way out of Boston, first by bridge over the Charles River to Cambridge, then by dirt roads northwest toward Lowell.

The air was clear but cold, encouraging them to travel along at a fairly steady rate. In the afternoon they found shelter in an abandoned cowshed and had a lunch of bread, cheese, and cider purchased in a small town on the way.

With a sigh, Mr. Drabble became engrossed in his volume of Shakespeare. As he read, he ran a finger along the text, now and again closing his eyes as he committed a passage to memory.

Laurence, alternating between hugging himself to keep warm and eating, gazed out at the meadow before him, a sight he had never experienced. Remnants of snow spotted the ground. A bright red bird—he did not recognize it from anything he had seen at home—landed on a bush, cocked an eye at him, then flew away.

Mr. Drabble began to nod. Before long, his head drooped, and though he still kept his precious book upright in his hands, he was soon fast asleep.

Mr. Grout, meanwhile, watched Laurence with wonderment, telling himself yet again that the boy was not only alive but only a foot away. When he realized that the actor was slumbering, he tapped Laurence's arm.

"Laddie," he said, speaking in a rough whisper, "seems to me that yer and I need to 'ave a bit of a chat."

"There's nothing to talk about," Laurence said primly, and turned back to the meadow.

"Now see 'ere, laddie, all I'm sayin' is that we'll 'ave to find some understandin' if we're goin' to be together a spell."

Laurence ignored him.

"I did get yer some boots, didn't I?" Mr. Grout said.

Laurence shrugged, though he was, in fact, delighted to have them.

"The thing is," Mr. Grout continued earnestly, "I'm truly 'umble and regretful about me takin' all that money from yer back in London. It was me old self, not wot I am now. Why, if I'd known we two were goin' to be in this 'ere strange land such as we are, why, I wouldn't 'ave done the deed even if it meant gettin' me bad eye turned right."

With some discomfort Laurence wondered what the man would say if he confessed that he himself had stolen the money.

"And it's true I took yer for a ghost," Mr. Grout allowed, "though yer not one, as I can now see perfectly well. But yer did get me to renounce me sins, which I'm thankful for. The point is, I'm goin' to work 'ard to get all that money back to yer."

Laurence turned. "How can you do that?" he asked.

"Look 'ere, laddie, I think the name Clemspool might mean something to yer."

"Clemspool!" Laurence cried out in alarm.

"Shhh!" Mr. Grout said, gesturing his thumb toward Mr. Drabble. "Clemspool is the one 'oo prigged yer lolly. Took it from me."

"But . . . he was in England," Laurence stammered.

"No more. 'E's in America now."

"*America!*" Laurence's mouth dropped open. "Wh-Wh-Where?" he sputtered.

"I don't know, and it's a big place, this America. But, laddie, I swore a vow to find 'im, and when I do, I'll get the money and give it back to you."

"Will you . . . really?"

Mr. Grout touched his heart. "I swear. So yer mustn't be fearful of me. Thing is, I'd like us—us two—to be workin' together to find that villain. All I'm askin' is for yer to find the 'eart to give me a chance to make decent. Wot do yer say, laddie?"

Laurence gazed at Mr. Grout. There was an earnestness, a forthright manner in the words that Laurence could not deny. "Does . . . does Mr. Clemspool really have the money?" he asked.

"As sure as there's a nose on me face."

"And is he truly here . . . in America?"

"Came on the same boat."

"He did?"

"Same stateroom."

Suddenly Laurence remembered his search for the money in the stateroom. There *had* been two people there. "And can we really, truly get the money back?"

"If we don't, it won't be for want of tryin', laddie."

"I do want it back," Laurence said.

Mr. Grout grinned and extended his hand. "Now, laddie, a shake of the old 'and is the proper way to do business. Give me yers so we have a deal."

After a moment's hesitation, Laurence put out his small hand. Mr. Grout took it into his two large ones and squeezed it gently and gratefully. "Me repentance is gettin' better minute by minute. 'Cause now we're partners."

Chapter 145
The O'Connells Reach Lowell

The O'Connells reached Lowell by midday. The station was smaller than the one in Boston, but a greater sense of order and decorum was everywhere in evidence. Young women were to be seen in considerable numbers, their long aproned skirts sweeping the ground. They moved about in groups of three and four, arms linked as they shared animated conversation. Even those alone walked briskly, heads held high, eyes bright and lively. Maura saw that these young women were very much bolder and more independent than she.

Men, fewer in number, were dressed in black frock coats, dark trousers, and boots. Almost all wore hats. Beards and mustaches were clearly fashionable. To Patrick's eyes, each and every one of the men looked rich. His bare feet embarrassed him.

Nathaniel guided his charges out of the station and into the cold but sunny day. The first thing they saw was a channel of water spotted with bits of thin ice.

"That's the Merrimack Canal," Nathaniel informed them. "Lots of canals in town. It's waterpower that runs the mills. Down there," he said, pointing along a wide street upon which stood many brick buildings, "is Dutton Street. Fine homes. There's Saint Anne's Church. Used to be all mill operatives had to go there. Not so anymore. Your father went to Saint Patrick's. I'll be happy to show you where it is.

"There's the City Hall. Along that way you can see Lawrence Mill, Merrimack Mill, Boott Mill. Big, aren't they?"

Not a quarter of a mile away—in the direction Nathaniel indicated—stood a great mass of huge redbrick buildings. Their height fairly blocked out the rest of the world.

"Lowell folks are always bragging they've got ten mills here," Nathaniel continued. "Claim more than ten thousand people work in them."

"Did my father work in one of those?" Maura asked softly.

"Not those. We were over to the Shagwell Cotton Mill, out by the Swamp Locks and Pautucket Canal," he said, pointing south. "I'm still there. But I don't think you'll want to work there," he said.

"Mr. Brewster," Maura said, determined that the young man should know the worst, "by the Holy Mother, you don't

228

seem to understand our situation." She pushed her hair away from her face and turned her blue eyes squarely upon him.

Nathaniel, both fascinated and a little frightened by those eyes, felt obliged to take off his hat. "Only if you want me to know, miss," he said shyly.

"Mr. Brewster, as I told you, by God's truth, we have nothing in our pockets," Maura said. "Just a few pennies. We were believing our father had become rich and would be caring for us."

Nathaniel glanced away. "Well," he finally replied, "your father wasn't rich. Not by a long shot. Oh, sure, he had some dollars saved up. And don't you doubt but I'll get them to you quick. But, no, he wasn't rich."

"We don't know a thing about America, Mr. Brewster," Maura cried. Though she tried to hold them back, tears came.

Bridy, looking from Nathaniel to Maura, clung to Maura's arm.

Nathaniel held up his hands as if to shield himself from Maura's distress. "Look here, Miss O'Connell, I found a place where you can stop, an independent boardinghouse not far from here. Eighty-seven Cabot Street. It's run by a good woman by the name of Mrs. Hamlyn. Her husband's around but bedridden. She takes in Irish girls."

"What kind of place is it?" Maura asked, recalling Mrs. Sonderbye's.

"A respectable place, Miss O'Connell," the young man assured her. "I wouldn't suggest any other."

"And what of my brother?" Maura asked. "Would he be staying there too?"

"Afraid it's just women there. But he can stop with me. It's where your father stayed. Nothing fine, mind. But it'll do. Not far from Mrs. Hamlyn's."

"How far?"

"Maybe a quarter mile."

"And Bridy?" Maura asked.

"You'll have to speak to Mrs. Hamlyn about the girl. She was expecting your mother, but I can't think it'll be a problem."

Maura closed her eyes. Though Nathaniel looked and acted as if he were honest, some of what he said reminded her of the way Ralph Toggs talked in Liverpool. Was he just the same? Then Maura reminded herself that he was, after all, her father's friend. Besides, what else were they to do?

She opened her eyes. Patrick, Bridy, and Nathaniel were looking at her, waiting for her decision.

"Mr. Brewster, if you'd be good enough, I'll do what you're suggesting."

Chapter 146
A Lowell Lodging

Nathaniel Brewster led them west along Merrimack Street, a wide well-paved avenue full of fine office blocks, shops, and municipal buildings. Well-dressed people were everywhere on the sidewalks. Street boys were offering to shine boots.

Further along, in the area known as the Acre, there was little commerce save liquor stalls and small groceries. Almost all the houses were three- and four-story wooden tenements, red or white in color with three dull wooden steps leading to porches or narrow front doors flanked by deteriorating wooden columns.

"Here we are, Eighty-seven Cabot Street," Nathaniel said,

coming to a stop before a large white clapboard house. It rose to a height of three stories and had a gray slate-covered roof, dormer windows, and chimneys at either end.

While hardly a new building, it was certainly not in a state of collapse, as Maura had expected. That was reassuring. Even so, she had made up her mind that if her impression of this Mrs. Hamlyn was poor, she would refuse to stay.

Nathaniel banged the door knocker. A small woman looked out. Her pale forehead was high, her eyes large but mild, her mouth a Cupid's bow. On a gray head of hair— parted in the middle and tied behind her neck—was perched a white house cap. She wore a dark green floor-length dress with long sleeves. The only touch of brightness was a multi-colored striped bow at her throat.

Maura thought her severe.

"A good day to you all," the woman said in a surprisingly soft voice. "May I be helpful?"

"Good afternoon, Mrs. Hamlyn," the young man said, hastily removing his cap. "I hope you remember me? Nathaniel Brewster. I came by last week, inquiring about boarding for friends."

"So you did . . . ," the woman said. Her eyes swept over Maura, Patrick, and Bridy, taking note of their poor clothing as well as their bare feet. All she said, however, was, "Won't you come in out of the cold." Pulling the door fully open, she beckoned them to enter.

The parlor to which the woman led them was a large room dominated by a deep fireplace. Some ten unmatched chairs had been placed randomly about. There was a horsehair sofa and a table upon which lay a large Bible and a few small token books. Faded pictures of flowers hung upon blue-papered walls. In one corner stood a tall grandfather clock, ticking loudly. The floor was partially covered by an oval braided rug of many colors.

Neither Maura, Patrick, nor Bridy had ever been in such

a fine warm room. To them it spoke of riches. Maura was certain they could not afford to stay in such a grand place.

"Please be seated," Mrs. Hamlyn urged. Only Maura sat, and it was on the edge of a chair. Patrick and Bridy stood nervously by her side. Nathaniel also stood.

Once her guests had arranged themselves, Mrs. Hamlyn seated herself, folding her delicate hands neatly in her lap.

"Well now," the woman began, "as I recall, Mr. Brewster, you spoke of a young woman and her mother. Are you the mother of this girl?" she asked Maura.

"If it please you, mistress," Maura replied very quietly, "I'm the young woman."

"And your mother?"

"She chose . . . not to come," Maura said with difficulty.

Mrs. Hamlyn's brow furrowed briefly. "I see. And you've come from Ireland?"

"Faith, only yesterday."

"And was it a fair voyage?"

"We're glad to be in America, mistress."

Mrs. Hamlyn allowed herself to smile. "And your name, my dear?"

"Maura O'Connell, if you please."

"Tell me about these other young people."

"This is my brother, Patrick. And here . . . my sister, Bridy."

Bridy, hearing the word *sister*, looked around at Maura in surprise.

"Miss O'Connell," Mrs. Hamlyn continued, "as I understand it, you've come to America expecting your father to meet you."

Maura looked down. "By the Holy Mother, that's true."

"But Mr. Brewster has informed me that, alas, he has passed away. I am most sorry."

Grateful for the sympathy, Maura nodded and made herself look up at the woman.

232

After a moment's silence, Mrs. Hamlyn said, "My dear, this must be hard for you."

"Yes . . . please," Maura whispered, already convinced that Mrs. Hamlyn was a good person.

Mrs. Hamlyn went on. "Mr. Brewster," she said, "has inquired as to whether you could board here with us."

"Yes, please. It would be for me and Bridy here," Maura said, clasping the girl's hand.

"And your brother?"

"He can stay with me," Nathaniel interjected.

Mrs. Hamlyn nodded. "We keep a simple home, Miss O'Connell, just girls. Mostly Irish. My husband is confined to his bed. We passed his room when we came down the hall. In all probability you'll not see him.

"Our rules are simple. This room is shared with other boarders, all young women like yourself. If you have visitors or gentlemen callers, they may come to this room between the evening hours of eight and nine. The town curfew bells ring at ten. We require you to be in by nine. Exceptions can be made upon a suitable request. The front door is locked at ten. All lights out by ten-thirty. That clock there"—she pointed to the corner clock—"chimes the hours quite accurately. I wind it every day. There are full meals, of course. We do not allow spirits in the house. And strict moral behavior is expected, or you will be asked to leave.

"We can offer you a small room, with a bed you can share with your sister. You will keep it clean yourself. As to the fee, it is one dollar and twenty-five cents a week, payable in advance. Will that do?"

Maura, having no sense of American money, looked up at Nathaniel.

"Her father left some cash," the young man said. "Enough for a few weeks. And she'll be looking for work."

"An operator in the mills?" inquired Mrs. Hamlyn.

"If it pleases," Maura replied.

Mrs. Hamlyn pursed her lips. "They are hard places to work. It's there my husband . . ." She checked herself and forced a smile. "But that's neither here nor there. Since Adam and Eve were driven from the Garden, we must toil. Isn't that so? Perhaps I can even be helpful in finding employment for you. A landlady's recommendation will often suffice.

"But for now, would you like to inspect the room?"

"I'll be pleased to have it," Maura said in a low voice.

Mrs. Hamlyn nodded. "Then, Miss O'Connell, consider it yours. You may have your things brought directly to the house."

"Please, mistress," Maura whispered in deep shame, "we have nothing."

Mrs. Hamlyn considered Maura anew. "How old are you, my dear?"

"Fifteen."

"Miss O'Connell, if I may be so bold, there is much of life to come."

Chapter 147
The Room

Leaving Patrick and Nathaniel in the parlor, the landlady gathered up her skirts and led Maura and Bridy up two flights of steep stairs to the top of her house. In an alcove she opened a door and invited the two to step inside.

The room was spotlessly clean, with a gabled window that flooded the small space with sunlight. There was a single bed covered by a quilt of many colors, as well as a small chest of drawers upon which sat a white pottery basin and water pitcher. The walls were white too, adorned with a print of George Washington praying in the snow on bent knee.

To Maura's eyes the room was the most beautiful she had ever seen. Its warm simplicity filled her with peace. "It's wonderful fine," she said softly.

"Oh, yes, the necessary is out back."

"The necessary?"

Mrs. Hamlyn blushed. "The privies. Now then, we don't have keys for the rooms. We trust one another."

"Thank you, mistress," Maura whispered.

"You'll want to say good-bye to your brother, I'm sure."

"If it pleases," Maura agreed.

As they were going down the steps, Mrs. Hamlyn paused. "Miss O'Connell, some of the other girls and young ladies who have boarded left any number of garments and shoes. If you'd care to have some of them, that will be fine. No doubt we can find something for your sister too. I'll lay them outside your door. You may pick and choose."

"You're a fountain of blessings."

"Miss O'Connell, I take my Bible seriously. 'And if a stranger sojourn with thee in your land, ye shall not vex him.' I'm quoting from Leviticus."

In the parlor Maura took Patrick aside to say good-bye. "Now, Patrick," she said to her clearly troubled brother, "Mr. Brewster said you'll not be far at all. So it's no real parting, is it? And as I'm standing here, I'm vowing by all that's holy that as soon as we have money enough, we'll find a place for the three of us."

"Can I see you later?" Patrick asked. "Today?"

"Faith, of course you can." Quickly they agreed to all meet again in Mrs. Hamlyn's parlor at eight that evening. Nathaniel promised to bring the money Mr. O'Connell had left.

235

As soon as the young men went, Maura and Bridy returned to their room. Once there, they stood in the middle of it, afraid to touch anything.

Maura sighed. "Jesus, Mary, and Joseph," she said, "it smells so sweet and fine, I'm thinking of a spring flower."

Bridy nodded.

With some trepidation, Maura sat on the bed. She touched the quilt gently, thrilling at the fine work, the multitude of colors. She marveled too at the thickness of the mattress, almost two inches.

Now exhaustion seized her. Her whole body felt leaden. She yawned. She lay back and closed her eyes. The bed was wonderful.

After a moment she opened her eyes. Bridy was still standing nearby.

"Come, Bridy," Maura said, patting the place by her side to entice the girl. "There's room for you."

Bridy, as silent as ever, lay down, arms stiffly at her sides.

Maura stared up at the ceiling. There were minute cracks upon it. It made her think of the innumerable wanderings of the many streams back home in Ireland.

By her side, Bridy stirred slightly.

"Are you like me then, Bridy?" Maura asked softly. "Awful tired but unable to sleep?"

"Yes."

"Bridy, love, I've been thinking how peaceful it is here in this new world. Sure, but America is as fine as people say. What would you be thinking?"

"Am I . . . ," Bridy faltered, "am I really to be your sister?"

Maura shifted her head. The girl—her brow furrowed—was staring at her with eyes full of sadness. Her mouth—soft and moist like an infant's—was trembling.

"Bridy Faherty," Maura said gently, "aren't you already a sister to me? And don't you know that I have no better friend?"

When Bridy said nothing, Maura reached out and put her arms about the girl and hugged her close. In response Bridy pressed herself against Maura and began to cry, the first time since her family died.

"It's a kind and gentle place, Bridy," Maura whispered into the sobbing girl's ear while softly stroking her hair. "And look up at the sun on the ceiling now. Sure, but it's dancing with a kind of joy."

Bridy looked to see for herself, but her eyes were too full of tears. She turned back to Maura, who smiled, closed her eyes, and fell asleep.

For a long while Bridy watched Maura's face. Then she leaned forward and softly kissed her cheek. In her sleep, Maura sighed and drew the girl closer. Bridy smiled.

Chapter 148
On Adams Street

*P*atrick struggled to keep up with Nathaniel's long strides. The young man was absorbed in thoughts he chose not to share, so Patrick—hugging himself against the cold—contented himself by looking about the neighborhood. What he had seen of America, he liked.

"Mr. Brewster," he finally asked, "is there no one living here about?"

Nathaniel laughed. "Sure there are. But they're working."

"All of them?"

"Lowell is nothing without work. Lots of it goes on in rooms. Women doing sewing. Or stitching shoes. It's not bad out today but still too cold to be sitting in the sun."

"Do you work?"

Nathaniel laughed again. "Of course I do. I took the time off to fetch you."

"I'd like to earn some money," Patrick said after a while.

"How old are you?"

"Twelve."

Nathaniel shook his head doubtfully. "You can try, but it won't be easy. There's not too much work to be had these days, and they're kind of particular in the mills."

"Faith, I can do what they ask," Patrick said stoutly.

"Better wait until you see one," Nathaniel cautioned. "Some of the foremen can be fussy."

After they had gone a bit farther, Nathaniel said, "Can I ask you a question?"

"You can ask me anything."

"Does your sister have a beau?"

"A what?"

"A fellow she's keen on?"

Patrick looked up at Nathaniel. The young man looked very somber. "Not that I know," the boy said.

Nathaniel smiled.

It was not long before they went down the side of a building, then through the back door and up the stairs to the small cold room that Nathaniel called home. Once there, he lit the lamp and set to work getting a fire started in the stove.

Patrick remained standing tentatively by the door.

"That was your father's bed," Nathaniel said gently, pointing. "You can have it if you'd like."

Patrick stared at it. "Did my da . . . die there?" he asked softly.

"He did."

The boy crossed himself.

"I reckon you'll want some shoes," Nathaniel said finally.

He pulled his storage box out from under the bed and extracted a pair of boots. Though not new, they looked sound. "They were your father's," he explained. "Maybe you can use them." He held them out.

Patrick took the boots into his hands. "Did he get them in America?" he asked.

"He did."

Patrick sat on the floor, the boots before him. He looked at Nathaniel. "Sure, but he'd want me to be wearing them, wouldn't he?" he said.

"I think so."

Patrick pulled one onto his lame foot. "It's a bit big," he said with disappointment.

"Nothing to it. We can get some paper and stuff them with it," Nathaniel suggested.

"Could I be getting some now?" Patrick asked, pulling the boot off.

"I think I saw some around the front of the house," Nathaniel said. "People leave it."

"Can I look?"

"Go on down the way we came."

Feeling a sense of adventure, Patrick easily made his way down the steps. By the front of the house, on the porch, he found a stack of old newspapers.

And then he heard voices. He turned around. Three boys were watching him from the street.

In a glance Patrick saw that they were all older than he, certainly bigger. Their coats were bigger still. Each carried a small box on which was crudely written, SHINE, 2C. Patrick had no idea what that meant.

"What are you looking at?" the biggest boy called to him in a sneering voice.

"Sure, nothing much at all," Patrick answered in as neutral a voice as he could muster.

The three boys grinned at one another. The biggest said, "Jeb, Tom, I think we've got a Paddy. That right?"

"What?" Patrick asked.

"A dumb papist. An Irishman," Jeb said sarcastically. "Eh, Nick?"

Patrick stared at them, baffled by their hostility.

"Can you fight?" Tom demanded. Though Patrick saw no humor in the question, the other boys laughed uproariously. "Or have you already had too much to drink?" the boy asked. This remark was considered even funnier by his companions. They laughed louder than before.

Patrick took a step back.

Nick advanced toward the porch. The two others followed, pushing and shoving at each other. "Come on down here," Nick called.

Patrick, alarmed but not knowing what else to do, moved nervously toward the corner of the porch steps.

"Now we'll let you go fair and square. All you have to do is fight one of us. You can take your pick as to who. Biggest"—he thumped himself on the chest—"or smallest." He pushed at Jeb's shoulder.

"F-F-Fight?" Patrick stammered. "But why?"

"Because you're Irish, and we don't like Irish," Tom cried shrilly. "You're all a filthy lot."

"But . . . I'm . . . not . . . ," Patrick managed to say.

"Not Irish or not filthy?"

"I'm not filthy."

"But you are Irish," Nick said. "Look at you. You don't even have shoes." He came up the steps and thrust his face close to Patrick, who retreated, tripped, and fell backward.

"There, you see," cried Nick with glee. "All you have to do is breathe on them, and they fall down!"

Patrick tried to get up.

"Give him a poke, Nick," Tom called.

Nick reached out, put the flat of his hand on Patrick's shoulder, and pushed, throwing him back again.

"Go back to where you came from, Paddy," Nick cried. "You're not wanted here!" He brushed off his hands as if they had been dirtied.

Jeering and laughing, the three boys marched off.

Full of humiliation, Patrick watched them go. Eyes welling with tears, breathing hard, he gathered up some paper and carried it back to the room.

It was much warmer than when he had left it. Nonetheless he shivered.

"Find any paper?" Nathaniel asked over his shoulder.

Patrick, unable to speak, held it up. Then he sat down on his bed and began to crumple the newspaper and shove it into one of the boots' toes. As he did, tears rolled down his cheeks.

"Here, what's the matter?" Nathaniel asked. "Is it your father's boots?"

Patrick shook his head. Then he said, "Mr. Brewster, do they not like the Irish in America?"

"What makes you ask?"

"Sure, out on the street just now, weren't there three mocking me, wanting to fight."

"Three who?"

"Boys."

No sooner did Patrick speak than Nathaniel ran from the room, down the stairs, and out into the street. The boys were nowhere in sight. As he climbed back to the room, he wondered if they were the same ones who had brought on Mr. O'Connell's heart attack. He was not sure what he should say to Patrick.

"Did you see them?"

"Nope," Nathaniel replied.

"They wanted me to fight. And pushed me down."

Nathaniel knelt before the boy and helped him pull on a

boot. "There are some like that. But not many." He looked up. "Anyway, a strong lad like you will be able to take care of himself."

Patrick, stuffing the second boot with paper, was not so sure.

Chapter 149
Mrs. Hamlyn's Place

At eight that evening Patrick and Nathaniel knocked on Mrs. Hamlyn's door. A girl in a maid's uniform—white apron over a long calico dress—opened it. When Nathaniel explained who they were, the maid bade them step inside and go directly to the parlor.

The room was nearly full. Four young ladies sat talking in one corner. Another laughed on the sofa with a young man. Mrs. Hamlyn sat in her own chair at work with her needle. She spoke to no one, merely looking up now and again, then returning to her work. A fire in the hearth filled the room with warmth.

Maura sat with Bridy by her side.

When Patrick and Nathaniel came in, Mrs. Hamlyn welcomed them with a quick smile of recognition. The four young ladies also paused to look but soon resumed their conversation. While Nathaniel stopped to talk to Mrs. Hamlyn, Patrick hurried to his sister.

"And have you settled yourself?" she asked.

"It's a fair room," he said. "And Mr. Brewster gave me Da's boots."

Maura looked down at them. "Do they fit?" she asked, knowing perfectly well they did not.

"I've stuffed them with paper," Patrick confessed. "But I have to tell you what happened," he said, his face clouding. In a low, anguished voice, Patrick told Maura about his confrontation with the street boys. "I'm thinking they don't like the Irish here," he finished.

"They're nothing but some bullyboys," Maura assured him. "Look how kind Mr. Brewster's been. And Mrs. Hamlyn too."

"Did she feed you some?" Patrick asked, not wanting to talk further about the incident.

"Patrick O'Connell, you cannot imagine how much she set before us," Maura enthused. "There was bread and soup, as well as a kind of fish—such as I never heard of before—along with a boiled meat, potatoes, and cabbage. And they finished it all with the sweetest-tasting thing in the world. A pudding she called it. By the Holy Mother, we surely have eaten well, haven't we, Bridy?" The child nodded her head in sleepy agreement.

"No cornmeal then?" Patrick asked with a rueful smile.

"None at all."

Patrick, whose dinner had not been nearly so fine, looked away.

"And the other young women here," Maura went on, "they are all Irish too. Two from county Clare. A pair from Dublin, and I don't know where else. Kind they are, and full of chatter. They work in the mills here. Operatives they call themselves. And didn't they promise to tell me all I'll need to know about what to do when I find employment myself."

Nathaniel came toward them. Maura looked up. "Mr. Brewster," she said, "you've been kindness itself. A blessing on you."

Feeling awkward, the young man could only nod. He reached into a pocket and withdrew a handful of money.

"Here's the cash your father left, Miss O'Connell. It comes to almost five dollars."

Maura took the money and considered it. It seemed like a great amount, but she was not sure. "But Patrick," she said, looking up, "surely he needs to pay you rent."

"It's fine for the moment," Nathaniel said. "It can wait. Your father and I had paid in advance. Besides, your brother was asking about work."

"Faith, Mr. Brewster, we'll all be needing some of that."

"They work you long hours, Miss O'Connell. These days the first bell is at four-thirty in the morning. Evening bell doesn't come till seven-thirty."

"These other girls do it, Mr. Brewster," Maura said firmly. "How can I expect to do any less?"

Nathaniel laughed at her earnestness. "I'm sure you'll do fine."

"And what about me?" Patrick asked. "Can I be working there?"

"I'll take you along with me in the morning," Nathaniel said.

Shortly before nine, Nathaniel and Patrick left the Hamlyn house. "This way," Nathaniel said. "The faster you walk, the less cold." He strode off, hands deep in pockets. Patrick started to follow but paused when he noticed that there was a man standing across the street. By the house lights, he could only see that his hair was white, and he had a fringe of white whiskers.

"Patrick!" called Nathaniel from down the street. "Come on now. It's cold!"

Patrick hurried along.

Chapter 150
Patrick at the Mill

At four-thirty in the morning the city bells rang. Patrick, asleep in his clothes with a blanket pulled over his head, failed to hear them. It took a severe foot shaking by Nathaniel to get him moving.

"Come along, my friend," the young man called cheerfully. "First bell. Four-thirty. Getting-up time."

Patrick sat up slowly and, with his knuckles, worked the sleep from his eyes. By the light of the candle, he could see his frosted breath. And when he set his feet upon the frigid floor, the chill made him recall his boots. He pulled them on gingerly, crunching down the newspaper wadding.

Atop the cold stove Nathaniel sliced a loaf of bread, a piece of which he handed to Patrick. The remainder—along with a lump of cheese—he placed in a small sack.

"You can eat it as we go," he suggested. "Won't be any breakfast until seven-thirty. I'm bringing enough for you too. Lunch at twelve-thirty. Evening bells come at half past seven. Can you remember all that?"

Hoping he would, Patrick nodded.

On the street, people were already hurrying by, filling the predawn darkness with sounds of shuffling feet. With heads bowed and hands deep in pockets or wrapped in shawls, they walked as if not fully awake. Some carried pails or sacks as Nathaniel did. Though most walked in twos and threes, few spoke. The cold wind was numbing.

Patrick, limping by Nathaniel's side, felt the large boots chafe but tried to ignore it. Now and again he bit into his bread and, from long habit, chewed slowly.

"In case we miss each other at the end of the day," Nathaniel said, "you'll need to look sharp so you can find your way back on your own. Remember, our room is on Adams Street."

"Faith, I'll know," Patrick said, though he worried that in the darkness most of the houses looked very much the same.

"Crow Street," Nathaniel announced, making a left turn. Then, as he started over a footbridge, he continued, "We're crossing the Western Canal. Almost there."

As they drew closer to the mill, the streets grew more crowded. Patrick noted that most of the walkers were women. From the way some wore their shawls, he was sure they were Irish.

"Mr. Brewster," he asked, "are there many Irish who work in the mills then?"

"More and more."

"And do Americans like them?"

"You're still worried about those boys, aren't you?"

Patrick nodded.

"Your father was a worrier."

"Was he?"

Nathaniel smiled at the memory. "He didn't have many laughs."

"But, Mr. Brewster, I'm still wondering if Americans like us here."

"I suppose we all came from somewhere," Nathaniel said, trying to sound lighthearted. "But you can always find a mean one if you look under enough rocks. I just hope that . . ."

"Hope what?" Patrick asked when Nathaniel didn't complete the sentence.

"That it'll be all right."

Ten minutes later, Nathaniel halted. "There it is, the Shagwell Cotton Mill Company. Not as big as some of the others in town, but big enough."

Patrick gazed with wonder. With so many windows lit up, the huge building made him think of a beast with multiple eyes. He thought of Cork and the statue of St. George and the dragon. Here was a gigantic dragon indeed.

"The gates will be opening soon," Nathaniel told him.

Sure enough, bells began to ring. "Second bell," he said. "We'd better move."

As they drew closer, Patrick became aware of a great wall surrounding the mill and a pair of iron gates—fifteen feet tall—that were swinging open. The crowd surged forward.

"I'll log in," Nathaniel explained, "then we'll speak to the overlooker."

"And what's the overlooker?"

"The floor boss."

They passed through the gates. Patrick could see that the mill consisted of two dark brick buildings. The bigger was six stories high. The other building was but two.

"I'm working on the first floor," Nathaniel said, gesturing toward the larger building. "Unpacking cotton and getting it ready for the carding."

"Would that be where my father worked?" Patrick wondered.

Nathaniel nodded. "At the carding machines."

Patrick crossed himself.

"Come on now," Nathaniel urged again. "If I'm late, they'll dock me."

"Dock?"

"Cut some of my pay."

"And do you mind me asking, Mr. Brewster, how much you earn?"

"Four dollars a week."

"Then it's a rich country, I'm thinking."

Nathaniel laughed.

Along with other men—no women here—they went inside.

"Brewster!" Nathaniel called to a man who stood by the door, checking names off in a ledger book.

The interior of the building was illuminated with glowing gas lamps. The hot white light revealed large bales of cotton standing among many wheelbarrows. Next to these were rows of men—not talking, not moving, but waiting. Patrick thought of the sailors on the *Robert Peel*, how they were never still.

Atop a two-foot-high wooden platform stood a man wearing a derby, green vest, and baggy trousers. Rolled-up sleeves revealed bulging muscles. While one hand kept stroking his bushy mustache, the other held a large pocket watch at which he was staring.

"The overlooker," Nathaniel whispered to Patrick as they approached. "Mr. Mosscut, sir," Nathaniel called.

The man glanced up quickly, only to return to his watch. "Yes, Brewster. What might I do for you?"

"Got a boy who's looking for work."

Another glance. "How old?"

Nathaniel looked at Patrick for the answer.

"Twelve, if it please Your Honor."

Hearing the sound of the Irish accent, Mr. Mosscut grimaced. Eyes still on the watch, he shook his head. "We're not taking on any more Irish, Brewster."

"Mr. Mosscut," Nathaniel pleaded, "it's Gregory O'Connell's son. He just came over."

The overlooker took another look at Patrick, more kindly than before.

"Sorry, Brewster," Mr. Mosscut said gruffly. "Orders from above." He checked his watch and suddenly shouted, "Commence work!" Even as he spoke, bells rang.

The men on the floor began to pull apart the bales, load-

ing large clumps of cotton—like armfuls of dirty clouds—
onto the barrows.

"Mr. Mosscut . . . ," Nathaniel said.

"Mr. Brewster, in another minute you'll be docked."

Patrick looked up at Nathaniel.

Nathaniel, at a loss for words, shook his head. Then he
said, "You better go home. I'll be there tonight after
seven-thirty."

Patrick, brokenhearted, didn't move.

"Go on now," Nathaniel said sadly. "You can't stay, lad.
You heard Mr. Mosscut. It'll only bring trouble. Can you
find your way back?"

Patrick nodded, turned, and limped out of the building.
Once beyond the gates he stopped, looked back, wiped his
eyes of tears. He dreaded the thought of spending the day
in a windowless room on Adams Street. Instead, he turned
toward the chilly center of Lowell.

Chapter 151

An Encounter

*P*atrick soon found himself staring down into a channel
of fast-running water some fifty feet wide. It looked like
a canal, but he was not certain. Clumps of ice floated by.
Alongside the water stood a few spindly trees that, in the
dim gray dawn, looked like a row of emaciated spirits. Broken branches lay scattered on the ground. Not far off was a
small footbridge.

Patrick wondered if it was the same bridge he'd crossed
with Nathaniel earlier. Fairly certain it was not, he sat down

on the bank, drew up his knees, and hugged himself to ward off the chill, then stared absentmindedly into the churning current. Wishing there was more light, he decided to wait until the sun rose.

A splash made him look up. Across the way a boy was tossing stones into the water. As he looked through the gloom, Patrick, with a start, realized the boy was the largest of the trio—Nick—who had pushed him about the night before at Mr. Brewster's house.

Not wishing to provoke a skirmish, Patrick chose to ignore the bully. Perhaps the boy would not recognize him. Only when a second stone landed even closer, splashing him with icy water, did he involuntarily jerk his head up.

Nick grinned. "Just wanted to give you a bath," he jeered. "When was the last time you had one?"

Patrick's anger flared. "Leave me alone!" he cried.

"There's some rocks on your side," the boy challenged from across the canal. "Or are you too weak to reach me?"

Wanting no part of any fight, Patrick stood and began to back off.

"Running away?" Nick called as he started for the footbridge.

When Patrick realized that the boy intended to come after him, he turned to run. But his large boots hampered him greatly and prevented him from moving fast.

Nick pursued him, pausing to pick up rocks and hurl them. One struck Patrick's shoulder.

Ignoring the pain, Patrick cut down what he thought was a street, only to come up against a bend in the canal. There was no bridge here to escape over. Fearful of being trapped, he spun about and started back just as Nick appeared around the corner.

The instant Nick realized that Patrick had no place to go other than into the canal itself, he slowed, grinning tauntingly. "Thought you'd get away, didn't you?" he sneered.

Patrick retreated.

"Now you *have* to fight. That or take a swim. Hope you know how to, Paddy boy. It's cold in there."

Patrick kept inching back, checking to see how much space there was between him and the canal. When he reached the edge, he halted.

"Come on," Nick challenged, fists up, ready to brawl. "You can do something, can't you? Fight or swim." He sauntered closer.

Trapped, barely thinking of what he was doing, Patrick lowered his head and charged, butting Nick in the chest. Taken by surprise, Nick reeled backward. Grimacing with pain, he gasped for breath.

"Leave me alone!" Patrick cried, too angry to be aware that he had gained the momentary advantage.

"Dirty Paddy!" Nick shouted. He edged forward again, but more cautiously, keeping his distance by circling around Patrick.

Heart pounding, Patrick moved the opposite way so that the boys reversed positions. Now it was Nick who had his back to the canal.

"You were lucky, that's all," Nick jeered. "Lucky. Come on, try that again. Come on. I dare you."

Patrick, fists up, panting, inched toward Nick.

"That's it," Nick said. "Come on, take your licking. Come on!" He threw a punch, but it didn't land.

Patrick, trying what had worked before, lowered his head and charged once more. Though this time he took a few blows, he managed to strike Nick again. The boy staggered backward, tottering on the edge of the canal. When Patrick made another feint, Nick recoiled, lost his balance, and fell head over heels into the canal with an enormous splash.

"Help! Help!" he cried as he flailed about in the water. "I can't swim. Help!"

Patrick turned, saw a branch on the ground, and snatched

251

it up. Flinging himself down at the canal bank, he extended it toward Nick. The boy grabbed it and, with Patrick holding on, struggled toward the edge of the canal.

He reached it, found a footing, and began to haul himself out of the water. As soon as Patrick saw Nick was out of danger, he withdrew an even greater distance.

Thoroughly soaked and shivering, Nick, having clambered back to the bank, took a menacing step toward Patrick. "You dirty Irish fighter," he cried, "I'll get you for this. See if I don't."

Nick did take a few steps but quickly gave up.

Patrick, feeling much safer, headed down one street, then another. He wanted to see his sister, to tell her everything about this morning. Suddenly, he stopped. Would Maura even be at Mrs. Hamlyn's house now? Wasn't she seeking work herself? He didn't want to upset her, not now.

Hoping she was having better luck than he had, he turned down a third street.

Chapter 152

Mr. Clemspool Visits the Mill

Y ou might want these," Mr. Shagwell told Mr. Clemspool. He held out two balls of white cotton.

"And what shall I do with them, sir?"

"I suggest you put them in your ears. If you've never been in a mill before, you can't imagine the noise."

"Do you wear them?" Mr. Clemspool asked.

Mr. Shagwell smiled. "I'm used to it."

"Then I'm sure I won't need them either."

"As you wish, sir. Now step this way."

To begin the tour, Mr. Shagwell led his guest into the courtyard. There, he explained how the cotton was shipped from the southern states to Lowell. "Once it's here, sir, the process is quite simple. The cotton is broken up and cleaned. Then it's turned into thread. The thread is woven into cloth. The cloth is shipped to the world, as far away as China.

"We do it all in vast quantities, sir, with great numbers of operatives working in one place. The Lowell system. We are justifiably famous for it."

"And is all this—are all these people—under your control, sir?" Mr. Clemspool asked, truly impressed.

"Each and every one of them! Come along now!"

The mill owner led the Englishman onto the first floor of the large building where the cotton was being unloaded. Mr. Clemspool watched the bales being broken up, after which masses of cotton were worked through carding machines that cleaned the fibers and drew them out into thick slivers.

"Now, sir," said Mr. Shagwell, "I'll show you where the crude thread is made."

They moved to the second floor. Here, the air was humid and the noise of the clacking machinery so tumultuous that Mr. Clemspool felt compelled to shield his ears with his hands. Mr. Shagwell offered the cotton balls again.

Mr. Clemspool shook his head and looked about.

Overhead power belts raced in a continual whir. Other belts looped down like elastic arms to power the machines. He watched a woman move back and forth among the machines, darting—or so it seemed—into their very midst to make adjustments.

While Mr. Shagwell and Mr. Clemspool were so engaged, the overlooker, Mr. Osmundson, approached and doffed his derby. "Good morning, sir," he shouted to Mr. Shagwell over the din. "Gratifying to see you, sir!"

"Mr. Osmundson, this is Mr. Clemspool. A visitor from England."

The two men shook hands.

Mr. Shagwell said, "Show us your best operative, Mr. Osmundson."

"That would be Betsy Howard, sir. Follow me."

The three men made their way among the machines.

"Here she is, sir," said Mr. Osmundson with pride. "Your best."

Betsy Howard was overseeing three machines. Now and again she lifted a full bobbin off one and placed it in a wooden box.

"She can't talk much, sir," Mr. Osmundson said into Mr. Clemspool's ear. "Too busy." The overlooker sidled up behind her. "It's Mr. Shagwell, sweetheart. With a guest."

Without stopping her work, Betsy Howard peered over her shoulder, saw who it was, and flushed.

Mr. Shagwell beckoned Mr. Clemspool closer. "How long have you worked here?" Mr. Shagwell asked his operative in a loud voice.

"Five years, sir."

Mr. Shagwell turned to Mr. Clemspool. "Do you see how loyal the operatives are?" He turned back to his operative. "And have you any complaints?" he asked her.

There was no reply.

"Speak up," Mr. Shagwell urged. "Our visitor from old England needs to know what a free country this is."

Betsy Howard glanced from Mr. Shagwell to Mr. Clemspool to Mr. Osmundson. The overlooker, beaming, nodded. She heard Sarah Grafton, at the next station, cough harshly.

"You'll not suffer for anything you say," Mr. Shagwell persisted. "You have my promise."

The woman looked at the mill owner's gray eyes as if to judge the full measure of his words. Taking a deep breath, she said, "Please, sir, they've speeded up the machines again. They're going much too fast."

Mr. Shagwell's eyes filled with astonishment. His normally pale cheeks turned red. His mane of gray hair seemed to swell. "I beg your pardon!" he exclaimed.

"And the air, sir. It's impossible to breathe with all this cotton flying about. We need it fresher. If we could only open the windows, it'd be so much better."

"Are you suggesting that you know how to operate my mill better than I?" a now indignant Mr. Shagwell cried.

Betsy Howard's face grew ashen. "You asked me to speak, sir, and I'm just saying what's true. We can hardly keep up. With the speed and the heat, it's truly hard."

Mr. Clemspool tried to keep from smirking.

"Complaints in front of a stranger," Mr. Shagwell cried. "A guest! I'll thank you to keep your comments to yourself next time." So saying, he turned on his heel and stalked away.

As he passed the next station, Sarah Grafton was seized by another fit of coughing. Mr. Shagwell stopped and fixed his eyes upon her. "Mr. Osmundson," he cried, pointing, "I want this girl turned off. Do you hear me? Right away! We can't have sickness here. She's contagious!"

Sarah stared at Mr. Shagwell in horror. "Sir, please, you mustn't. . . ."

Mr. Shagwell wheeled about. "Mr. Osmundson! Find a replacement for that girl. Immediately! Mr. Clemspool, this way, please. There's more to see." He marched off, Mr. Clemspool hurrying to keep pace.

For a moment Mr. Osmundson gazed after the mill owner. Then he turned to Betsy Howard. "Oh, my dear, why ever did you say such a thing? You only provoked him. And look what you've gone and done to poor Sarah. Sarah, my dear," he said, hastening to where she stood, dumbstruck. "I'm afraid you must go. There's nothing I can do. I am . . . what can I say . . . terribly sorry."

Speechless, Sarah Grafton fell to weeping. Behind, her machines snarled, tangled, and began to snap threads.

Chapter 153
Maura Goes to the Mill

I do admire your willingness to work, Miss O'Connell," Mrs. Hamlyn said as she guided Maura away from Cabot Street. It was seven-thirty in the morning. "But while it's true we must all toil, you need to know mill life is not easy."

Maura wore one of the dresses from the pile of cast-off garments her landlady had provided. A too-large calico dress, it nonetheless felt clean and comfortable. Not so comfortable were the pair of high shoes she had selected. It had been a long time since Maura had worn shoes, and these were tight. Still, she was grateful to have them and walked as best she could, her shawl wrapped about her. Though nervous, she was excited, hardly minding the cold.

"Faith, Mrs. Hamlyn, I'm sure I can manage," Maura replied stoutly. "And by the Holy Mother, we have only the few dollars my father left us. We can't be living on air."

"When you begin," the woman warned, "they pay very little."

"In Ireland, mistress, a body is lucky to have any money at all."

"Just remember," said Mrs. Hamlyn, "there are other jobs to be had here. In shops. Or as a maid."

"Please, mistress, I should like to do as my father did."

When they entered the Shagwell Mill courtyard, Maura saw many young women sitting, despite the weather, in the open air. They had napkins on their laps, and they were eating. A fewer number of men—sitting separately—were taking their food out of tin pails. There was an air of concentration upon the operatives' faces, almost an urgency, that puzzled Maura.

"They have only a half hour for breakfast," Mrs. Hamlyn explained.

The older woman went directly to the smaller of the brick buildings where a sign, MANAGER'S OFFICE, had been placed on the door. As she was about to knock, she cast an appraising eye over Maura. "You might just smooth your hair back from your face," she said. "And straighten your dress."

Maura did as she was told.

"If they ask you questions, say as little as possible," the woman warned. Then she knocked.

A boy answered. Though he wore a suit and a peaked leather cap, to Maura's eyes he appeared to be no older than Patrick.

"What do you want?" he demanded.

"My name is Mrs. Hamlyn," the woman said. "I should like to speak to Mr. Farrington, please."

"What's it about?" came the response.

Mrs. Hamlyn was determined not to be irritated. "I am seeking employment for this young lady."

The boy squinted up at Maura. "Irish?" he asked.

"She is."

"Well, I don't know. It's not likely," the boy advised. "I'll go see if Mr. Farrington's about."

"You must mention my name," the woman said severely. "It's Mrs. James Hamlyn."

The door slammed in their faces.

Maura, recalling Patrick's story about the boys who picked a fight with him because he was Irish, felt her stomach knot.

"Faith, Mrs. Hamlyn," she whispered, head bowed, "I don't wish to be where I'm not wanted."

"Stuff and nonsense," the woman snorted. "He's just a sassy boy. I don't like such talk. Besides . . ."

The door opened again. "He'll see you both," the boy said. "But only because it's you," he told Mrs. Hamlyn.

Pressing her lips tightly to keep from speaking her thoughts, the woman stepped forward, touching Maura on the arm to encourage her to follow.

They entered a busy office alive with the sounds of scratching pens and turning pages. Clerks, sitting on stools, worked on great ledgers.

Without checking to see if he was being followed, the boy marched toward a door at the far side of the room, rapped on it, and held it open for the two women to pass. "Here's Mrs. Hamlyn, sir."

The room was quite small and lined with piles of papers. A large desk, its surface exceedingly cluttered, stood in the center of the room. Behind the desk sat a man dwarfed by the crowded conditions around him. The look on his face was pinched. His eyes conveyed worry.

When the women entered his office, the man stood up and leaned over his desk, hands down and splayed, rather like a bulldog taking a fighting stance.

"Mrs. Hamlyn," he said brusquely. "Good morning to you."

"Good morning, Mr. Farrington. I trust you are well."

Mr. Farrington shook his head. "Trying to keep our heads above water," he said. "Not the best of times."

"I'm sorry to hear it."

"Well, well, that's of no interest to a lady. How's the mister?"

"As well as can be expected."

"And what can I do for you today?" he asked.

"This is Maura O'Connell. She's a boarder at my house

258

and is seeking employment. She is Irish," Mrs. Hamlyn said firmly. "You might as well know from the first."

"Knew it from the moment you walked in," Mr. Farrington snorted.

"Is there any work to be had?" Mrs. Hamlyn asked.

"Don't know as to the weaving rooms. . . . How old are you, girl?" The question was directed at Maura.

"Fifteen, Your Honor."

"Not educated, I suppose."

"I can read, Your Honor."

His look suggested doubt. "Can you read that?" he asked, pointing across the room at a wall poster.

RULES TO BE OBSERVED
BY THE HANDS EMPLOYED IN
THIS MILL

Listed below were twenty-one rules, each numbered.

"I think so," Maura replied.

"Read number two," Mr. Farrington snapped.

Maura studied the poster and read, " 'Any person coming too late shall be fined as follows: for five minutes, two pennies; ten minutes, four pennies; and fifteen minutes, six pennies.' "

"And the sixteenth?"

" 'The master would recommend that all their workpeople wash themselves every morning, but they shall wash themselves at least twice a week, Monday morning and Thursday morning, and any found not washed will be fined three pennies for each offense.' "

"Good enough," Mr. Farrington admitted. "Try number twelve."

Again Maura read: " 'All persons in our employ shall serve four weeks' notice before leaving their position, but A. Shag-

259

well & Company shall and will turn any person off without notice being given.' "

"All right, that's sufficient," said Mr. Farrington. "You're in luck. This morning an operative in the drawing section left suddenly because of illness. You can start right away at one dollar and fifty cents a week. You'll work under Mr. Osmundson. Yes or no?"

"Yes, please, Your Honor," Maura said eagerly.

"Mind, I only do it for Mrs. Hamlyn," Mr. Farrington said severely, "not you. We're not supposed to take on any more Irish. But I can make exceptions. Just make sure you read, learn, and act by the rest of those regulations. They're posted about. What's your name?"

"Maura O'Connell, Your Honor."

"All right, Maura, on your way out, speak to the door clerk. He'll sign you on and give you a pass. Report to the overlooker, Mr. Osmundson. Second floor of the mill." He sat down and gathered up some papers, making it perfectly clear he was done with them.

After saying good-bye to Mrs. Hamlyn—and hearing some further kindly advice—Maura made her way apprehensively to the second floor of the large building. In her hand she clutched the note she'd been given in the manager's office that would introduce her to the overlooker.

She felt excitement as well as fear. Here she was, her first full day in Lowell, and she would be earning money for herself, Patrick, and Bridy! Life *was* going to get better. Suddenly glad, Maura smiled.

But when she stepped onto the second floor, her smile withered. Before her—in a room far bigger than she'd ever seen before—ranged row upon row of clacking, churning machines. The noise was staggering. Ceilings were laced with whirling power belts of gigantic proportions. The floorboards upon which she stood trembled. The air was so hot and cloudy, she found it hard to breathe.

How, she asked herself, could she exist, much less work, in such a place? What did she know of machines, she who had never worked with any machine before, *ever?*

When a wave of nausea swept through her, Maura squeezed her hands so tightly, her nails bit into her flesh. The pain served to steady her.

From somewhere—Maura did not see him coming—Mr. Osmundson appeared.

"Can I help you, sweetheart?" he cried, his voice loud enough to be heard over the noise.

Maura, incapable of speech, presented the note she'd been given with an unsteady hand. Mr. Osmundson read it.

"New operative, eh? Maura O'Connell," he said, looking her over. "Irish, I suppose?"

Feeling uncomfortable, Maura nodded even as she stared at her feet.

The overlooker started to frown but caught himself and smiled. "Well, you're needed. The girl you're replacing got ill, poor thing. Ever work in a mill before, sweetheart?"

Maura managed to shake her head.

"Nothing to it," Mr. Osmundson said. "The other girls will be happy to teach you. I'll put you next to the best. My Betsy. Come along, my dear."

Full of fear, Maura followed, passing among rows of machines, painfully aware of the eyes of the other operatives appraising her.

"All right, my dear," cried Mr. Osmundson as he approached Betsy Howard's station. "Here's Maura O'Connell, Sarah's replacement."

Betsy Howard glanced at Maura over her shoulder. Brief as the look was, Maura caught the unmistakable glint of anger in the woman's eyes. The girl shivered.

Mr. Osmundson, noticing nothing, said, "Betsy, darling, it'll be your job to teach Maura what she needs to know. Maura, Betsy is the best girl we've got. Mind her, and you can't go wrong. Step over here, my dear," he called to Maura. "These three machines are yours."

Maura, avoiding Betsy Howard's hostile eyes, stood helplessly before one of the drawing machines assigned to her. With its rollers and wires, its seemingly random strands of cotton poking out here, there, everywhere, it was so incomprehensibly complex, she felt humiliated. Tears came to her eyes. Wanting to run, she looked about.

To the right and to the left, young women seemed to know what they were doing, though what it was Maura had not the slightest idea. One or two of them—those nearest—turned from their machines and looked at her now with friendly faces. One went so far as to smile and nod. Somehow, Maura managed a small smile in return.

The realization that women were doing all the work on the floor gave Maura a spark of hope. If they could do it, might not she?

There was a tap on her arm. Betsy Howard was by her side.

"Look here, Miss Paddy," she said sharply, "you're replacing as good a friend as ever lived. Turned off because I was stupid enough to open my mouth. Her only fault was being ill from this air." She made a gesture that encompassed everything in the huge room.

"And you're Irish, aren't you?" the operative went on. "So you might as well know, I don't like Paddies, and I don't intend to like you either."

"Yes, miss," Maura whispered, caught up in a swirl of shame and fury all at once.

"The first thing you need to know is there's no place for a soft voice here. Now let me show you how this goes." She moved toward the first machine.

Maura closed her eyes briefly, crossed herself, and followed the woman.

Chapter 154
Bridy Alone

*A*fter a good night's sleep, Bridy had washed herself with cold water, then dressed in the clothing Maura had selected for her. Old though it was, the girl had never had a finer dress.

Downstairs she was treated to a breakfast of Indian bread, tea, savory sausage, and beans. Happily full, she wrapped herself in a shawl and went outside to sit on the wood front steps.

It was a bright day and, though cool, considerably warmer than the day before. The Hamlyn house, situated on the northern side of Cabot Street, was bathed in sunlight. From time to time, as Bridy sat playing with her fingers or singing snatches of tunes, people passed by. Sometimes they greeted her, sometimes not. When they did, the girl responded with a shy, friendly greeting of her own.

Bridy did think of her parents and her brothers, but already she'd begun to sense that they belonged to a life that was gone. A certain vagueness about them had crept like mist into her mind. Though still uncertain exactly where or what America was, she accepted that she was there. Maura was near, wasn't she? And Maura had become the most important person in her life, the one whom Bridy loved and trusted.

After an hour or so of sitting and dreaming, Bridy realized that someone was standing between her and the sun. She looked up.

It was Mr. Jenkins.

"Do you live here?" he asked, speaking calmly so as not to alarm the girl.

"Yes, Your Honor," Bridy whispered.

"And are you a guest of Mr. James Hamlyn?"

Bridy was not at all sure she understood the question.

"I won't harm you, girl," Mr. Jenkins said. "Just tell me who you are and what business you have with Mr. Hamlyn."

Bridy hardly knew what to say.

"I had a child your age," the man informed her. "And so I say to you, beware of James Hamlyn. Indeed, my dear, you must give him a message from me. Can you do a simple thing like that?"

Bridy nodded.

"Good girl. Tell him that Jeremiah Jenkins came to call. Tell him that I haven't forgotten. That he shouldn't forget me or my child. Can you repeat what I just told you?" he asked.

"What?" Bridy whispered tremulously.

"Give Mr. Hamlyn that message." Mr. Jenkins attempted to smile.

"Mr. Jer—," Bridy stammered.

"Jeremiah," the man coached.

"Jeremiah Jenkins," Bridy managed to say.

Word by word Mr. Jenkins led her through the complete message two more times. "Now please tell the man exactly what I said. But, my dear, because I like children, I urge you to get away from this house. It's a bad house."

With that said, Mr. Jenkins strode off.

Bridy, upset and puzzled, watched him go. She was not at all sure what he had said, much less what the words meant. She knew Mrs. Hamlyn, of course, but also knew she'd gone off with Maura. As for Mrs. Hamlyn's husband, she had no knowledge of him at all.

It was the housemaid who found Bridy crying in the hallway.

"And what would be the matter with you, missy?" the young woman inquired kindly. "Are you fretting for your sister now?"

Bridy shook her head.

"Then what is it, pet? You can tell me, I'm sure."

"It was a man . . . ," Bridy sobbed.

"What kind of man?"

"He was asking for . . . Mr. . . . Hamlyn."

"For the master?"

Bridy nodded. "He said I should be telling him something."

"Well then, so you can. Nothing to be afraid of at all. He's a kindly man, though he must stay in his bed with his affliction. Come now, I'll take you to him." Giving her hand to the child, the servant led Bridy along the hallway, then knocked softly on a door.

Hearing a "Yes," she poked her head into the room and explained who Bridy was and why they were calling.

"There! You're welcome to go on in, my dear. And don't you worry none now." The maid led the frightened girl into the room.

Mr. Hamlyn was sitting up in his high bed. To Bridy, he looked very strange in his nightcap, jacket, and gloves.

"Here's the girl, Your Honor," the housemaid said.

Mr. Hamlyn looked down. "Come along closer, my dear," he called. "There's nothing to be afraid about, my girl. It's just that I can't get out of bed."

The maid gave Bridy a gentle shove forward. Bridy took two steps but stopped.

"All right now," Mr. Hamlyn said, "be good enough to tell me what this message was."

Bridy closed her eyes. "Mr. Jerry Jenkins . . ."

"Who?" cried Mr. Hamlyn, so altering his tone that Bridy jumped.

"Jerry-myra Jenkins . . . ," Bridy managed to say.

"I don't believe it!" Mr. Hamlyn murmured, and he pulled off his gloves and nightcap as if they were impediments to his hearing. "Go on," he said with barely suppressed impatience. "What did he say?"

Slowly, awkwardly, and with much coaching, Bridy repeated the message. When she'd done, Mr. Hamlyn lay back on his pillows and closed his eyes. He looked grim.

"Will that be all, master?" the maid asked.

Mr. Hamlyn opened his eyes. "You may go, Kate. Let the girl stay."

After whispering words of encouragement into Bridy's ear, the maid slipped out of the room, closing the door behind her.

For a long time Mr. Hamlyn—lips pursed, brow furrowed—remained silent, lost in thought. Bridy, most uncomfortable, scratched a leg. At last the man looked down at her and smiled. "What's your name?" he asked kindly.

"Bridy."

"Bridy, I'd like you to do something for me."

"Yes, please," Bridy whispered.

"You'll know the man—the one who gave you the message—if you see him again, won't you?"

Bridy nodded.

"He's an evil man, Bridy. A man who intends me harm. I want you to watch for him. If you see him again, you're to tell me right away. Do you understand? At once. Can you do that?"

"Yes, Your Honor."

"Mind, you mustn't fail. I'm counting on you."

"Yes, sir."

"Good."

As soon as Bridy left the room, Mr. Hamlyn set about writing a note to Mr. Tolliver.

Chapter 155
Mr. Drabble Reaches
Another Stage

*I*t was midday when Laurence, Mr. Grout, and Mr. Drabble trudged into Lowell. Having walked fifteen miles on each of two days—sleeping one night in a warm barn with the permission of a farmer—they were tired, chilled, but in reasonable spirits.

"It's all very well to be here," Mr. Drabble observed. "But now what do we do?"

Mr. Grout said, "We 'ead for a place I know, that's wot. The Spindle City 'Otel and Oyster Bar."

"And how, sir, do you know about this establishment?"

"That's where that Mr. Jenkins—the one 'oo promised me a quick job—told me to go."

Mr. Drabble shook his head. "Without telling you what the job is."

"See 'ere, Drabble, as long as it means money, we can't be too particular, can we? Yer the one who said we should walk 'ere, and yer right. We don't 'ave much."

"Sometimes, my friend," said Mr. Drabble, "I think you are too trusting."

"It's me new nature," Mr. Grout returned agreeably. "But if we're goin' to find Clemspool and get that money back, risk is wot we 'ave to take. Ain't that so, laddie?" He clasped Laurence's shoulder by way of showing him that their partnership was very much in effect.

"I think so," agreed Laurence, who wanted only to get to a warm room.

"I knew yer would," said Mr. Grout. With that under-standing, he approached a working man and asked for and received information regarding the location of the hotel. Calling on his companions to follow, he started off.

Their way took them along busy Merrimack Street. Sud-denly Mr. Drabble stopped.

"Great heavens!" he cried. "Look!" Across the way, among some business buildings, was a structure that had the distinct look of a church, though its steeple had been lopped off. A large sign stretched across its facade.

BOSTON MUSEUM AND STOCK
COMPANY
Strictly Moral Plays
Tonight: LOVE'S SACRIFICE
Seats 25c–50c
8:00 P.M.
Roderick Wyman, Manager-Actor

Coming soon! The Tragedy of
HAMLET

"They do have theaters in America!" Mr. Drabble ex-claimed with delight. "There may be a place for me after all!"

Mr. Grout studied the sign. "I can't make it all out," he confessed. "Yer have to read it to me."

Mr. Drabble obliged, explaining that *Hamlet* was a play by Shakespeare.

Mr. Grout whooped with excitement. "Mr. Drabble," he said, "as soon as they know yer 'ere in town, they'll be desperate to 'ave yer. I congratulate yer on yer success."

Mr. Drabble paled. Thin as he was, he seemed to dwindle further before Mr. Grout's and Laurence's eyes. "Well . . . I do have to meet them first," he managed to say, his low voice becoming almost childlike in its meekness. "But, yes, of course, I can hope for the best."

"Never mind 'ope," Mr. Grout urged. "Yer need to go to them right away."

"*Now?*" Mr. Drabble cried with alarm.

"Yer want the work, don't yer? And yer know 'ow fine yer are. Why, they'll be beggin' yer to take part soon as they clap eyes on yer, won't they? Besides, it'll pay for some food and lodgin' while we're 'ere."

"Well, yes," the actor felt obliged to agree. "I suppose."

"Mr. Drabble," Mr. Grout enthused, "a man doesn't 'ave much in the way of time except the right now, does 'e? Take 'old of yer chance. Don't yer worry about the laddie and me. We'll take us a room at the 'otel to get out of this weather. Yer can join us as soon as they shake yer 'and."

"But . . . but I'm not sure I'm . . . prepared."

" 'Ere now, Mr. Drabble, yer the best in the world."

The actor turned red behind his curtain of hair. "But . . . I've never been on a real stage before," he blurted out. "Oh, I've tried," he fairly wept, "and I do know the words well— perfectly, in fact—but that has never been enough. I think it's because I don't look tragic. I look the fool. But believe me, friends, inside I *am* tragic!" He hid his face with his hands.

"Now see 'ere, Drabble," Mr. Grout said with gentle gruffness, "don't go blowin' yerself down. What might be foolin' in England is more than likely tragic 'ere in America."

Mr. Drabble, clutching his volume of Shakespeare, took a deep breath and stared across at the theater. He swallowed hard. "But . . ."

"Yer 'ave to," Mr. Grout insisted. "It's yer fate."

"Well then," replied the actor meekly, "who am I to contradict my most loyal audience?" He bowed low, straightened up, then commenced a painfully slow crossing of the street.

Nervous to the point of trembling, the actor approached the theater building. He tried the front door but—to his great relief—found it locked. He turned about. Mr. Grout and Laurence were watching.

"There's another door by the side!" Mr. Grout bellowed.

Feeling he had no choice, Mr. Drabble walked to the right where he saw an open door. Mr. Grout, nodding by way of encouragement, waved him on.

Heart knocking against his thin chest, Mr. Drabble entered a shadowy hallway hung with forests, oceans, castles, cliffs, and raging rivers—all painted on canvas. At the far end he heard the sound of voices. Struggling to control his anxiety, Mr. Drabble crept forward.

The room he entered was large and bare, striped by multicolored light streaming through a stained-glass window high above. On an ill-swept floor six men and two women, blank faces expressing boredom, shuffling feet and twitching fingers suggesting irritation, were listening to a man.

This man was short, fat, and toothless, his bulk made even more voluminous by the velvet cape that reached from his thick shoulders to his buckled shoes. "It is art we serve, dear friends, *art*," the man was saying. "Not money. For you to ask for more is—" He paused, becoming aware that someone had come into the room. Instead of simply turning, he gathered up his cape and spun about so that the velvet swirled around him.

"Sir?" he inquired. "Do you have business with me?"

Mr. Drabble threw himself into the deepest of bows, so low his long fingers scraped the floor. Then he righted himself and threw back the hair from his face. "Sir," he began tentatively, "my name is Horatio Drabble, late of the Liverpool stage, just arrived from England."

"Roderick Wyman at your service," the American returned in a voice that boomed like a cannon. "But what, sir, might I do for you?"

"I've . . . I've only just come . . . to this fair city," Mr. Drabble stammered, "and . . . seeing the sign before your theater, I thought . . . perhaps that . . . I might make application to be part of your . . . illustrious company."

"What roles, sir, are you familiar with?"

"I know *Hamlet* in its entirety. But I am . . . best suited to play the . . . noble prince himself."

"Are you, indeed!" Mr. Wyman cried. "Let us observe act three, scene one," he said.

Mr. Drabble braced himself, looked heavenward, and extended one arm high. "To be, or not to be: that is the question: whether—"

"I'm terribly sorry, sir," Mr. Wyman interrupted, "that's not our style. It may do for the Old World but not the New. In any case, *I* am to play the role of Hamlet. I thank you for your interest and encourage you to become a member of the noble audience."

So saying, the manager swirled about and once again began to harangue his company.

Mr. Drabble was too stunned to do anything but stand where he was. But as Mr. Wyman continued to ignore him, the English actor turned and made his way sadly out of the theater. Oh, why, he kept repeating to himself, did I ever leave Liverpool!

He glanced across the street. To his relief Laurence and Mr. Grout had moved on.

Utterly dejected, Mr. Drabble trudged along the city streets, heading where he cared not. As far as he was concerned, his acting career was over. He would have to find something else to do with his life, a life that had become a tragedy without an audience.

271

"Everyone," Mr. Drabble moaned, "has a place in life but me."

Indeed, he would have to forget about Maura O'Connell. Oh, if only he could see her again. If only he could render her some service! If only he could find some way to prove his love for her. . . .

When he reached a canal, Mr. Drabble stared into its flowing waters for a long time. Tenderly, as though laying a flower on a grave, he set his volume of Shakespeare on the bank, cried, wiped at his tears, and slowly walked away.

Chapter 156

Mr. Clemspool and the Money

M r. Clemspool, fresh from his morning's tour of the Shagwell Cotton Mill, entered the Merrimack Valley Consolidated Bank and Land Company building in central Lowell.

"I need a safe-deposit box," he informed a gentleman who inquired if he might be of service. In an inner office, he was introduced to a Mr. Artridge, a pale-faced, thin-lipped, clean-shaven man of middle years who informed Mr. Clemspool—as if he were sharing one of nature's deep secrets—that he was vice president of the bank.

"I've only just come from England, sir," Mr. Clemspool explained grandly, "with a large quantity of British bills. I should like to change the pounds into dollars and provide for their safekeeping in a locked security box—with my own key, of course."

Nothing could be easier. Papers were produced, the relevant information recorded, fees explained, and Mr. Clemspool was gently asked for the English money.

With silent dexterity Mr. Artridge counted the pile, then pronounced—as if it were another secret—the American value as four thousand six hundred and thirty-two dollars and sixteen cents.

"A tidy sum, sir," the vice president said. "May I inquire . . . will you be staying with us long?"

Mr. Clemspool smiled. "I'm thinking of investing here."

Mr. Artridge folded his well-manicured hands together. "We might be able to give advice," he suggested.

"And I should be happy to receive it."

"Were you thinking of any particular kind of investments?"

Mr. Clemspool fingered the air and then, as it were, plucked out the words "Cotton mills."

The merest hint of a smile played about Mr. Artridge's lips.

"Say," continued Mr. Clemspool, "the Shagwell Cotton Mill."

Mr. Artridge frowned.

"Not sound?" Mr. Clemspool returned, quick to take the hint.

"There are . . . better prospects. Far better."

"Can you say more?"

The banker stared at his hands and then lifted his clear blue eyes. "In financial difficulties," he said.

Mr. Clemspool responded with a sage nod. "Sir, I have heard your advice and shall take advantage of it."

More papers were signed, a receipt given, the money deposited in a box—with a little held out for daily use. The box was then placed in the bank's vault and the key handed over to Mr. Clemspool.

"That key, sir, is your pass to the vault. You need not speak to me to gain entry. Merely show it to the teller. You'll notice it has the bank's name engraved upon it along with the number of the box. It is now your responsibility. Do keep it in a safe place."

"I shall," said Mr. Clemspool, taking the key tenderly and stowing it with care in an inner vest pocket.

When Mr. Clemspool emerged from the bank onto Merrimack Street, he was filled with a serene sense that everything was moving along just as he wanted. He had secured Lord Kirkle's money for himself. He was settled in Mr. Shagwell's house. He had discovered just how weak the mill owner's position was. The perfect moment for squeezing the man for all he had. "Get them while they're weak," he murmured with relish. Perhaps, he thought, he might even take over the mill himself. Intensely gratified by his own intelligence, judgment, and luck, he patted the bank key in his vest pocket.

Mr. Clemspool, suffused with a deep contentment, sauntered along busy Merrimack Street, looking into shop windows, watching the crowds. He even purchased a newspaper—*The People's Voice.*

"Blacken your boots!"

Hearing the cry, Mr. Clemspool looked about. When he saw a shoe-shine boy, the Englishman decided that polished shoes were *exactly* in keeping with his mood. With a flamboyant gesture, he hailed the boy and requested that his boots be cleaned as well as blackened.

"What's your name?" Mr. Clemspool asked expansively.

"Jeb Grafton, sir."

"Now, Jeb, my boy, I want those shoes extrabright."

Jeb was only too happy to oblige. After suggesting that Mr. Clemspool lean back against a building and place his foot upon his box, he set to work.

Mr. Clemspool opened his newspaper and began to read, casually skipping from item to item, from time to time lowering the pages to gaze along the street. He was just about to conclude that Lowell was quite the perfect place for him when he saw—walking side by side and coming his way—Laurence and Mr. Grout.

Chapter 157

Mr. Clemspool Takes Action

Great Heavens! Matthew Clemspool was so stunned by the sight that he nearly jumped into the air. As it was, his foot slipped off the shoe-shine box, and Jeb had to replace it firmly.

Panicky, Mr. Clemspool hastily lifted the newspaper to hide his face, then peeked out from behind it again. Mr. Grout, he noted, was no longer dressed as a gentleman but looked like an American workingman. As for Laurence, though he seemed thinner and paler than Mr. Clemspool remembered him in the ship's stateroom, searching for the money, there was no question as to who he was. The mark on his right cheek—just barely visible—was sufficient proof of that.

Mr. Clemspool's reaction passed quickly from panic to fury. That these two should be together, looking for all the world as if they were friends, was—in his view—a betrayal of the highest order! His whole body quivered with indignation.

Questions poured in upon him. How did they come to be together? How did they get to Lowell? Why were they here, of all places? As far as Mr. Clemspool was concerned, to ask *that* question was to answer it: They were pursuing him and the money! Oh, the effrontery!

Nonetheless, it took but a second for Mr. Clemspool to grasp that all his plans for Lowell would be in jeopardy with those two lurking about. The boy—alone—was not a danger. Who would listen to him? But his powerful father, Lord Kirkle . . .

As for Toby Grout, the young man knew a great deal too much about Brother's Keeper. If people started to listen to him and believed what they heard—that Mr. Clemspool had spirited away many boys from England—Mr. Clemspool would not be able to stay in Lowell.

Mr. Grout and Laurence passed only a few feet from the agitated man. Once they moved on, Mr. Clemspool lowered the newspaper—such was his rage that his fingers shook and made the paper rattle. He watched them enter the Spindle City Hotel and Oyster Bar.

"That will be two cents," Jeb informed him.

With a start, the Englishman thrust his hand into a pocket, found some coins—inspected them to make sure he was not giving away too much—and handed them to the boy.

Mr. Clemspool pondered. Should he flee? That was the last thing he wished to do. What with Mr. Shagwell ripe for plucking, he was about to become a truly wealthy man. But to achieve his goal, he would have to get rid of Laurence and Mr. Grout and do it fast—lest they interfere.

"Something the matter, mister?" Jeb asked.

"Quickly," Mr. Clemspool said. "Go into that hotel."

"The Spindle?"

"See if a man with an eye patch and a boy are registering to stay. I'll give you ten cents! Hurry."

Jeb leaped up and ran for the hotel entrance. When he was gone, Mr. Clemspool tried frantically to think of a way to get rid of the two.

Breathless, Jeb returned. "They were signing in," he announced.

"Villains . . . ," hissed Mr. Clemspool. He looked down at the boy. "Is there a constable headquarters somewhere near about?"

"A what?" Jeb asked.

"A law officer. A . . ."

"A policeman?"

"Exactly."

"There's a station just over to Worthen Street."

"Can you take me there?"

"I suppose I could."

"I'll pay you. But hurry. This is an emergency!"

Chapter 158

In the Spindle City Hotel

With the expectation that he would soon have money in his pocket from his job with Mr. Jenkins—and that Mr. Drabble would be earning even more—Toby Grout requested a decent room from the man at the registration desk.

"Do you 'ave a gent by the name of Jenkins stoppin' 'ere?" he inquired, once matters of accommodation had been settled.

"We do indeed, but I don't think he's in at the moment," was the reply.

"When 'e does come, yer can tell 'im Toby Grout's arrived and ready to work."

"I certainly will."

The room Mr. Grout took was rather small and, despite a window, quite airless. With four beds it looked more like a dormitory than a hotel room. The mattresses, stretched over rope webbing, were hardly more than thick blankets. The pillows were thin as doormats.

"Yer can take yer pick of the beds," Mr. Grout urged Laurence. "Whatever yer want."

Laurence chose one and sat on it.

"I'm goin' to take meself a walk to see what I can do about findin' Clemspool," Mr. Grout announced. "Do yer want to come along?"

"I'll stay here," Laurence said, thinking he would rather go out on his own and start looking for Patrick.

"Suit yerself," agreed Mr. Grout. "I suspect Drabble will be along after a while. Then we can celebrate 'is success."

When Mr. Grout left, Laurence remained sitting on the bed, the first time since he had left the bottom hold on the ship that he'd been alone.

He took a deep breath. So many extraordinary things had happened to him. He thought of that time—how long ago it seemed!—in his father's study, where he'd suffered his brother's cruelty. He thought of his flight, his days in Liverpool, the long, lonely voyage. Yet here he was in America. That very day he had walked fifteen winter miles. He had become friends with a London thief. Truly, he was no longer what he had been. Then he thought about what Mr. Grout had promised—the return of his father's money.

What would he do if they actually did get the money back from Mr. Clemspool? Would he return to England? Should he? Laurence had to acknowledge he had no answers. Instead, he thought about Patrick, happy to think his friend was not far away. And though he was eager to start looking for him, the long walk of the past two days, the excitement, had taken its toll. With a yawn, he lay down and fell into a sleep.

Chapter 159
Sir Albert Comes Across

The *Yorkshire*, true to her reputation as the fastest ship in the North Atlantic fleet, had crossed the ocean in twenty-seven days, a near record. Sir Albert Kirkle, slouching over the quarterdeck rail, gazed across the bay at the city of Boston. From out of his greatcoat sleeves, his hands dangled as if they were marionette hands cut from their strings.

For the young lord it had been an excessively boring voyage. Even the constant good if chilly weather held no pleasure for him. While he had been keenly interested in the plentiful food available at the captain's table, he had kept to himself. It was much too distasteful to explain the reasons for his voyage. He was also too lazy to lie about it.

Now, as Sir Albert contemplated the American city that rose before him, he felt the annoying obligation to concoct some strategy to find Laurence. After all, though Lord Kirkle said he was not to return to England without the boy, Sir Albert's only reason for going to America was to make sure his brother *did not* return. No, he had no intention of sharing his father's money with anyone.

But the United States was immense. No saying where Laurence actually was. It might be impossible to find him. That, mused Albert, was his great hope. How much better it would be if the boy disappeared on his own—without any assistance from him.

But, if assistance was what it required to keep the boy on this side of the Atlantic, assistance was exactly what he was prepared to give. And that meant finding Mr. Clemspool, since the man claimed he was holding Laurence. Furthermore, Sir Albert assumed that Clemspool would—for a price—be willing to *do* something about the boy.

Alas, Albert's only clue to Clemspool's whereabouts was the unfortunate letter that the proprietor of Brother's Keeper had written to him and that his father had intercepted. Clemspool was reachable through a Mr. Ambrose Shagwell of Lowell, Massachusetts.

Albert wished he could avoid this Shagwell fellow entirely, but his father had seen the letter. If Lord Kirkle made contact with the American and discovered Albert had not called upon him . . . No, he must see the man.

The young lord had taken the trouble to learn that the city of Lowell was but a short distance from Boston, hardly more than an hour's railway ride. First thing tomorrow, he supposed, he would have to go. How boring!

Chapter 160
Mr. Clemspool Complains

A nd how much do you make a day blacking boots?" Mr. Clemspool asked Jeb as the boy led him to the police station.

Jeb pulled at his cap and looked up at Mr. Clemspool suspiciously. "How come you want to know?"

"Because I wish to employ you."

"Doing what?"

"To watch someone. But how much do you earn?" the Englishman asked impatiently.

Jeb pondered the question. That morning, just before he was supposed to go out onto the streets to work, his mother had come back from the mill with the terrible news that she had been turned off. Nothing her husband or Jeb could say or do would comfort her. When Jeb finally took up his shoe-shine box, he left with the dismal realization that he was the only one in the family who was bringing home any money.

"Come, come," Mr. Clemspool pressed. "What do you earn, boy?"

Jeb, nervous about giving too high a figure, said, "I've made twenty-five cents."

"Excellent," said Mr. Clemspool. "I will pay you"—he poked about in the air—"twenty cents for your time. But you must wait for me while I speak to the police. Do I make myself clear?"

"I guess so," Jeb replied, trying not to show just how thrilled he was by the offer.

Jeb led Mr. Clemspool to a small nondescript brick building with little to suggest its function other than a sign over the dark green door:

LOWELL CITY POLICE

"Wait here," Mr. Clemspool said.

"I will," the boy promised.

It was a dingy room into which Mr. Clemspool stepped. Four oil lamps with smoky chimneys sat one each on four old, scarred desks. These were placed behind a wooden railing that ran around the room in the shape of a large U, effectively keeping callers, such as Mr. Clemspool, at bay.

Three of the desks were unoccupied. Behind the fourth sat Mr. Tolliver, reading a stack of mail. In his hands was a note from Mr. Hamlyn. Seeing Mr. Clemspool, he lowered it. "Yes, sir, what can I do for you?"

"I need to speak to a police officer."

The man nodded. "You are, sir. The name is Tolliver. I'm captain here. May I help you?"

"My name, sir, is Matthew Clemspool, recently arrived from London, England."

"And welcome you are, sir."

"I am the guest of Mr. Ambrose Shagwell."

"Of Shagwell Cotton Mill Company?"

"I suppose he is," said Mr. Clemspool with a show of indifference.

Mr. Tolliver sat a little straighter in his chair. "Very well, sir, how does this fact pertain to the police?"

"It is," Mr. Clemspool allowed, "somewhat embarrassing. On the ship upon which I came to America, the *Robert Peel*, out of Liverpool, I found myself harassed by a fellow passenger. His name is Toby Grout."

"What do you mean, *harassed?*"

"I'm sure you know how it is, sir. On the ship there was some card playing. This Mr. Grout, whom I assure you I never met before, swore he would have his revenge after losing some trifling sums of money to me. He is not—to make my point precisely—a gentleman."

"And?" a puzzled Mr. Tolliver prompted again.

"Well, sir, he has followed me to your fair city, no doubt with the intent of doing me bodily harm."

"*Has* he done you bodily harm?"

"Not yet," Mr. Clemspool conceded. "But why else would he follow me here?"

"No doubt your Mr. Grout would have a different story."

"Thieves and beggars usually do," Mr. Clemspool acknowledged with an easy smile. "He did brag about being a thief in London."

"Describe the fellow."

Mr. Clemspool did so.

"Do you know where he's staying?"

"I certainly do. The Spindle City Hotel."

Mr. Tolliver frowned, picked up Mr. Hamlyn's letter, then put it down. "Ever hear of a man named Jeremiah Jenkins?" he inquired.

"I'm afraid I've not had the pleasure."

"He stays there."

Mr. Clemspool shrugged.

"Sir," Mr. Tolliver said, "what exactly would you like me to do for you?"

"This Toby Grout is dangerous. I am concerned about my safety. I should like you to apprehend him."

"Will you file an official complaint?"

"Of course."

Mr. Tolliver offered a form to the Englishman. "Just fill this in, and I shall be able to proceed."

Pen in hand, Mr. Clemspool set down what he had told the policeman, to wit, that he was being followed and harassed by a dangerous English brute. After signing it and handing the paper over, he took his leave.

Mr. Tolliver gazed after him, then examined the complaint. It all seemed suspicious to him. An Englishman—an associate of Mr. Shagwell, or so he claimed—complaining, in Lowell, about a petty London thief? This Mr. Grout had not yet *done* anything. Mr. Clemspool's story was hard to believe. Yet, Mr. Tolliver thought, there must be something here. This Clemspool fellow would bear watching.

The police captain reached for the rest of his morning's mail and noticed a particularly elegant envelope addressed to "The Lowell Police Headquarters." He opened it and unfolded an embossed piece of fine paper upon which was engraved:

THE EMBASSY OF THE COURT OF ST. JAMES

A short note followed:

283

It was signed by the British ambassador.

Outside the police station Jeb was waiting.

"Very well, young man," Mr. Clemspool said to the boy when he had drawn him away from the police station, "listen well. There's a boy staying in that hotel—"

"The Spindle City?"

"Exactly."

"I need to have that boy watched. You shall be the one to do it and keep me informed about him. Can you do that?"

Jeb considered the man. "You going to pay me?"

"Of course I shall! And well too." The Englishman fished in his pocket, drew out some coins, and gave Jeb a twenty-five-cent piece. "Here's some payment in advance." He went on to describe Laurence as he had seen him on the street. "Do you think you can recognize him?"

Jeb, excited by the promise of making more money, asked, "And you say he's got a mark on his cheek, here, right?"

"You are a smart boy," Mr. Clemspool said, patting the boy on the shoulder. "Go back to that hotel entrance. If he comes out, stick with him. If he remains within, I shall want to know that too. It's most important you get with him and find out what he's doing here in Lowell.

"Now I shall come by the hotel entrance at eight this evening. You will give a full report. Do you understand all this?"

"Yes, sir, I do."

"Good. Do as I ask and you will continue to be well paid. Young man, consider yourself lucky to be in my employ."

"What's your name?"

"Mr. Matthew Clemspool, gentleman, from England. Can you grasp the importance of that?"

"Yes, sir, Mr. Clemspool, I can."

After watching Mr. Clemspool go off, Jeb looked at the coins he had received with pleasure and relief. Maybe his mother could feel a little better now. Committed to earning lots more, he headed back to the Spindle City Hotel and Laurence.

As for Mr. Clemspool, he had fully recovered his confidence. The police would deal with Mr. Grout. And as for Laurence, he would take care of the brat himself.

Indeed, Mr. Clemspool was so confident—striding resolutely along—he had not the slightest notion that Mr. Tolliver was following him.

Chapter 161
Mr. Grout Takes His Walk

Toby Grout, having left Laurence in the hotel room, made his way down to the hotel lobby. Once there, he searched for Mr. Jenkins but found no trace. He did inquire again at the main desk, yet gained no further information as to the man's whereabouts.

So Mr. Grout put his mind to what he considered more important business, the finding of Clemspool. And for that, he needed to find Ambrose Shagwell.

The attendant—a young man with his hair slicked down—asked, "That the Mr. Shagwell who owns the mill?"

" 'E did say 'e ran a mill 'ere in Lowell," Mr. Grout acknowledged. "So I suppose it's 'im."

The young man examined Mr. Grout with some amusement. "And what might be your business with him?" he could not resist inquiring.

"Yer might say 'e's an old friend of mine, that's what," the one-eyed man said with the utmost seriousness. "Where can I find 'im?"

"At his mill, I suppose," came the reply. "Not far from the Swamp Locks and Pautucket Canal."

After getting more specific instructions, Mr. Grout set off and reached the mill gates in a short time. The size and noise of the mill not only took him by surprise but made him uneasy. Perhaps he had misjudged Mr. Shagwell. Perhaps the man *was* as important as he'd claimed. Mr. Grout began to wish he had not exchanged his London clothing.

Then he recalled his vow to retrieve Laurence Kirkle's money and acknowledged that there was little choice except to press on.

He found the mill yard an exceedingly busy place. Many workers—women and men both—passed to and fro, and each and every one of them, or so it seemed to Mr. Grout, was intent upon some duty or other. He hailed the first man to come near him. " 'Ere now, can yer tell me where I can find a Mr. Ambrose Shagwell?"

The man looked up at Mr. Grout. "The owner?" he asked.

"That's 'im."

"You might look in the office building," the man said, indicating the smaller of the brick structures.

After thanking the man, Mr. Grout went directly to the building indicated. Seeing but one door, he knocked. A boy looked out. When he saw Mr. Grout, he scowled.

"What do you want?" he demanded.

"If yer don't mind, laddie, I'm lookin' for a Mr. Shagwell."

"And who are you?" the boy asked in such a tone that it was perfectly clear he did not think Mr. Grout was much.

"I'm a friend of 'is."

"You and George Washington!" the boy scoffed.

"Just give 'im me name, laddie," Mr. Grout said menacingly. "Grout. Toby Grout."

The boy was not impressed. "He can't be bothered."

"Can't 'e now?"

"No," the boy said, and shut the door in Mr. Grout's face.

Vexed and rather nonplussed, Mr. Grout tried to decide what to do. Perhaps he could discover where Mr. Shagwell lived. It might be easier to see him there. In the meantime he made up his mind to return to the hotel and search out Mr. Jenkins. Yet when he reached the hotel, all he found was a note:

Meet me at the Cotton House Tavern.
Hurd Street. 8 P.M. J. Jenkins

Feeling hungry after all his efforts, Mr. Grout repaired to the bar, ordered some food, and struggled to read his message.

Chapter 162

A Meeting at the Mill

W ell, sir," said Mr. Shagwell, "you lost no time in coming." In his office the mill owner was sitting behind his massive desk, fingers linked over his bulky stomach as he leaned back in his chair the better to consider Mr. Jeremiah Jenkins.

Mr. Jenkins nodded. "You've been away too long, Mr. Shagwell," he said. "I'm not so sure you know what's been happening at your own business."

The mill owner gestured amiably toward a chair. "Then you must tell me."

Mr. Jenkins took the proffered chair, then bowed his head as if gathering strength for what he needed to say. After a few moments he looked up. "Mr. Shagwell, sir," he began, "talk is all very well in its place. But people need to see something that will demonstrate our power."

"Ah, sir, you're always in a hurry," Mr. Shagwell returned.

Mr. Jenkins shook his head. "While you were gone, sir, Irish have been taken on at your mill."

Mr. Shagwell stopped smiling. He opened his hands as if to show he held nothing secret. "As you said, I have been away."

"But now that you're back, I presume you'll put a stop to it."

Mr. Shagwell ran his fingers through his mane of gray hair, thrummed them, and said, "I may or I may not, sir. My business associates have had reasons—"

"Hang your reasons!" Mr. Jenkins burst out. "You're betraying your own countrymen. What about the Order of the Star-spangled Banner and your oath to that organization?"

"Keep your voice down, Mr. Jenkins," the mill owner urged, then continued after a thoughtful pause. "Sir, secret oaths are all well and good. But the crucial fact is, the mill's earnings are down—"

"So is the price of cotton."

Mr. Shagwell struggled to maintain his temper. "It is. But because of increased competition from other mills, I am under constant pressure to cut costs. To be more efficient. Increase the rate of production. Lower wages."

"What's that have to do with hiring Irishmen?"

"For a clever man, Mr. Jenkins," Mr. Shagwell said, laughing scornfully, "you can be quite dense. You know as well as I do that I much prefer the native worker. But they resist the natural requirements of the mill. The Irish, however—"

"They're nothing but thieves!"

Mr. Shagwell scowled but continued all the same. "The Irish are willing to take lower wages. Nor do they complain about the faster machines."

"Because they're ignorant beggars."

"They do the work nonetheless," Mr. Shagwell replied.

"Sir, you're a hypocrite!" Mr. Jenkins cried. His fringe of whiskers seemed to bristle.

Mr. Shagwell refused to be provoked. "If we hire a few of these Irish workers—a mere handful," he threw back, "it's our way of reminding the native worker that he had best not ask for too much. Else . . . more Irish. It happened just this morning. Pay no mind to it."

"But I do mind it," Mr. Jenkins exclaimed. "You swore you wouldn't do so."

"Merely business," Mr. Shagwell retorted. "Merely business."

Mr. Jenkins sighed and closed his eyes. Then—as if he

had made up his mind—he sat up and glared at Mr. Shagwell. "My funds are low," he announced.

"As to funds, here you are," Mr. Shagwell said. From his desk he took up and held out an envelope. Mr. Jenkins took it, opened it, and—to the mill owner's great annoyance—checked its contents. Only then did the man pocket the money.

"Mr. Jenkins," Mr. Shagwell said with growing irritation, "over the past year you have received a considerable amount of money from me, is that not correct?"

"And I did what you wanted: made sure your operatives knew the Irish were ready to take their jobs. Of course," Mr. Jenkins added sarcastically, "you wouldn't really do such a thing, now would you?"

Mr. Shagwell's smooth pink cheeks turned pinker. "Be careful, sir, that I don't cut you off entirely."

"And replace me with an Irishman?" Mr. Jenkins sneered. "I don't want any more talk!" he burst out. "I organize every day. From this city to that. I want something to happen!"

Mr. Shagwell pressed his hands together so as to contain his anger. "Mr. Jenkins, I cannot speak with you thundering."

"I don't believe you anymore," returned Mr. Jenkins.

Mr. Shagwell's face turned a fiery red. "The truth of the matter is, sir, the Shagwell Cotton Mill Company is close to ruin."

Mr. Jenkins jerked up his head. "Ruin?"

"Bankruptcy."

Mr. Jenkins stared at the mill owner in disbelief.

"The competition has been too fierce," Mr. Shagwell continued angrily. "Manchester, Taunton, Concord, not to mention Rhode Island, press us. I am losing money, sir, a great deal of it, and very quickly too!"

"What do you propose to do?"

With effort Mr. Shagwell pushed himself out of his chair and paced the floor. Then he said, "There is a certain individual—a British investor—currently in the city. A very wealthy man. And a guest in my house. If he can be coaxed properly, he is prepared to put money into the company. If he does—all will be well."

"A foreigner, eh? What's his name?"

"Does it matter?"

"I like to know names."

"If you must know, it's Clemspool. Matthew Clemspool. A gentleman from London." With a show of disinterest, he contemplated his wall of ledger books.

Mr. Jenkins—remembering what Mr. Grout had informed him regarding Clemspool—laughed derisively. "The man's a swindler."

Mr. Shagwell whirled around. "I beg your pardon!"

"A fraud. A crook."

The mill owner felt a sudden shortness of breath. "Why— Who provided you with your information?"

"A man I met."

"A man you met," Mr. Shagwell cried, his anger now boiling over. "You are absurd, sir!" But feeling weak, he, all the same, dropped heavily into his chair.

"I'm only telling you what I heard. Look here, what if this Clemspool doesn't provide the help you need?" Mr. Jenkins asked.

"I . . . I don't know," Mr. Shagwell admitted. "I can apply to the local banks."

"And if *they* say no?"

"A plague on all your questions!" Mr. Shagwell cried. "Just leave me. I have work to do. I'll call you if you're needed."

With a look of cold anger, Mr. Jenkins left the room.

For a long while Mr. Shagwell, trying to calm himself, remained seated behind his desk. He wished he had not lost his temper and blurted out what he had. But the man was annoying. Demanding. Manipulative. Then and there, the mill owner made up his mind to have nothing more to do with him.

But there was one thing Mr. Jenkins had said that he took very seriously. Did the man truly know something about Clemspool or was he bluffing? And if he did know, what truth was there to the notion that the Englishman was a swindler?

Mr. Shagwell decided he had best engage in a frank conversation with Mr. Clemspool as soon as possible.

As for Mr. Jenkins, he left another note for Mr. Grout at the hotel. It read,

> I can tell you where your Mr.
> Clemspool is to be found. Make
> sure you come to the Cotton
> House Tavern this evening.
> Jenkins

Chapter 163
Patrick's Day

After his fight with Nick, Patrick walked aimlessly about Lowell, not sure where he was or even where he wanted to go. Any number of times he huddled in doorways to keep warm. Twice he went into shops but was chased out.

Why, he kept asking himself, are they so mad at the Irish?

After walking some hours, he decided he simply had to speak with his sister. And, though it took him a while, he finally made his way to the Hamlyn house, where he found Bridy sitting on the front steps. She smiled at the sight of him.

"Maura went out this morning," she said. "The house-maid told me."

"Was it to look for work?"

"I think so."

"You'll tell her I've been by then, won't you? And that I'll be back. And thanks."

Hoping that Maura had found employment and thinking how grand it would be if she had, Patrick continued to walk about, taking in the sights of Lowell. Despite the cold, he still had no desire to go to Nathaniel's room.

It was while walking aimlessly about that he came upon a great Catholic church, bigger by far than any he had ever seen before. The church he knew in Kilonny was tiny and in a bad state of repair. This was something grand. ST. PAT-RICK'S CHURCH, a sign said. "Jesus, Mary, and Joseph," he whispered, "everything is so big in America."

Patrick remembered that Nathaniel had said his father came here.

For a long while Patrick simply gazed at the structure, the grandeur of the spire, the massive doors. Not at all sure he would be permitted to enter, he approached cautiously.

Inside the church it was much warmer than outside. A delicate smell of incense wafted through the air. Dark pews stood row upon row like waves. The cross on the altar gleamed in the soft light of the stained-glass windows. Patrick, standing by the entrance, was enthralled.

After dipping his hand in the font of holy water, he crossed himself and genuflected. Then he slipped into a back pew, sat quietly, and gazed about. Finally, he leaned forward and rested his forehead against the pew before him, allowing the smooth coolness of the hard wood to fill him with calm. He prayed silently.

It will be good in America, he told himself finally, it will.

It was an hour later when he felt a tap on his shoulder. Startled, he looked about. A man—short and stooped, with an old, weather-beaten face—was standing there.

"Are you all right, lad?" he asked in a hushed voice.

Patrick stood up quickly. "Yes, sir."

"Just taking a bit of a rest, are ye?"

"Yes, sir."

"You're not alone, are ye? Have some family about?"

"My sister."

"Blessings on her. I was just wanting to be sure you're fine. Peace be with you, lad." The man moved away.

Patrick settled back down in the pew.

Chapter 164

In Which Laurence Finds
an Occupation

*L*aurence woke later than he'd planned. Remembering that he had wanted to start searching for Patrick, he jumped up and looked about. Neither Mr. Grout nor Mr. Drabble was there.

Wondering if they were in the lobby, he hurried downstairs. A fair number of men were sitting about smoking and talking, but there was no sign of his friends. Frustrated, the boy stepped onto the street.

"Want your boots blackened?" a voice called to him.

Laurence turned about. There was something almost comical about the shoe-shine boy who spoke to him, nearly hidden as he was in a large greatcoat that all but reached his toes. His cap, moreover, was pulled so low that it was hard for Laurence to see his face.

"I beg your pardon?" Laurence replied.

"I said your boots could use some blacking. How about it?"

"No, thank you," Laurence said, and turned to look again along the street.

He felt a pull on his arm. "Hey, fellah," Jeb said. "You got a funny way of talking. Where you from?"

"England," Laurence replied.

"That's pretty far, isn't it?"

Laurence merely nodded and once again turned away.

"Who'd you come with?" Jeb tried.

"Friends."

"Been here long?"

"Couple of days."

"You going to stay? You like America?"

"It's fine," Laurence answered. "What's that?" he asked, pointing to the shoe-shine box.

"It's my work," Jeb informed him. "Blacking boots and shoes. Just two cents a shine. I'm telling you, you could use one."

"I don't have any money."

"You don't? Then how come you're staying here?" Jeb gestured back to the hotel.

"My friends are paying."

"How come you came to Lowell?" Jeb asked in hopes of getting some of the information Mr. Clemspool wanted.

"A friend is looking for someone."

"Who's that?"

Laurence hesitated. "Why do you want to know?"

"Just curious, that's all. That person you're looking for," Jeb persisted, "is it someone living in Lowell?"

Laurence, wanting no more questions, said only, "I'm not sure."

"Look here," Jeb said, trying desperately to find a way to keep the boy by his side, "if you don't have any money, I bet you'd like to get some, wouldn't you?"

"I guess . . . ," Laurence admitted.

"How about working with me?" Jeb suggested. "Blacking shoes?"

"Me?"

"Sure thing. You can make ten cents a day, easy."

"Is that a lot?" Laurence asked.

"My father wouldn't say no to it."

"I'm not sure how long we'll be here."

"Don't matter. As long as you're in Lowell, you could do it. What do you say? Split the work. Go shares on the cash."

Laurence considered. Perhaps Mr. Grout had already begun his job. And no doubt Mr. Drabble would be working in the theater. Might it not be better if he began to make some money on his own? Besides, if he were on the streets, he could always be on the lookout for Patrick.

"All right," he said. "I'll do it. But you'll have to teach me how."

"Come on then!" Jeb opened his shoe-shine box and took out two bottles as well as a large dirty cloth. It was about six inches wide and two feet in length. "First thing," he said, "is to show you how to do things.

"This here is the blacking," Jeb explained, holding up a bottle of inky fluid. The second bottle was filled with a bubbly gray substance. "Soap and water, see? You clean their shoes or boots with it first. Just don't tell them what it is."

"Why not?"

"They'll think it's cheap, which it is. If they asks, say, 'Cleaning mix.' "

"Do I have to talk to them?"

Jeb looked at the English boy with puzzlement. "Ain't you ever worked before?"

Laurence blushed. "Not really," he admitted.

Jeb scrutinized him from under his cap. "You telling me this is your first job?"

Sheepishly, Laurence nodded.

"You are something," Jeb said. "Well, it's good work. You're going to like it. And you'll do all right as long as you stay with me. Now, watch, I'll try to catch someone." One hand cupped about his mouth, he called, "Black your boots! Black your boots!"

After some twenty minutes of vigorous calling, an elderly gentleman approached and murmured, "Here, boy."

"Yes, sir," Jeb cried. "You lean up against the wall here, and we'll do you fine and bright." To Laurence, he said under his breath, "Watch me close now."

Jeb knelt before the man. "Put your shoe here, sir," he said. The old man placed his right foot on the box.

Working quickly, Jeb put a dab of the "cleaning mix" onto the toe, then worked it about with the cloth. The cloth took on a black hue. After cleaning the shoe, he poured a spot of blacking on the toe, smeared it around with his fingers, then began to rub it in hard. Then he flung his cloth over the shoe and, holding on to both ends, whipped it back and forth. Now and again he pulled it off and—Laurence couldn't figure how—snapped the cloth to make a sharp cracking sound. Then he worked the heel of the shoe in the same flamboyant fashion. Laurence smiled at the performance.

The right shoe done, Jeb tapped it. Without looking, the man took his foot away and put up the other. Jeb started right in. Laurence continued to watch intently, trying to absorb all that he saw.

When the blacking was finished, Jeb sounded a final double crack of his cloth and looked up. "That's two cents," he said.

The man thrust a hand into a pocket, drew out some coins, gave Jeb three pennies, and walked away.

"There," Jeb said, holding out the money so Laurence could see. "Three cents. Nothing to it."

Laurence looked at the coins and wanted nothing more than to earn some on his own.

With Jeb's guidance, a nervous Laurence began to call, "Black your shoes! Black your shoes!"

Ten minutes later he secured his first customer, a rather fat gentleman with a ruddy face.

Excited, Laurence knelt before him and began to do the shoes. To his relief, Jeb, at his side, helped with comments and suggestions. When the job was done, Laurence looked up. "That's two cents," he whispered, hardly believing he would get paid.

The man examined his shoes, gave a grunt of satisfaction, and dropped two pennies into Laurence's hand.

"There you go," cried Jeb, giving a playful punch. "You're a natural."

Laurence looked at the two coins in the palm of his hand. Never had he felt so proud.

Chapter 165
Nick Seeks Revenge

Where's Jeb?" was the first thing Nick Boswell asked Tom Pelkerton when the boy arrived at their shanty. "How come he's not here?"

"Doing something for that Jenkins fellow maybe," Tom answered.

It was late afternoon, and Tom, shoe-shine box under his arm, was returning from his day's work. By the light of the candle Nick had stuck in a bottle, Tom's round face looked like a dirty full moon. The smell of boot blacking was strong.

"It's meeting time," Nick said, sulking. The three boys were supposed to meet every other day. "And I need him too."

"I'm here," Tom said, and he put his shoe-shine box down near the candle. Then he sat on the box and held his hands near the flame for warmth. "Something happen?" he asked.

Nick studied his boots. At last he looked up. "I ran into a gang. An Irish gang."

"Why . . . ," Tom stammered, "what do you mean?"

"See, this morning I wasn't doing much of anything—just stopping by the Western Canal, getting ready to go to work. A whole gang of them Paddies jumped me."

Tom's eyes grew wide. "How many?"

"Maybe ten, twenty. Came on so quick and sneaky, I couldn't count them very well. I tried to fight them," Nick said convincingly. "And I bloodied a few noses."

"I bet you did!"

"Only there were too many. What they did was, they threw me in the canal."

"In the canal!"

Nick looked into his friend's frightened face. "You can bet I got a good soaking. Cold too. I had to get out on my own."

"You swim?"

Nick nodded. "Then I came here. Tried to dry myself out."

"You should have gone home."

Nick shrugged. "Didn't want to."

After a moment Tom said, "We going to do something about it?"

"Sure thing. What do you think?"

"They all bigger than you?" Tom whispered.

"Sure were."

"They come from Lowell?"

Nick shrugged. "They came at me so fast—like a regular swarm of bees—I only recognized one of them."

"Who was that?"

"Remember, just yesterday—along Adams Street—there was that Paddy . . . ?"

"The little kid?"

"Well, yeah . . . ," Nick said, made a bit uncomfortable by the description. "He was one of them."

"That why you wanted Jeb, so we could catch him?"

"The three of us could, easy."

"Just that one?" Tom jeered, feeling a little easier. "Why, the two of us could do it. Let's go looking for him."

First they went to the building on Adams Street where they had seen Patrick the day before. After waiting a while, Tom said, "Never mind him. I know where we could find us a Paddy."

"Where?"

"That church. St. Patrick's. You can always find some there."

Chapter 166
Patrick Meets Someone
He Knows

Patrick, having spent a warm if solitary time in the church, decided that enough time had passed. Perhaps his sister had returned to the Hamlyns. Eager to find her, he left the church. But no sooner did he start down the steps than he saw Nick, the boy he had fought that morning.

Patrick stopped.

Nick grinned. "Looks like Tom and me surprised you, eh?" he said.

"What . . . do you want?" Eyeing the big boy and not wishing to fight anymore, Patrick darted a look back over his shoulder. That was when he realized that Tom had slipped behind him. There was no one else about.

"You didn't think you could get away with dumping me in the canal, did you?"

"You're the one who started it," Patrick cried.

"All I know is I'm going to end it," said Nick, advancing.

Patrick tried to back away only to come up against Tom. He turned back toward Nick. The boy's hands were balled into fists.

Knowing he had to do something, Patrick spun about and tried to push by Tom so as to get back to the church. But Tom was ready for him and shoved him so hard that Patrick fell down. There he lay, momentarily stunned.

When he looked up, Nick was standing over him, grabbing at his shirt. "Do you want any more, Paddy? Do you?"

Patrick was too frightened, too groggy to answer.

"Come on now," Nick cried. "On your feet." He pulled Patrick up.

"What we going to do with him?" Tom asked.

"Grab his arm," Nick ordered. "Twist it up and around."

Patrick felt his arm grabbed and shoved up, making him double over in pain.

"We'll take him to the shanty. We can keep him there till we decide what to do."

"What if someone comes looking for him?" Tom asked.

"Don't worry about that. No one will know what we're doing. Come on now, Paddy."

With Tom holding his arm behind him and Nick poking at him, a dazed Patrick was led away.

Chapter 167
Mr. Shagwell and Mr. Clemspool Have a Talk

*I*n the Shagwell home, Mr. Clemspool was ready for tea. Just before leaving his room, he touched the bank key in his vest pocket—making sure it was safe—and paused. Would it not be more prudent to secure the key rather than carry it about on his person? If Mr. Grout attacked him . . . The man at the bank did say anyone might walk in and use it.

Mr. Clemspool surveyed the room and its furnishings: a bed with a small table next to it, a chair, a dressing table, a wardrobe. The small table had a drawer in it.

He slid the drawer open. Inside was a slim book of poetry extolling the virtues of Lowell. Mr. Clemspool took it up and carefully placed the key between the cover and the endpaper. Then he returned the book to the drawer, closed it, and went down to tea.

In the best parlor a cheerful fire blazed in the fireplace. Mrs. Shagwell served tea and small sandwiches with an elegant silver tea set that came, she claimed, from the hands of Paul Revere himself. Though Mr. Clemspool had not the slightest idea who Paul Revere was, he allowed as how he would have expected no less in so fine a home.

"I understand you were given a tour of the mill this morning," Mrs. Shagwell said.

"It was—to make my point precisely—inspiring," Mr. Clemspool observed.

"I trust you know, Mr. Clemspool," Mrs. Shagwell confided in a low voice, "it is one of the most prosperous mills in the city."

Mr. Clemspool's face glowed. "I'm not the least surprised to hear you say so," he cooed.

His hostess leaned forward. "And you must realize, sir, that my husband does not accept *any* investor. Only the right people—such as yourself—are welcome."

Mr. Clemspool smiled and took another sip of tea.

It was not long before Mr. Shagwell arrived. Though seeming rather agitated to the Englishman, he settled himself into his favorite commodious chair and worked hard to be congenial, chatting about mill business and how much there was to do, particularly now that he had been gone for such a length of time. "They all depend on me," he said expansively, "more than I would like."

But in time the conversation fell into a lull. At last the mill owner turned to his wife. "My dear Mrs. Shagwell," he said, "I wonder if you would be so kind as to leave us. I have some particular words to exchange with our guest. Matters," he said with a knowing nod, "of business."

"Of course, Mr. Shagwell," his wife replied, and swept out of the room, shutting the parlor doors behind her with a firm snap, the sound conveying just as much knowing as her husband's nod.

Mr. Shagwell leaned back in his chair and briefly closed his eyes as if preparing for battle.

Mr. Clemspool watched his host with sudden apprehension, for clearly the man's manner had changed.

"Mr. Clemspool," the mill owner finally said, clasping his hands over his broad chest, "I have heard some unsavory reports about you."

"From a boy?" cried Mr. Clemspool, ready to leap from his chair. "From Grout?"

The look of bafflement on Mr. Shagwell's face was sufficient to make Mr. Clemspool wish he had not reacted so.

"Not at all."

"Then from whom came these reports?"

Mr. Shagwell cleared his throat. "Does the name Jeremiah Jenkins mean anything to you?"

Mr. Clemspool made a mental note that this was the second time that day Mr. Jenkins's name had been mentioned.

"No," he replied tersely. "I have not had the honor of the gentleman's acquaintance."

"Curious," allowed Mr. Shagwell. "He seems to know of you."

"Does he? How?" Such was Mr. Clemspool's nervousness that he began to wonder if—despite Mr. Shagwell's denial—there was some connection between this Jenkins, Grout, and Laurence.

"You might recall, sir," continued Mr. Shagwell, "I spoke to Mr. Jenkins from the carriage in Boston."

Mr. Clemspool did remember, but the encounter was so fleeting, his impression was at best vague.

"He is a business associate," Mr. Shagwell continued, "someone with whom, from time to time, I meet and share views."

"What was he saying about me?" inquired Mr. Clemspool.

The mill owner considered his guest with his small gray eyes. His company was in need of money, but it would only make matters worse if he became entangled in anything fraudulent.

"I am afraid, sir," Mr. Shagwell said at last, "the word was not flattering."

"You know," Mr. Clemspool said, eager to strike a blow of his own, "that when I met with my banker here in town to transfer some of my investment funds, I made some inquiries about you . . . and your business." He offered up a patently false smile.

304

Mr. Shagwell flinched. "And pray, sir, what did this banker say?"

"I am afraid," said the Englishman, "it was not very flattering either."

The two men contemplated each other with growing suspicion. On one side, Mr. Shagwell was increasingly certain his guest was exactly the swindler Mr. Jenkins had said he was. For his part, Mr. Clemspool was becoming more and more convinced that Mr. Grout and Laurence were, in some way, behind Mr. Shagwell's altered attitude toward him.

Mr. Clemspool leaned forward. "Let me tell you, sir, what my banker said pertaining to the Shagwell Cotton Mill. In regard to investment, he said, it might be best to look elsewhere. He told me, sir, that your business is . . . in financial trouble."

Mr. Clemspool studied his host to see if he had hit the mark. He was quite certain—from the look of distress upon Mr. Shagwell's face—that he had.

Indeed, Mr. Shagwell felt compelled to cover his eyes with a hand. If there was word abroad that his mill was in difficult straits, he was closer to the edge of ruin than he had thought.

His thin lips twisted in a sickly grin. "Well, sir," he replied, "the reports regarding you were not altogether pleasing either. I heard the words *swindler, thief, fraud.* Is that possible?"

"Grout did talk to you!" cried Mr. Clemspool.

"I assure you, I have not seen Mr. Grout since we were on board the *Robert Peel.* Nor do I have any intention of seeing him."

"Then a boy. A boy by the name of Laurence."

"I am not in the habit of taking advice from boys."

"It's all lies anyway," Mr. Clemspool burst out. "Do I work very hard? Do I sail close to the wind? Am I willing to take advantage and squeeze when necessary? I hope I am, sir. Does that make a man a crook? It does not.

"Do you read your Bible, sir?" Mr. Clemspool suddenly asked.

"Of course," returned Mr. Shagwell with growing vexation.

"Genesis. Chapter four. Verses five through nine. Cain and Abel. 'Am I my brother's keeper?' The answer, of course, is *yes*. And, sir, I prefer to think of you, to make my point precisely, as my brother."

Mr. Shagwell grew hot. "You are not my brother, sir!" he cried. "Do you or do you not have money to invest?"

"I do," returned Mr. Clemspool with as much heat.

"How much?"

"Thousands."

"Where does it come from?"

"You have been to England. Does the name Kirkle mean anything to you? I represent Lord Kirkle. But I will not invest his money in a failing business. Honesty is very important to me, sir. Is your business in trouble or is it not? I suspect it is. Now, I may promise to give you what you need. But you must return the favor before you see any cash."

Mr. Shagwell looked at his guest quizzically. "What could you possibly need from me?" he asked.

"I wish to establish a business. I want you to make a public statement as to my virtues, value, and position."

"Why?"

"So that I may raise money, sir. Capital."

"For what purpose?"

"Why should you care? Why do you want money? For the same reasons I do. That should be a sufficient answer."

Though his face had turned red, Mr. Shagwell's small gray eyes turned harder than usual. "Mr. Clemspool, sir, I must ask you to leave my house, *immediately*."

"I beg your pardon," the startled Englishman cried.

"You have been playing me for the fool, sir. I am not interested in taking the part."

"But . . ."

"Out!"

Mr. Clemspool rose on shaky knees. "Very well, sir, I shall just go to my room—"

"Never mind your room. Leave at once. Send word where you may be found, and I shall arrange to have your things sent on to you."

Mr. Clemspool gasped. "But . . ."

Mr. Shagwell opened the door of the parlor. "I am asking you to leave, sir."

All Mr. Clemspool could think of was the bank-vault key he had left in the bedside table drawer. "There are certain items—"

"Have you no self-respect, sir! *I have asked you to go!*"

Ashen-faced, Mr. Clemspool walked out of the room and house.

Mr. Shagwell remained sitting, now and again running his fingers through his mane of gray hair. He had, he realized, made a terrible mistake in regard to Mr. Clemspool. Thank goodness he need have no more to do with him!

Chapter 168
Mr. Clemspool Paces

*M*r. Clemspool, bald head glistening with perspiration, paced back and forth in the small hotel room he had taken only minutes before. Now and again he lifted agitated hands and snatched at the air with frustration.

Who was this Jenkins? How did it happen that a stranger was saying vile things about him?

And what of being banished by Shagwell? Was not his house the one to which Sir Albert Kirkle would be sending his money? It was! How was he to get it now?

Finally, what was he to do about Laurence and Grout, the two of them so irksomely in Lowell?

Presumably the police would take care of Grout. Laurence, however, was quite another matter. Would it be worthwhile to get hold of him again? If he held the boy for ransom from Lord Kirkle—why, that could mean months. . . . And how was he to live?

He could only hope that boy—Jeb, wasn't it?—had found his way to Laurence and had been able to pry out some information about him. It would be exceedingly useful to know what young Kirkle and Grout were about.

But most vexatious was the matter of the key to the safe-deposit box. *He had to retrieve it*. The question was, How?

The room was at the back of the Shagwell house, on the second floor. A window looked out upon a garden. Might it be possible to enter that garden, climb in through that rear window, and reclaim the key from the book in the bedside table? Mr. Clemspool sighed. He could not do it. But someone else . . .

Then he thought again of the boy he'd hired to watch Laurence. The thought made Mr. Clemspool smile. Jeb Grafton was just the one to retrieve the key. And they were to meet at eight.

With collar turned up against the night chill, Mr. Clemspool walked through the streets of Lowell. He was glad it was a dark night.

As he approached the Spindle City Hotel, he saw someone he knew: Mr. Tolliver. Mr. Clemspool stopped and watched the policeman go into the hotel.

Good! thought Mr. Clemspool with a spurt of hope. Perhaps the policeman's come to arrest Grout! The Englishman searched for an appropriate observation spot and found one across the street, in the entryway of a shuttered store.

After fifteen minutes had passed, there was no sign of the policeman, but now Jeb Grafton appeared from around the corner. With him was, of all people, Laurence Kirkle, shoeshine box under his arm. From the way the two hiked along, side by side and chatting, it appeared as if the boys had become friends.

Mr. Clemspool grinned broadly. This Jeb was a winner! Just the lad to get the bank key.

With a wave, Laurence went into the hotel, leaving Jeb alone.

Mr. Clemspool sprang forward. "Well done!" he cried, turning Jeb about and guiding him forcibly back across the street, where the two of them would be less conspicuous.

"It was easy," Jeb said. "We're working together."

"Doing what?"

"Shoe shine. I've been teaching him how. So I can stay with him. I even lent him my box, so he'll be sure to show up tomorrow morning."

"Did you find out why he's in Lowell?"

Jeb shrugged. "With his friends."

"Nothing more?"

"They're looking for someone."

Mr. Clemspool's heart jumped. "Who?" he asked.

"He wouldn't say," Jeb replied. Then he asked, "You going to pay me?"

"Yes, yes, of course." Mr. Clemspool reached into his pocket, found some coins, and gave the boy a twenty-five-cent piece. "Now then," he said, "you have pleased me so much, I will offer you another job. How would you like to earn . . . ten dollars?"

"*Ten dollars!*" exclaimed Jeb. He'd have earned almost

eleven dollars that day. More than the cost of a doctor's visit for his mother.

"That's what I'm offering."

"I guess I would," Jeb said eagerly. "What do I have to do?"

"I assure you, it will take very little effort on your part."

Jeb gazed up at Mr. Clemspool. "It's not doing anything bad, is it?"

"Dear boy," cried Mr. Clemspool as he led Jeb in the direction of Mr. Shagwell's house, "you must not even entertain such thoughts!"

Chapter 169
Earnings

*L*aurence was lying on his bed when Mr. Drabble came into the room.

"Look!" the boy cried, bounding up and holding out his hand, where some coins lay. "I earned eleven cents!"

Tired and dejected, Mr. Drabble made a perfunctory glance at the money. "And how did you get that?" he asked dully.

"I was working. Shoe shining. Blacking boots. You see, I met a boy, and he taught me. It isn't hard."

"I'm sure it's not," the actor said as he slumped down on his bed and clutched his thin knees. "And where is Mr. Grout?" he asked.

"I haven't seen him all afternoon," Laurence replied. "Have you been at the theater?"

After a moment Mr. Drabble slowly shook his head.

"Why not?" a puzzled Laurence asked.

At first Mr. Drabble said nothing. Then he sighed. "I am, as the poet said, 'bound in shallows and in miseries.' "

"I don't understand."

"Mr. Laurence . . . unlike you, I was not offered a position. I was, in fact, rejected."

"But Mr. Grout said they would hire you for sure."

"I was invited—merely—to sit with the audience."

"Oh."

"You, young man," said Mr. Drabble as he lay back, put his arms under his head, and stared at the ceiling, "have climbed far higher than I. And you are dealing with boots."

"Would . . . would you like my money?" Laurence asked.

Mr. Drabble shook his head.

Laurence held the coins out anyway. "I'll be sure to be earning more tomorrow."

Tears dropped from Mr. Drabble's eyes. "I'm sure you will," the actor said, and turned away.

Chapter 170
Maura after Work

I t was nearly eight in the evening by the time Maura reached Mrs. Hamlyn's house. Her head throbbed. Her back ached. Her feet were so sore that she carried her shoes, preferring the cold ground to the pain from the leather.

In the hallway she was greeted by Bridy, who gave her a great hug, babbling about someone named Jenkins even as she dragged Maura to the dining table.

Dinner, with Mrs. Hamlyn presiding, had already begun.

The eight other young women were there, busily eating like wolf cubs but finding time to chat too. A chair was drawn out for Maura. She sat, sighed audibly, and watched amazedly as her plate was filled with food.

"Your first day, my dear?" asked one of the other lodgers, a lemon-haired, dimple-cheeked young woman in her late teens.

Maura could only nod.

"Then bravo to you, and well begun," the young woman cried. "I don't doubt but it was the worst day of your life. You can rejoice you'll not have to meet its like again."

There was a chorus of boisterous agreement from the other boarders, who commenced exchanging dreadful stories of their first days in the mills.

At first, Maura felt too tired to eat, and merely picked at her food. But, heartened by the talk, she soon regained some strength and devoured all she had been given.

As she ate, she paid close attention as the others offered now this suggestion, now that to help her with tomorrow's work.

Dinner done, Maura made her way to the parlor, and at eight-thirty Nathaniel arrived, smiling. But the moment he saw Maura and Bridy, the smile vanished.

"Isn't Patrick with you?" he asked.

"Patrick! To be sure," Maura said, "I've not seen him since last night, when you left. I thought he'd be with you."

"He was," Nathaniel explained. "We went to the mill this morning, but they wouldn't take him on."

"No. . . . Why?"

"He's too young, they told him, and . . . and . . . because he's Irish."

"They took me," said Maura.

Nathaniel could only shake his head. "I thought he'd be in my room. He wasn't."

Maura closed her eyes. A wave of weariness engulfed her.

"By the Holy Mother," she said, "hasn't he gone off like this before? No sooner did we reach Liverpool than he vanished. The same on the boat as well."

"Do you think he's all right?"

Caught between her great tiredness and worry, Maura hardly knew how to respond. What she did know was that she needed to rest. "Faith, Mr. Brewster, if I worried each time he did his mischief, I'd be having more lines on my brow than there are in a spider's web."

"And your job," the young man said. "Was it very hard?"

"To be sure, I've never known such a day. I'm ready to sleep this moment."

Nathaniel quickly came to his feet. "Forgive me. I shouldn't be keeping you," he said.

"You're always kind," Maura replied, standing herself. "When Patrick returns to you, you can give him a scolding from me, and tell him to come tomorrow evening sure."

Chapter 171

Mr. Shagwell's House

Mr. Clemspool found the way to Mr. Shagwell's house with little trouble.

With his coat close about him, Jeb trudged behind, wondering about the job ahead when he was not wondering about this odd man.

"We can stop here," Mr. Clemspool announced.

Jeb looked around. He recognized the neighborhood as an area where rich people lived, not a place he came often.

"Do you see that house?" Mr. Clemspool asked, pointing across the street.

By the light of the moon, Jeb saw a large stone building. Save for a few spots of candlelight behind first-floor windows, it was quite dark. "What about it?" the boy asked cautiously.

Mr. Clemspool had spent time pondering how best to explain what it was he wished Jeb to do, so as not to frighten him. "It's a thief who lives there," he said.

"What do you mean?" Jeb asked, alarmed.

"The kind of man who turns on you cruelly," the Englishman said, his voice low with anger.

Jeb's eyes grew wide. "He do that to you?"

"To make my point precisely—yes."

"How?"

"He lured me into his house by pretending to be my friend. Then, when I had left my possessions in the room he provided, he insisted upon my immediate departure, thereby forcing me to leave behind what was my own. I don't care for most of it. But I did lose something of particular value. A key."

"What's it for?"

"My most precious property. I shall give you ten dollars to get that key back for me."

Jeb looked from Mr. Clemspool to the house. "What's the man's name?"

"Shagwell," the Englishman spit out.

"Shagwell? Of Shagwell Cotton Mill?"

"The same."

"I hate that man!" Jeb hissed. "He's worse than a thief!"

Mr. Clemspool smiled broadly. "I'm delighted to agree with you."

"How we going to get the key?" Jeb said with new enthusiasm.

The man glanced up and down the street. "Come with me," he said, and started toward the house. Jeb stayed close.

Silently, they moved onto a narrow path at the side of

the house. It led them into a yard, a blooming garden in warmer days.

Jeb studied the house. "Which window, mister?" he asked in a hushed voice.

Mr. Clemspool considered. "I believe it's that one," he said, indicating a second-floor window at one corner of the structure. From inside he had noticed that the window looked out upon a roofed extension of the house.

"Nothing to it," Jeb whispered after taking it all in. "I can get there easy."

"Can you?"

"See that barrel?" Jeb said, pointing to a large rain collector by a downspout at the corner of the house. "I'll get on it, then climb to your low roof. From there I can reach that window in nothing flat."

"Clever boy," Mr. Clemspool enthused, patting Jeb on the head. "Wonderful boy. I'm glad I have you with me."

Jeb unbuttoned his coat. "Would you mind holding this?"

"A pleasure."

"Just tell me where the key is."

"Once you're in the room, look for a small table next to the bed. The table has a drawer. Open the drawer and you'll find a book. Inside the book's cover lies a key."

Mr. Clemspool held a ten-dollar bill up to the moonlight. "This will be yours," he said, "when the key is mine."

Jeb ogled the money for a moment, grinned, handed his coat to Mr. Clemspool, then turned back to the house.

After stuffing his cap into a back pocket, he hoisted himself onto the barrel. With his two hands on the cornice and with one kick of his leg, he levered himself up to the roof.

Mr. Clemspool looked on with satisfaction, then dropped Jeb's coat on the ground. There was a clink of coins. Making sure Jeb had his back to him, the Englishman quickly checked the coat pockets, found the boy's money, and took it out. Mr. Clemspool smiled. The boy's efforts to reach the roof were so easy, Mr. Clemspool decided he would give Jeb only one dollar instead of ten. What's more, he would use the boy's own money.

Once on the roof, Jeb crept cautiously toward the window. When he reached it, he glanced back down at Mr. Clemspool, who waved his encouragement.

Jeb peered into the room. It appeared deserted. The window sliding up with ease, he stuck his head inside and looked about. Moonlight revealed just what Mr. Clemspool had described.

The boy slithered inside. Two steps took him to the table, where he opened the drawer. In it lay the book with the key exactly where it was supposed to be. All but laughing with delight at the trick he was playing on his family's enemy, Mr. Shagwell, Jeb placed the key in a pocket, then scurried back to the window and searched below for Mr. Clemspool.

Seeing a man standing in the middle of the garden, he started to climb out. Suddenly he stopped and ducked back into the room. The man was not Mr. Clemspool!

"All right, Clemspool," a voice called out. "Just stay where you are. It's Tolliver, from the police."

The next thing Jeb heard was the sound of running. "Stop, thief!" came a cry, followed by a blast of a whistle and more running.

Frightened, Jeb dived under the bed. There he lay, heart hammering, praying no one would come look for him.

Ten minutes later he was still hiding when the door to the room opened. Jeb saw the flickering light of a candle.

"He must have wanted to come in here," said a voice.

"Well, Mr. Shagwell," said another, "this Clemspool claims he only wanted his own possessions back. There, you see, the window is open."

"I thought you said he didn't enter the room."

"I didn't think he had."

"Perhaps it was open before." From under the bed, Jeb heard the sounds of the window being shut.

"Mr. Tolliver, sir, the man was a guest in my house. Fortunately, I was warned he was not to be trusted, and I ordered him to leave."

"What can you tell me about the man?"

"Very little. Hardly know him."

"You had him as a guest."

"Business. . . ."

"All well and good, sir, but do you want me to charge him or not?"

"I don't think that's necessary, Mr. Tolliver. May I suggest you keep him in jail for a day or two and then encourage him to leave Lowell. That seems best for all concerned."

"I'll do so, sir," returned Mr. Tolliver.

Taking the light with them, the two men left the room.

Jeb held still until he was quite sure the men were not coming back. Then he tiptoed to the window and opened it. In moments he worked his way to the end of the roof, jumped to the ground, and ran off.

Five blocks later he remembered he'd given his coat to Mr. Clemspool. With the money from the day in its pocket! His heart sank, and he all but burst into tears. He did consider going back but was too fearful of being caught.

Disgusted, he thrust his hands in his pants pockets. All he found was Clemspool's key. He looked at it but in the darkness could make little of it. In a rage of frustration, angry at everything and everybody—not the least himself—Jeb trudged home.

Chapter 172
Mr. Jenkins Meets with Friends

Mr. Jenkins and Betsy Howard sat across from each other at a table in the crowded and smoky Cotton House Tavern. A small candle in a cracked cup provided a spot of light between them. "Thank you for hearing me," Betsy Howard said.

Mr. Jenkins shrugged. "There are some who care nothing for what women say. That's not me."

"I needed to tell you what happened today. You are speaking tomorrow, aren't you?"

"I am. Tell me your news."

The woman proceeded to tell Mr. Jenkins what happened in the mill that morning, the turning away of Sarah Grafton.

With growing anger, Mr. Jenkins heard it all. "Did they replace her?"

Betsy Howard nodded. "A Paddy."

"I knew it!"

"Then they asked me to teach her how to work the machines!"

"Insult to injury!" cried Mr. Jenkins. "Now," he said, "do I have the name—Grafton—right?"

"Yes."

"Does she have a boy? Blacks shoes?"

Betsy Howard nodded.

"I know him well."

"Do you? I suppose he's the only one in the family making money now."

"Miss Howard, I promise you, I shall use all of this as an example at my meeting tomorrow. It's exactly what people need to know. Make sure to be there. Big things will be happening."

"What?"

Mr. Jenkins leaned forward and whispered, "Revenge."

Betsy Howard looked into Mr. Jenkins's eyes, then, feeling uncomfortable, stood up. "It's near to curfew time," she announced. "I have to be at lodgings."

"I'd see you there, but I'm meeting someone else. Miss Howard, do come to the meeting."

"I will."

Twenty minutes later Mr. Grout appeared. As soon as he sat down, he said, "Look 'ere, Jenkins, I came to this city searchin' for Matthew Clemspool. Yer promised yer'd tell me where I could find 'im."

Mr. Jenkins looked at the Englishman slyly. "And I will tell you, sir. But not till tomorrow evening, when you will have completed your work for me."

Mr. Grout grimaced. "I keep askin' yer, wot kind of work is it?"

"It's very simple, sir. Tomorrow evening I will be holding a meeting. At Appleton Hall. Eight o'clock. I shall be doing the speaking."

"Wot's the subject?"

"The dangers of immigration to this country. I'll propose a call to action."

Mr. Grout squinted his one good eye. "Wot kind of action?"

For a moment Mr. Jenkins said nothing. Then he hunched forward and, speaking in a low voice, said, "I want a demonstration outside a certain place."

"Why?"

"It will do the most good there," he said.

"And wot am I supposed to do?"

319

"You will lead the people to that place."

Mr. Grout considered the man with suspicion. "That's it?"

Mr. Jenkins smiled grimly. "That is it."

Taking a piece of paper from his pocket, he said, "Here is the name of the street to which you are to guide the demonstration."

Mr. Grout picked it up and, in the dim light, struggled to read the writing.

"Cabot Street," coached Mr. Jenkins. And he repeated the name but held back the number. He was not sure he could trust this man.

"What you must do, young man, is during the day go and find that street. Then you'll know how to lead the people there. But you must tell no one what you're doing."

"Why?"

"An unplanned event should look unplanned," Mr. Jenkins allowed, then pointed to his eye and his nose and made a circle with his thumb and forefinger.

"Yer full of mystery, ain't yer?" said Mr. Grout.

"I know nothing," replied Mr. Jenkins with a grim smile. "But, sir, once the unplanned demonstration is over, you have my solemn vow I will tell you where to find your man. Thus, you will know something."

Mr. Grout, not entirely happy with the conversation, left the tavern.

In contrast, Mr. Jenkins was happy indeed. Having arranged that Mr. Grout would lead the crowd to James Hamlyn's address, he felt confident he could shed responsibility for any incident that occurred there. Let Grout carry the blame for what the American hoped would happen. The man was a foreigner.

320

Chapter 173
Maura Doesn't Worry

Maura could hardly bear the tolling of the first morning bells. How she longed to stay in bed! But though her back, legs, and feet ached, she scolded herself for being lazy. Was she not in America with employment, earning money? "Thank you, Holy Mother," she murmured.

Then and there she made a vow that she would ask Mr. Brewster where she could find her father's church, so she might confess and take the sacrament. She must also ask the whereabouts of Da's grave.

After a prayer, she made the sign of the cross, then got up, trying not to wake Bridy.

In haste now—for the room was dark and cold—Maura slipped on her new clothing and tight shoes, washed her face in the cold-water basin, then bent over Bridy and brushed a soft kiss on her brow. For this, she was rewarded by the girl reaching up and hugging her around the neck.

"Are you awake then?" Maura murmured.

"Yes," Bridy replied drowsily.

"I'll be going off to the mill now and will return when day is done," Maura told her. "Will you be finding yourself something useful to do?" she asked.

"I'll watch the house for Mr. Hamlyn," Bridy said.

Maura, not really understanding what the girl was talking about, merely replied, "Sure, that will be fine."

While swallowing a quick cup of hot tea and a piece of warm buttered corn bread, Maura told Mrs. Hamlyn that her brother had disappeared.

"You must be worried about him," the woman said.

"Faith, mistress, I am and am not," Maura explained with a rueful smile. "You can't believe how often the boy's gone off, but he never fails to come back safe and sure. And truth to say, mistress, last night I was too exhausted to be looking for him. But if he does come to your door, I'd be grateful if you'd tell him I expect a visit from him tonight."

Mrs. Hamlyn promised she would, and Maura left the house in the company of one of her sister boarders.

"Please, Miss Polly," she said to her companion, "can you explain the meaning of all those bells again?"

Chapter 174

Mr. Drabble Wanders

At the Spindle City Hotel, Mr. Drabble, too troubled to sleep, also rose from his bed when the first bells rang. Leaving a sleeping Laurence and Toby Grout, he crept out of the room and onto Merrimack Street. There, the cold, dark, and deserted street helped him indulge the illusion that he was the only person in the world. As well as the most wretched.

Mr. Grout had found work. So had Laurence. But not him. Perhaps, he thought, it was better to have been rejected than to have looked foolish before an audience. No, he wished that he had a role, any role.

His thoughts drifted to his love for Maura. " 'Let thy love

be younger than thyself . . . ,' " he murmured, quoting from his adored bard.

He regretted now having left his volume of Shakespeare by the canal. The more he thought of it, the more he wanted it back. Glad to have some goal in mind, he set off—head bowed, hands deep in pockets—through the gloomy streets.

A few people passed. Mr. Drabble supposed they were going to the mills. Shivering, he envied them. Then the notion struck him that perhaps he might apply for a mill job. Not only would it provide necessary money, but he would, at least, then be able to stay in the same city as Maura.

The idea so appealed to him, he stopped meandering and studied the other predawn passersby. It was while watching them that he thought he saw Maura. His heart tumbled. The clothing this woman wore was quite different. But her tall, straight way of walking and the brown hair that flowed down her back were much like Maura's. And when, by the light of a street lamp, the actor saw that the shawl wrapped about her was dark red, he became certain it *was* his beloved.

Maura presumably had found work. Why else would she be about at such an hour? His first impulse was to cry out her name and rush to her side. She was walking, however, with another young woman, and from time to time the two exchanged words. The thought that Maura might rebuke him again—and in front of a stranger—was more than he could bear.

Besides, Mr. Drabble told himself, what could he say of *his* achievements? Nothing. Better to see where she went.

Accordingly, he fell in behind her, but not so close that she might notice. Never losing sight of her, he saw her turn in at the gates of the Shagwell Mill.

He knew he could wait for her—the whole day, if necessary—for he assumed that it was here that she had been fortunate enough to find employment. Or he could return to the street where he'd first seen her. She must live near there with her father, he thought. Mr. Drabble was certain he would recognize the man.

With renewed energy, the actor retraced his steps. Some minutes later he found Cabot Street. And there he spied Bridy, emerging from a doorway. She too was in a new dress. With a shawl wrapped about her, she sat on the top step and looked right and left along the street, sending Mr. Drabble ducking into a doorway.

He peeked out. From the look of the house in front of which the child sat, Mr. O'Connell had done well for himself. The realization caused Mr. Drabble a new pang: While he had fallen in the world, Maura had risen. She would never look at him again.

He must establish himself. Then and only then could he let his presence be known. He noted the number of the house—eighty-seven. He repeated it to himself—"Eighty-seven Cabot Street"—as if the phrase were a magical charm. Merely knowing where she lived, knowing that, secretly, he could see her every morning as she left the house for work, gave Mr. Drabble new courage.

Now that he had again found his very heart, he bustled off to find his Shakespeare volume, his very soul.

Chapter 175

A Surprising Pair of Shoes

Y ou forgot your coat," Laurence said, yawning, as he came out of the hotel to find Jeb waiting for him.

"Guess I did," Jeb mumbled, hardly wishing to explain what had happened the night before. "If the sun shines, this can be a warm spot. And in the morning you get a good class of gents."

Though the sun was barely up, he had been awake for hours, worrying about the stolen key and about how angry his parents would be if they found out he had it—and how he got it. Light though the key was, he could almost feel its weight in his pocket. He kept telling himself he should get rid of it or at least hide it—maybe in the shanty.

Even worse than his worries about the key was the sound of his mother's cough. All through the night, he had heard it. It seemed deeper, harsher than before. Was it that way because she had no job, because Jeb was the only one working . . . ? The boy had shuddered at the thought. It was all so frightening.

"When do they start coming?" Laurence said. For him, it was still early. He wished he could have stayed in bed.

"Soon as the first train from Boston pulls in, we should get some business. Just one thing."

"What's that?"

"Better scruff up your face a bit. Hide that mark. The gents don't like to see rough stuff. Makes them uncomfortable." Jeb poured a spot of the blacking on his cloth and smeared Laurence's face. "There you go. Now you look decent. Who's going to shine first, you or me?"

"You can," Laurence said, trying to suppress another yawn.

Jeb set the box down a few feet from the hotel entrance. Then he began his call, "Black your boots! Black your boots!"

Laurence, glad he didn't have to work right away, sat on the ground, legs drawn up, back propped against the hotel wall. To protect himself against the cold, he bent over and hugged himself.

Thirty minutes passed before Jeb found his first customer. Laurence strove to watch carefully, wanting to be sure he wouldn't forget how to do the job properly. Instead, he dozed.

"Hey, wake up, fellah," he heard Jeb call into his ear. "I got you a customer!"

Startled into wakefulness, an embarrassed Laurence—trying desperately to open his eyes—scurried over to where the gentleman was waiting. Automatically, he knelt before him and the shoe-shine box, then set the man's boot firmly on the box.

Paying strict attention to the boot, Laurence worked hard. Only when the first boot was done did he remember Jeb's instructions, that he should look up and smile. Which is exactly what he did. The man whose boots he was blacking was none other than his brother, Albert.

Chapter 176
Brothers

*L*aurence felt as if he were caught in a vise. In a panic, he ducked his head over his brother's boot and worked away with trembling hands.

As for Albert, he took no more notice of the urchin at his feet than of the pavement itself. Instead, he gazed up and down, looking at the city to which he had just come by railway. He had already decided Lowell was a tiresome place and was resolved to spend as little time here as possible.

"The other boot," Jeb whispered into Laurence's ear.

Laurence tapped Albert's foot. The second boot was put in place.

As Laurence worked, his mind raced furiously. How his brother had tracked him to Lowell was beyond his understanding. It made little difference. He had no doubt but that Albert was there to do him harm. All Laurence could think was that he had to get away.

The boot blacking was done. Laurence, without lifting his head, his voice pitched higher than normal, said, "Two pennies, sir."

Albert reached into a pocket and drew out a fistful of change. "Confounded money," he murmured. "Here, take this." He dropped a coin into Laurence's raised, shaking hand and walked off without a backward look.

Laurence stared after his brother. He seemed to be going no place in particular but merely lumbered along, pausing now and again to gawk about.

"How much he give you?" Laurence heard Jeb ask as though from a great distance.

With a start, Laurence turned, then glanced down at the dime in his hand. Numb, he handed it to Jeb.

"Crackers!" Jeb exclaimed. "A whole dime. Beginner's luck!"

Laurence, still on his knees, turned again to stare after his brother.

"What's the matter?" Jeb asked. "What you looking at?"

"That . . . that man there . . . ," said Laurence, still in a daze.

"The one you just blacked?"

Laurence nodded.

"He is dressed fancy, ain't he?" Albert was wearing greatcoat, top hat, and gloves.

Laurence bolted up. "I . . . I have to get away," he stammered.

"What do you mean?"

"He's . . . That man is trying to catch me."

"Him?" Jeb said, gazing with puzzlement at Albert, who had already gone a considerable distance along the street. "If he's trying to catch you, how come he's going that way?"

"He didn't know it was me," Laurence said in a choked whisper.

"What's he want you for?"

"He wants to harm me. I know he does."

Jeb considered Laurence anew. First it was Mr. Clemspool who had wanted this boy watched. Now here was someone the boy was running from. Jeb wished he knew just who Laurence was and what it was all about. "What about your friends in the hotel?"

"I have to get away," Laurence gasped.

"Where?"

An anguished Laurence looked at Jeb. "Anywhere. *Please*. Help me. You can keep that money."

Suppressing a grin, Jeb put the dime in his pocket. As he did, he felt the key and remembered he wanted to hide it. "I know a place you can keep out of sight for a while."

"Where?"

"It's a pretty good shanty my pals and I put together. Nothing says you can't stay there for a bit. It's not so far."

"Please . . . ," Laurence implored.

"Come on then," Jeb said, and he picked up his shoe-shine box and tucked it under an arm.

The two boys set off down the street, Laurence anxiously looking back over his shoulder from time to time.

Suddenly Jeb spied a policeman ambling in their direction from the other end of the street. Fearful that Mr. Clemspool might have given the police his name and that they might now be coming after him for housebreaking, the boy stopped short. If they arrested him and found the key in his pocket, his situation would be awful.

"Look here," he said to Laurence, extracting the key. "I need you to do something for me."

"What is it?"

Jeb held the key out. "It's my father's. I've been carrying it. Only my pockets are so full of holes, I keep worrying I'll lose it. Would you mind holding it for me?"

While Laurence stowed the key away, Jeb kept a wary eye on the policeman. As it was, the officer merely meandered by, not even looking at the boys.

Though much relieved, Jeb decided he'd let Laurence hold the key until he got to the shanty. It would be safer.

The farther they walked, the calmer Laurence became. First he reminded himself that he was in America, not England. He need not be so fearful. And wasn't he a new person with a new name? "I am not Sir Laurence Kirkle," he whispered to himself. "I'm not."

A poke from Jeb startled Laurence out of his thoughts. "How come," the boy asked, "that gent is after you?"

"He hates me."

"Why? What you do to him?"

"Nothing."

"He English like you?"

"Yes."

Jeb shook his head. "You sure have a lot of Englishmen looking for you."

Laurence came to an abrupt halt. "What do you mean . . . a lot?" he cried. "Is there someone else?"

Too late, Jeb realized he'd blundered. "Look here," he said, "I'm willing to help you—don't know why I shouldn't—only you have to tell me what your game is."

"Who else is looking for me?" Laurence demanded with sudden fierceness.

Somewhat cowed, Jeb said, "Ever hear of a man by the name of Clemspool?"

"Clemspool!" Laurence cried. "In Lowell?"

"Sort of fat, bald, round-faced fellow, with fingers that fidget a lot and a mouth that likes to talk."

"That's him."

"Then he's here."

"Is he looking for me too?"

"I suppose," Jeb replied, wishing he hadn't said anything.

"Where is he?" Laurence said. He'd begun to think it was a mistake to have left Mr. Grout this morning. "How do you know about Mr. Clemspool?"

"I was just shining his shoes, and he asked me to help him," Jeb answered truthfully. "What's it all about anyway?"

Laurence glanced at Jeb, wondering how much he could trust him. "I ran away from home," he said.

"That's nothing," a disappointed Jeb returned with a shrug. "A ton of boys do that."

"From London, England," Laurence went on. "And those men, they've come after me."

"To haul you back?"

"But I won't go," Laurence said with a burst of resolve. "I won't. Only I have to go back to the hotel," he added, wanting now to tell Mr. Grout what he had discovered.

"Just hold on a minute," Jeb said. "We're only a bit from the shanty. I need to leave that key there. Then we'll go."

"Will you promise to take me back to the hotel then?" Laurence asked.

"Sure thing," Jeb said sincerely. "The shanty's just over here."

Chapter 177
Albert Looks for His Man

A lbert, unaware that it was his brother who had blackened his boots, continued his stroll through Lowell. To his disgust, all he could see were businesses and shops. No fine tailors, no sweetshops, no betting parlors. As for the people, they walked too fast and talked too loudly, and no one appeared to be of any importance. As far as he was concerned, the sooner he found this Mr. Shagwell, the better. When he saw some waiting hackney carriages, he approached the first in line.

"I say," he called up, "I need to find a man by the name of . . . Ambrose Shagwell. Any idea where the chap might be?"

The driver, an old man with a slouch hat set low about his ears, pulled at his thick mustache. "Don't know, but there's a Mr. Shagwell of the Shagwell Cotton Mill. That the one you're looking for?"

"Look here, I haven't the faintest idea *what* he is. And I don't care. I just need to find him."

"Well, if that's your man, he might be at the mill."

"Then take me there." Albert climbed into the carriage, and off they went. The city being quite small, the ride seemed hardly to have begun before the coach stopped and the driver called down that they had arrived.

Albert—who had not considered what he might say to Mr. Shagwell—stepped from the carriage and found himself before the mill gates. The size of the establishment took him by surprise.

"And you say this Mr. Shagwell is in charge of this . . . place?" he asked his driver.

"Owns it," was the curt reply.

Albert was impressed. Not that he wanted to show it. "Stay here till I get back," he ordered.

"Long as you pay, mister."

Trying to act casual, but squeezing his knuckles with nervousness, Albert strolled into the mill yard and looked about. All was busy. Any number of people were at work. From the larger of the buildings, a great clatter of mechanical noise poured forth.

Feeling uneasy, Albert turned toward the smaller of the structures, where the manager's sign was posted, and knocked upon the door.

It was the boy who answered. When he observed Albert—top hatted, wearing a knee-length overcoat, hands in leather gloves—he immediately opened the door wide.

"Yes, sir," he said with deference, "what can we do for you?"

"Yes . . . ," Albert drawled. "Is there a fellow named Ambrose Shagwell about?"

"Mr. Shagwell, the *owner?*"

"I suppose he is." Albert reached into a pocket and produced a calling card with his name embossed on it. "Show him this," he directed.

332

The boy squinted at the card. "You might as well come in," he said.

Albert took indifferent note of the men working at their ledgers. Not liking to be associated with business in any way, he turned his back, gazing instead upon a map of the world pinned to the wall. How he wished he was home in England!

"He'll see you, sir," the boy said upon returning, and led Albert into Mr. Shagwell's office.

The mill owner had received the young lord's card with both shock and perplexity. After all, Mr. Clemspool had claimed he represented the Kirkle interests. Now here, at his door, was someone announcing he *was* a Kirkle. Mr. Shagwell hardly knew how to react. Though he felt compelled to be wary, he was curious as to who was calling and why.

And when Albert walked into the room, Mr. Shagwell was even more taken aback. Here was merely a very awkward youth who, nonetheless, as indicated by the way he dressed, appeared to be of the first rank.

"How do you do, sir," the mill owner managed to say, feeling obliged to step out from behind his desk and offer to shake the young man's hand.

Albert, making no concession to friendliness—and not even removing his hat—demanded, "Look here, are you Shagwell?"

"Ambrose Shagwell at your service, sir. And you"—he glanced at the calling card—"are Sir Albert Kirkle. What, sir, may I have the honor of doing for you?"

"Actually, I'm . . . looking for someone." Albert reached into his vest pocket and removed the letter Mr. Clemspool had written to him. "My younger brother, you know. Ungrateful scamp ran off . . . from home."

Once again Mr. Shagwell was puzzled. "And what, sir, does that have to do with me?"

333

"He's here in America somewhere," Albert explained with a general gesture. "But I don't know where. The thing is, he was brought here by a fellow by the name of Clemspool. That name . . . mean anything to you?"

"It might," Mr. Shagwell replied with caution.

"This Clemspool fellow said I could reach him through you."

"Did he?"

"That's what he wrote."

"What, sir," Mr. Shagwell asked Albert, "are your connections to this Mr. Clemspool?"

"He was doing some . . . little business for me."

The answer startled Mr. Shagwell. Could it be that he had made a mistake in thinking Mr. Clemspool was a swindler? Perhaps he *did* represent the Kirkle interests. "Is he, sir, an associate, a friend?"

"Friend!" Albert exclaimed with a sneer. "The man's a scoundrel!"

This response brought Mr. Shagwell much relief. "Well, sir," he allowed expansively, "your man has been in Lowell."

"Confound the fellow," said Albert. "Did he have a boy with him?"

"I know nothing about a boy, sir. But, you see . . . ," Mr. Shagwell faltered, not exactly sure how to explain without doing himself a disservice.

Albert came to his help. "Look here, Shagwell, I don't like the man. I just need to find him."

Mr. Shagwell smiled. "Well, sir, if you must know, your Mr. Clemspool is presently in . . . well, the city jail."

"Jail!"

"As of last night."

The young man grinned. "I rather like that. What's he there for?"

"He was . . . trying to rob my house."

Albert burst into laughter. "Rob your house! That's the fellow! Was the boy with him? He in jail too?" he asked hopefully.

Mr. Shagwell was not amused. "I told you, I know nothing about a boy."

"Where's this jolly jail?"

"Exchange Street."

"And you don't know anything else about Clemspool?"

"Ummmmm . . . no, sir," Mr. Shagwell said. "But may I ask you, sir, if you or your family has any interest in investing—"

Albert cut him short with a wave of his gloved hand. "Appreciate your information, Shagwell. Imagine that, in jail. . . ." And without another word, he strode from the office, leaving the mill owner as puzzled as he had been when the young lord arrived.

Chapter 178
In the Shanty

*T*here it is," Jeb said to Laurence as he pointed to the shanty in the far corner of the deserted lot.

Laurence looked about, not exactly sure what Jeb was pointing to.

"We built it," Jeb said with pride about the pile of wooden sticks and slabs. "Me and my chums. You get in through the back. Soon as I hide the key, I'll take you to the Spindle City."

He guided Laurence around the structure, pulled aside the old rug used to cover the entryway, and stepped into the shadowy interior.

It took a moment for Jeb's eyes to adjust to the dank darkness. Only then did he see a boy sleeping in one of the corners. Jeb gazed at him. It was not that unusual for one of his friends to spend the night when they were unwelcome at home. But this was a boy he did not know.

"Hello!" Jeb cried. "Who are you? What are you doing here?"

Startled into wakefulness, Patrick tried to twist around, but his hands were tied with an old muffler and his legs were bound. His dirty face bore the streak marks of many tears. "Please," he whimpered, teeth chattering. "Help me. I'm freezing."

Laurence had come into the shack right behind Jeb. He too needed a moment to adjust to the dark. When he saw a boy on the ground before him, he started. He realized who it was. "Patrick!" he cried.

Patrick, recognizing the voice, felt a surge of joy course through him.

"Laurence!" he exclaimed. "By the Holy Mother, you must help me!"

Laurence jumped forward, knelt, and began to untie his friend's bonds.

Recovering his wits, Jeb said, "Who brought you here?"

"Wasn't it some boys who caught me and dragged me," Patrick answered as much to Laurence as to Jeb.

"Was it Nick?" asked Jeb. "Was it Tom? Are you Irish? That why they brought you here?"

Supported by Laurence's steadying hand, Patrick, unbound, struggled to his feet. "Laurence," he begged, rubbing his hands together for warmth, "get me away!"

"I will," Laurence said. Holding on to his friend's arm, he moved him toward the entryway.

"You're not going till you tell me what's happened," Jeb threatened, moving to block their departure.

"He's my friend," Laurence replied. "I have to take him away from here."

"Not till I know what's going on," Jeb said, refusing to budge.

Frustrated, Laurence took a stride forward and attempted to shove Jeb aside. Jeb resisted by grabbing Laurence's arms. The boys tumbled to the ground. Patrick, seeing the way was clear, all but dived out of the shanty.

Laurence, meanwhile, managed to untangle himself from Jeb and jump up. Then he too bolted.

"Come on," he cried to his friend, and led the way, running, toward the street. Patrick, his muscles cramped, limped after him as best he could.

Inside the shanty, a dispirited Jeb picked himself up and brushed himself off. Things had happened too quickly. Who was that tied-up boy?

Cautiously, he went outside. They had already fled. Feeling both anger and relief, Jeb slouched back into the shed and retrieved his shoe-shine box. Suddenly he remembered something: The English boy still had the key.

Chapter 179
Tales Are Told

Where are we going?" Patrick gasped.

"I'm not sure," Laurence cried, glancing back along the street. "We just better get away from that boy."

Patrick halted. He had suddenly remembered Jeb from his first encounter with the boys who taunted him. "Do you know him?"

"Who?"

"That boy you were with. Is he your friend then?"

"Jeb? He's a shoe-shine boy. He was teaching me the trade. I just met him yesterday. Patrick, I think we should go farther before we stop."

Not until they had gone four more streets was Laurence willing to halt. "There," he said. "I think we're safe now." Even so he checked to see if Jeb was following. Seeing no one, he asked, "Patrick, why were you there? Who tied you up?"

As quickly as he could, Patrick told Laurence how Nick and Tom caught him as he came out of the church, how he had been forced to go to the shanty, and about his awful night trussed up.

When the tale was told, Laurence said, "Did they really tie you up just because you're Irish?"

"That's the only reason they gave," Patrick replied. "Faith, it's the only reason anyone gives," he added bitterly.

"It's not fair," Laurence said, and he glanced behind them again as if somehow the answer lay there. Then he said, "Is your father near?"

"Ah, Laurence, you never knew. He died."

"Died!"

"We learned it the morning after you left us."

"I'm . . . sorry," Laurence whispered. "How did it happen?"

"His friend, Mr. Brewster, who came for us at the ship, told us. Said it was my father's heart. Then the fellow brought us here."

"Did Maura and Bridy come too?"

"To be sure. They're in lodgings with a Mrs. Hamlyn. And a fine place it is too, Laurence. You can't imagine how grand it is, with more food than a body can eat."

Laurence grinned. "Are you staying there?"

Patrick shook his head. "Mrs. Hamlyn's is only for gals, so I'm stopping with Mr. Brewster. But, Laurence, I need to know. . . . When I saw you enter that terrible place, it was like the coming of a saint. How did you get there?"

"Mr. Grout and Mr. Drabble brought me to Lowell. And, as I told you, that Jeb was teaching me how to shine shoes."

"Well, whoever he is, the boy did me the favor of getting you there. And that Mr. Grout, is he the one Mr. Drabble was working for on the boat?"

"I don't know," Laurence said, suddenly unsure how much he wanted to tell Patrick. He looked down the street again. "Maybe we shouldn't be going to your home."

"You're right," Patrick agreed. "Those boys know I'm staying on Adams Street. They might come after me again."

"Can you go to your sister's?"

"It would be best," Patrick replied. He started off.

Laurence held back as he tried to decide if he shouldn't first tell Mr. Grout what he had learned from Jeb, that Clemspool was in Lowell. But then he reminded himself that Albert was lurking and decided he'd rather stay with Patrick.

For a while the two boys walked in silence. Finally, Patrick said, "Sure, Laurence, you told me who brought you to Lowell. But you haven't said a word as to the why. Was it so that Mr. Drabble could court my sister?"

"He didn't say so to me."

"Then why?"

Laurence glanced sideways at Patrick. Though he wanted to tell his whole tale, he felt great uneasiness as to what his friend's reaction would be. Nervously, he said, "Mr. Grout is looking for some money."

"Is he now? What do you mean?"

"It was . . . money that was . . . stolen."

"Stolen? Lord forbid. Who was it taken from?"

The word *me* caught in Laurence's mouth. He could taste it. But he could not get it past his lips.

Patrick, sensing something was wrong, stopped and contemplated Laurence.

Afraid to meet Patrick's questioning eyes, Laurence finally

said, "It was taken from . . . me." He spoke so softly it was difficult for Patrick to hear.

The Irish boy's eyes narrowed. "I'm not understanding."

"Patrick," Laurence stumbled on, "it was money . . . I . . . stole. In London."

"Faith, I remember now." Patrick nodded with grave understanding. "In Liverpool—on that queer church boat—wasn't that minister fellow saying you ran away from home? And weren't all those people looking for you? Was it all about money then?"

Upset, Laurence started to walk away. Patrick hurried to catch up. "Was it a great amount?" he asked.

Heart heavy, Laurence had to stop again. "A . . . thousand . . . pounds."

"A thousand pounds!" Patrick cried in disbelief. "Go on now! You're talking daft! That's the coin of kings and queens. And, sure, in Liverpool you had nothing like."

Laurence felt as if he were dying. His eyes were full of tears. "It was taken from me."

"Was it that runner Toggs?"

Laurence shook his head.

"Who then?"

"Mr. Grout."

"Mr. Grout!" Patrick exclaimed. "Laurence, you have me spinning! Didn't you say he's the one you're with?"

Laurence nodded. "He's trying . . . to get the money back from the man who . . . took it from him."

"Jesus, Mary, and Joseph," Patrick muttered. "You're living a tangled tale. Where in the name of Saint Patrick himself did you get that kind of loot?"

Laurence closed his eyes.

"Surely now, Laurence," Patrick pressed, "you can trust me. Haven't we become like brothers? Faith, I'll never tell a blessed soul." He made the sign of the cross to show how seriously he took the vow.

"I took it from my father," Laurence blurted out.

"Your father!"

"Yes. . . ."

"Holy faith, Laurence," Patrick said with wonder even as he took hold of his friend's sleeve, "from the look of you, I'd never have thought. But where would the likes of a father of yours be having that kind of money?"

"He . . . owns . . . land," Laurence stammered.

"*Land?*"

"I think so."

"Where?"

"Places. . . . In Ireland."

"Ireland," Patrick echoed, and his hand fell away from Laurence. He stepped back. "Laurence, there's something else you're fearing of telling me, isn't there?"

"Yes. . . ."

"What is it?"

"My . . . name."

"I don't understand."

"It's Laurence . . . Kirkle," the boy said as though ashes filled his mouth. "Sir . . . Laurence Kirkle."

"*Kirkle,*" Patrick repeated.

Laurence nodded.

"By all the saints," Patrick whispered. "Are you saying then . . . it's the same Lord Kirkle who owns . . . the land of . . . Kilonny?"

"I think so . . . ," Laurence replied bleakly.

Patrick's eyes grew wide with dismay. "What makes you think so?" he asked.

"Before I ran away I . . . saw a paper on my father's desk—with that name on it."

"Holy Jesus," a shocked Patrick murmured. "Laurence, does the name Mr. Morgan mean anything to you?"

"No."

"He's your father's agent. Him that collects the rents. And

341

a cruel man, Laurence. Something awful. He drove us—and many others—away. And always he was doing it in your father's name. There's blood on Morgan's hands. Buckets of it. And didn't those hands work for your da."

Laurence, crying now, gazed at Patrick. "I didn't know."

"And didn't that Morgan have the soldiers shoot at me? And didn't he want to throw me in jail? Laurence, I have to know. Why did you leave your home?"

"It was my brother, and my father, they . . . didn't treat me well."

"That mark on your face," Patrick said. "It was new when I met you. Was it that?"

Laurence nodded.

"And who was the one who did it?"

"My brother," Laurence said. "But my father let him. And Patrick," he added, "my brother is here, in Lowell. You have to help me."

"By all that's sacred," Patrick replied with the utmost gravity, "I'm not so sure I should."

Chapter 180
In Search of Safety

P atrick," Laurence pleaded, "I didn't have anything to do with Ireland or your Mr. Morgan, and I—"

"Sir Laurence Kirkle," Patrick said bitterly, "how can you be my friend while your father's a great enemy?"

"I'm not your enemy," Laurence cried. "I just helped you, didn't I?"

Patrick looked away.

"And you helped me in Liverpool," Laurence pressed, "and on the ship."

They walked on. A silent Patrick stared straight ahead. Laurence kept stealing glances at him. After some ten minutes the Irish boy stopped. "Laurence," Patrick said, facing him, "that money you're looking for . . . by the Holy Mother, don't you see? Some of it must have come from Kilonny!"

"But I don't have it," Laurence cried. "And it wasn't me who took it from your village!"

Patrick ran his fingers through his black hair. "I hardly know what to be saying," he admitted. "But I suppose you need not worry. Didn't I swear I wouldn't be telling your tale? I can't be going back on my oath. For now, it's my sister I need to be talking to, and over there is the house she's lodging at. Do you want to come along or not?"

"Will you still be my friend?"

"I have to be thinking about it," Patrick replied.

"Then I guess we should go," said a disappointed Laurence.

As they drew nearer to the Hamlyn house, they saw Bridy on the front steps. As soon as she saw Patrick, she ran toward him gladly.

"There you are, Bridy," Patrick called to her. "Look who I found on the streets."

Bridy gazed up at Laurence and smiled shyly.

"And what were you doing out here?" Patrick asked.

"I'm watching," the girl said.

"Are you now. For what?"

"It's my job," Bridy said solemnly. "Mr. Hamlyn wants me to watch for someone."

"Then you're being helpful," Patrick said with amusement. "Do you know if Maura is in?"

"I think she's still working."

All the same Patrick knocked on the door. It was the housemaid who answered. "Please, miss," Patrick said, "I'm

Maura O'Connell's brother, Patrick. I need to be speaking to my sister. It's something urgent."

"Just wait a bit then," the young woman said, shutting the door. Within moments it opened again, and Mrs. Hamlyn looked out. "Master Patrick," she said. "I am glad to see you. Your sister was worried about you."

"Can I be speaking with her then?"

"Oh, no. She's at the mill. Is there something the matter?"

"I'm in a kind of trouble, mistress."

"Trouble?" the woman asked. "What kind?"

Patrick explained what had happened to him. "You see, I'm afraid to go to Mr. Brewster's rooms," he said when he'd told it all. "And I need to be talking with my sister."

Mrs. Hamlyn, having listened to the story with sympathy, gave a sigh of regret when Patrick was done. "I'm sorry about what occurred," she said. "It's nothing but wickedness. And I think you're right. It wouldn't be wise to roam the streets if those boys are looking for you. Besides, you need something to eat. You must be famished and cold. You can wait here until your sister returns."

"Did she go off looking for work?"

Mrs. Hamlyn smiled. "She's been employed at the Shagwell Mill."

Patrick grinned. "I'm glad to know it," he said.

Mrs. Hamlyn drew open the door to allow the boy to enter. Laurence, not sure what to do, remained standing below the steps.

"And who is this?" Mrs. Hamlyn asked.

Patrick looked back. "His name is . . . Laurence, mistress."

Mrs. Hamlyn scrutinized the boy before her. "Where does he come from?" she said, finding him scrawny and dirty.

"He came to America on the same ship we did."

Mrs. Hamlyn pursed her lips. "He's very ragged. Is he from Ireland too?"

344

"England."

"But a friend of yours?"

Laurence and Patrick looked at each other.

"Is he?" Mrs. Hamlyn asked again.

Patrick said, "He saved my life, twice."

"Did he? Then he must be a good friend indeed. I presume he knows your sister."

"Yes, mistress."

"Then perhaps he could deliver a message from you to her. I'm sure she'd like to know you're all right. And he might tell her to come home immediately after work. Are you willing to go?" she asked Laurence.

"Yes, ma'am."

"Fine. I'll give you directions. As for you, Patrick, you must stop here. It will be safer. Miss Bridy, will you be coming in too?"

"No, please," the girl replied, cozy in the secret she shared with Mr. Hamlyn. "I need to be watching."

Chapter 181

In Which Mr. Clemspool Has a Visitor

Mr. Clemspool had spent an insufferable night. First he had been thrown out of the Shagwell house. Then he had been arrested by Mr. Tolliver as a common thief for attempting to rob the mill owner. Next he had been booked at the police office, taken to jail, and locked in a cell that was not just dingy and dirty but rancid with the stench of all the common prisoners who had been kept there.

Even so, the cell was not the worst of it for Mr. Clemspool. Far worse was his belief that the bank key remained in the drawer of the bedside table—or with that boy from the street! Just the possibility that he had lost access to all that money was enough to drive him into a perfect frenzy.

When he interrogated his jailer about his rights as a freeborn Englishman, he was told that he could be free in two days, not before. Mr. Clemspool hastened to point out that, for an earlier release, he would be able to offer the jail keeper a handsome bonus.

The jail keeper, a grizzled fellow with a bulky, sagging pear-shaped body, merely guffawed and walked away.

Swearing many a foul oath against the man, Mr. Clemspool took to the cell's wooden bench, which the jail keeper had insisted was the bed.

That night, the sole proprietor of Brother's Keeper, Ltd., tossed and turned so that he slept little. By breakfast time—breakfast consisting of boiled coffee, stale bread, and a sinewy pull of cold beef—Mr. Clemspool was reduced to muttering, "Bloody all Kirkles!" in a rage, desperately desiring to wring their collective aristocratic necks like so many chickens set for a stew.

Midmorning, Mr. Clemspool was pacing up and down his cell, fuming and focused principally on Laurence. As far as Matthew Clemspool was concerned, the boy was the cause of all his problems! Bad enough in England. Here he was in America, blighting him again. . . .

A clanging on his cell door startled Mr. Clemspool. "You've got a visitor, mister," the jail keeper announced through the bars. "Says he's a friend!"

"A friend!" Mr. Clemspool exclaimed, wondering who in the world might be coming to his aid. "Who is it?" he asked. "The British ambassador?"

"He wouldn't give his name. Want to see him or not?"

"I suppose I do." Mr. Clemspool hastened to smooth

down his few licks of hair and put on his jacket. But hardly had he the chance when who should walk in but Sir Albert Kirkle.

"I've left the door open," said the jail keeper to Albert. "Just shut it when you leave."

A disbelieving Mr. Clemspool stared at the young man. He even stretched his plump fingers into the air and made a feeble attempt to brush away the dream that he presumed Albert was.

"Didn't think it would be me, did you?" the young lord began, finding great amusement in Mr. Clemspool's astonishment. He smirked and squeezed his hands until his knuckles cracked.

"*Is* it you?" Mr. Clemspool returned nervously, wondering if he had, perhaps, lost his mind as so many did who suffered lengthy prison stays.

"It's me, all right."

"But . . . but why—how—are you here?" Mr. Clemspool stammered.

"You wrote to me, didn't you?"

"From the ship . . . I suppose I did."

"Asking blackmail money—"

"Sir! Blackmail? Heaven forfend! You wrong me! I was merely asking you for the money you—to make my point precisely—owed me."

"Well, you can thank my father for this visit," Sir Albert said. "He intercepted that letter and passed it on to me. You said you had my brother. Well, where is he? My lord father has said—in a most unseemly temper—that I'm not to come back unless I bring Laurence with me."

"And do you," Mr. Clemspool inquired carefully, "intend to . . . take him home?"

Albert snorted with disdain. "Take him home! Look here, Clemspool, I came to this awful place to make sure you did what you promised to do, get rid of him, for good. My father

347

won't let the Kirkle name go to nothing. He can settle for me. I'm the real thing. Not Laurence."

Mr. Clemspool, feeling a rush of his old confidence, flipped the tails of his jacket, sat down on the bench, and leaned back against the wall. "All very well for you to talk, Sir Albert," he replied in his best haughty tones. "Don't think I haven't devoted myself to your cause. Indeed, I wouldn't be here"—he waved his hands in a gesture that encompassed the jail cell—"if *you* had not managed to make a muddle of things."

"Me?"

"No point in going into details," Mr. Clemspool said airily. "In order to achieve your desired object, sir, you must deal with me. To begin, you must get me out of here."

Albert shook his head. "I'm not interested in you, Clemspool. Just my bothersome brother."

Mr. Clemspool smiled blandly. "Sir, I appreciate your frankness. But without me, you can't get him, can you? Mind, your brother and I have become great friends. You should also know that I'm aware of the money he took."

"How much of it is left?"

"Oh," Mr. Clemspool said with his best shrug of indifference, "most of it."

"Where is it?" asked Albert, suddenly alert.

Mr. Clemspool smiled shrewdly. "If I may be so bold, Sir Albert," he said, "I should like to offer an arrangement. Help me get out of this place, and you and I—together—shall go to Laurence. Have no fear. I'll take care of him. As for the money, sir, why, you can have it all."

"How do I know I can trust you?" Albert asked.

Mr. Clemspool drew himself up with dignity. "Sir, I consider myself an honest man, a moral man. Have you read your Bible, sir—"

Albert cut him off. "Cut the cant, Clemspool. Where's my brother?"

"No, sir," Mr. Clemspool replied grandly, "you either help me or you can forget about the money. As for your brother, he will—"

"Will what?"

Mr. Clemspool reached into the air and snatched at it. "Why, sir, I will be forced—on strictly moral grounds, you understand—to aid your brother in his desired return to England . . . and, to make my point precisely, *encourage* him to go to your father."

"All right," Albert interjected quickly. "Just tell me what I have to do."

"I told you. Get me out of here."

"How?"

"That oaf of a jail keeper left the cell door open. I shall walk out."

"But—"

"Your task is to go find the blockhead. Detain him. Busy him for ten minutes. I shall bide my time, then take my leave."

"I have a carriage waiting just outside."

"Better and better. I'll just get in it. Follow at your leisure."

"Look here, Clemspool—"

"Sir Albert, do you wish to have that boy taken care of? Do you desire the money? Or do you want him—and the money—to return to England?"

Albert gave a grunt and slipped out of the cell. Mr. Clemspool hovered by the door. After five minutes he walked out of the jail quite unnoticed.

Chapter 182
The Bank Key

M r. Clemspool glared out the carriage window at the passing streets of Lowell.

"The world," he snarled at Albert, who sat slouched across from him with a vacant look on his face, "the *entire* world would be better off without young people. Look at Adam! Look at Eve! And young, weren't they? Well then, consider the harm they did! How difficult for the rest of us! Yes, it's young people like that who cause most of the problems in the world. What a pity *I* wasn't there to advise them."

"I'm young," Albert drawled.

"You make my point precisely," snapped Mr. Clemspool. "But no doubt I shall be happier when I return to my room, take a bath, shave, and find some clean clothing. I don't like jails. Never have."

Albert leered. "Been in them before, eh?"

The top of Mr. Clemspool's bald head turned quite pink. "That, sir, is none of your business. I will only say, if governments insist upon putting citizens in such places, they might have the courtesy to make them comfortable. Hello!" he suddenly cried, and banged on the roof of the carriage. "Stop!"

"What's the matter?" demanded Albert, startled by the outburst and the lurching halt of the carriage.

"There! You see that boy!" Mr. Clemspool cried, pointing out the window at Jeb Grafton.

Jeb was walking down the sidewalk, shoe-shine box tucked under an arm, cap pulled low over his face.

"What about him? He looks dirty enough."

"He must be detained!" cried Mr. Clemspool. "Money, Sir Albert, money. . . ." He thrust open the door and, pulling Albert along with him, tumbled out of the carriage. "We'll be right back," he cried to the carriage driver. "Don't move." Then he ordered Albert, "You go ahead of the boy. I'll catch him up from the rear. Hurry!"

A reluctant Albert lumbered along the street, pushing his way by pedestrians until he had passed Jeb. Mr. Clemspool, simultaneously, crept up behind him.

"There you are!" he cried as he clamped his hand tightly upon the unsuspecting boy's right shoulder.

Startled, Jeb twisted about and saw who had apprehended him. He then tried to pull free and run only to have Albert block his way.

"What do you want from me?" Jeb cried.

"Come along quickly," Mr. Clemspool insisted. Holding tightly to one of the boy's arms with both hands, he dragged him toward the carriage.

"I don't want to go," Jeb cried, trying to resist.

"You'll come with me or go to the police, do you hear!" Mr. Clemspool hissed into the boy's ear. Albert helped by shoving the boy from behind.

Jeb, seeing that there was no one to rescue him, gave in to the pressure.

"In you go!" cried Mr. Clemspool as he pushed Jeb into the carriage. Then he too climbed in and took a place directly across from the boy to make sure he stayed. Albert squeezed in next to Jeb.

"What do you want with me?" Jeb, feeling overwhelmed, sniffled.

"What do I *want* with you?" bellowed Mr. Clemspool. "What do you think I want? I want what's mine. You got into that room in Shagwell's house. Where is my key?"

"Don't know what you're talking about," Jeb said.

Mr. Clemspool leaned forward and shook a fat fist before the boy's nose. "Wretched youth! Of course you know what I'm talking about. The *key*, you dunce, the one I sent you into the room for. Where is it?"

"I don't have it," Jeb said tearfully. "I don't! You can search all my pockets. I don't have it!"

Albert looked across at Mr. Clemspool. "What's all this about a key?"

"Never mind," the man snapped. "He knows what I'm talking about. You say you don't have it. *Did* you have it?" he demanded of the boy.

After a moment Jeb nodded.

"You contemptible swindler! I knew you did. You probably called in the police too, didn't you?"

"I didn't, mister! I swear I didn't!"

"Then what happened to that key?" Mr. Clemspool roared.

Jeb, wilting before the onslaught, sniffled, smeared his nose with the back of his hand, took a breath, and said, "A boy took it from me."

"A boy?" cried an exasperated Mr. Clemspool. "What boy?"

Jeb squeezed himself farther into the corner. "The same one as you wanted me to watch."

"Laurence?" Mr. Clemspool screeched.

Jeb nodded.

"Look here," Albert said, finally interested, "is he talking about my brother?"

Jeb glanced at Albert, realized it was the man Laurence was running away from, and grew even more frightened.

Ignoring Albert's question, Mr. Clemspool leaned forward so that his hot face was close to Jeb's. "Are you telling the truth, boy?" he demanded with loathing.

"Yes, sir. . . . He and another boy took it," Jeb said.

"What other boy?"

"I don't know his name. But he's Irish."

"Irish? What difference does that make?" Mr. Clemspool shouted. With a spasm of anger, he heaved himself back into his seat. Then, full of rage, he snatched at the air as if it were Laurence himself. "Now answer this," he cried at Jeb. "Is Laurence *aware* of what that key is for?"

"You just said it was for some precious property. And I didn't even tell him that."

"Where is he now?"

"He ran away."

Mr. Clemspool flung his head back. "I hate that boy!" he screamed.

"I say," interjected Albert, "what *is* this all about?"

Mr. Clemspool leaned forward again and pressed an accusatory finger on Jeb's nose. "Get out, and don't ever let me see you again. If the police catch you—and I have a good friend in the police—you'll spend the rest of your contemptible life in prison. Do you understand? The rest of your life! Now get out and go away!"

Jeb stared at Mr. Clemspool, trying to decide if he should believe the man or not. Cautiously, he sat up, wiggled toward the carriage door, threw it open, and leaped out.

Albert pulled the door shut.

"Clemspool," he said again, "what *is* all this?"

The man cast a withering look at the young lord. "Your brother, sir, is about to recover all that money."

Albert sat up. "My *father's*—Lord Kirkle's—money?"

"And if he does, sir, I have not the slightest doubt he will gallop home to Belgrave Square, and that, sir, will be the end of *you*."

Albert's face reddened and grew blotchy with alarm. "But you said you knew where Laurence was," he gasped.

"I do."

"Then . . . then," the young man stammered, "don't you think we should seize him?"

Instead of answering, Mr. Clemspool leaned out of the

353

carriage window and instructed the driver to take them directly to the Spindle City Hotel.

Once there, however, Mr. Clemspool was at some perplexity as to how to proceed. Though he longed to find Laurence, he had no desire to confront Mr. Grout. He decided, therefore, that it would be much more prudent to wait and watch.

"Remember, sir," he said to Albert, "it's your brother we're seeking. Keep an eye out for him."

By way of a reply Albert gave a grunt.

"As we have the time," said Mr. Clemspool, "I shall tell you what happened in Liverpool. And you will see, sir, that no fault can be attached to me. Indeed, on your behalf—to make my point precisely—I have suffered much."

Chapter 183
Mr. Drabble Returns

Mr. Drabble, his recovered volume of Shakespeare under his arm, and excited by his discovery of Maura's dwelling place, returned breathlessly to the Spindle City Hotel. Wanting to make certain he did not forget his beloved's address, he asked at the clerk's desk for pencil and paper.

On the paper he wrote:

Where Maura O'Connell lives:
87 Cabot Street

Neither Laurence nor Mr. Grout was in the room. With hardly a thought of them, Mr. Drabble secreted the paper under his pillow, stretched out on his bed, and—his head propped up with his hands—gave way to romantic imaginings. Once more he looked into Maura's blue eyes. The vision made him sigh.

Chapter 184
Laurence Meets Some Friends

"Tell my sister I'm here and not to worry," Patrick requested as Laurence was about to leave the Hamlyn house.

"Shall I say what happened to you?"

"I suppose you'd better. But I'm thinking you should also be letting her know it was you who rescued me."

"Why?"

"It will do you some good."

Laurence looked at Patrick earnestly. "Are you still my friend then . . . ?"

"By the Holy Mother, Laurence, I'm still thinking it over. It's a bit of a thing, isn't it, not knowing your friend from your enemy, and him the same person? Faith, I'm saying the truth. If I'd known in Liverpool what you've told me, I wouldn't have helped you."

"But why?" replied a shocked Laurence.

"Ah, Laurence, you don't know the misery your father dealt!"

"But maybe he didn't know."

"If he's taking the money from us, he should be knowing!" Patrick replied with anger.

"But I didn't know."

Patrick suddenly shrugged. "Sure then, the innocence of babes," he said bitterly.

Laurence, afraid to say any more on the subject, muttered, "I'll come back as soon as I can," and set off.

It was not long before he was standing in front of the Shagwell Corton Mill, gazing at the buildings. Impressed by the noise and numbers of people he saw, he hesitated as to whether to go forward or not. Not that anyone paid him any notice.

Preparing to wait for Maura—Mrs. Hamlyn had said the lunch break came at twelve-thirty—Laurence sat against one of the mill walls. There, in a spot bathed in warm sunlight, he gave himself over to musing about his confession to Patrick.

Laurence could hardly believe the facts of his life as he'd told them to his friend. Though he knew perfectly well his father was Lord Kirkle, their privileged world seemed very remote. Once again he told himself he was no longer a part of it. That made Patrick's hostility all the harder to bear. Even so, the question arose again: Would he—if he got the money back—return to England?

With a sigh, Laurence acknowledged he didn't know the answer. "I'm not Sir Laurence Kirkle," he said aloud, "I'm Laurence Worthy." With a rueful smile, he recalled how he'd gotten the name Worthy. From a muffin man in London. . . . Yet perhaps he was not Laurence Worthy either but someone new. Not that Patrick noticed, he thought sadly.

Laurence assumed that Albert meant to bring him back to London. Even if he did return, it wouldn't be Albert who took him. Upon that Laurence was resolved. "Maybe," he said out loud, "I am John Faherty. If I am, I have no brother in this world."

But over and over again the boy's thoughts circled back

to the question of Lord Kirkle's money. Perhaps if he could get it back, all his questions would be answered.

As the sun shifted, Laurence began to feel chilly. In search of warmth he thrust his hands in his pockets and felt the key Jeb had given him. He had forgotten all about it. On the key shank he read the words:

MERRIMACK VALLEY CONSOLIDATED BANK
AND LAND COMPANY

How, Laurence wondered, had a boy like Jeb come by such a key? And what was it for? He was about to toss it away when the city lunch bells startled him. Half past twelve! Maura! Cramming the key back in his pocket, Laurence scrambled to his feet.

As he looked on, hordes of people burst from the large building and swept out from the yard, making their way to boardinghouses where meals would be waiting for them. They had thirty-five minutes to get there, eat, and be back to their work.

Those who did not leave the mill sat or strolled, alone or with others, eating from buckets, kerchiefs, or leather pouches.

Laurence searched the crowds for Maura. It took some fifteen minutes before he spied her. She was leaning against a sunny wall, eyes closed, face turned toward the warmth. By her side was a young man who now and again seemed to be speaking to her, though, for all Laurence could see, she did not reply.

He approached cautiously. "Miss O'Connell," he called.

Maura looked about, staring at him with puzzlement. Then she realized who it was. "Faith and glory," she cried, "it's Laurence himself!" Not only was she surprised to see him, she found herself glad too. "And what might you be doing here?"

"It's Patrick. . . ."

Maura shook her head and smiled. "I should have guessed it was only you and he in mischief again." She turned to Nathaniel. "This is Laurence, a poor English boy that Patrick befriended in Liverpool. He was on the ship with us."

"Welcome to America," Nathaniel said.

"Miss O'Connell," Laurence said, "Patrick is perfectly fine. But he wasn't when I found him."

Maura's smile faded. She put a hand to her throat. "Why, what do you mean?"

Laurence told her what had happened to her brother, how and where he found him, and that he was now with Mrs. Hamlyn.

"Jesus, Mary, and Joseph," Maura said, flinging her hair out of her face with a snap of her head, "are we Irish to get no peace in this world? Laurence, I've done you wrong," she conceded. "It's twice now you've been kind to my brother. Once is friendship. Twice is more like kith and kin. I'll ever be thankful to you."

Laurence, wondering what she would say if she knew what he had told Patrick, made no reply.

"Mr. Brewster, do I have the time to see him now?" Maura asked Nathaniel.

"Not nearly," said the young man. "But at least you know he's all right."

"Are you the man he's staying with?" Laurence asked.

"I am."

"He said the boys knew where he lived, and he's afraid to go there. He's staying at Mrs. Hamlyn's."

"He is probably wise," agreed Nathaniel grimly. "I'll go back with you tonight," he said to Maura.

"I'll come too," Laurence offered.

Maura, worried now, looking down, said only, "That would be fine."

"But I have to go to my friends first and tell them where I am," Laurence said.

Maura lifted her face. "Would that be Mr. Drabble?" she asked.

"Yes."

The young woman hesitated, even blushed when she remembered how she had bid the actor leave her at the Boston wharf. "Laurence . . . you can tell Mr. Drabble . . . for friendship's sake . . . I should like to see him."

Promising to do so, Laurence dutifully set off for the Spindle City Hotel. When he reached it, he paused and looked for Jeb at his shoe-shine post. But other than a carriage stationed opposite the door, everything appeared exactly as when he left early that morning.

Within moments Laurence was in his room, where he discovered Mr. Drabble stretched our on his bed, reading his volume of Shakespeare. Mr. Grout was not there.

"Well, here you are," exclaimed the actor. "I've been worrying about you. Are you all right?"

"I'm fine," said Laurence.

"Truly, Master Laurence," Mr. Drabble chided gently, "we must really keep each other better informed."

Laurence was perfectly willing to tell the actor all that had happened regarding Patrick, including the news of Mr. O'Connell's death. This he did at some length, mentioning but briefly the role of Jeb Grafton in the affair. He also told Mr. Drabble how he had gone to Maura and delivered Patrick's message.

The thin man popped up like a drawbridge. "And . . . did Miss O'Connell ask . . . anything . . . about me?"

Laurence nodded.

Mr. Drabble closed his eyes and commenced to breathe deeply. "Pray tell, what . . . did she . . . say?"

"She said she'd like to see you."

"Oh, my heart!" cried the actor, his face taking on a perfectly crimson hue of delight. Hugging his Shakespeare volume to his chest, he leaped to his feet. "I shall go to her immediately," he announced.

"She's working at a mill," Laurence warned. "She won't be going home until the work is over."

"But I know where she works," Mr. Drabble replied, full of trembling excitement. "I'll wait at the gates."

"Mr. Drabble, do you have any idea when Mr. Grout will be—," Laurence began to say only to have the door burst open and Sir Albert Kirkle step into the room.

Chapter 185

A Family Reunion

Laurence stood like a small animal trapped in surprise. Albert, leaning arrogantly against the door frame, grinned with glee.

"You wretched, insufferable thief!" he declared. "What do you say to my marking up the other side of your insolent face?"

Albert's words jarred Laurence out of his shock. In its place, anger and hatred began to boil.

Mr. Drabble, though just as startled as Laurence, leaped forward to stand between the brothers. "I beg your pardon, sir," he cautioned Albert. "This is a private room."

"Keep aside, fellow," Albert replied, flapping a dismissive hand in the actor's face. "I have some matters—private matters—to discuss with my brother."

This declaration of a family connection caused Mr. Drabble to look from one to the other hastily. There was—he now saw—a resemblance between the two.

"Laurence," Mr. Drabble inquired, "is this young gentleman what he claims to be?"

"I hate him!" Laurence cried. "I hate him."

Mr. Drabble drew himself to his full height. "Sir," he declared to Albert, "considering what my young friend has said, I must ask you to leave."

"He's my younger brother, isn't he?" Albert sneered. "And I've come a rather long way to give him the punishment he deserves."

"Punishment? Pray tell, for what offense?" Mr. Drabble asked.

"That boy's a thief," the young lord drawled with contempt. "So stand aside and let me take him. He's stolen something I want." With that he made a sudden if clumsy grab at Laurence.

The boy leaped back upon Mr. Drabble's bed.

"And what, sir," Mr. Drabble persisted, "did Laurence steal?"

"Money," gasped a frustrated Albert as he edged closer to his brother.

Laurence, who kept inching away, tried to defend himself by snatching up the pillow and holding it before him like a shield.

"How much, sir," Mr. Drabble pressed, "did he take?"

"A thousand pounds."

The figure, Mr. Drabble recalled, was the exact amount of money Mr. Grout admitted to taking from the boy. "But where," he asked, "did Laurence get the money?"

"Look here," said Albert, after yet another futile lunge at his brother, "don't you know about this scamp? He stole it from my father, Lord Kirkle."

Mr. Drabble's eyes grew very round. "Are you asserting, sir, that this wretched boy is the *son* of *Lord Kirkle?*"

"The *younger* son," Albert took pains to say as he made still one more ineffectual grab at Laurence. "To tell the

361

truth, the governor don't care a snap for him. All he wants is his money back. That's why he sent me over."

"Liar!" cried Laurence.

"Sir," Mr. Drabble interjected, "I hasten to inform you that this boy has only a few pennies to his pocket."

Worn out, Albert stopped trying to reach his brother. Perplexity gathered on his face. "Where's the rest of the money then?" he asked.

"A man named Clemspool stole it!" Laurence shouted.

Albert, thinking he had caught Laurence in a lie, broke into a grin. "All right," he said, "let's ask the fellow directly." So saying, he stepped to the door and made a beckoning gesture. Into the room walked Matthew Clemspool like a Roman general marching through a triumphal arch. His face fairly glowed with pleasure; a benign smile played upon his lips. His plump hands spread wide—as if ready to grasp the entire world.

"Well, young sir," he said to Laurence, "I am—to make my point precisely—*delighted* to see you again. There is something about a hotel room. . . . Now then, if you would be so good as to give me—"

Mr. Clemspool did not finish the sentence. Laurence, seeing his two great enemies standing side by side, was now utterly inflamed with rage. So powerful was his anger that he hurled the pillow he was holding into his brother's face with such force, it drove the young man back against the wall. Laurence followed up this blow by jumping from the bed and flinging himself upon Mr. Clemspool, knocking that gentleman to the floor. Even then Laurence did not stop but tore out of the room as fast as he could.

All this occurred so quickly that Mr. Drabble needed a moment to grasp what was happening. Once he did, he too hurried from the room.

"Laurence, wait!" he cried as he ran out of the hotel and saw the boy running pell-mell down the street.

362

Laurence looked back. When he realized that it was only Mr. Drabble trying to catch up to him, he halted.

"Where are you going?" Mr. Drabble demanded.

"To Patrick," Laurence panted.

"Is that where Maura will be?"

"I think so."

"Then I'll go with you!" Without another word, man and boy rushed on toward Cabot Street.

Across the street, Jeb Grafton, wanting to take up his shoe-shine post again, watched Laurence run off. Ruefully, he wondered if the boy still had the key with him. Should he follow, Jeb wondered, as Mr. Clemspool had employed him to do? He was, he knew, a little frightened of the boy. He looked small, but he was fierce. And now there was a man with him too. Even so, Jeb decided he would hardly place himself in harm's way if he followed at a distance to see where they were going. Perhaps if he told Mr. Clemspool where the boy was, he might yet get something. Jeb didn't like Mr. Clemspool, but there was his mother's illness. And if ten dollars could cure her . . . After all, he had been promised that amount to fetch the key.

Chapter 186
Further Adventures in the Hotel

*I*n the hotel room it was Albert who recovered his composure first. He trudged to the room door and made a nervous check of the hallway. Neither Laurence nor Mr. Drabble were in sight.

"This has become an exhausting business," he said, turning back into the room and shutting the door firmly behind him as if that would put an end to the business.

A scowling Mr. Clemspool sat on the floor, methodically checking his bones.

"I say, Clemspool," Albert complained, "have you noticed, every time you make a plan things go smash?"

Mr. Clemspool darted a wrathful glance up at the young lord. "You, sir," he sneered, "are nothing more than an insufferable buffoon." With much groaning and moaning, he got up and brushed himself off. Then he looked at his pocket watch.

Albert cracked his knuckles. "What are we to do now? Does the boy have this bank key or not?"

"He must."

"Don't you think we should pursue him?"

"How do I know where he's gone?"

"Then what are we to do?"

"You just told me, sir, that everything I plan goes badly. Now you presume to ask my advice. I can see why your father prefers his younger son to his elder. At least he's got some pluck. Are you not capable, sir, of any thoughts on your own behalf?"

"Look here, Clemspool," Albert protested, "the boy said *you* took the money. Did you?"

"I *had* it," Mr. Clemspool snapped, "but I put it in a bank vault to keep it safe for you. Then Laurence stole the key. That's what we need. It may yet be here somewhere. He left quickly."

The two began a frenzied search, turning over the beds, stripping them of blankets, even flipping through the pages of Mr. Drabble's Shakespeare.

"What about this?" Albert asked, finding a piece of paper, the one on which Mr. Drabble had written:

Where Maura O'Connell lives:
87 Cabot Street

364

Mr. Clemspool snatched at the paper, considered it momentarily, then flung it away with indifference. But though the two searched thoroughly, they found no key.

Exasperated, Mr. Clemspool sat upon one of the now righted beds and pondered what they might do next.

"That boy you had in the carriage," Albert suggested, "do you think he knows more than he said?"

"Now how would I know that?" Mr. Clemspool replied.

"He just might be worth trying," Albert offered.

"You simpleton! I don't know where he is either!" cried Mr. Clemspool, reaching out as if to find some answer in the air. There was none.

But outside the door there were footsteps. In the next moment the doorknob rattled. Startled, Mr. Clemspool looked up. Sir Albert's face paled like a boiled potato.

"Hide yourself behind the door!" Mr. Clemspool hissed. Hardly had Albert done so than the door swung open and into the room stepped Mr. Grout.

It was with considerable and mutual surprise that Toby Grout and Matthew Clemspool gazed at each other.

Mr. Clemspool affected a sickly smile. "Ah, Mr. Grout, sir," he exclaimed, his bald head sweating profusely. "How very pleasant indeed it is to see you again."

Mr. Grout fixed his glittering eye upon his former partner. "Wot yer doin' 'ere, Clemspool?"

"Why, good sir, having learned that you were in town, I decided to make a social call in hopes that we could let bygones be bygones."

"Clemspool! Where's the money yer took from me?" was the rejoinder. "I wants it back."

"Sir," Mr. Clemspool protested, "I will swear upon my immortal soul that I have not so much as one penny at my disposal."

Mr. Grout raised his massive fists and took a step forward.

Retreating in haste, Mr. Clemspool crashed against a bed and sat down.

"You took that money from me!" Mr. Grout roared.

"Let me merely say . . . ," Mr. Clemspool cast about for a reply. Then remembering that Albert was hiding behind the door, he said, "Mr. Grout, sir, back on the ship you expressed your desire to return the money to the esteemed Kirkle family. Did you not?"

"I said it when I thought the laddie was dead. Only 'e's alive so it's to 'im I'll be givin' it back."

"Well now," said Mr. Clemspool, doing his best to feign surprise, "I am truly delighted to learn the boy is alive, especially since you informed me you'd seen his ghost. But if he is alive, I rejoice and will work to restore the money to the family directly. Happily we are well served. For here, sir," he said with a flashing smile, "is the very one to receive it. Will you come forth, sir?"

With some uncertainty, Albert emerged from behind the door.

"May I introduce Sir Albert Kirkle," Mr. Clemspool said sweetly. "Laurence's elder, affectionate brother. He came all the way from London to rescue the boy and return him to his loving home, where he is deeply missed.

"Sir Albert, this gentleman is Toby Grout, a man, I assure you, of the highest moral values and the will—not to mention the strength—to put them into effect. He worked with me"—he gave a knowing wink—"on many projects."

Albert nodded curtly. "Pleased to meet you, sir."

Toby Grout considered Albert with suspicion. "Yer really the laddie's brother?" he asked.

"I am."

"And did Clemspool 'ere give yer the money 'e prigged from me that I prigged from yer brother?"

"Mr. Grout, I have received nothing. But it has been promised."

366

"Promised! By 'im? And are yer really thinkin' the villain will give it to yer?"

"I believe Mr. Clemspool to be an honorable man," Albert avowed.

"Then yer the biggest block'ead in the world," said Mr. Grout, leaning suddenly over Mr. Clemspool. That gentleman leaned away. It was not far enough. The one-eyed man clamped his hands on Mr. Clemspool's shoulders and dragged him up.

"Sir!" cried Mr. Clemspool.

"Yer a villain!" cried Mr. Grout. "A liar! Yer came 'ere lookin' for somethin'. Wot is it?"

"Sir, you are quite mistaken. And, to make my point precisely—"

"I'm sick of yer persnickety precisely points!" yelled Mr. Grout, shaking Mr. Clemspool so hard, the man's teeth clicked like a baby's rattle. "I wants to know where the money is!"

"Sir Albert," bleated Mr. Clemspool. "Get some help!"

Albert took a step toward the door only to be stared into stopping by the force of Mr. Grout's look.

The onetime prizefighter now transferred his large hands to Mr. Clemspool's neck. "Clemspool," he threatened, "tell me where that money is or yer won't be able to manage one more lyin' breath."

"I don't have it," the man gasped. "I don't!"

"But yer were lookin' for somethin', and that tells me yer knows somethin'. Tell me now or—" His hands squeezed.

"I don't know!" Mr. Clemspool screamed.

Mr. Grout squeezed even tighter.

"It's in the bank!"

Mr. Grout released his grip slightly. "Wot's in wot bank?"

"The money is in the Merrimack Valley Consolidated Bank and Land Company. Here! In Lowell!"

"Get it," Mr. Grout said.

"I can't!"

"Why?"

"It requires a key. I thought it might be here."

"Did yer find it?"

Mr. Clemspool managed to shake his head.

"Where is it then?"

Mr. Clemspool coughed. "Unhand me, and I'll tell you what I know."

Mr. Grout loosened his grip. Mr. Clemspool promptly subsided onto the bed and worked his fingers about his neck as if to make sure his head was still attached in proper fashion.

"The truth is, sir," he began through heavy breathing, "I was informed Laurence had it."

"Laurence! Yer lyin'!"

"It's true!"

"Empty yer pockets," Mr. Grout demanded.

"Sir!"

"Do it!"

Mr. Clemspool did so. Nothing but coins.

"Yers too," Mr. Grout said to Albert.

"I say . . ."

"Do it!"

Albert's pockets revealed no key.

"And yer sure yer don't know where the key is?" Mr. Grout said to Mr. Clemspool.

The man lifted his hand as though in court. "I swear."

Stymied, Mr. Grout backed away from the bed, perplexed about what to do next. He wished Laurence or Mr. Drabble was there so one of them could tell him. All he could think of was to say, "Get out! The both of yer. And don't let me see yer 'ere again, Clemspool. Ever. It'll go much worse, I warn yer."

Mr. Clemspool picked himself up and walked hastily to the door. "I wish you much luck, sir. Truly." And he fled the room. Albert scurried after him, slamming the door.

Mr. Grout, much troubled, thought he should at least put the chaotic room in order. It was while doing so that he found Mr. Drabble's note.

Where Maura O'Connell lives:
87 Cabot Street

Too impatient to struggle through the words, Mr. Grout stuffed the paper into his pocket.

When the room was at last more or less in order, the big man turned his mind to Mr. Jenkins. The reason he was working for the American was to find the whereabouts of Mr. Clemspool, but—by heaven—he had done that himself. There was no more reason to seek Jenkins out. Hastily, Mr. Grout rebuked himself: Hadn't he told the man he would help in his demonstration? He had! And wasn't part of his reformed character the keeping of vows? It was! Knowing he would be the better man for keeping his word, Mr. Grout resolved to do as he had promised.

But, oh, how he wished Mr. Drabble and Laurence would return! This matter of the money, a bank, and a key was all much too confusing!

Chapter 187
Jeb Follows Laurence

Keeping a careful distance, Jeb followed Laurence and the man until they reached their destination. The place took Jeb by surprise. It was the same house Mr. Jenkins had pointed out to him, the one owned by that hateful Irishman, James Hamlyn.

Sitting on the front steps was a girl. Laurence and his friend spoke to her, then knocked upon the door.

The door opened and a woman looked out. Jeb watched as Laurence and the man disappeared inside, leaving the girl on the steps.

What would Laurence have to do with Mr. Hamlyn? Jeb wondered. He waited and waited only to realize that the boy, for whatever reasons, was staying inside. With a shrug, he turned and headed back into the middle of town. If he could find Mr. Clemspool, he could at least report the boy's whereabouts. He paused to memorize the address. "Eighty-seven Cabot Street," he said out loud to make sure he remembered it.

The winter sky was already turning dark as he walked. He saw a man pasting up an announcement on a wall.

EMERGENCY PUBLIC MEETING!

A Call to Action

The Horrors and Dangers of Immigration!
How the American Worker Suffers!
A Cruel Local Example!
The Corruption of Our Language!
The Evils of Foreign Religions!
Our Liberties Swept Away!!

Appleton Hall
8:00 P.M.

Jeremiah Jenkins, Speaker

Jeb stopped. "What's that say?" he asked the man posting the sign.

The man read it to him.

"Is Mr. Jenkins really going to talk?"

"That's what it says."

"He's a friend of mine."

"Is that so?"

On the spot Jeb made up his mind to be there. Mr. Jenkins always made him feel better. And maybe he'd have some work for him.

Reaching Merrimack Street, Jeb spied a hansom cab outside the main entrance to the Spindle City Hotel. He slowed, wondering if it could be Mr. Clemspool's.

Nervous, Jeb approached the carriage and peeked inside. Sure enough, Mr. Clemspool and his friend were there. Did he wish to deal with them again? Then he thought of his mother and the money. . . .

Taking a deep breath, Jeb tapped on the cab's door.

Mr. Clemspool's face appeared at the window. "I thought I informed you I never wished to see you again," he snapped.

"I know where that boy Laurence has gone to," Jeb said quickly.

"My good young friend," Mr. Clemspool exclaimed, "you have done well! And where is he?"

Jeb took another deep breath. Then he said, "It'll cost you ten dollars."

Not long after, the hansom cab was inching its way up Cabot Street.

"That's the house, right there," Jeb said, pointing out the carriage window.

"You're quite sure?"

"I saw him go in."

"He might have come out," Mr. Clemspool said.

The carriage driver, having no orders to stop, continued on. Two streets later, Mr. Clemspool called to him.

"All right then," he said to Jeb. "What do you know about that house?"

"It's a boardinghouse. They take in Irish boarders."

"Anything else?"

"There's a Mr. Hamlyn who owns it."

"What about him?"

"Nothing. He's Irish too."

"Oh, hang the Irish," Albert interjected. "What's my brother doing there? And how, Clemspool, do you expect to get him out?"

"I'm not sure," the man growled.

"Mister," Jeb asked, "can I get my money now?"

"Money? You have the effrontery to ask for money when I don't even *know* he's inside. You might be lying. Indeed, you probably are."

"He is there!" protested Jeb.

"Come on, Clemspool," drawled Albert, "give the boy some money."

After first giving Albert an annoyed glare, Mr. Clemspool reached into his pocket, drew out a fistful of coins, selected one, and offered it to Jeb.

The boy looked at the half-dime piece. "You said ten dollars," he objected.

"For the key!" hissed Mr. Clemspool. "Not a piece of fraudulent information. Consider yourself lucky to get anything."

Reluctantly, Jeb took the coin, pushed open the door, and stepped onto the pavement.

Mr. Clemspool shook a fist at him. "Now get away from here!"

Jeb spit on the ground and walked off.

Mr. Clemspool slumped back into his seat.

"Here, I'm frightfully hungry," Albert announced.

"Then take yourself away," Mr. Clemspool said in a sulky voice.

"What do you intend to do, just sit here?"

"Sir, I intend to draw the carriage closer to that house and wait for your brother to come out. He's got to sometime or other. And when he does, I will get the key."

"But it's dark," protested Albert. "And I'm exhausted! He could be there for the night."

"I doubt it. He's staying at the hotel."

"Then why don't we wait for him there?"

"Because then we might have to deal with those others. This could be easier. But if you wish to go back, you're welcome to."

Albert shook his head. "And leave that money to you? To make *my* point precisely, I don't trust you."

"The feeling is mutual, sir," Mr. Clemspool snarled.

"What time is it?" Albert asked.

Mr. Clemspool drew out his pocket watch and squinted at it. "Seven-twenty."

Chapter 188
Maura Returns

When the seven-thirty bells rang at the Shagwell Cotton Mill, Maura fairly flew out of the yard and, all but running, raced for Mrs. Hamlyn's. Though her work at the mill had exhausted her, there was nothing that would keep her back. This time she paid no mind to her aches.

At her side trotted a grim-faced Nathaniel.

When they rushed into the house, they found Patrick, Bridy, Laurence, and Mr. Drabble in the parlor. Mr. Drabble was relating tales of the theater to an enchanted Mrs. Hamlyn. But no sooner did Maura burst upon them than he turned quite pale, stopped speaking, and rose to his feet.

"Patrick!" Maura called. Her brother jumped up and greeted her with a hug.

"By all the blessed saints, Patrick O'Connell," she exclaimed as she returned his embrace, "you're forever being lost and found. Praise God you're safe."

She greeted Bridy and Laurence, then nodded shyly to Mr. Drabble, who immediately flung himself into a bow.

Flustered, Maura turned to Mrs. Hamlyn. "Have you met Mr. Drabble then?" she asked. "He's an old friend who helped us much in Liverpool and on the ship."

The actor beamed.

Then, at his sister's insistence, Patrick told the story of what had happened to him. All listened intently.

"And do you think," Maura asked tearfully, "that those . . . hooligans . . . would have left you there to perish?"

"I don't know," Patrick admitted.

"Thank God Laurence came to rescue you," his sister said, turning to the English boy. "You have a faithful friend here, Patrick, and you must never forget him."

Patrick looked into Laurence's eyes. But neither boy said a word.

"Mrs. Hamlyn, Mr. Brewster," Maura went on, her hands clasped tightly together, "what's to be done? I don't know this country. I'm fearful those boys will be looking for my brother again."

"I suppose they might," Nathaniel agreed. "Mrs. Hamlyn, could you let the boy stay in the house—maybe in the basement—for tonight and maybe the next?"

"I think it could be done," Mrs. Hamlyn replied. "It is a terrible thing that's happened. But the boy will be safe here."

"You're more than kind," Maura said.

Agreement was quickly reached. For that night, in any

case, Patrick would stay in the basement. Laurence was invited to stay too. Mrs. Hamlyn would talk to her husband as to what might be arranged beyond that. She assured them he was on friendly terms with the Lowell police. They too might offer some advice.

Shortly thereafter Nathaniel excused himself. Though he said nothing about it, he was anxious to see if there were any of those boys lurking about his house. He promised to return as soon as possible.

Mrs. Hamlyn, her arms about Bridy's thin shoulders, took Patrick and Laurence into the kitchen.

Mr. Drabble and Maura were left alone.

For a moment neither spoke.

"Mr. Drabble," Maura began finally, "I am owing you a deep apology. I spoke badly to you in Boston on the quay. There was no call for it. I was that upset."

"Miss O'Connell, you don't have to make any excuse."

"Our father has died."

"Laurence told me. I offer my heartfelt sympathy."

"Mr. Drabble," Maura said softly while staring at the floor, "you were very kind to us."

"Miss O'Connell," the actor returned with a gentle, hesitant smile, "I could be even kinder."

Without looking up, Maura shook her head. "Please, you mustn't speak of that."

Mr. Drabble swallowed hard. "My dear . . . never?"

Maura lifted her eyes and looked straight at him. "Not at all." Then she said, "Mr. Drabble, I'm willing to be your good friend. It can't be more."

It was the actor who bowed his head this time. "There is, as the poet said, a 'love that comes too late.' "

"Faith, Mr. Drabble, can't there be love in friendship too?" And she held out her hand.

After a moment, the actor took it, held it, suddenly folded himself over, and kissed it. "I shall honor thee forever," he said, bowing, and with a straight back walked out of the house.

Maura let him go.

The regular meal was served for the boarders. There being no room at the table, Patrick and Laurence remained in the kitchen, where they ate, if anything, more than the others. At first they consumed their food in silence.

Halfway through their meal, Patrick put down his spoon. "Faith, Laurence, haven't I been thinking hard," he announced.

Laurence, fearful about what might be said, stared into his plate.

"As much as I think I should, I can't be your enemy. I can't. Jesus, Mary, and Joseph, there's been too much life between us. I'm thinking," he said, "we should be forgetting about what happened beyond the Western Sea."

"I want to," Laurence managed to say.

Chapter 189
Mr. Jenkins Speaks

By seven forty-five the meeting-room floor of Appleton Hall had been swept clean and the hall's flaring gaslights lit. The stage was draped in red, white, and blue bunting that was a bit frayed at the edges. There was, however, one new banner—provided by Mr. Jenkins himself—which he had attached to the wall behind the podium. It proclaimed ALL MEN ARE CREATED EQUAL!

Mr. Jenkins had also provided, near the front entrance of the hall, a stack of seven pitch torches, ready for lighting.

As soon as they could, an impatient crowd of fifty surged into the hall and arrayed themselves in seats scattered here and there about the room. Only one person was brave enough to take a chair in the front row. That was Betsy Howard.

The audience was varied: mill operatives, women and men both, shopkeepers, businessmen. Even Mr. Tolliver was there, though he stayed toward the back and sat low in his seat so as not to draw attention to himself.

Not far from the policeman slouched Jeb Grafton. Full of anger and resentment, he felt robbed by Mr. Shagwell, bullied by Mr. Clemspool, tricked by Laurence. Nothing was going right. Nobody cared about him or his family. If only there was something he could *do*. Maybe he could talk to Mr. Jenkins and ask for help in getting his father a job. . . . Jeb looked toward the chair on the stage.

Mr. Jenkins's rumpled suit and flaring whiskers gave him the air of an embattled warrior. On his lap he fingered the speech that Mr. Brown had written for him, hoping it would be strong enough for his audience.

As he studied the crowd, he now and again nodded solemnly to someone he knew—like Betsy Howard. But the one he kept searching for, Mr. Grout, had yet to appear. He had hoped to speak to him privately. Mr. Jenkins was growing concerned. Time was running out.

More people arrived. There were now about one hundred in the hall. And finally—to Mr. Jenkins's great relief—Mr. Grout arrived.

As soon as the speaker saw him, he put all caution aside and immediately stood, walked to the edge of the stage, and beckoned. A number of people in the audience swiveled about to see who merited such special attention. Even so, it took a moment for Mr. Grout to realize it was he being summoned. Feeling self-conscious, he made his way to the stage.

Mr. Tolliver, remembering Mr. Clemspool's description at the police station, recognized the one-eyed man immediately. That he appeared to have a connection to Jenkins interested the policeman mightily. He wished he knew what that connection was. Unable to hear anything from so great a distance, he had to be content with intense watching.

"I'm glad to see you, sir," said Mr. Jenkins, holding out a hand, which Mr. Grout felt obliged to take. "I was beginning to think you wouldn't come."

"I almost didn't," Mr. Grout admitted.

Mr. Jenkins raised his dark eyebrows questioningly.

"I found Clemspool on me own."

Mr. Jenkins frowned. "Does that mean, sir, you won't perform the service you agreed to?" he asked.

"I said I would, didn't I? And the new Toby Grout keeps 'is word, don't 'e?"

"I should think you would," Mr. Jenkins said in as pleasant a voice as he could manage. Then he squatted down and—so no one in the audience could observe what he was doing—drew forth a folded piece of paper from his pocket and handed it to Mr. Grout.

"No! Don't look at it now," he cautioned. "Put it away. You don't want people to see. But when you return to the back of the room—where I should like you to be for my speech—you can look at it. I've written the number of the house on Cabot Street where the demonstration must be held. You can read, can't you?" he suddenly asked.

" 'Course I can," Mr. Grout said with pride. "I've been workin' at it too."

"Excellent. And you remember the name of the street?"

"Cabot, isn't it?"

"Correct. Do you know where it is? How to get there?"

"Went there this morning."

"You do keep your word," acknowledged Mr. Jenkins with a wily smile. "Now all I ask is that you cry out the full address at the appropriate moment, then lead the way to that place."

" 'Ow will I know when to make the cry?" Mr. Grout asked.

"When I pound my fist—like this—on that podium, three times in a row, that will be your signal. Not once or twice, sir, but *three* times." Mr. Jenkins mimed three strokes.

"I get it," Mr. Grout assured him, "though I can't see why yer can't do this all yerself."

Mr. Jenkins smiled. "I assure you, it's merely an old speaker's trick. It will be better coming from the audience. Much more dramatic than if I were to do it.

"And, sir, I can assure you further, no harm will come of it. Oh, yes, I did say I'd pay you. You've found your man. Excellent. Shall we then say five dollars for your efforts tonight?" he asked casually.

"That's a lot."

Mr. Jenkins reached into his jacket pocket and partly removed a wallet for Mr. Grout to see. "You need not fear. I have the money with me. Now get on with you to your place."

Mr. Grout paused. "There's not goin' to be any trouble, is there?"

"Of course not," replied the man with a bland smile.

Mr. Grout studied Mr. Jenkins's face for a moment, then put the paper into his pocket and returned to the back of the room.

As he passed Mr. Tolliver, the policeman—wishing he knew what had passed between the two men—shifted around casually, the better to consider Mr. Grout.

Mr. Jenkins, meanwhile, rose, took up his speech, and approached the speaker's podium. "I should like to call this meeting to order," he announced loudly. Mr. Tolliver turned back to the stage. The audience quieted. The only sounds were the shifting of feet and an occasional cough.

With elaborate ceremony, Mr. Jenkins spread his speech before him, looked out over the crowd, cleared his throat, and began.

"My fellow Americans, we have come together during a moment of great crisis in the history of our republic. A crisis for us. A crisis for our children." In a voice laced with anger, Mr. Jenkins cited the numbers of immigrants who had been coming to the United States—most of them, these days, from Ireland. He called them ignorant, debased. He spoke of their religion with contempt, a danger to republican institutions.

Mr. Grout, listening, began to feel uncomfortable with the speaker's wrath. He hoped Jenkins would calm himself.

Instead, Mr. Jenkins grew more belligerent, referring to the increase in crime and poverty and illness, which, he claimed, was all the fault of these same immigrant Irish paupers. "And what happens when they arrive?" he asked loudly. "They take our jobs. And yet"—he pointed to the banner behind him—"we are supposed to be equal!"

"That's true," someone in the audience called.

Mr. Jenkins, dramatically putting aside his written text, continued at a high pitch. "I shall give you but one example of injustice brought to my attention by one of the noblest citizens of Lowell, a woman who has labored long and hard in the cotton mills.

"When this woman had occasion—expressly at the urging of the owner—to speak of affairs in the mill, she politely, humbly, protested the lack of good air and the enforced speedup of the machines."

"She was right too," someone was heard to murmur.

"This so outraged the mill owner that, in a fit of pique and to brandish his own power, he turned away a woman operative—one Sarah Grafton—whose only crime was that she suffered the cotton cough!"

The story brought an angry stir from the audience. Jeb,

who had been paying only scant attention, nearly jumped out of his seat when he heard his mother's name. Now he gawked at Mr. Jenkins with nothing less than adoration.

As for Mr. Grout, the more he heard, the more convinced he became that Mr. Jenkins was trying to stir up trouble. He began to ask himself what he should do.

The speaker went on: "Who was this hardworking native-born American woman replaced with? An indolent, ignorant Irish girl who accepted less pay for more work!"

There were a few hisses from the audience. Someone cried, "Unfair!" Another, "Treachery!"

Returning to his prepared speech, Mr. Jenkins went on. "But there are some so-called citizens of Lowell who make a profit by bringing in these Irish immigrants, taking them into their homes, and taking that same pay that should be yours."

At the back of the room, Mr. Grout reached into his pocket and pulled out the piece of paper Mr. Jenkins had given him. Carefully, he unfolded it, shifting around in the gaslight so he could read the writing. It read,

87 Cabot Street

As was his way, Mr. Grout read the words slowly, murmuring out loud to himself to make sure he understood them. He did so once, twice. Vaguely, he sensed that he had seen the address written elsewhere but could not quite place where. He turned back to listen to Mr. Jenkins.

"If we are to drive these people out of the city—and thus secure our rights, liberties, and sacred privileges"—here Mr. Jenkins banged the podium with his fist two times, bringing Mr. Grout's attention into sharp focus—"then we must *do* something! It is our children we must protect!"

There was some applause from the audience.

"And I say to you, my friends and fellow native citizens,

the time for action is now! And it must be *severe* action."
Once again he banged the podium twice.

Mr. Grout, now convinced the speaker was stirring up the
people to no good, braced himself. Though he knew he had
promised to cry out, he was beginning to feel it was the
wrong thing to do.

"We must set an example," Mr. Jenkins went on, "lest
every Sarah Grafton in Lowell be pushed aside by ignorant
Irish immigrants!"

The audience cheered and clapped wildly.

The speaker began to shout. "We need to take our cause
to the streets! Who among you can suggest a likely site for
showing these foreigners that we mean business, that they
are not welcome to America? Anyone? Shall someone be
brave enough to speak of such a place?" So saying, he
banged his fist on the podium *three* times.

With a start, Mr. Grout drew in his breath and readied
himself to stand when suddenly he remembered where he
had seen the Cabot Street address before. When he did, his
stomach seemed to roll over. He plunged his hand into his
pocket and pulled out Mr. Drabble's note.

Where Maura O'Connell lives:
87 Cabot Street

"Who can suggest such a place?" cried Mr. Jenkins, looking straight at Toby Grout.

His great hands trembling, Mr. Grout compared the two
pieces of paper, the one from Mr. Jenkins, the one from Mr.
Drabble, and read for himself that the address was the same.
Horrified, he looked up and stared, speechless, at the
speaker, who once again struck the podium three times.

The full import of what might happen now burst upon Mr.
Grout. As soon as it did, he turned and ran from the meeting.

From the stage, Mr. Jenkins saw Mr. Grout race away

from the hall. Furious, he was just about to cry out the address himself when Jeb Grafton leaped to his feet.

"I know where to go!" the boy shouted. "It's where James Hamlyn lives. He's a Paddy who lets other Paddies live with him!"

Mr. Jenkins was thrilled. "And where is that?" he cried with fervor.

"Eighty-seven Cabot Street, that's where!" Jeb shouted.

"Eighty-seven Cabot Street!" echoed Mr. Jenkins. "Let us bring our protest there! Eighty-seven Cabot Street!" he shouted again. So saying, he leaped off the stage, strode up the aisle, gathered up the torches, and headed out into the street.

A large part of the audience—cheering and yelling—followed him. Quickly, he distributed six torches among them and lit the seventh. Soon all the others were burning brightly, revealing the excited faces of people swept up in mob action.

"Let's show those Irish what trueborn Americans can do," Mr. Jenkins shouted. "You, boy," he cried to Jeb, who had pushed his way to the man's side. "Lead us to Eighty-seven Cabot Street!"

Wild with enthusiasm, Jeb started off.

Mr. Tolliver, to his own chagrin, found himself taken by surprise. For a moment he thought he might be able to charge into the crowd, apprehend Mr. Jenkins, and defuse the situation. But he perceived that the crowd was already overwrought. They would never let him take the speaker. Instead, Mr. Tolliver wheeled about and began to run toward the police station.

The crowd streamed off into the night, calling to one another to keep up their angry spirits. Now and again someone darted from the mob, accosted a startled onlooker, and tried to drag him along for the march.

Jeb, in the front of the crowd, with Mr. Jenkins at his

side, cried, "That was my mother—Sarah Grafton—you were talking about, sir."

Mr. Jenkins had been consumed with thoughts of at last having his revenge against Mr. James Hamlyn. And when he looked at Jeb, he was overwhelmed by a vision of his own boy marching by his side. In a rush of emotion, he thrust the flaming torch into Jeb's hand. "Hurry on!" he cried. "Faster!"

Upon leaving the meeting, Mr. Grout headed straight for the Spindle City Hotel. He found Mr. Drabble lying on his bed, boots off, gazing vacantly into the air with a look of gentle melancholy. A small candle—like some votive memorial—glowed feebly by his side. It was as if the actor were performing the final scene in a tragic play.

"There you are," he intoned languidly when Mr. Grout burst in.

"Yer gal, she's in the way of trouble!"

Mr. Drabble's theatrical air dropped away like a cast-off cloak. "Why, what do you mean?" he cried, springing to his feet.

"Wot does this read?" Mr. Grout demanded, thrusting Mr. Drabble's own note into the actor's hands.

"Why, it's where Maura O'Connell is staying. I wrote it."

"Yer might want to know there's a mob 'eadin' there right now, and it's going to put 'er in awful trouble unless we do something quick."

"Good heavens!" exclaimed Mr. Drabble, and in frantic haste he pulled on his boots.

Within moments, the two men were out of the room, out of the hotel, and racing toward Cabot Street.

Chapter 190
The Mob

Though dinner was done and boarders and guests were gathered in the parlor, Bridy was sitting on the outdoor steps, Maura's red shawl wrapped tightly about her against the night cold. The feeling that she was doing something useful for people who were being kind to her gave Bridy deep satisfaction. She loved the idea that she had a job watching for Mr. Hamlyn—though why it was so important she neither understood nor cared to know. The main thing was she had a job—just like Maura.

Then, from the corner, Bridy heard shouting. She made little sense of it. Indeed, at first she was not even sure what she was seeing, other than a crowd of people, several of whom held flaming torches. She thought this might be a parade.

It was only when the crowd drew closer that she recognized Mr. Jenkins. His face was lit up by the torch carried by a boy walking at his side. The man's fringe of white whiskers was unmistakable. It was as if, by virtue of the reflected torch flames, he himself were ringed with fire.

As soon as Bridy realized the man was Jeremiah Jenkins, she stumbled up the steps and pushed the front door open. It was not the parlor, where so many of the household—including Maura—had gathered, to which she ran. Instead, she turned to the other side of the hallway, to Mr. Hamlyn's room.

Heart beating wildly, the child rapped lightly on the door.

The sound, however, was so small and tentative, it received no response. With a look over her shoulder—for Mr. Jenkins himself might be following—Bridy knocked again, this time more loudly.

"Come in!"

She pushed the door open and went into the room on shaking legs.

As usual, Mr. Hamlyn—his sleeping cap tied around his head—lay in bed beneath a pile of blankets. A fire glowed brightly in the fireplace. In his hands he held a book.

Seeing it was Bridy who had come into the room, he put down his book and smiled warmly at her. "Yes, my dear," he said. "What is it? Did you wish me to read to you again?"

"He's . . . come," the girl stammered. "I saw him."

Mr. Hamlyn could not grasp her words. "Did you say someone . . . has come?"

"Yes."

"But . . . who?"

"That man," Bridy said, her voice quivering. "Himself. The one . . . the one you said I should be watching for."

Mr. Hamlyn started. "Do you mean . . . Mr. Jenkins?"

Bridy nodded.

"At the door?"

Bridy shook her head. "He's outside. With a crowd of people."

This time Mr. Hamlyn did understand. He sat up so quickly his book tumbled to the floor. Faintly now, as though from a considerable distance, he heard raucous chants and calls from outside. Through his front window, he could see the glow of the torch flames. Mr. Hamlyn's pale face grew even paler.

"Quickly, Bridy!" he cried. "Fetch my wife! Hurry, girl!"

The urgency in his voice caused Bridy to freeze with fear.

"For heaven's sake, go!" the man shouted.

Jarred into action, Bridy ran across the hallway and into the parlor.

Mrs. Hamlyn, Maura, and the eight other young women boarders as well as Nathaniel Brewster were crowded about the front windows, staring into the street.

When Maura saw Betsy Howard in the first rank of the crowd, she felt a terrible chill. Was this demonstration aimed at her?

"Down with the Irish! Drive the foreigners out," the people chanted.

Bridy squirmed her way to Mrs. Hamlyn and tugged at her dress.

Greatly agitated, the woman demanded, "Why, what is it, girl?"

"It's Master Hamlyn, mistress," Bridy whispered fervently. "He's wanting you to come."

Mrs. Hamlyn frowned, then clapped her hands smartly. "Girls! Go to your rooms! Away from the windows now! Go! Quickly." She pulled a key from her dress pocket and held it out. "Someone lock the front door from the inside. Hurry! Do as I say!" One of the boarders snatched at the key and hurried out into the hall. As soon as she was gone, Mrs. Hamlyn darted about the room, snuffing out candles.

The other boarders, not sure how they should react to the scene outside—with fear or curiosity—backed away reluctantly from the windows.

"Come along now," Maura insisted to Bridy, only to stop at the parlor door. "The boys," she suddenly said. "Where are they?"

"I'm not certain," Nathaniel replied. "I think in the basement, bedding down."

"You must tell them to come to my room," Maura said. And, grasping Bridy's hand firmly, she hurried from the parlor and up the steps to the third floor.

Nathaniel started down the hall toward the basement only

to be restrained by an outstretched hand on his jacket sleeve. It was Mrs. Hamlyn.

"Mr. Brewster, sir," she said urgently. "You must come! I need help with my husband."

"Yes, ma'am," the young man replied. Putting aside his first mission, he followed the woman back toward the front of the house.

Mr. Hamlyn was already sitting on the edge of his bed, the short stump of his left leg sticking straight out like a broken post, his right leg dangling uselessly. He kept straining to look through the window. The chants had grown louder than before.

"How many are there?" he asked in great agitation.

"Maybe fifty," his wife replied.

"It's that man Jenkins. He's led them here. He must have come for me."

"We'll leave by the back door," Mrs. Hamlyn said.

"Let's pray they're not out there too. Nelly," Mr. Hamlyn said to his wife, "we can go to neighbors till this quiets down. Take a candle from the hall."

Mrs. Hamlyn turned to the young man. "He can't walk. You'll have to carry him."

"Yes, ma'am."

"Once you dump me," Mr. Hamlyn told Nathaniel, "you're to go get the police. Do you hear me? Fetch Mr. Tolliver."

Mrs. Hamlyn snatched up a blanket and wrapped it about her husband. Then Nathaniel bent over the man and lifted him. He was very light. Mrs. Hamlyn ran to the door and held it open.

"Which way?" Nathaniel asked once he had carried the man out of the room.

"To the left," Mr. Hamlyn said. "There's a door at the back."

They hurried down the hallway, Mrs. Hamlyn following.

At the far end, Mrs. Hamlyn edged open the door and peeked out. "No one's there," she said with relief, and pushed the door open the rest of the way. Nathaniel stepped into the cold dark.

"Mind yourself," Mr. Hamlyn cautioned as the three went down a short flight of steps.

In the open air, the chants of the crowd seemed more insistent. Leaping light—thrown by the torches—danced on the walls of neighboring houses.

They moved into a small bare yard. "Go directly across," Nathaniel was told. "There's a gate there. Once we get through, we should be safe."

Nathaniel, carrying Mr. Hamlyn, all but ran to the neighbor's house. There, Mrs. Hamlyn knocked on the door, then told the alarmed householder what was happening. The door was pulled open, and Nathaniel deposited Mr. Hamlyn on a parlor sofa.

"Nelly," Mr. Hamlyn cried as he was set down. "Get the other people out of the house! Young man, run for the police. Tell them to come quickly!"

Mrs. Hamlyn and Nathaniel ran outside.

"Go!" Mrs. Hamlyn shouted to the young man. "I'll take care of the others."

Nodding his understanding, Nathaniel tore around the side of the neighbor's house and raced as fast as he could toward downtown.

Hiking up her skirts, Mrs. Hamlyn ran back to the house. Once inside, she climbed to the second floor and began throwing open the doors of her boarders' rooms one after the other. "Leave by the back way!" she ordered. "Hurry! Neighbors will take you in."

The young women, all too aware of the danger now, gathered up capes and shawls and rushed out of the building and into neighbors' houses.

When Mrs. Hamlyn reached the foot the steps to the third

floor, she was met by the housemaid coming down. "Faith, mistress, what is happening?" the young woman cried. "What are they wanting? Are we in awful danger?"

"Get out of the house and you'll be safe!" Mrs. Hamlyn told her. The young woman started away. "Wait! Stop! Is Miss O'Connell still up there with her sister?"

"I think so," the frightened young woman replied.

"Then go back and tell them to leave immediately!"

"Yes, mistress." The young woman turned toward the stairs.

Satisfied she had done her best, Mrs. Hamlyn hurried out of the house through the back door.

The maid, following orders, was halfway up the steps when, panting for breath, she stopped to listen.

"Down with the Irish!" she heard. "Get rid of them all! Kill them all!"

With a gasp, and fearing for her life, the young woman turned about, hurried down the steps, and dashed out the back door, leaving Maura and Bridy unknowing in their room.

Out on the street, Mr. Jenkins saw—through the window of the room—the glow of the fire in the fireplace of James Hamlyn's bedroom.

He looked down again at Jeb. But it was not Jeb he saw. It was the image of his own child, dead at Mr. Hamlyn's hand.

In the basement, Laurence and Patrick, unrolling blankets on the dirt floor, heard the muffled shouts of the crowd. At first they paid no attention. But the din persisted.

"Laurence," Patrick asked suddenly. "What do you make of that?"

Laurence listened. "Some people shouting."

"Can you catch what they're saying? I think it's about the Irish."

Laurence went halfway up the narrow cellar steps to hear better.

"There!" cried Patrick, just behind him. "Did you hear that? 'Down with the Irish!' "

"What's it mean?"

Instead of answering, Patrick eased by Laurence. Once he reached the top of the steps, he looked up and down the empty hallway.

He grew alarmed. "Laurence," he called down. "There must be something bad happening."

The two boys crept into the first-floor hallway. By the light of the few candles still burning, they could see and sense that the house was deserted.

"What is it?" Laurence said, feeling the need to whisper. "Where is everybody?"

"Jesus, Mary, and Joseph, I don't know. . . ."

Outside, the shouting intensified.

"I'm going to the front," Patrick said. "I have to see what's happening."

They slipped into the dark parlor. Flashes of torchlight seemed to dance about the room.

The boys looked out through the windows at the crowd. Patrick shuddered. In the reddish light, faces seemed contorted, with bodies oddly angular and grotesque. The shouting, calling, and shaking of fists continued unabated. "Out with the Irish!" "Get rid of the foreigners!" "America for Americans!"

"Holy Jesus," Patrick whispered in fright as he crossed himself. "Will you look at that?"

Laurence pressed his face to the window. "What do they want?" he asked.

"Look there," cried Patrick, pointing. "It's that boy—the one you said was named Jeb. Do you see him?"

"Where?"

"He's holding a torch. Standing by the fellow with the ring of whiskers."

Laurence, seeing them, only nodded. Then he turned to look down the street. That's when he saw a carriage.

"Why are all these people here?" Mr. Clemspool demanded with indignation.

Albert, at his side, looked out the carriage window. "Perhaps they want that key too," he drawled.

A look of horror came into Mr. Clemspool's eyes. "But how dare they—" Abruptly, he opened the carriage door and stepped out.

The crowd, having attracted people from nearby streets, was growing larger and angrier.

"See here," Mr. Clemspool said, grasping the elbow of a man looking on, "what's this all about?"

The man barely looked to see who had spoken. "It's to get the foreigners out," he said.

"Out of where?"

"The house. It's full of 'em."

A much relieved Mr. Clemspool retreated toward the carriage. "It's to get rid of foreigners," he told Albert.

"But Laurence is not a foreigner," his brother objected. "He's *English*."

Mr. Clemspool started to say something but turned back to the house. "That Jeb did say he was in there."

"What a confounded nuisance!" Albert declared. "Now you can see for yourself what an insufferable bore my brother is. I tell you, he's not worth all this bother."

"Sir, I intend to get that key."

"Oh, hang the key!" Albert bleated. "I don't like any of this. I want to go back to Boston." He squeezed his knuckles until they cracked. "I want to go home!"

"Do you wish to lose the boy now? Or that money? This is fine. The crowd will flush him out, and then we'll pounce on him."

Albert, with considerable reluctance, stepped out of the carriage.

Mr. Tolliver had been able to round up only three policemen, one of them the old jail keeper. He had also commandeered a wagon and instructed the startled farmer—whose wagon it was—to get the policemen to Cabot Street fast. With a nod, and calling upon his horses to do their utmost, the fellow snapped his whip in the air, and the wagon rattled away down the rutted and poorly lit streets of Lowell. There was nothing for the policemen to do but hold on anxiously.

But at Cabot Street Mr. Tolliver's heart sank. The cries, the flames of torches, the palpable anger of the protesters alarmed him. All he could think of was a nest of churning poisonous snakes.

He ordered the driver to urge the horses and wagon directly into the crowd in hopes it might intimidate them. "Right in front of the house, if you can," he cried.

The farmer did attempt the maneuver, but the mob was packed too tightly and was, moreover, determined not to give way. The wagon could go no more than a few feet before being forced to stop.

"There aren't enough of us to do anything but contain them and keep things from getting worse," Mr. Tolliver told his men, shouting to make himself heard over the tumult. "No point in agitating further. But arrest anyone provoking violence. Bring them back to the wagon." Truncheons in hand, the three policemen waded in among the people.

"This is the Lowell police," Mr. Tolliver shouted through cupped hands. "You will cease this riot! This is the police! Disperse at once or you will be subject to arrest!"

So great was the noise, only a few in the crowd even heard the warning. Some of them edged away a foot or two. And all the while new people kept arriving.

*   *   *

When Mr. Jenkins saw the wagon and realized it was a policeman shouting from its seat, he became incensed. How dare the police offer help to foreigners!

He surveyed the angry people about him with feelings of pride. Had he not created this mob out of his own will? Was it not he alone who commanded them? Was not this boy—like his boy, who had so cruelly perished—devoted to him?

"I know nothing!" he shouted at the police, and shook a fist. He would show them what he knew. No police force in the world could stop *him*.

"Give me that," he cried, snatching the flaming torch from Jeb's hands. Startled, the boy watched as Mr. Jenkins broke from the crowd and strode toward the house, the torch held high. "Follow me if you dare!" he shouted above the din. "We'll show these Paddies what we're all about!"

Only Jeb followed him.

Mr. Tolliver heard the man's cry and looked about. When he saw Mr. Jenkins—torch in hand, advancing upon the house—he leaped from the wagon and strove to make his way through the crowd.

Aghast, the police captain saw Mr. Jenkins whirl the torch around his head and with all his might fling it like a javelin. His aim was accurate. The torch—burning like a comet—flew through the window into Mr. Hamlyn's room.

The sound of the crashing, shattering glass brought a gasp from the crowd. One moment the air had been full of boisterous cries. The next, people suddenly stilled to watch an orange glow in the room blossom like a flower. In moments, fingers of flame spiked up. From the crowd, as if in one voice, there arose an "*Ahhh!*" Now those in the mob stood in passive, shocked silence as they absorbed what was happening.

Horrified, Jeb cried, "You set . . . the house afire!"

"Revenge!" Mr. Jenkins shouted with a terrible smile. "Revenge!"

Jeb stared at him, seeing him for the first time, a man consumed by hate. It filled him with fright. Muffling a cry, the boy turned and fled and did not stop until he reached home.

Someone in the crowd shouted, "Fire brigade! Get the fire brigade!" A half dozen of those who had been yelling anti-Irish slogans now peeled away and began to race down the street.

Mr. Tolliver, in pursuit of the arsonist, broke through the front line of the crowd. "Mr. Jenkins," he shouted. "You are under arrest!"

Mr. Jenkins turned to see the police captain striding toward him. Infuriated, he hastened to the window of Mr. Hamlyn's room and looked in, desperate for proof that he had destroyed his enemy. But the flames and smoke were already too thick. Using the back of his hand, Mr. Jenkins punched out what remained of the window. Then he hoisted himself up and crawled into the room.

Flames were creeping up the walls, causing the wallpaper to curl down in yellowish ribbons. Bedclothes were smoldering. Burning wood snapped and popped. Areas of the floor seemed to be boiling with low blue flames. Mr. Jenkins could hardly breathe for the smoke, could hardly see. But one thing was clear to him: Mr. Hamlyn was not in the room.

Swearing violent oaths, Mr. Jenkins wrenched the bedroom door open and slammed it behind him.

The hallway was dim, deserted. Snatching a candle from the wall, he plunged toward the back of the house in search of the basement.

Frightened but spellbound, Patrick and Laurence were watching through the parlor windows when they heard the crash of breaking glass.

"What's that?" Laurence asked.

"Faith, I don't know. It came from across the hall."

The boys ran out of the parlor.

At the far end of the hall, Mr. Jenkins loomed up only to disappear into the dimness. The boys had no idea who he was.

Instead, they tried the door opposite, Mr. Hamlyn's room. The handle was hot. Patrick pushed the door open and looked inside. The room was ablaze.

"Holy Jesus!" Patrick cried, leaping back and bumping into Laurence. "The house is burning!" He shoved the door shut; then both he and Laurence ran to the front door. It was locked.

Outside Mr. Hamlyn's burning room, Mr. Tolliver stood by the smashed window, trying to see in. He was afraid to move, afraid not to. His mind roaring, he slowly hoisted himself up and crawled through the window into the billowing smoke.

Mr. Hamlyn was not there, but neither could he see Jeremiah Jenkins. Eyes smarting from the smoke, Mr. Tolliver went to the bedroom door, opened it, and stepped into the hallway and looked about. Sick to his stomach and fearful of the worst, he saw—dimly—movement at the far end of the hall. He began to move toward it, heart pounding.

By the time Mr. Grout and Mr. Drabble found their way to Cabot Street, the acrid stench of burning pitch was heavy in the night air. Torches cast a speckled light over a mob of ruddy and perspiring faces. Angry cries kept ringing out: "Down with the Irish. Throw the foreigners out! America for Americans!" Behind the anger there was also a certain glee as people, laughing, egged one another on.

"What is it?" cried the actor. "What is this?"

"Keep behind me, Mr. Drabble. I'll try to get us closer so we can find out."

Mr. Grout, using his broad shoulders and strength to shove

aside those who blocked his way, pushed into the crowd. Even so, the going was difficult.

"Mr. Grout," cried the actor. "Look! It's Mr. Clemspool! And Laurence's brother too."

"Where?"

"There! You see! On the other side of the mob."

"Mr. Drabble, is Laurence in the 'ouse?"

"He was when I left."

"Then those rascals must be tryin' to get 'im. We 'ad better get to 'im as well as yer love! Come on!"

The two men broke through the crowd and rushed up to the house. "There's a fire inside," cried Mr. Drabble. He struggled with the knob of the front door but could not turn it. After banging hard on the door to no avail, he gave an imploring look to Mr. Grout.

"Keep to one side. I'll get it," said the one-eyed man. So saying, he hurled himself forward, shoulder low. Though the door cracked, it did not give entirely. Shaking off the shock, Mr. Grout stepped back, braced himself, and heaved himself at the door a second time. With a shriek of splintering wood, it fell in.

Mr. Grout stumbled into the dim hallway, where he heard a cry of astonishment. "Mr. Grout! Mr. Drabble!"

It was Laurence and Patrick being herded forward by Mr. Tolliver.

"There you are, laddie!" cried a joyful Mr. Grout when he saw Laurence.

"Patrick," Mr. Drabble shouted, "where's Maura?"

"I don't know," the all but breathless boy replied. "We saw some man back there, but there doesn't seem to be anyone else about at all."

"Who was this man?" Mr. Tolliver demanded.

"I don't know."

"Get these boys out!" cried the police captain to Mr. Grout. Then Mr. Tolliver raced back down the hallway.

"Tell me where Maura's room is!" Mr. Drabble demanded of Patrick.

"It's at the top," the boy replied. "But I don't know exactly where or if she's there."

"Show me the steps!"

"This way!" Patrick cried.

Laurence started to follow only to be restrained by Mr. Grout. "Laddie," he called, "yer've got to get out of 'ere."

"I have to go with Patrick!" Laurence pleaded.

"Don't yer worry. Drabble can attend. We need to get out before yer burn like a cinder."

Mr. Tolliver had run to the end of the hallway only to be confronted by a closed door. He yanked it open and looked into the kitchen. One glance told him no one was there. He retreated quickly.

To his left was another door. He pushed it open and saw that it led to the outside. He wondered if Mr. Jenkins had gone out. But where was James Hamlyn?

He opened the door at the opposite side of the hall. He saw steps leading down, to the basement presumably. It was dark. Knowing Mr. Hamlyn's infirmities, the captain didn't think the man would be there. In haste, he shut the door and ran out of the house through the back door.

In the yard, Mr. Tolliver looked at the neighbor's houses and saw people staring out of windows at the fire. Perhaps Mr. Hamlyn was in one of the houses. He ran to check.

He needed only moments to find the Hamlyns and their boarders safe in the neighbor's house. "Is everyone out?" he demanded.

"I'm not certain," Mrs. Hamlyn replied. "There were two sisters at the top and two boys in the basement. They're not with us."

Mr. Tolliver tore back to the front of Eighty-seven Cabot Street.

"Is anyone still in there?" he asked an onlooker.

"I don't know," the man answered.

Mr. Tolliver looked about. Mr. Grout was kneeling by Laurence. The boy was sitting on the ground.

"I don't care wot yer want to do," the one-eyed man was telling the boy, "yer to keep away from the building." The next moment Mr. Grout leaped up and dashed back into the house in pursuit of Mr. Drabble.

Mr. Tolliver grabbed two onlookers and pulled them into position before the house. "Don't let anyone else in there!" Mr. Tolliver commanded. "They'll be killed!"

Inside, Patrick and Mr. Drabble had reached the steps. "Where are we?" the actor asked. Smoke eddied about their feet.

"Maura's room is up there somewhere," Patrick shouted.

"For the love of God, boy, hurry!" Flipping the hair out of his face, taking the steps three at a time with his long legs, the actor tore up the stairwell. Suddenly he stopped and turned, blocking the boy's way. "Patrick!" he cried. "Get yourself out of the house!"

"But . . ."

"Do it!" the actor shouted. "It's too dangerous here!" Without waiting, Mr. Drabble continued up.

For a moment Patrick watched him go, then—albeit reluctantly—he headed back toward the first floor. There, he saw a twist of flame poke out from beneath a door like a cat's paw. Even as he watched, the wooden floor near the doorway darkened. Tongues of fire leaped to the steps. Heart beating madly, Patrick turned. He had to warn Mr. Drabble.

On the second floor, Mr. Drabble shouted, "Maura! Are you about? Where are you?" Receiving no reply, he ran up and down the hallway, opening and shutting doors. Finding no one, he headed for the floor above. By this time, Patrick was back, just a few steps behind him.

"Mr. Drabble! Mr. Drabble," he called.

The man ignored him. "Maura!" he shouted. He found her behind the second door. "Thank God!" he cried. "Quickly! Quickly!"

Maura sat on the bed, arms tight around a wide-eyed Bridy on her lap.

"Mr. Drabble!" she said with surprise. "What is it? What's happening?"

"The house is ablaze," the actor shouted. "You must get out!"

Needing no further words, Maura caught up Bridy's hand and ran into the hallway. Patrick came to her side. With a free arm, she drew him close, then let him go.

"Down the steps," Mr. Drabble cried. "All of you! Down the steps!"

"But you can't," Patrick shouted. "They've already caught fire!"

"All of them?"

"The ones near the first floor."

"We'd still be better off on the second," the actor shouted, and galloped down. Patrick and Maura—holding the terrified Bridy close—hurried after.

Mr. Jenkins, candle in hand, found the basement cluttered with boxes and old furniture. For a while he just stood there, hoping to hear a sound. When he heard nothing, he began to thrash about wildly, turning everything over. But of James Hamlyn he found no trace.

Wildly frustrated, he climbed back to the first floor. "Hamlyn!" he thundered through the thickening smoke. "Hamlyn, I know you're here. . . ."

* * *

Outside, before the house, a rather dazed Laurence looked around, trying to get his bearings. Scores of faces were staring at him.

"Who is he?" someone asked from the crowd. "What was a boy doing in there?"

Then a voice cried, "Laurence!"

Laurence turned. There at his side were Albert and Mr. Clemspool. The boy tried to escape only to have Mr. Clemspool snare him by the collar while Albert gripped one of his arms. They began to drag him through the crowd away from the house.

"The key!" Mr. Clemspool shouted, trying to shove his hand into one of the boy's pockets. "The key!"

Laurence resisted by twisting wildly. "Let me go! Let me go!" he cried. Struggling fiercely to free himself, he struck out and hit now Albert, now Mr. Clemspool.

The man was forced to pull away his hand. Albert ripped off his top hat and began to whack his brother with it repeatedly.

Finding the brawl diverting, some of the crowd of onlookers completed a ring about the combatants and cheered them on.

One of the policemen broke through the ring. "Break it up!" he cried. "Break it up! No brawling!"

Albert restored his crumpled hat to its proper place and drew himself up. "Look here, chap, who do you think you are?" he demanded.

"The Lowell police, that's who! Here now!" he cried, pointing right at Mr. Clemspool. "I had you in jail this morning, didn't I? And you," he said to Albert, "helped him escape." Using his truncheon, he knocked Albert's hat off.

When Mr. Clemspool realized the man was the jail keeper, he dropped his grip on Laurence and made a desperate effort to break through the crowd and flee. Albert tried another direction. The jeering crowd, however, would not let either Englishman escape.

Laurence, seizing his chance to get away from his brother and Mr. Clemspool, squirmed through the circle of onlookers.

Nathaniel Brewster had run to the middle of Lowell only to find the police station deserted. Anxiously, he hurried back to Cabot Street and pushed his way to the forefront of the crowd in search of Maura. Smoke was now billowing from the building.

"Have they got everyone out?" he asked an onlooker.

"Don't know," said Betsy Howard. "But if not, that's where they'll be staying."

Nathaniel turned back through the crowd in hopes of finding one of his friends.

In the hallway, Mr. Grout called, "Drabble! Where are yer?"

A door along the hallway flew open. Mr. Jenkins loomed like an apparition through the rolling heat.

" 'Ere!" cried the one-eyed man. "It's yer! Look wot yer done!"

Giving no reply, Mr. Jenkins bolted down the hallway and charged up the steps. Flames licked at his heels.

"Drabble!" Toby Grout shouted, his words nearly swallowed by an ominous crackling noise behind him in the hall. "Where are yer?"

Horatio Drabble, with Maura, Bridy, and Patrick, had fled into one of the boarders' rooms on the second floor. Once there, Maura yanked open a window and looked down to the ground.

"It's too far to jump," she exclaimed.

She heard a loud clanging noise. The fire-brigade wagon, pulled by its fifteen members, was turning into the street.

"We'll have to try the steps," Mr. Drabble shouted. He broke from the room. As he did, Mr. Jenkins appeared, rushed up to him, and stared madly into his face.

"Where's Hamlyn?" he shrieked.

Mr. Drabble could only shake his head and step back. Mr. Jenkins roared away, opening and shutting doors.

Mr. Drabble looked back. Maura, Bridy, and Patrick emerged. The actor peered down the steps. Wild flames surged up.

"We'll have to risk it this way," he called. "Maura, take up the girl again. Stay close. Cover your nose and mouth. Keep your heads low. Try not to breathe the smoke! And for heaven's sake, stay right behind me." Dramatically, he gestured upward, cried, " 'O! who can hold a fire in his hand . . . ?' " and started down.

Maura, with a crying Bridy in her arms, came right after. Her eyes were tearing, her head dizzy with fear. Patrick, holding on to her skirt, followed closely.

The walls of the stairwell were smoldering. The balustrade was too hot to touch. Sparks and stinging cinders whirled through the air.

When they reached the first-floor hallway, Mr. Drabble cried, "Which way?"

"I know," Maura shouted. "Let me go first! You follow!" Still carrying Bridy, she slipped in front of him.

Maura led now, groping slowly down the smoke-filled hallway toward the front door. Once, twice she looked back to see Patrick. As for Mr. Drabble, he had disappeared in the clouds through which flames shot like lightning.

"We're almost there," she cried, her eyes streaming. It was no longer possible to see where they were going.

Bridy, whimpering and trembling, pressed her face against Maura's neck.

Suddenly a figure stood before them. Maura halted in fear. It was Mr. Grout.

"Give me yer hand," he called.

Maura complied, and he led them toward the door.

Gasping for breath, their faces covered with soot, coughing violently, Mr. Grout, Maura, and Bridy stumbled out of the burning building and down the wooden steps.

Members of the fire brigade—who had been fruitlessly tossing water from leather buckets at the house—gave way. The same mob that had been so angry now parted, making sympathetic murmurs. "Give them room. Let them pass!"

The three sank down in the middle of the street. From out of the crowd first Nathaniel appeared, then Laurence.

"Where's Patrick?" Nathaniel asked.

Maura started and looked around wildly. "Holy Jesus!" she screamed. "He must be still inside."

Laurence leaped up and raced for the building. Maura thrust Bridy into Nathaniel's arms and followed. The fire-brigade members tried to hold the two back. They were able to restrain Maura, but the small boy darted under their grabbing hands. In one bound, he leaped through the doorway.

"Patrick!" he screamed. "Where are you?" He tried to go forward. The intensity of the heat forced him back. Dropping to his hands and knees, he began to crawl. Halfway down the hall, he found his friend lying on the floor, unconscious.

Gasping for air, Laurence grabbed Patrick by his shirt collar and began, by crawling, to drag him toward the door. Patrick's shirt tore. Laurence, crying with exhaustion and frustration, rubbed his tearing eyes and tried to wipe the sweat and soot from his hot face.

"Patrick!" he screamed. "You must move!" When no answer came, Laurence pushed the boy up to a sitting position. Then he bent over, wrapped his arms around his friend's chest, and, bent double, started to haul him backward again.

Straining with every small step he took, Laurence moved

along the hall. He didn't even know when he reached the door, but when he did, he all but fell out.

Outside he was met by a weeping Maura and Mr. Grout. "Merciful Jesus," she cried, "you found him! Is he alive?"

"I don't know," said Laurence, crying and wheezing, trying to soothe his stinging eyes by rubbing them.

A few people came forward—among them, Betsy Howard—and reached out for both boys. But it was Maura and Mr. Grout who carried them a distance from the burning building. There they laid them on the ground.

Laurence, groggy, sat up. "Is Patrick all right?"

"By the living Jesus," Maura whispered as tears ran down her cheeks, "he's alive, and didn't you save him."

Suddenly Mr. Grout looked about. "But where's Drabble?" he cried.

Maura gasped. "Didn't he come out?"

"No."

"Then he's still in there!"

Mr. Grout jumped up and raced for the house only to be confronted by members of the fire brigade. They blocked his way.

"You can't go in!" they shouted at him.

"My friend's in there!" screamed Mr. Grout, fighting desperately to get by. Six men restrained him. He could not get through.

"Drabble!" he cried at the house. "Do yer 'ear me! Find yerself an exit!"

Mr. Jenkins had reached the top floor. "I know you're hiding, Hamlyn!" he shouted. "I know you are!"

He stormed into one and then the other of the upper rooms. He found no one.

Bellowing with rage, Mr. Jenkins ran crazily back to the steps.

"You can't get away from me, do you hear, Hamlyn!" the

man cried. "I'll find you!" And he descended into the inferno.

From their neighbor's window, Mr. and Mrs. Hamlyn watched as their house became engulfed. Their boarders stared with horror. Mrs. Hamlyn, covering her ears to veil the sound of the roaring flames, again and again sobbed the words. " 'Ashes to ashes, dust to dust. . . .' "

"Stand back!" the police and members of the fire brigade kept shouting. "Stand back!"

Slowly, they pushed the crowd—blinking in awe at the heat and light—away from the spectacle. Never once did Mr. Grout, Maura, or Nathaniel take their eyes from the building.

Flames—like serpent tongues—licked out from the windows of all three stories. Patches of red appeared upon the roof. Black smoke obliterated the stars.

With a sudden roar, the Hamlyn house seemed to expand like a balloon. Then a moaning, sucking sound filled Cabot Street, and the building collapsed upon itself.

Betsy Howard buried her face in her hands.

Chapter 191

From the Ashes

Presumably, Jeremiah Jenkins had perished. His body was not found. As for Mr. Drabble, his was discovered in what had been the parlor. It was the surmise of Mr. Tolliver that, trying to get out, the actor had taken a wrong turn in the smoky darkness and had been trapped.

Maura wept by his body. Standing just behind her, Toby Grout wept too.

Patrick provided particulars to the police captain about who Mr. Drabble was and where he came from. Nathaniel offered his address on Adams Street if any more information was needed.

So it was that he, Maura and Patrick, Bridy, Laurence, and Toby Grout gathered sadly before his small stove in the room on Adams Street.

Maura, eyes full of tears, spoke of Mr. Drabble's many kindnesses since they had met in Liverpool. Mr. Grout spoke of how smart the actor had been and what a patient teacher. Patrick talked of the man's bravery.

As he spoke, a soft knock was heard at the door. It was Mr. Tolliver again.

He nodded solemnly to all, then, pointing to Laurence, he said, "Young man, I need to speak to you."

"Me?" Laurence asked with a quiver of nervousness.

"If you will be so good as to step outside."

"You can speak here. These are my friends."

Mr. Tolliver considered. "All right," he said. "This evening we arrested any number of people over what happened. Among them were two Englishmen. Their names are"—the police captain consulted a piece of paper from his pocket—"Matthew Clemspool and Albert Kirkle.

"The officer who took them in claimed they were brawling. But when I spoke to them, they said it was nothing but a family dispute. And that you, young man, were the cause. Do you know anything about them?"

"They're thieves," Mr. Grout said immediately.

"I was asking this boy, sir."

"Right. And 'e can tell you 'oo they are better than I can."

"Do you know them?" Mr. Tolliver asked Laurence again.

"Maybe," Laurence said.

"I know it's very late," said Mr. Tolliver. "But if you could come along with me to the jail, I could sort this matter out."

"May I take someone with me?"

"Don't know why not."

Laurence turned to Mr. Grout.

Mr. Tolliver brought them to the jailhouse in his own carriage. Holding a lamp, he led them down the stone hallway to the same cell Mr. Clemspool had occupied earlier.

Albert lay asleep on the floor. Mr. Clemspool slept also but sitting on the bench. Their clothing was soiled and, in Mr. Clemspool's case, somewhat torn. Their hands and faces were smudged with dirt.

Mr. Tolliver banged on the cell bars.

Mr. Clemspool blinked at the light. When he saw who it was, he reached over to poke Albert. The young lord woke with a start, saw Laurence, and jumped up.

"There you are! You took your time, didn't you?"

Laurence stared at him.

"Well, go on then, tell this foolish policeman that you and

408

I are brothers, that this is all a family quarrel. Then we can leave this disgusting place."

Laurence said nothing.

"Didn't you hear me?" Albert cried, squeezing his hands so tightly, his knuckles cracked.

Mr. Clemspool grunted. "I suspect the boy is not sure he wants to recognize you."

"Why, what do you mean?" Albert shrieked. "Of course he recognizes me. I'm his older brother. The future Lord Kirkle."

Mr. Clemspool grinned. "He's not, to make my point precisely, very *fond* of you, sir."

"But I'm his brother!" Albert protested. "His devoted brother."

"What'll 'appen if the boy says nothin'?" Mr. Grout asked Mr. Tolliver.

Rocking back on his heels, the police captain, hands deep in his pockets, felt the British ambassador's letter. "Not much. They'll stay here for a week. Maybe less. Disturbing the peace. This fellow escaped from jail early yesterday morning. But he was already due to be let out." He shrugged. "They'll be warned to leave the country. Long as they do and promise not to come back, there's nothing to worry about."

Mr. Tolliver looked from Albert to Laurence. "*Are* you brothers?" he asked Laurence.

After a moment the boy said, "No."

Albert blanched. "What do you mean *no?*" he cried in shock. "Once a brother, always a brother! Anyone knows that." He clutched at the bars. "For heaven's sake, Laurence, tell him so. Clemspool, tell him that bit from the Bible you like to quote. Of course he knows me!" Albert shouted. "What's more, he stole money from our father. He's a thief. He's the one who should be here!"

409

Mr. Tolliver bent over Laurence. "What's your name then?"

Laurence considered Albert coldly. Grimly, he said, "I don't know who he is. My family died on the ship coming over. My name is John Faherty."

"Good enough for me," Mr. Tolliver said.

"That's a lie!" squawked Albert. "An absolute lie!"

"Laurence! Laurence is his name," Mr. Clemspool shouted as the boy began to back away. "Read your Bible. Genesis. Chapter four. Verses five through nine. Cain and Abel. 'Am I my brother's keeper?' Read it and learn!"

In the carriage that Mr. Tolliver had provided for their return to Nathaniel's room, Laurence and Mr. Grout were silent for a time.

Finally, Mr. Grout said, "Do yer know wot that Clemspool told me yesterday afternoon?"

Laurence shook his head.

" 'E said that all that money was put in a bank. And that unless 'e found some sort of a key to it, it would stay there—forever."

Laurence turned, his eyes wide. "A key?" he said.

"Right. From a bank 'ereabouts. Something like a Mannibeck . . . Merrimack. But then 'e always was one for makin' up stories."

Laurence reached into his pocket, pulled out the key, and held it out for Mr. Grout to see.

In spite of himself, the one-eyed man grinned.

Later, lying on the floor of Nathaniel's room, staring into the darkness, Laurence whispered, "Patrick, are you awake?"

"Faith, I can't sleep either. Too much has happened."

"I told my brother I didn't know him. Can . . . can I be your brother?"

Patrick hesitated only a moment. "Faith, I'm proud to have you for that. But will you go back to London?"

"I'm not yet sure. What would I *be* there?"

In another corner Nathaniel murmured to Maura, "You must know, Miss O'Connell, I . . . I loved you even before I saw you. It was your father's way of talking."

Maura shook her head. "You mustn't say that. It's not my dear da's words that should do the wooing," she said gently. "I'd rather be cared for . . . for what I am myself."

Nathaniel nodded. "I'll not say more. But I will tell you what I think I'm going to do."

"And what is that?"

"I'm going to California to search for gold."

"And do you think, Nathaniel Brewster, you'll find it?"

"I do. But it won't be as fine as what's here," Nathaniel said with a shy smile. "Maura O'Connell . . . will . . . will you . . . wait for me to come back?"

Maura was silent.

"Will you?"

"You're a fine young man, Mr. Brewster. I can only say I'll not forget you."

Chapter 192
Lord Kirkle's Money

Neither Maura nor Nathaniel went to work that day. Instead, she made the suggestion that Nathaniel should fetch the money from the bank. Laurence was only too willing to let the young man do it.

There was not the slightest problem. Nathaniel showed the key to the teller, who led him to the vault, indicated the locked boxes, and left him alone. Nathaniel opened the box, took out all the money, handed in the key, and walked out to the street.

For a long moment Laurence looked at the bills and small change, then put them all in his pocket and held them tightly until he returned to Nathaniel's room.

Mr. Grout could now arrange for Mr. Drabble's funeral. Laurence insisted.

The service was held the next day in a small cemetery on the edge of Lowell. Mrs. Hamlyn was expressly invited by Maura.

The narrow pine box—upon which the actor's volume of Shakespeare had been placed—was lowered into the earth. Mr. Grout spoke the final words. " 'E was a good man," he said, "and a friend with a 'eart wider than 'e 'imself was. 'Ere's 'opin' God blesses 'im."

When the funeral was over, the mourners repaired to a restaurant on Merrimack Street. There was very little talk, but when the table was cleared, Laurence stood up. "I have to say something," he announced in his small voice. He nodded to Mr. Grout. From his pockets the one-eyed man took a number of envelopes.

"I have all this money from my father. I shouldn't have taken it. But I can't give it back now. It needs to be used." He slid one envelope to Mrs. Hamlyn.

"That's a thousand dollars to find another house."

He handed another envelope to Maura. "There's two thousand dollars to help you and Patrick and Bridy make your way in America."

"Jesus, Mary, and Joseph," Maura gasped.

"The rest is for Mr. Grout, Mr. Brewster . . . and me. We're going to California. And when Mr. Grout and I have made back all the money I took from my father, we're going to take it to him. Mr. Brewster will keep his own fortune and can do what he wants with it."

412

Nathaniel glanced across the table at Maura. She was holding Bridy on her lap and stroking Patrick's hand. She lifted her tearstained face briefly, looked into Nathaniel's eyes, then turned back again to gaze at Laurence.

Chapter 193
Departures

M r. Clemspool and Sir Albert stood upon the quarter-deck of the clipper ship *Good Fortune*. They did not face each other but gazed separately at the New England coast fast fading behind.

"See here, Clemspool," said Sir Albert, "we need to buck each other up. I'm going to tell my father that Laurence died. You'll have to give evidence, you know."

"As long as you testify that I had nothing to do with his going to America."

Albert hesitated. Then he said, "Of course."

Mr. Clemspool, noting the hesitation, winced. All he said, however, was, "Then we should get by."

"Jolly well too," returned Albert, though there was little conviction in his voice. "What's my father going to do, disown his only son and heir? Cause a scandal? Not him."

Mr. Clemspool, saying nothing, stared glumly at the undulating sea.

"Well then," Albert pressed, "you should be glad to be going home."

"Sir, considering the way things have transpired—being obliged to flee England, forced out of America—well, sir, I am not, to make my point precisely, altogether *pleased*." So saying, he turned upon his heels and walked off toward his steerage berth.

Not long after, Maura, Patrick, and Bridy stood on the well-lit platform of the Lowell & Boston Railway station in Lowell. From the rear deck of the last car, Laurence, Mr. Grout, and Nathaniel smiled down at them.

Suddenly the train's whistle shrieked, causing Bridy to press her hands to her ears. Great clouds of smoke and steam blew forth. With much clanging, the train began to pull out. "Good-bye! Good-bye!"

Patrick, Bridy, and Maura waved back.

In silence the three walked out of the station and into the chilly dimness of the predawn air. Bridy was anxious to return to their new home—Mr. Brewster's old room. Patrick kept wishing he could have gone west, but he knew that he needed to stay with Maura. They would make a new life. And hadn't Maura told him that with the money Laurence had given them she would continue working, but he could go to school as well as look after Bridy. Though Patrick did wonder how long it would be before the others came back from the west and what adventures might befall them, he was excited by the thought of school. Who knew what might become of him!

For her part, Maura thought of her mother alone in Ireland. She would write her a letter, telling her about Da's death and all that had happened. She thought too of Nathaniel Brewster and what he would be like when—and if—he returned. How would she be, by that time, herself?

Looking up, Maura saw that it was dawn. She stopped and listened. All was still. Suddenly, her heart began to beat with joy. She felt herself teetering on the edge of possibilities.

DON'T MISS ANY OF THE STORIES BY AWARD-WINNING AUTHOR AVI

Available in Bookstores Everywhere or See Below for Ordering Information

☐	AMANDA JOINS THE CIRCUS	80338-0/$3.99 US/$4.99 Can
☐	KEEP YOUR EYE ON AMANDA!	80337-2/$3.99 US/$4.99 Can
☐	THE BARN	72562-2/$4.99 US/$6.99 Can
☐	BLUE HERON	72043-4/$4.50 US/$6.50 Can
☐	THE MAN WHO WAS POE	73022-7/$4.99 US/$6.99 Can
☐	POPPY	72769-2/$4.99 US/$6.99 Can
☐	POPPY AND RYE	79717-8/$4.99 US/$6.99 Can
☐	PUNCH WITH JUDY	72980-6/$4.50 US/$5.99 Can
☐	ROMEO AND JULIET TOGETHER (AND ALIVE!) AT LAST	70525-7/$4.50 US/$5.99 Can
☐	S.O.R. LOSERS	69993-1/$4.50 US/$5.99 Can
☐	SOMETHING UPSTAIRS	79086-6/$4.99 US/$6.99 Can
☐	THE TRUE CONFESSIONS OF CHARLOTTE DOYLE	72885-0/$4.99 US/$6.99 Can
☐	"WHO WAS THAT MASKED MAN, ANYWAY?"	72113-0/$3.99 US/$4.99 Can
☐	WINDCATCHER	71805-7/$4.99 US/$6.99 Can